ANIMIST

Tor Books by Eve Forward

Villains by Necessity

ANIMIST

EVE FORWARD

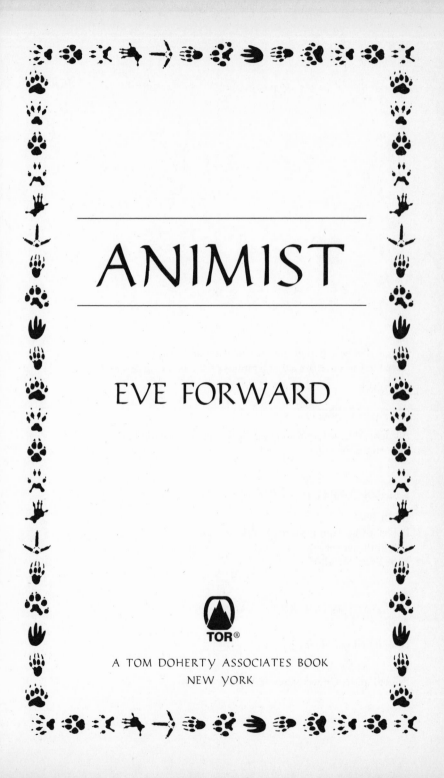

TOR®

A TOM DOHERTY ASSOCIATES BOOK
NEW YORK

ANIMIST

Copyright © 2000 by Eve Forward

Edited by David G. Hartwell

A Tor Book
Published by Tom Doherty Associates, LLC
175 Fifth Avenue
New York, NY 10010

Tor® is a registered trademark of Tom Doherty Associates, LLC.

Design by Lisa Pifher

ISBN 0-312-86891-X
Printed in the United States of America

For Nathan, who believes in me

ACKNOWLEDGMENTS

With special thanks to:
Dr. Robert L. Forward, Luke Campbell, and Donald Tsang

And to the staff and students, human and otherwise, of the
Exotic Animal Training and Management Program
America's Teaching Zoo
Moorpark College

ANIMIST

ONE

It was night, dark over the island of Highjade. The sea shifted in the blackness, more felt than heard.

Flickering torches marked the walls and towers of the College of Animists, riding a ridge above the jungles and the sea. On the slowly rising slopes, the thick rustling night marked the forests of the Lemyri. Here and there, the canopy glowed with fireflies, or the lamps of a crownhome. Beyond the College, along the coast, were the brighter and wider lights of Humani dwellings. On the border of Humani and Lemyri lands, a downhill walk from the College, was a sprawl of particularly bright lights, and noise, and music.

The tents spread out like skirts around the trunks of the massive trees, to protect the revellers from anything dropped by the Lemyri in the branches above. They also served to concentrate the smoke and smells of the cooking fires, and the noise, and the people. Humani and Lemyri and even a few Rodeni moved from tent to tent, talking, drinking, bartering, shouting. It was Trade-Meet, a festival held to celebrate the many differing species of the Archipelago, and to encourage them to work for their mutual benefit.

Right, thought Alex wearily, as he watched a small but spry Lemyri artisan proceed to deliver a thorough and painful beating to a Human who'd been too drunk to avoid crashing into the Lemyr's display of dried fruits. Other Humani came into the fray, and then more Lemyri, and soon a mass brawl of fur and skin and profanity was raging in the ruins of the stall. Meanwhile, a Roden hopped cautiously up and started shoveling the spilled fruits into a sack. Maybe Trade-Meet meant something on other islands, where it was held with religious significance, but here on Highjade it was only a tradition, along with such other traditions as insults, prejudice, and blood feuds. Alex wished he'd stayed at home, at the College.

"Whaaoo! Party!!" shouted Jocin, right in his ear. She was walking along next to him. On his other side, his other friend, Phyl, laughed as Jocin flung her drinking gourd. It splashed somewhere into the melee, but went unnoticed. All three of them were already very drunk. Alex, being the cause of the other two's celebration, was even more so. Jocin and Phyl had to help him stagger along to the next drinking-tent. Since they were fairly tall, and Alex quite short for a Human, they looked like an unsteady W as they wove through the crowds.

"T'kren, I think we ought to go back now," Alex managed to protest as he was dragged along. "I've got a lot to do t'morrow . . ."

"Ah bisht you do," snorted Jocin, dragging him into a tent. "Listen to some babble, get your pendant, and then off you go, and we'll never see our favorite takre again."

"He's graduating, not being executed," Phyl protested gently, helping Alex to collapse onto a smooth wood bench, while waving a hand at the frazzled Lemyri drinkseller. "He'll come back after his spirit quest, won't you, Alex?"

"I'll have to," mumbled Alex. He wasn't feeling well. Even though he was sitting down now, the room still seemed to be staggering around him.

"Even so, he'll never have another chance to get drunk with us, his bestest takren," Jocin insisted. Graduated Animists were forbidden to drink alcohol or, indeed, take intoxicants of any form. Alex felt he'd already had enough for a lifetime. "Takren" meant "siblings" in the Lemyri language; but these three were not related, as a casual glance revealed. All three had their hair cut short, as was the tradition for students, but there the resemblance ended. Phyl was tall and graceful, older than Alex by a decade. Jocin was a year younger than

Alex and seemed to bristle with wild energy. Alex himself was barely five feet high, almost frail-looking, with the pale skin (tanned now from Highjade's endless summers) and the dark eyes and hair of a northern clime. He was sixteen, and despite the difference in their ages, he was graduating tomorrow, and his two friends would still have some years to go.

"Drinking contest!" Jocin shouted, grabbing a ceramic mug and pounding it so hard against their table that it shattered. She threw out a string of polished bone beads in trade-payment. "Run a tab! Drinking contest! Get out the hard stuff, m'tosho tak-takuni! Tik!" she added in slurred and rather rude Lemyri to the proprietor. The Lemyr pinned his ears back angrily, but turned to fill new mugs from the casks.

"Hard stuff it is, then, pestilent Human," he grumbled in his own language to himself, as he poured.

Another Lemyr dropped down from the branches above and landed lightly on their table. Phyl and Jocin drew back warily, even as the smirking proprietor set a tray of mugs on their table, in front of the furry spiderlike toes of the newcomer.

"Drinking contest, is it?" purred the Lemyr, its golden eyes set in the black foxlike mask of its face, giving it an air of menace. The thick fur was piebald in black and white and brown, and the long, erect furry tail waved like a cat's. The Lemyr was the same size as Alex. Its hands and feet had long, thin fingers, without claws, but a lift of its lip showed the sharp white teeth in a parody of a Humani smile. Most fearsome of all was the thick ruff of fur around its neck and shoulders that indicated it was a female, the dominant and more aggressive gender of the species.

She sat on their table, a breach of etiquette asking for trouble, and grabbed one of the mugs while she stared fixedly at them. "Apprentices, by your shorn pelts. Does Kataka know you are here?"

"Well, furrfu, why should the Head Animist care? We're not from that dumb College, are we, takren?" Jocin lied quickly. Alex and Phyl shook their heads. Alex fell off the bench and had to climb back up.

"No students allowed to sneak off. 'Specially me," he explained drunkenly, as he clung to the table.

"Only because you try to run away at least twice a year, takre," Jocin chided him. "Anyway, we're not from there."

"I should hope not," rumbled the Lemyr. "To have some of her students involved in a disgraceful drunken incident at Trade-Meet would cause a great dishonor to Kataka."

"We're just travelers," put in Phyl.

"Musicians," suggested Alex.

"Idiots, is what you are," snorted Jocin, giving them a shove, as she grabbed her mug. "You can drink, too, fuzzbutt," she invited the Lemyr. "Us Humani can outdrink our throwback primate cousins anytime." Alex almost threw up in fear as Jocin thereby likely bought herself an instant death-duel for her insubordination, but the Lemyr seemed more amused than offended and, with no more than a restrained twitch of her tail, raised a mug, and they all drank.

Alex was rather thirsty, despite his already drunken state, and the new drink was actually very good, with a fruit-juice tang to it. It couldn't be very strong; he couldn't taste any alcohol in it, and it was much better than the palm wine and fermented coconut milk they had been drinking. He had another taste.

The female Lemyr's name turned out to be Hashana, and it turned out that she didn't much like Kataka any more than the three students—erm, travelers—did. Despite their earlier attempts at deception, they found themselves chatting with Hashana like old friends, even telling her about Alex's upcoming graduation.

"Well, congratulations, then," Hashana said, tipping her mug to him. They'd all been matching each other drink for drink, though Alex, who had been talking less than the other two, noticed blearily that the proprietor seemed to be using a different pitcher to refill the Lemyr's glass. *Probably giving her better stuff than this fruit juice,* he thought to himself, but since Hashana had offered to pay for the rounds he didn't say anything. He realized he'd had more than enough to drink already, and was glad to be slacking off now. He still felt really drunk, even worse than before, really. It must be sitting down that was doing it.

"Yeah, not bad for a slave-boy, huh?" Jocin said, punching Alex on the arm and knocking him over again.

"Jocin!" cried Phyl reproachfully. "Come on, we weren't going to mention that, remember?" Alex climbed back onto the bench, his face in odd shades of white and crimson and green.

"Aw, blow, I'm sorry," Jocin swore. "Here, have another drink." Alex took it and took a big gulp, to hide from the fixed yellow stare of Hashana.

"A slave, really? At the College?" she asked, her tail waving. Alex nodded wearily, to drunk to care. Reality seemed to be fading in and out anyway, so it probably didn't matter.

"Yeah, his parents were so poor they had to sell him," explained Jocin, waving her mug around. "But a talent scout for the College spotted him and bought him. Once he graduates, see, then he'll go on his spirit quest."

"And then once I've got my Anim, then I come back here," Alex added, bunking one finger on the tabletop for emphasis. "Here. Finish my training."

"And then he'll get bought," Phyl said, giving Alex a chummy pat on the back that made him bang his head on the table.

"Hired!" protested Alex from face-down on the table.

"Hired, right, to pay off his slave-debt . . ."

"Lemyri do not keep slaves," Hashana said coolly. "I am surprised that Kataka allows it."

"Shhh! It'sa sssseeecret," Jocin hissed, winking broadly. "He's the only one. My father paid my way in."

"Mine, too," added Phyl.

"What do you think about it, boy?" Hashana asked, her thin furry fingers gripping the short wool of Alex's hair and lifting his head off the table so she could look at him. "What is it like, to be bought and sold so?"

"Don' like it," Alex grumbled. "All this time and I'm a thing. Six years of shit and work and sweat and lessons and getting bit by things, and at the end of it all I'm still a . . . a thing."

"You're a thing worth a lot more now, though," Phyl pointed out to him.

"Not so much," Alex argued, finishing his drink and attempting to get to his feet. "Look at me. Short. Scrawny. Human. I'd have to bond a fanglion or something to get any respect. Ha!" he shouted, and passed out, falling over backwards into a party of Lemyri, who did not take his intrusion kindly. Jocin and Phyl attempted to pull him out and found themselves embroiled in a screaming brawl, in which the rest of the bar quickly joined, except for Hashana, who retreated quietly back up into the rafters, and Alex, who regained enough consciousness to crawl away blindly.

Something was very wrong, he realized dimly. Obviously the fruit juice he'd been sucking down was indeed alcoholic, and very much so. He couldn't walk, could only crawl. He fumbled through the tent fabric, and out into the mud and loam. People of all races stumbled over him, swore, kicked him, and he fell, and rolled, and threw up. It didn't seem to help. He kept crawling, but everything was dark.

"You gave tilka to *Humani?*" Kintoku asked incredulously. The Lemyri Animist had been summoned from the College when Jocin and Phyl had at last been pulled from the brawl by the Lemyri police. Both were unconscious and breathing hard.

"They asked for strong drink," shrugged the proprietor. "It was the strongest I had."

"Were there any others? I know these two. There would have been another."

"Another, a male I think. Small. I do not see it now," the proprietor replied.

Kintoku swore. "Alex. Curse you, if you've cost us . . ." He pulled a leathery bundle from the fur of his back, and it unfurled itself into a small fruit bat. The other Lemyri drew back, muttering and flattening their ears against this display of the Animist's power. The Animists were the only type of magic the Lemyri would tolerate, but they still remained wary.

Kintoku exchanged a glance with his Anim, stroking the soft fur with a fingertip, and the bat chirped softly in response. "Miska, go, find Alex." He sighed. "Again." The bat launched itself with a flapping storm of wings, barely clearing the door opening.

It was all a blur for Alex; crawling through something stinking and then falling down a gully. He had suddenly realized he was alone, and

for a moment then, free. Even through his drunken si⟨
ing was intoxicating. He thought he could hear the ⟨
find the shore, maybe he could find a boat, maybe he ⟨⟨
way away, off the island, away. The thought that tomorrow he would
have been allowed to leave anyway didn't stop him.

He'd run away before, as Phyl had said. It was futile, always futile.
The Animists could always find him—with their Anims, animals of
all species that could run faster and see farther and track him by smell
and sound. And the people of the College would come and collect
him, trying to be understanding but never quite managing. The
Humani seemed to think he was ungrateful, that since they'd given
him shelter and food and education and care, he had no right even to
want to escape. He'd never been any more harshly dealt with than any
other student. And yet he wasn't free.

He made it to the beach this time, before the chittering squeal of
a bat sounded overhead, and furry shadows materialized out of the
palm trees. As Kintoku stepped up, eyes almost glowing with anger,
Alex managed to throw up over him and then passed out.

The sky was growing lighter, and with it came the noise. Usually the
singing tree-apes started it, with short hoots that peaked rapidly into
high-low screams of such volume that they carried for miles and effec-
tively woke up everything else. The great cats would break in, with
great hollow, sawing roars in round chorus, and the hyenas would
begin to whoop. The canines began then, as though in protest at the
noise, barking, yapping, yowling, with the wolves howling low and
deep below it all. Shrill whistling came from the mustelid pens, and
roaring barks from the pinniped colony down on the beach below.
The cockerels in the feeder pens crowed loudly and repeatedly, and
the striches gave their hissing honks, and the native parrots either imi-
tated one of the other beasts or else did their own free-form raucous
screaming. Some of the hoof stock gave belches or bleats or barks or
brays or bellows in general contribution, while myriad smaller creatures stayed silent through the cacophony, in response to their secre-
tive instincts. Finally, as the sun at last broke over the horizon,

burning gold over the sea, the College's Lemyri population gave their eerie, structured chorus of chattering ululation in ritual salute to the dawn.

Alex moaned and tried to wrap a pillow around his head to shut out the sound. It didn't work. It hadn't worked in all of six years, but the fact that today he might have actually slept in—at long, long last—made him try. The hangover wasn't too bad, at least; the College's allopathist had forced him to down a lot of purging draughts, in preparation for today.

His two roommates had already abandoned their hammocks and were shrugging into clothes with the sleepwalking air of long practice. Phyl, also wincing from his hangover, had a black eye. The other roommate, Mikel, grabbed hold of Alex's hammock rope and started swinging it back and forth. (Jocin, of course, was in the girl's dormitory . . . unless she'd already sneaked out again on some other mischief.)

Mikel swung the hammock harder and harder. It would have made Alex throw up again, if he'd anything left to do it with.

"Aaaalex, get uuuup," sang Mikel.

"M'graduating. I don' hafto," Alex mumbled through his pillow.

"Smug little puppy," Mikel snorted, and spun the hammock. Alex was used to this, though, and didn't fall out, though he ended up hanging upside-down from the hammock, like a sloth. "If you were a *real* student, they'd have expelled you after that stunt last night. They'd have done it years ago." On the woven roof above their heads, a series of thuds marked the leaping progress of the Lemyri, moving from their dawn-worshipping perches to the day's work.

"Leave him alone, Mikel," said Phyl, wincing. "None of us got expelled. Even the Director was young once."

"Kataka was plenty upset, though. And Kintoku looked like he wanted your hide on the wall, after what you did to his. You'd better get out there before he comes looking for you." Mikel started pulling on his boots. "Or are you just going to make another run for it? Furrfu, Alex, the least you could do is learn to escape successfully."

Alex swung underneath the hammock, trying to right himself, but not quite managing. "I'm getting out of here today, Mikel, and that's more than you'll do for a looong time, you clean-shirted first-year," Alex muttered. Mikel pretended not to hear.

"You might as well get an early start, Alex," Phyl suggested, not unkindly. "If I don't see you again before you go, good luck."

"Yeah, don't get killed or something," Mikel added, pulling on his oiled-canvas coveralls for the morning cleaning. Phyl had already dressed in simple, loose cotton robes, for his meditation classes. Mikel still had many long months of hard work, cleaning out and watching over the animal pens of the College's menagerie, while Phyl had advanced into the more metaphysical aspects of Animist training, though still continuing to work with some of the species on the campus.

The College of Animists was not prestigious, nor was it easy. Many students left after having to deal with the hard, filthy, endless work. Others were expelled for failure to adhere to the strict rules, or failure to live up to the expectations of the instructors. Some left for other reasons . . . but that was their choice, as free persons. Alex didn't have that option. He was property, and couldn't leave. Failure meant punishment, sometimes very strict—he still bore scars from being caned by a Humani professor. The Lemyri hadn't bothered last night, or else were saving something else up for him. Alex didn't realize that the Lemyri, who prized their own freedom above all else, secretly admired his spirit.

He let go his failing grip on the hammock, and thudded gracelessly to the basalt floor. Mikel rolled his eyes and Phyl gave him a friendly pat on the head as they left the small dorm room, the wicker door banging behind them.

Alex grumbled mentally as he dressed and packed. Technically, as a graduate, he should have been entitled to respect from the underclassmen, even though they happened to be older, and taller, than himself. In practice, though, it probably wouldn't happen until he returned to the College with his Anim. Hopefully, it would be some particularly impressive and exotic creature, and they would all feel very sorry that they'd acted this way. And all the girls, too, would be impressed—the College's Humani students were female in the majority, which should have meant improved chances for the few males.

But again, in practice, the girls tended to see Alex as a "friend," as in, "let's just be friends." It didn't matter much, anyway; you tended to lose romantic infatuation with someone when you saw them every day, frequently covered in dirt and feces.

Alex packed everything he owned; it wasn't much. A cloth satchel held a pair of pants, socks, undershorts, and shirt. His own work shirts were faded, and stained, and the stains faded, as was the mark of a sixth-year student. He wore the other set of clothes, and good leather boots, waterproofed though weathered with the dung of many species. Over that he wore a coat, of llama's wool patched with leather at the collar and sleeves and hems; it was warm but light. All his clothes were undyed, remaining the grey or white or brown or green of nature. A wooden whistle he'd made for his passing test in wood-carving, a piece of cord with the Knots tied in it, a little box with a rawhide membrane that made a sharp clicking noise when pressed with the thumb, and a leather strap with a few rooster spurs on it. His lucky rock went in a pocket; it was almost completely round, and grey-green, and he'd picked it up from the beach while waiting with his father for the slave-trader. From that point on, things had tended to improve, so maybe it was a little bit magic; the kind of quiet magic that Animists couldn't detect.

A leather trinket pouch went around his neck. Within were a few small items of value that might be worth something in trade: a tirg's tooth, a couple of obsidian scalpel blades wrapped in a bit of wool, a matched pair of bright kestrel primary feathers folded into a scrap of paper, a tiny clay pot that contained two ounces of civet scent. Also in the pouch was a recipe for a salve for treating botflies, and a tiny irregular pearl. With thousands of islands and many races with many different cultures and standards of value, the way of the Archipelago was trade; what might be worthless to one person could be a worthy curiosity to another, or a rare prize to yet someone else. Only metal, rare and precious, had any absolute value. Bronze was the best for tools, but silver and gold were rare enough to be used only for jewelry.

Also around his neck went the necklace of beads, each with its cartouche that signified classes taken, levels of training passed. The largest one, a flat disk of hard clay imprinted with his thumbprint and a few symbols, had been handed to him last night by Kataka, head-master of the College.

He'd been sitting there in bleary sickness, drinking yet another disgusting sickly-sweet potion mixed by Doctor Peddae, the College's resident allopathist and veterinarian. Kataka arrived from above, as Lemyri usually did, bouncing down from a walkway on her long, limber legs. Kataka was grey, with a white ruff around her neck and shoulders, symmetrical black patches on her chest and hips, and a black tail. Her eyes were bright orange, the pupils tiny slits in the bright light. No Humani expression could fit that face, but Alex knew well enough, from the set of her tail and ears, that she was furious, though controlling it well, as all Lemyri could.

The Lemyri race looked down on Humani, in more ways than one. The College's student population was almost half Lemyri, but there were only a few of them that Alex would count as friends. The rest wanted nothing to do with him.

"You. Immature. Foolish. Careless, headstrong, and stupid. It galls me to send out such a student as yourself, but anything to be rid of you, if only for a time." She'd thrown the ceramic token at Alex; it hit him in the face, and stung, but he caught it as it bounced. Alex, unsure, dipped his head in respect and stammered, "Thank you, mirr'tika shi shinta . . ."

"See the Director Humani before you go," Kataka had said coldly, interrupting Alex's long formal expression of respect and thanks. "There is something he will have to explain to you." With a leap, then, the Lemyri had vanished back into the maze of scaffolding that crawled over the basalt stones of the College.

Alex finished packing his meager belongings, and took a last look around the room that had been his home for so long. Then he turned, and let the door bang shut behind him, forever.

Then he remembered something, and went back in. The hammock was his, too; he'd made it in Nets and Snares class. He unhooked it and folded it up, and stuffed it in his pack. Then he left the room for the last time.

The Director Humani was in charge of supervising the Humani students of the College. At about this time, he'd be making his way through the menagerie, checking that everything was alive and that the students, Humani and Lemyri both, were slogging away with buckets and shovels. Alex went down to find him, through the buildings of the College itself, composed of hexagonal basalt blocks (the building had once been an ancient temple of some kind, now long abandoned, and built over now with timber, bamboo, and woven wicker Lemyri construction). He left the dark walls and set off down the twisting paths along the ridge of the hill, with the animal pens sloping away to either side, all sectioned off into walled compounds by species type: herbivores, large carnivores, small carnivores, etc. Some were actually stone buildings, divided inside into glass-fronted or stonewood-barred cages. Some of these had their own heating fires built in, to warm the floors for the delicate species that could not tolerate even the mild winters of Highjade. Some were open corrals or wooden barns and stalls, or stone enclosures with bars of rare and precious bronze, the only material strong enough to hold some of the animals. Complex mazes of one-way gates and guillotine doors led from pen to pen. There were animals from all over the Archipelago; some were the descendants of Animulae past, others had been imported and bred when possible, in hopes that they might someday provide an Anim for someone.

The Animists generally believed that all things, animals and even plants and stones and weather, had spirits, souls. Sometimes they could see them, through the eyes of an Anim. And of course there were many greater gods and spirits, not usually embodied in an earthly form. But only the spirits of animals, and only mammals among those, shared enough metaphysical ground with the mammalian Animists to become the bonded spirits known as Animulae. Not every Anim could bond with every Animist. In fact, it was suspected that an Animist's likelihood of bonding with any given Anim was slim indeed. Somewhere out there was a compatible Anim, and the spirit quest was taken to find it.

Professor Cynde had explained it by showing them some glass whistles, used in training. "If I blow this one," she'd said, demonstrating, "you all can hear it?" The class had nodded. She'd selected another, and blown. "Hear that?" The Humani students had shaken their heads, while the Lemyri students had solemnly nodded. "It's a question of . . . of pitch. Animulae all seem to exist on different pitches; only certain Animists can sense certain pitches."

Alex walked quickly past most of the animal pens, but here and there he had to stop to bid farewell to friends—some of them fellow students, some of them animals. Despite his excitement at his graduation, he felt a lump come to his throat as Motati, one of his few Lemyri friends, had shown a totally untypical display of emotion and hugged him gingerly, her fur soft on his face. And he felt his eyes tearing up as he scratched the College's ancient lion through the bars of its cage, listening to the rumbling growl as the beast placidly sucked its own tail-tip, a habit it had picked up in infancy. The lion had been here far longer than Alex had, and he knew, even though he'd be returning, that he wouldn't see the lion alive again. He stroked the matted mane gently with a fingertip, all the while watching to make sure the beast didn't casually turn and bite his finger off. Some of the newer students, busy at the chores of cleaning, looked on enviously; for the first few years of their training, new students were forbidden to talk to, touch, or even make eye contact with any of the animals.

Alex tried to keep his visitations short, but nonetheless he was delayed, and only caught up with the Director at the last pens on the campus.

Here were kept the feeder animals, animals raised for food for the students and animals of the College. Pens of pigs and goats, a large enclosure of chickens, ducks and geese in a pond, a few pens of cavies cooing and bubbling. Stritches wandered and honked in a wide field down one hillside, while the other was taken up with a herd of tough, long-horned water buffalo. Beyond the animal pens the ground sloped away more gradually; and here the earth was cut into terraced fields, guarded by hundreds of rock borders, and irrigated by drainage ditches that made the most of the College's abundant supply of manure. Fields and fruit trees stretched away all around the College, wherever the land could be made flat enough to hold them. The fields were worked and maintained by the students; Alex saw several of them working on repairing the rock borders.

The Director Humani, whose name was Welson, was leaning

over the fence to poke at the lead bull buffalo, who was sulking by the fence, not wanting to be led out with the rest of the herd. He was getting on in years (the bull, not the Director), and didn't want to walk down the steep hillside. The two students in charge of herding the buffalo down to the river to drink and graze were both standing by nervously.

The Director gave the bull another tap, then reached out and pulled its tail. The bull rounded on him with surprising speed, huge crescent horns swinging, and the Director jumped back just in time, losing his balance and falling over backward on the safe side of the fence. The bull snorted, then slowly moved off down to the river, the students following it cautiously.

The Director was standing and dusting himself off, grinning though trying to maintain some of his dignity as Alex approached. The Director's Anim, a scruffy brown long-tailed monkey, sat underneath a lemon tree nearby, opening her mouth in threat at the retreating water buffalo. It was rare that an animal as intelligent as a monkey could be bonded, but the Director's training and skill were exceptional. The monkey turned and gave a half-hearted threat gesture at Alex, more out of species habit than any real aggression, and the Director turned at an unheard prompt from his Anim.

"Oh, there you are, Alex," he said, seeing him. "Ready to leave?" he asked, noticing Alex's satchel.

"Yes, sir," Alex replied. "Kataka said I should talk to you before I go, though."

"Ah, right," said the Director, taking a quick look around and then sitting down on a low stone wall. This brought him down to Alex's eye level. He was tall, with dark hair and blue eyes and a manner that seemed friendly but hid a core of stern discipline. His monkey, whose name was Rhese, ran over to Alex and jumped onto his arm. "As you know, we invested a certain amount, to purchase you and have you brought to Highjade. Because of your initial price, right now you're a net loss if, for example, you head out on your quest and are killed. We don't want that to happen, of course."

"No, sir," agreed Alex. Rhese was now grooming his hair.

"Or if we were to lose you, any other way," Welson added. "If you just, oh . . . ran off, for example."

Alex didn't respond to this, but felt his ears burning. Rhese pulling them didn't help.

"So we have to protect our interests. Like any other student, you graduate; you find your Anim. You come back. And in your case, we find you a working position and get you started in paying off your debt, through whatever salary your employer determines."

Alex nodded. "Yes, I know."

"But most students learn Separation as soon as they return from their quest. In your case, you work off your debt to us with your new employer, and then, and only then, we'll teach you Separation." He gave a whistle, and Rhese left Alex, to return to her master.

"What? But . . . but if I don't know Separation—" Alex protested.

"You have to understand, Alex, that Animists have a certain amount of power, and we're valuable. If you owe us money, we want to be sure that debt is paid. You've shown that we can't exactly trust you."

Alex looked down again, stifling his protests, as the Director continued.

"We have to have insurance. You'll need the College to teach you Separation. And we won't do it until your debt is paid. Understood?"

"But if my Anim dies, without Separation, *I'll* die! Then you'll have lost everything—"

"It's a gamble we've decided to take. The odds are good. I'm sure you see that the fear of death is a stronger motivation than some kind of tenuous loyalty to a College from which you take every opportunity to escape."

"Is this negative reinforcement, or positive punishment?" Alex asked sarcastically. The Director smiled, but without much humor.

The bond between an Anim and Animist was strong, so strong that they could feel each other's emotions, experiences, pleasures, and pains. The two souls, beast and being, were interwoven. Only the careful discipline of Separation could loosen that bond; without that training, when one of the pair died, the other would suffer a terrible wrenching trauma to the mind and the spirit, like a gaping psychic wound. The lucky ones died instantly, following their Animulae into the realms beyond the Oether. A few lived a little while, if catatonia and constant seizures could be counted as living.

"I'm sure I'll be able to pay you back without any problems, sir," Alex said, with more confidence than he felt. Rhese gave him a suspicious look, and opened her mouth at him, and the Director sighed.

"Well, yes, Rhese, he's hiding something." Alex tried to look innocent. "Let me see. Probably something along the lines of, 'Sure, once I get on a ship out of here I'm never going to come back,' right?"

Alex looked down. "The thought did cross my mind," he added quietly. "I mean, I know I'm supposed to be an Animist, but . . . I'd rather be free."

"Alex," Welson sighed. "Why do you think we bought you? You have talent. Your mind stands out in the Oether like a lighthouse."

"Can't I just not Call?" Alex asked, plaintively. "Can't I just, you know, be an animal trainer, or something?"

"As I said, you stand out. All this training we've put you through only makes you more receptive . . ." The Director's tone became stern. "You can Call, and be an Animist . . . or you can be Called, and become something else." His eyes were cold. "And then you'll *never* be free. Power always has a price."

Alex shuddered. "I guess . . ."

"Don't worry, Alex," said Welson, smiling again. "I'm sure you won't have any problem paying your way clear with us. We'll find you a good job. True, you're not very impressive in appearance but I'm sure you'll find a good, suitable Anim to back you up. Oh, you did try to Call on the grounds, didn't you?"

"No, sir . . . I thought I should check with you first?" Alex asked.

"Yes, good. Thank you," he added. "You wouldn't believe how few people give me that courtesy. All those students down hanging around the baby tirgs, Calling away constantly. It's not like we can't hear them, after all. And there was one girl who Called the first day we'd taught her. It worked, too; she'd bonded one of the piglets in the feeder pens." The Director shook his head, remembering.

"Really, what happened?" Alex asked. He hadn't heard of this before; most of the College's feeder animals were carefully bred for low intelligence and low susceptibility to bonding.

"She tried to keep it a secret, because she knew she wasn't supposed to be Calling so early. Of course we found it out; pig missing, girl not showing for classes . . . we found her. No one's going to hire an Animist with a pig! We'd have been a laughingstock. And if we'd just taught her Separation, gotten rid of the pig, and sent her out on her quest, we'd be at risk that she'd go freelance. She was a bit like you, and she got a bit upset over the matter . . . So we ended up doing a chemsep."

"A what?"

"Chemsep, chemical Separation. Put her into a coma with drugs, basically shut down the parts of the mind affected by the bonding. Euthanize the Anim, and bring her back out; the mind has a chance to recover and it doesn't take the shock of the death. Then she could go on like it never happened."

"And did she?"

"Um, well." The Director looked embarrassed. Rhese put her head on Welson's knee, and the Director stroked the coarse fur absently. "She actually didn't. I think . . . well, the other students gave her a hard time about it. There was a bit of a scene; she didn't want us to kill her Anim, of course. We had to force her. The piglet didn't suffer, and we buried it, you know, all proper, we *didn't* cook it, I'll swear that, and we gave her counseling, but . . . there were jokes. You know how students can be . . ."

Alex nodded. Anyone who thought wild animals were vicious had never seen the interplay among a group of teenaged girls.

"And, well . . . she killed herself." He looked down, and Rhese looked up at him, and raised a paw in a sort of comforting way. The Director sighed, then looked up again. "Still, no point lingering on this stuff, eh? Go ahead and Call."

"What, now? Here?" Alex looked around. A couple of ancient nanny goats looked at him scornfully, but there were no other students around.

"Sure, why not?" The Director looked around, saw Alex's gaze. "What? You're not going to end up with them, Alex. Those goats are almost as old as you are. Go on."

"Um, I'd really rather . . ." Alex began, but the Director interrupted him.

"You're not going to sneak out of it that way. You have to prove to me you can do it, before we'll let you leave. And if you think you can avoid it later . . ." He shook his head. "When my first Anim, Coosha, died, I felt awful. I never wanted to go through that again. I said I wouldn't Call again, ever. Then one day Mirkosho came in with this filthy, starving puppy he'd found and was planning to take to the kitchen . . . I glanced at it and—" He snapped his fingers. "Like that. That was Grub, the brown dog in the mural in my office."

"I wondered why you'd named her that," Alex said, smiling despite himself.

"That's right. It's the way we are, Alex. Even without your training, you're an Animist at heart. The College is a family. Sometimes we're harsh, but your original family wasn't much better, was it?" Alex shook his head. "Go ahead and Call, Alex, and then you're free to go. For now, anyway." He shut his own eyes.

Alex sighed, and sat down, and leaned against the wall to steady himself. "I haven't done it before," he warned. "I don't know—"

"Just try," insisted the Director. "I'll watch."

He didn't want to. He still held out hope, despite the Director's words, that he could just go about his life as a person; not as a Animist, not as a slave. But here and now, Welson wouldn't let him go unless he proved he *could* Call. And at least, there were plenty of impressive animals in the menagerie of the College. The baby tirgs, cute and playful in their orange and black stripes, were particularly appealing.

Alex kicked off his boots, and assumed the position for his meditations; the soles of his feet both touching, the palms of his hands touching, head down, eyes closed. The sun was warm on his head, and the smell of manure was in his nose.

Slowly he counted his breaths, seven counts in, seven counts out. He listened to that soft susurration, until it filled the mind and left nothing else. The gurgle and swish of the goats chewing their cud, the distant chatter of the campus, the sounds of the outside world seemed to diminish and vanish.

He concentrated on letting his muscles relax, joint by joint, tendon by tendon, slowly letting control slip away. His limbs seemed to drift into nothingness, but there remained the sensation of warmth, on the soles of his feet and the palms of his hands. He could hear his pulse, a steady beat to the slow counterpoint of his breath.

Watching through the Oether-eyes of Rhese, the Director saw Alex go from a faint imprint on the Oether into a slowly expanding sphere, bright and strong. Welson took a quick glance around, wary of other spirits, but all was quiet.

In Alex's mind, he formed the essence of himself into a single note, and struck it: a Call of *here I am*, a broadcast of self, of a pattern seeking a compatible match for a missing part of itself.

In the Director's mind the Call rang out like a bell, like a huge bronze bell that tolled a single note and sent the lights of the Oether rippling and shuddering; it made him flinch back and cover his ears against a sound only his brain had felt, and Rhese gave a coughing bark of surprise and annoyance.

The echoes rang out like ripples in a pond and Alex could feel/see them go, felt them shiver slightly with contacts from other spirits, Animulae, Animists in the Oether, and pass on, unmatched. There was no response, no echo back. He felt the waves pass out to their farthest point; past the walls of the College, he was sure, and some ways into the forest, for he felt a touch of the confusion of woods spirits before the waves faded into nothing. Nothing. Relieved, but also disappointed, he slowly backed himself out of his trance, slowly bringing himself back to reality, to the sun hot on his head and the wall digging into his back and his butt having fallen asleep. The Director was watching him hopefully.

"Anything?"

Alex shook his head. "No . . . but it did work, didn't it? I did it right?"

"Oh, certainly. Quite loudly, too. Yes, you certainly have talent. Worth every rill we paid for you," he added, meaning it jokingly, but Alex only grimaced. He stood up briskly, then had to sit down again as the blood rushed from his head, then, once recovered, he followed the Director back to the front gate. "It was worth a try, anyway. It always is. Someday we'll be able to do away with this quest thing altogether, just breed all the Animulae we need, here at the College. Speaking of, where did you say you were thinking of looking?"

"I thought . . . thought I'd go home, actually," Alex answered, stretching and rubbing his eyes. "See my parents."

"Are you sure that's a good idea?" the Director asked warily. "I mean, they sold you into slavery. You don't resent that?"

"We were starving." Alex shrugged. "They did what they had to do. Maybe someday I can help them, give them a better life. Maybe they're already dead, but . . . I have to know. Besides, there's these animals on Drylast . . ." He glanced away, lost in distant memory. "Snowfoxes. White, almost as big as the wolves . . . I used to see them far away, playing on the hills. I always wanted to pat them but they never came close." He sighed. "Maybe this time one will."

And besides, he thought, *in those distant, cold lands, there's a good chance the College won't even bother to come looking for me.*

He made his way down the winding path from the College, through the green of the jungle and down to the shore, where a coastal trail wound along the hills with the black sand beach on one side and the green slopes on the other. On many other occasions he'd walked the same road, traveling to trade with the Humani or Lemyri villages on Highjade.

He passed through the trading village of Lemyri, where he'd disgraced himself so badly with Jocin and Phyl the other night. He hurried through, keeping his head low, and hoping none of the bounding furry shapes recognized him.

He traveled on until he'd reached the town on the coast where he'd first arrived on the island: a Humani city of no great size, but still worthy of note for the trader. In addition to the presence of the College, which was always a buyer for rare animals, herbs, and metal, Highjade provided fine obsidian, rare Lemyri wines and chutney made from the fruits of the forest, fresh water, coffee, tea, cocoa, and other herbs and spices and medicines, ceramics, worked and crafted items, as well as timber.

There were no ships in port heading north at the time; Alex found a small farm willing to let him sleep in the shed and share in meals, in exchange for mucking out the striches and goats. Alex was happy to oblige.

The work kept his mind off the worries of his life; the fact of his debt to the College, the uncertainty of his future, and increasingly, his loneliness. After being surrounded by well-known acquaintances, if not friends, for so many years, he felt lost without the familiar greetings. He found himself now talking to the goats, and made himself

stop; all he needed was accidentally to bond with a goat, and he'd be
worse off than that girl with the pig.

It was with some relief, then, when he saw the trading ship afloat
in the bay one morning, and heard from the dockmaster that it was
indeed bound in a roughly northerly direction. Good enough,
thought Alex to himself; at least get myself to a more well-traveled
port, and I should be able to get passage to Drylast soon enough.

The *Charmed* turned out to be a three-masted Humani vessel,
simple and functional of line, with little ornamentation except two
large painted eyes on either side of her prow, which were supposed to
keep her away from reefs. She sat at the end of one of the deepwater
docks, her crew loading aboard the last necessities of the voyage. She
was sitting low in the water, holds full of goods to carry north; judging by the smell, coffee was at least part of her cargo.

Alex hailed the ship as he reached the end of the dock, and a
moment later a Roden jumped down from the railing to land before
him.

The Rodeni looked very much like large hopping rats, though
with larger heads in proportion to their bodies, eyes set farther forward and closer together to allow for some binocular vision, and tails
covered in short flat hair with a tuft on the tip. Alex had learned that
they were probably more closely related to desert jerboas than rats,
but the unknown distant species from which they'd evolved was long
extinct and "large hopping rats" was probably the closest you could
get in accurate description. They usually moved in bipedal hops, but
could also waddle along awkwardly step by step, and they could travel
on all fours quickly, and did, in their native desert tunnels. Their
hands, with clawed nails and knobby palms, had an opposable thumb.
The front incisors were yellow and long and sharp and very visible,
and this particular Roden stood, on his hind legs, only a foot shorter
than Alex. Many were smaller than this; they tended to live low in status, and Rodeni who were hungry in their early years would never
grow as large as those few who were well fed. Alex sometimes wondered if his own lack of height was due to those childhood years of
starvation.

This Roden, cocoa brown, was wearing wide, baggy trews that
tied up over the base of the tail, and was therefore a male. He flicked

his large ears forward in greeting, looking at Alex with a quizzical air. "Yes, what?" the Roden chirped in Trade. His voice was higher than a human's, and each consonant was sharp and clicking. Trade was a simple, elegant language of easy-to-make sounds, and it was known to all the Trading races—all the sapient species of the Archipelago. All had their own languages as well, often with many variants and dialects, but anywhere you could find a priest you would find a speaker of Trade. For Trade was also the holy language, the magical language of theists, theurgists, and thaumaturgists. Theists were the priests of the gods, theurgists were shamans of the spirit world, and the rare and powerful thaumaturgists were true wizards and witches. In comparison to any, Animists were mere dabblers—but they served a separate and dangerous function of their own.

"The Harbormaster told me you might be looking for an Animist to go along to Patralinkos," Alex said, giving a nod of respect that made his necklace clink.

"Animist, eh? Where's your familiar, then?" demanded the Roden, twisting his head to look behind Alex.

"I don't have one, not yet," Alex explained. "That's why I need to travel, you see."

"Then what good are you?"

"I can still weatherwatch for you; it just will take a bit longer. And I can . . ." Alex mentally ran through the list of the skills the College had taught. "Um, I can sew, bind and tend wounds, set bones, prepare foods, distill medicines, weave fence, baskets, and rope, carve wood, slaughter and butcher, cure leather, chip obsidian, divine from entrails, train and shape behaviors, tell enlightening animal stories, identify and interpret most species of mammal, tie the Fourteen True Knots and eleven other ones, and, as I said, I can see into the Oether if you give me a little time to do it." He didn't bother to mention Scooping Dung, Rock Border Repair, Being On Watch, and Digging Drainage Ditches, although it sometimes seemed as if most of College had been composed of that.

"Can you fight?" the Roden asked, squinting up at him.

"Some," retorted Alex, returning the gaze calmly, trying to show confidence. He'd had many days of being nerve-pinched into screams by his Lemyri teachers, and wrestling recalcitrant beasts, if that counted.

"Well, I suppose you won't eat much," sighed the Roden. "And maybe half an Animist's better than nothing. Rather have a priest of Shantovar, but . . ."

"You won't find any here; the god-ridden and the Animists don't get along well." Alex folded his arms on his chest.

"I'll have to clear it with the cap'n, but come aboard," the Roden said, springing straight up to grab the rough wooden side of the ship and hauling himself back up to the deck, his legs and tail waggling comically before they vanished. Alex took the longer route, up the gangplank.

On the deck, the crew, a mixture of Humani and Roden, bustled about; a few of them glanced in Alex's direction but did not challenge him. He saw the cocoa brown Roden talking to a man dressed in fine clothing, who soon came over to greet him.

"Captain Chauncer," he introduced himself bluntly. "You stay on call and weatherwatch for us at dusk and dawn, and whenever else we ask. We'll pay you in passage. Deal?"

"That's all I'm looking for, sir," Alex replied respectfully.

"Prang says you've got other skills as well; we'll expect you to help out as needed. For the most part, though, stay out of the way and let us know if there's anything in the Oether we should know about." He gave a nod of his head, and Alex bowed in acknowledgment.

Prang, the Roden, showed Alex to a cabin, little more than an enlarged cupboard, with a bunk he could lie down in if he tucked up his legs. A slatted-wood hatchroll gave some privacy, but made Alex feel that he was sleeping in the Director's roll-top desk. It was about the same size. Alex felt it was cramped and small until he saw the Rodeni quarters, where three Rodeni shared a space of equivalent size, curled up together in the tiny area. A tiny porthole provided some ventilation.

Cramped and small though it was, it was luxury compared to his last ship voyage, in the hold of a slave trader. That had been dark, crowded, and stuffy. True, they had been allowed out onto the deck once a day, but it had only made the hold seem stuffier upon returning. The cargo had outnumbered the crew, but among the crew was a theurgist—one who works magic with the help of the spirits. When one of the slaves had attempted to punch a crewman for an insult, this shaman had raised his hand—there had been a flash of light that made Alex and all the others watching flinch painfully—and then the slave was rolling on the deck, whimpering like a kicked dog. He'd had to be carried back down into the hold, and for the rest of the trip could not speak or raise his gaze to anyone.

The cabin was without much interest for Alex, so he went about exploring the ship. Alex quickly gathered that Prang was the first officer of the ship, an unusual position for a Roden. Many ships had a high complement of Rodeni, since their natural skills made them useful crewmen, and their minimum requirements in food and housing made them economical. You could have too many on board a ship, though. If their numbers grew too high, especially in mixed-gender groups, they would start to fight and could erupt into an almost berserk fury.

In cities, Rodeni were often pushed to the bottom of the social structure. They were seen by Humani as being little more than evolved rats, and the Lemyri despised their lack of discipline and ground-living habits. Most Rodeni lived in Humani cities; there were a few all-Rodeni cities and islands, but they were distant and, rumor had it, overcrowded and often stricken with famine and disease.

All the Rodeni on the *Charmed* were male; this kept the intergroup conflict down to a minimum. On other ships, Prang informed him some time later, the Rodeni crews were entirely female. No ship could be crewed solely by Rodeni, however; their distance vision was poor, making navigation difficult if not impossible without the help of a sharper-eyed being on board.

The crew was busy with its business; goods of trade were being ferried across the bay, and provisions were being replenished. Other goods were spread on the wide floating dock, and a group of merchants, Humani and Lemyri, looked over the bundles of rustling herbs, bolts of cloth, as well as jars, bags, and barrels filled with other things Alex could only begin to guess at. The captain and the trademaster watched them warily, and conducted deals. When darkness fell Alex went to his cabin and managed to curl himself into the tiny space, small and stuffy after years in his hammock at the College. He was using his rolled-up hammock as a pillow; there was no place to hang it in here, and he found the hard flat surface of the wood strange and uncomfortable, even with its thin mattress. The swaying of the ship made him feel constantly on the verge of being flipped out of bed, another problem with being used to hammocks. Unable to fall asleep, he performed his meditations instead, and just lay there, sensing the faint silvery patterns in the Oether, taking comfort in their random swirling dance. Deliberately, he did not Call. Here and now, he was free, he could do what he wanted. He was sixteen and the world was suddenly opening at his feet into a horizon of possibility. He sat quietly and listened to the Oether, unable to get more than faint impressions, but still, by his talent and his training, more than any normal person could sense.

There were the Visi, the weather-spirits, unaware and unfocused, little more than particles of energy. By them he could weatherwatch, as requested; this calm behavior meant the day would be calm tomorrow. The Visi drifted about aimlessly in his awareness, and he almost fell asleep then; but with a start, he halted, and backed himself out of his trance. It could be dangerous to sleep with an open mind; you never knew what might wander in. He finally fell into normal sleep in the small hours of the morning.

TWO

Alex awoke to a pounding; bleary-eyed, he pulled himself up and rolled up the slatted hatchroll to see one of the ship's Rodeni, black and white, peering in at him. The ship seemed to be swaying more now.

"Sun's up, *chus*," chirped the Roden. "Time you to work, yep."

Alex thanked him and shrugged into his clothing, and staggered out onto the deck to clear his head. The sunlight made him blink, but he saw that the *Charmed* was clipping quickly along the sea now, her sails filled overhead; Highjade was a receding green shape aft.

Watching it go, Alex felt a pang of homesickness; the blue of sky and sea all around suddenly seemed far too open and empty, and as blank as the future.

He sat down on a coil of rope on the deck. In the center of the coil was a black and gold spangled monitor lizard, kept on board to control the populations of rats that threatened the cargo. It was about three feet long, and raised its head and flicked its tongue at him. Alex nodded at it in greeting. It seemed to find him uninteresting, and went back to its basking in the sun. Alex shifted his position slightly, so as not to block the reptile's sun, and concentrated on his meditations.

The Visi still swarmed, in sky and sea, aimless and drifting. Keeping his eyes shut, Alex turned his head with the effort of trying to sense in all directions, to check the horizon, but saw nothing unusual. The weather should remain clear for now. He hoped.

He backed out of his trance and opened his eyes, and was startled to see a girl standing only a few feet away, looking at him in interest. She was perhaps a bit older than he, wearing the simple pants, shirt, and vest of the ship's crew. Her black hair was curly and brushed her shoulders. When she smiled at him, her teeth were white against her tanned skin.

"You looked like you were asleep," she commented. "Sorry to startle you . . . I just don't see that many magists and I was curious. I'm Jeena."

"Oh, no need to apologize—my name's Alex," Alex stammered quickly, and tried to smile. She was very pretty. "I'm not a magist, though. I'm not even an Animist, yet." *What am I, then?* he wondered, not for the first time.

"But you can see the Oether," Jeena pointed out, sitting on the rope next to him. The monitor woke up again, gave a peevish hiss and climbed out and away, vanishing down one of the hatches. "You're on the path, as they say."

"Well, but we . . . they, Animists, they don't consider themselves magists, anyway," Alex explained. "The Anim—Animulae, really, but we just call them Anims—are just animals. Animal souls, I guess. Simple things . . . and an Animist works with them, forms a bond, and works through one."

"I always wanted to be able to do magic," Jeena said with a sigh. "I really envy you. But if *I* had the talent for it, I think I'd want to do something more than Animism. Be a shaman, or a witch."

"I didn't have much choice," Alex said, with a sigh, but avoided her questioning expression. "Besides, I'm not sure being a shaman or even a thaumaturgist is such a good thing."

"What do you mean?" Jeena asked, puzzled.

Alex waved a hand. "I guess it's just part of the Animist philosophy. We don't trust the magists all that much. I mean, they're powerful. They can do things no one else can. Sometimes, that can make a person feel superior, give them an edge over everyone else."

"I don't see anything wrong in that . . . they *would* be superior! And they could use their magic to help others."

"I suppose, but . . . power is corrupting. They could also use it to manipulate others, or hurt others, or just mislead. That's why the Lemyri developed Animism."

"The Lemyri don't like magic . . . I've never understood that," Jeena said, shaking her head. "Probably because they can't do it."

Alex shrugged. "I don't know . . . it could be. But they certainly aren't telling."

Just then one of the other crewmen whistled for Jeena's help with a rope, and she stood up quickly and excused herself. Alex sat and silently berated himself for not being a more interesting conversationalist, and watched as Highjade slowly vanished away into the distance.

The days went by. Alex found he had little to do beyond his Oetherwise duties, and despite the novelty of travel, the time dragged. He still felt alone; the crew was polite enough, but if he tried to help he found he only got in the way. Trying to engage them in conversation was frustrating, for there was simply not enough common ground between them. Jeena was the exception; though for the most part she would only ask questions, about magic and the Oether. She didn't want to talk about herself, or hear his amusing stories about the animals at the College; she was interested in the theories of magic. Alex's education was not very helpful here. As he'd said, the practice of Animism was discovered by the Lemyri. Thus, Animism had at one time been violently opposed to all other forms of magic, as the Lemyri still were. Animism was developed as a way to view the Oether, to detect magical activity. With an attending Animist, a Lemyri tribe could refuse to deal with anyone wielding or influenced by magic. Sometimes, particularly if any sign showed in their own people, they would kill the magist.

Understandably, Animists were viewed with malice by magists and priests, and vice versa. A Human named Brez had learned of the Lemyri discovery, and set about trying it himself. He formed a small group of followers, and then presented himself, cautiously, to the Lemyri. After careful deliberations, the two cultures agreed to combine their knowledge, and the College had been formed. Humani influence had opened wider employment opportunities for Animists, and it was not unheard of for an Animist to go on, later, to become a true magist of some form. Such was frowned upon by the College, of course, but it did happen. Even so, Alex had only tenuous knowledge about most of the subjects upon which Jeena questioned him. Animism itself didn't interest her. As she came to realize that he couldn't help her with her ambition of some day joining the ranks of the magists, she began to lose interest in Alex's company. This only made him feel more alone; first his parents, then the College, and now even this girl were only interested in what use or value he might have, not in who he was.

It was while he was musing glumly on this one morning, after his weatherwatch, that the sails were adjusted and the ship's skipping pace slowed.

"Why've we stopped?" Alex asked a passing crewman, who was coiling ropes.

"Gotta summon the Delph escort," the man grunted. "We're in their waters now."

Alex looked around. The decks were being cleared of clutter, and rum was being distributed from a small cask, each man taking his share in a small ceramic cup. The air held a certain expectation. He noticed the Rodeni signal-drummer taking up his post by the great drum on the foredeck, and two men taking out instruments: a fiddle and a flute.

To the north the sea stretched wide and empty. Alex shivered despite himself, thinking of the dark depths beneath the waves, where, legend had it, strange creatures lurked. Then the music started up.

It was a sea chantey Alex had heard before, with typically salty lyrics. A group of five of the crewmen began belting them out in firm voice, and stomping around on the cleared deck in a dance that seemed less concerned with grace than with making as much noise as possible.

> *Hey-yup hup we rises*
> *Sing ho for a hornpipe crew*
> *Give us a wink an' we'll sink our dink,*
> *Any ol' port will do!*

The signal drum thudded out the pounding beat, counterpoint to the dancers' stamping feet. The fiddle squeaked and sang, the flute pattered out the quick melody, and the men's voices bellowed out. Hands clapped among the rest of the crew, or, in the case of the Rodeni, who lacked smooth palms, strong feet pounded in time against the deck and hull. Alex found his own foot tapping, and made himself stop. The thudding against the echoing ship would be magnified underwater, Alex realized, and this must serve as a signal to the Delphini.

The melody was really pretty simple. Alex took his own wooden flute from his pocket, and started to play along. A couple of the crewmen nearest him glanced his way, grinned and nodded. Encouraged, Alex kept playing. He tried to ignore the lyrics, which went on to describe various obscene practices that could be accomplished with most of the Trading races.

"Delphs ahoy!" shouted a man at the railing, and Alex looked in that direction. A shape burst up out of the water, flashing turquoise and silver, sleek and gilded with spray as it leaped higher than the deck. Alex caught a glimpse of a dark eye peering at the figures on deck, before gravity claimed the leap and brought the Delphin down. The Delphin turned gracefully as it fell, to splash as neatly as a falling knife into the water.

Other Delphini began jumping, like hybrids of jewels and lightning; emerald green, teal blue, white and grey and purple. The music continued, the Delphini timing their splashes now to crash like symbols at the beats. When the song finally wheezed to a close, there was a fusillade of jumping splashes, and spray blew cold and salty over the deck.

Captain Chauncer strode over to the railing; he'd been absent during the song, but someone had gone to fetch him at the first sign of the Delphini. Now he leaned over the rail, and shouted, "Greetings from the *Charmed*!"

"Ch-Ch-Charrrmed I'sure," creaked back a reply in Trade from one of the milling forms below, and there was a chorus of snapping, popping, squealing noises, and a few razzberries.

Ignoring this, the captain shouted, "We need to get to Patralinkos!"

The chorus protested.

"Aaarrr, toofarrr!"

"C-c-c-cold!"

"Merrrrk-k-k-konos!" one offered, as an alternate destination.

"Aeeedelwae!" suggested another.

"Mirrrap-posa!"

"Dusk-k-k-ward St-t-tret-ch!" added one.

"That's fine!" the captain shouted back. "Duskward Stretch is fine!"

The words of Trade slacked off, as the pod discussed the matter between themselves. Then there came a loud, shrill whistle. The captain turned to his men.

"Hoist sail! Let's go! Give these things a run for their trouble!" he shouted, and the crew leapt to obey. Prang jumped up over Alex, climbing into the rigging, while Alex peered cautiously over the railing at the Delphini. He knew they were used as guides in the open seas; they traded for ketchunal and other drugs, mainly, since they had no way to carry much of anything else. They traveled constantly anyway, and did not mind being escorts for navigation and protection in the process. He didn't remember seeing them on his first voyage, but on that passage they had avoided the open sea, hopping instead from island to island to keep the living cargo supplied with food and fresh water.

The Delphini were larger than he'd expected, on an average of fifteen feet from narrow nose to tail-flukes, sleek bodies snorting spray through the double-holes atop their bulging heads. He tried to count them, but they were moving too quickly, turning and diving and boiling up again, a flash of color in head and flukes before they vanished again.

With a slow creaking and strain, the *Charmed* surged out once again, her sails swelling with the wind. The Delphini took up positions on either side of her prow, three each, riding and jumping and diving over her wake. Slowly at first, with impatience as the ship gradually got up speed, then with greater leaps and arcing jumps they paced her. Alex noted that they were taking turns; after a time, a Delphin would vanish, and be replaced by another. Distant spray-signs far ahead of them made him realize that they were taking it in turns to scout ahead, forging through the water while their companions rode on the wake of the *Charmed*. There were monsters in the open seas that could swallow a ship whole, and sometimes a Delph scout was the only thing that could save a ship from becoming a snack.

Dusk came, and the winds slowed, the ship plowing along at a more sedate pace now, the Delphini invisible in the darkness but still audible, their creaking whistles and puffing respirations sounding over the creak and slap of wood and water. From time to time the crew would make a course correction at a shrill whistle from the escort. Alex sat on a coil of rope near the prow to do his nightly weatherwatch. He could have as easily done it from his cabin, but being out where everyone could see him would look better.

The Oether swarmed with Visi, aimless as usual. In the middle distance, however, he could detect ripples of something; something to do with the Delphini, he suspected. It was hard to tell what it might be; without an Anim, he could only get vague impressions, sensations that might be no more than false images thrown up by his own mind.

There was a sudden flash of something, close by and strong. It startled him, and frightened him. He could see it, and suddenly, he knew it could see him.

Panic slammed down his defenses; adrenaline flooded his system and jerked him back to himself, roughly. He hadn't been Calling, but had some spirit or demon sensed him anyway? He glanced around wildly, his head throbbing with the pain of his sudden return to full consciousness, his heart pounding. Warnings from the College rang in his mind: of what an unbonded Animist must always fear, that his trained and open and above all receptive mind might be an invitation for something else to inhabit. Something that would not be coaxed and invited, like an Anim, but that would attack and engulf and control. The higher spirits could do it, and they were not all the benevolent ones sought by magists. He concentrated on his thoughts, reinforcing himself, repeating his memories, until he calmed, and felt rather foolish. Whatever had come, had gone.

The next day dawned with blue skies, and the winds had picked up to a bracing speed. The Delphini, who seemed to be no worse for their nightly vigil, greeted the sun with many wild leaps and splashes, but it seemed odd to see the sun rise without hearing the rattling Lemyri chorus. Alex weatherwatched again, briefly and cautiously, and saw no change, and no sign of whatever it was that he'd seen in the night. He thought about telling the captain about the strange presence he'd sensed, but did not want to cause alarm when he didn't even know what the source might be.

Around noon the Delphini had all gathered to flank the ship on either side, and Alex was able to guess that the pod consisted of perhaps twenty individuals. As the wind picked up and the ship's speed increased, the Delphini became more active, leaping and bounding higher and higher. In between their clicks and calls, a single sound that might have been a word, blurred by speed and splash, began to be heard. It grew more and more prevalent until it was a repetitive chant, and many of the crew, Alex noted, were gathering on the deck and watching over the railing, and glancing warily at one another.

"What are they saying?" Alex asked Jeena, next to him at the port rail. "It sounds like 'Ride! Ride! Ride!' Do they want to come on board?"

Jeena was about to answer, when a shout erupted on the starboard side, and a splash, and Alex saw one of the crewmen struggling in the water below while a man on deck shouted down at him. And then before he could react, a Roden, teeth bruxing in laughter, and Jeena, grinning on his right, both grabbed his belt and lifted, tossing him over the rail. He twisted as he fell, trying to grab the rail, and in that extended perception of time that happens at such moments he was clearly aware of the merry faces watching him fall. Jeena waved.

"I can't *swi*—" Alex screamed, and then the water hit him like a plank across the back. It knocked the air from his lungs, and all he could replace it with was salty water. Cold and wet and shock and pain struck him like an all-over blow.

He flailed madly at the water as he sank, and something bumped into him, hard. He grabbed at it with the legendary frenzy of a drowning man, and found it slippery and hard to grip. He ended up astride it as it burst into the air, an explosion of hot air in his face and his answering choking gasp of water. He grabbed tight to this life support with both arms and legs. It was like hugging a rubber barrel.

"You hang on now, 'k-k-kay?" honked a loud voice in front of him, and he opened salt-stinging eyes to see a large purple fin directly in front of his face, and the thing he was clinging to was purple as well: the broad back of one of the Delphini. The creature was a solid tube of muscle that surged forward, tail flukes pounding. Alex wanted to close his eyes against the sting of spray, but fear kept his eyes wide and staring. He sank his fingernails into the rubbery skin and stared frantically up at the shape of the *Charmed,* looking for a rope, a ladder, anything. He saw Jeena leap over the side, and his heart gave a thud of hope that maybe she'd help him, and rescue him from these crazed beasts.

His head was turned to the side, facing the ship as the Delphin came alongside, and he saw the ship's timbers move past rapidly, in between the waves that smacked down over his head. He could not tell when the waves were coming, and in any case was too busy choking and coughing to hold his breath, which meant that he was sucking in about as much water as he was coughing out. Abruptly the barrier of the ship was past, and clear horizon showed in between the sudden blurry blue of the water. He hung on to the Delphin for dear life; if he let go, he knew, he wouldn't have the strength to try to keep himself afloat.

The rush of water tore at his sodden clothing, over his legs and into his boots, filling them and slurping them off his feet. The Delphin leapt high into the air; Alex could hear shouts from the crew of the *Charmed,* and the squeals of the Delphini, before the water smacked into him again. This time he attempted to hold his breath, gritting his teeth against the need to cough. His mouth was full of the taste of the sea, salty as blood.

They leapt again, and this time Alex caught a clear glimpse of another Delphin, and on its broad back was Jeena, seeming perfectly at ease. She hung on to the dorsal fin with her hands, legs gripping the blue-silver sides of the Delphin. She saw him, and let go one hand to wave as the Delphin cleared the water in a mighty leap. This proved to be a mistake, however, for the Delphin abruptly bucked and twisted in midair, splashing down sideways, and with a shriek Jeena was jolted off its back, visible free-falling for a moment before water poured into his face and eyes and mouth again.

The Delphin beneath him seemed to be getting more violent as well. It skipped like a stone through the water, the rapid shock of air-water-air-water-air-water disorienting Alex; he gave up on trying to see anything, and just buried his face against the slick hide, clinging like a leech. The creature dived then, down and down and down, the water pressing on his ears, his lungs burning in utter agony. The echoing heaviness of the water was full of sound: hissing roars, and clicks and pops and bangs and ticks, like a musical hailstorm against a sheet of tin. He felt the Delphin turn and forge upward again, and he tried to hold his breath until the air once again was available. He almost managed it, but not quite, and instead filled his sinuses with seawater.

Coughing and snorting again now in the rapid wild leaps, Alex could no longer feel his limbs. The few gasps of air he was managing to take didn't seem to be enough. He could feel his consciousness slipping, and his will with it.

Just then, the Delphin dived again, and before Alex had time to think, it was rocketing straight upward. They burst high into the air; Alex's eyes opened one last time in terror, to see quite clearly the ship's nameplate ten feet from his face in a sudden flash as the Delphin spun like a top. The centrifugal force hauled on him and he felt his grip slipping, but he was still clinging tight when the Delphin crashed back down into the water, on its back, on top of him.

He came to himself in spasms of agony on the deck, whooping for breath and coughing seawater. A crewman who'd been pounding him on the back stepped away, and there were shouts of relief (at having him alive) and accusation (at having him being at risk in the first place). He didn't pay them much attention. His body felt cold and wet and heavy, every limb numb, his lungs and chest and stomach burning.

"Get blankets, get him to his cabin," he heard the voice of the captain shouting. "What idiot threw him overboard?"

Jeena was demanding, "How were we supposed to know he couldn't swim? What's he doing on a ship and not able to swim?"

"Sorrrrry! K-k-k-k-now? Bet-t-t-terr?" came Delphini voices from below. There was a splash, and a moment later a large purple head appeared briefly over the railing before falling back again.

Prang helped him to his feet, as he continued to cough and retch, and half-led, half-carried him toward the cabin.

"Thanks," Alex managed, as he collapsed on his bunk. The ship used to seem to be shifting and unstable with its motions, but now it seemed so solid, so warm, so comforting. He never wanted to get within ten feet of the ocean again. Not even a tub of water.

"You need to get out of your wet clothes and dry," Prang insisted, helping him sit up. With the Roden's help he managed to change into a nightshirt-like arrangement that was too big for him, but warm nonetheless. Prang also tried to give him a large cup of rum, which Alex had to refuse. Even if he didn't intend to Call, the strictures against intoxicants for Animists were in place for a reason. Now that he was using his talent, he'd better abide by them.

"Why did they throw me in?" Alex asked. His lungs still burned with a heavy ache, and he worried about pneumonia. Prang flattened his ears, annoyed, but not at Alex.

"Just a joke. The Delphs like to play with you Humani, they try to show off how fast they can carry you, then they try to shake you off. It's part of how we pay 'em; let 'em use Humani for toys. But no one likes to get wet, so it's become a joke to try an' throw someone else to 'em. Jeena *likes* the fishy beasties and will go in with 'em, but they gotta have more than one of you to play with, so they can compete with each other." He shook his fur; Alex got the impression that the Rodeni were not considered good toys for Delphini, and that Prang was glad of this. "They didn't know you couldn't swim, or they would-n't have chucked you." His ears flicked up again, and he bruxed, grind-ing his teeth in the rasping equivalent of a Rodeni laugh. "I think you quite impressed their pod mama, that big one that carried you. Even half-drowned you hung on longer than Jeena or Dandals."

"Huh," Alex grunted, and fell asleep.

Jeena woke him a bit later with apologies, soup, bread, more rum, and a strange sort of clay smoking pipe stuffed with dried herbs. "Cap'n says you're to smoke that," she explained regarding the pipe. "It'll help dry your lungs out. I'm supposed to sit and watch you do it, in case you fall asleep and set the place aflame."

Alex sniffed the herbs, and didn't recognize them. "No, thanks," he said, as politely as he could manage. "I'm not . . . Animists can't risk taking things. Messes up the meditations—" he managed, before he started coughing for breath again. Jeena shook her head.

"It's perfectly safe, it's just medicine. And meditations won't do you much good if you don't recover. Come on."

"No, thank you," Alex insisted politely but stubbornly. He was still irked that Jeena had thrown him overboard in the first place. Her apologies seemed contrite.

"How long have I been asleep?" Alex asked, to change the subject.

"We're a few days out from Great Duskward," she told him. "The Delphs felt bad that you almost got killed, and they said they'd go all the way to Patralinkos with us anyway."

"Oh joy," Alex coughed sarcastically. Jeena looked annoyed.

"Alex, don't blame them, it's partly your own fault; you should have told us you couldn't swim before we hired you. And the Delphs are nice, really, when you get to know them. That purple one, I can't remember its whole name, wants to talk to you when you get better. You should be honored."

Jeena sat down on the edge of the bunk. Since there was so little room, her legs were in the gangway, and a passing Rodeni sailor had to hop nimbly over them to get by. "Alex . . . why *did* you become an Animist? It seems so . . . unimportant. Unambitious, I guess." She gave him a look of concern. "I think you're better than that."

"You do?" Alex managed. Jeena nodded.

"I mean, from what you've told me, if you have the talent to be an Animist, there's a chance you could become something more. Wouldn't that be worth it?"

"No," said Alex, flatly. He was too sick, too tired, to try and give a polite answer as he'd done to her queries before.

"What do you mean, no? Isn't working real magic better than cleaning up after an animal? You could do better, Alex!"

"Look," Alex said, and coughed, and managed to sit up, and tried again. "I'm an Animist because someone bought me and made me be one. Someone took control of my life and made me into something. I didn't ask for it, but I've done it now. I can't undo the past six years . . ."

"But you're free now!" insisted Jeena. "Leave it behind you, and move on to something better!"

Alex didn't know what to say. In a way, it was what he'd thought himself; and yet, Animism was all he'd ever learned. Could he really be something else? Something better? The thought of casting aside all the teachings of the College was frightening, but also tempting. If he could have power, real power, he'd never be a slave to anyone again.

Jeena, sensing this, pressed her advantage, and put her hand on his leg. Even this minor contact was enough to distract him wildly, but she was talking on. "I think you could even be a priest, Alex. You have talent, you could serve one of the Great Ones. That's real power."

But with that, a warning bell rang in Alex's mind. He shook his head slowly. "I . . . I don't like belonging to someone else. Being a priest is like that. You sell yourself to a faith; you take up what someone else wants you to believe and says you should do."

"No, it's not like that," insisted Jeena. "You just find friends, teachers, people with the truth. People wanting to help you, to be what you were meant to be, live the way you should."

"But . . . shouldn't that be up to me? How do I know they're right?" Alex asked.

"How do you know the Animists are right? From what you've told me, once you've found an Anim you won't be any good at any other magic. Why throw it all away like that?" asked Jeena.

"I . . . the Animists say that magic can't be trusted. It's power from something outside, something given by the gods and spirits, not from inside oneself, unless you're lucky enough to be born a thaumaturgist. And the Lemyri—"

"The Lemyri! They're a lot of arrogant bullies with no talent, who hate anything they can't control. They hate what they don't understand. They don't even like Humani! Magic is a part of the natural world, the spirits and gods are our friends and allies, they give us wisdom and counsel and guidance, and comfort and strength and power . . ." Jeena stared into the middle distance, with hunger in her gaze. "I'd kill for something like that."

"I'm sure," Alex said. "That's part of the problem, right there."

Jeena glared. "You think you've suffered, trained by the Animists? Do you have any idea what *I* went through? I was born in a whorehouse! What I suffered . . . no one valued *me* enough to buy *me* as a slave and train me! I ran away, I taught myself, and I'm going to learn magic, whether you'll teach me or not, and someday—"

"Someday you'll go back and *show* them, won't you?" Alex interrupted. "Furrfu, spare me! You think I haven't heard this before, from new students to the College? 'Oh, no one understands me, I'll become an Animist and bond a big tirg or a beautiful ornyx with a flowing mane, and then I'll go home with it and everyone will be so impressed . . .' Then they find out it's a lot of work and stink and persecution, and most of them leave. Maybe some of them go on to become magists. But is that any way to live your life? Living it, doing what you do, because of what some other people think and say and do? Isn't that just as much slavery as anything else?"

Jeena clenched her fists; for a moment Alex was sure she was going to hit him, but he was too tired to do anything about it. But instead she displaced her aggression, slamming one fist hard into the bulkhead, and then burying her face in her hands as she began to sob in a strangled fashion. Classic redirection of conflict/frustration impulses with overtones of both self-infliction and fear response. Despite knowing this, Alex felt himself to be a total conglomeration of fecal matter.

"It's not true . . . it's not. No one cares about me, and no one understands . . . only the gods might . . ."

"You'll have to find them yourself," Alex said, with a sigh. "I told you all the things I'm not supposed to do; why don't you go do them."

"I've been trying!" Jeena snapped at him, her face dark and wet with tears and anger. "The spirits won't talk to me! I'm not worthy! I'm not like you, Alex, I don't have some inborn talent. If I want magic, I'll have to work for it, work *hard.* I've been trying—" The Rodeni crew member came bouncing back, and halted at the turbulent scene, black eyes wide in puzzlement. "Go away, Kep!" Jeena screamed at him, and he leaped over her legs in terror and bounced up the stairway as fast as he could. Jeena sniffled. "All my life I've wanted to be someone special. Someone important, someone people would respect. Isn't that what everyone wants?"

"You are—" Alex started to say, but she interrupted him.

"Don't go telling me to be proud of myself, to be happy with what I have. Magic is my dream, my faith."

"That's fine, but you shouldn't have to stampede over other people, chasing after what you want. And it's an arbitrary sort of power, anyway. There's plenty of real, human paths to power and respect, magic's just . . . cheating!"

"It's not! It's the only true thing in a world full of lies. With your talent, you could become great . . ."

"And if you can convert a journeyman Animist to some cult or another, they'll be so grateful they'll allow you to join, too," Alex said, meaning it as a joke. But the sudden stiffening in Jeena's features wasn't funny at all. Even though he'd been warned of this by his tutors, his gut response was more sad than fearful. "No, Jeena. It's not going to happen. I've been living for other people for too long already. I'm not going to sign on for another seven years of labor, not even for the Instruments of Time. And not even for you, either." The rivalry between Animists and other magists was legendary, and he'd mentioned as much to her. Probably she *could* have used him as a bargaining chip . . .

Jeena's voice was cold. "I thought you could help me . . . but you won't even help yourself." She stood up, and gripped the hatchroll's handle as she looked at him with loathing. Her eyes seemed feverish. "You're a close-minded, paranoid, arrogant, selfish stupid bastard, and I hate you. I hope you die of the lung-rot." She slammed down the hatchroll so hard that one of the slats cracked, but she had already gone storming back up to the deck.

Alex curled into a small ball, pulling the blankets up around himself tightly as chills shook him. Jeena's voice still rang in his head, and he cursed himself; a few words, some simple advice, could have made a friendship . . . so what if she was a dreamer? Why had he said what he'd said? Why did he feel so much sicker, all at once?

Alex wrapped himself tighter in the blankets, shuddering with chill, his breath wheezing in his thickening lungs. The hours wore on. When he tried to open the hatchroll the broken slat stuck in the runner and jammed; he didn't have the energy to force it, and his voice was gone from coughing, so he couldn't call for assistance.

With the fever came fear, a cold evaluation of his sickness. He was too sick, too weak, much too sick. Something was very wrong. He might well be able to oblige Jeena by dying. He had never felt so alone, so helpless; a malignancy pressed on him, seeming stronger as

the light faded from the porthole and the tiny cabin, reeking of
sweat, grew pitch dark. He tried to fight off the smothering fear of
impending death with his meditations, but tumbled instead into a
hazy delirium.

The darkness of his dream was filled with lights and shapes twisting and spinning, like the Oether with the Visi swooped by storms.
Yet the lights were of shapes: triangles that pinwheeled past, structures
like the branches of trees but woven symmetrically, crystal lattices
forking out with multicolored lightning. A great cloud of spots, like a
massive flock of birds, flexed and formed around them all, its individual specks shifting in waving patterns. The specks like birds swooped
around him; he felt himself as though drowned, drifting limp, unable
to raise a hand to bat at the bird-specks as they pecked his flesh, his
eyes. There was no pain, only coldness, and terror; he couldn't move,
couldn't scream, could only wail in silent anguish his fear, his loneliness, his desperation. He felt the speckled, skittering blackness pull
around him, and watched in horror as the specks formed a spiral,
whirling around, opening up into a vast black whirlpool, with lightning crackling in its throat. He felt himself being drawn toward it,
and cried out again, a silent plea, a cry for help, ringing out through
the darkness.

Suddenly in the blackness something shot past like a falling star, a
single point of light. The specks boiled around it but could not touch
it; it moved too quickly. He found himself able to move, able to
crawl; slow and weak, every motion an effort as though he struggled
in the folds of a thick net. The point of light swooped back again,
menaced by the specks, and he reached out to it; it swerved in its
flight and came to him, and expanded. It flared into a brightness that
stunned him, and the specks of darkness boiled away from the light,
the tunnel collapsing into nothingness. The specks seemed to pull
away, searching, and then plunged away. Driven back from him, they
had found another target . . . but the warm light around him drove
such visions away.

He felt himself ringing perfectly with the light around him. There
was warmth, and the sense of a huge, surrounding presence, filling the
space around him. He could almost feel it breathing all around him,
one great pulse for each ten beats of his own. With the warmth came

a sense of peace and of love strong and pure. He could see rolling whiteness, like clouds, in slowly heaving billows on all sides of him, shining with a dim light.

So I've died, and this is the afterlife, Alex thought in wonder. *This great light . . . some kind of . . . god?* And then he started coughing.

Abruptly he awoke, back in the stinking, stuffy air of his cabin. He coughed, but the chills and ache had gone; the fever had broken. The sun was shining right into his little window. He was tired, and his lungs still wheezed a bit, but he felt better—better than he had in a long time. He reached up to pull back the blankets, and his hand touched soft wiggly fur.

?!

A sense of strange startlement and mild annoyance chimed through his mind, in addition to his own reaction—warning enough to prevent him from a reflexive flinging-away of the thing. He stared down in blank shock: Curled in the rolling whiteness of his blankets was a baby ship rat, small and grey, with black blinking eyes that had only opened recently. It sniffed his hand, and then licked it quickly with a tiny tongue.

peace love comfort

rang through his mind, and an impression of saltiness.

"A . . . rat?" Alex whispered, trying to wake up. This couldn't be happening. Dismay filled him. The rat looked up suddenly, and then climbed into his hand, pressing against it.

love! love love . . . sadness? love?

And with it came the impression of a star of light in the swirling darkness.

"There was something . . . and it was attacking me, through the fever. I called for help . . . Called, and you answered. You saved me," he said, staring at it, though he knew that Anims didn't really understand speech, only emotions and images and tones of voice. "But . . . Animulae aren't supposed to do that. They're terrified of higher spirits . . . and you're just a rat!" Dismay was briefly outflanked by amazement.

happiness

The rat snuggled up against his hand, and broadcast little waves of contentment. It was very small, very young; Alex wondered how it had even gotten here. Holding the rat cupped in his hand, he looked

around; it had either gotten in through the small gap in the jammed hatchroll, or possibly from some crack in the walls. Probably the latter; but even so, a rat barely out of nestling age that had managed to crawl all the way from . . . wherever its nest was, through a ship patrolled by monitor lizards and unsympathetic crew . . . you had to admire it. He stroked its soft fur with a fingertip, and felt a wave of
happy love contentment
sweep over him. With that, suddenly, he realized he was no longer alone, and he hugged the small loving shape gently, and tried not to weep with the conflict of emotions.

He gently inspected the rat; it (she, he amended mentally after quickly checking) seemed in good health. Her color was unusual, a dilution of black which made a blue-grey instead, and with a small spot of white on her brow, such as baby rabbits have. The white spot reminded him of how the small Anim-spirit had appeared in his Oether-affected fever dream, and he stroked it gently.

"Like a mote of light. Mote. Mote-Rat," he told her, and felt her contented acceptance of the name. He leaned back and tried to think, then, as the reality of what had happened sank in.

He was, of course, disappointed. He hadn't been sure he'd wanted an Anim at all. And this . . . a rat was worse than a pig. There was going to be trouble. The College wouldn't allow a debt-paying slave to have a useless Anim; no employer would want someone with a disease-carrying vermin animal as a companion—He had to keep checking his thoughts, though, because every time he started along these trains of thought, Mote would respond with plaintive sending. Though she couldn't speak in words, the message "I love you, why don't you love me?" came through so clearly he couldn't help but try to stop himself. And she was something unusual; she was brave and clever and obviously a strong Anim, odd to find one in such a small form. The feeling of completeness, of peace, of friendship, too, was so welcome after the long days of loneliness and misery.

Well, like it or not, he had his Anim now. His spirit-quest was technically over, though it seemed really like he'd only begun. The thing to do now was get back to the College . . .

Where people would be very understanding, but firm. He would be commiserated with. A rat! Poor Alex. That's no good. They only live a few years anyway, plus everyone and everything will be trying to kill it. Better off this way. Value invested in you, can't afford to risk it. Our decision, not yours. Chemsep. Euthanasia. What a reward for a tiny thing that had risked its own life to save his; thanks, now I'm going to kill you because you're not what I want. And on top of that, back to the College again? Without having anything more than this stuffy hold to be his experience of freedom? But what else was there to do?

Mote sensed his turmoil and tried to comfort him, which only made him feel worse. That was another problem; for all this rationalization, he realized he did care about the little thing. Part of this was, he knew, only the normal Animist reaction to the bonding process, but even so . . . she was cute, small and furry and grey. She was . . .

There was a creak from the hatchroll, a curse, and then the jammed slat snapped and the roll flew up, revealing the ship's cook with a mug of something in one hand.

"I brung you some—Blastrafters!" he swore, and lunged with a mighty hand toward Mote. "Gerroff him, ye vermin!"

"No!" Alex shouted, folding double to shield her with his body, grabbing her to his chest. The blow smacked into his nose instead and knocked him back. "Ouch!"

"There's a—" began the cook, but Alex talked over him, as best he could for the sore throat.

"No! Look, she's my Anim now, if you kill her I'll go into shock and die! Don't touch her!"

fear! confusion?

"But they said you didn't have . . ." the cook stammered, while thin soup spilled out of the mug held too loosely.

"I know, but she just showed up last night. It's hard to explain. Just don't hurt her."

"But they're all over the ship! How are we supposed to know which one's yers? And how are the monny-lizzies to know?"

"She'll stay with me, I'll keep her with me," Alex was explaining, when another crewman leaned over to peer into the bunk from the hatchway.

"You alive? Cap'n says he wants you to work, if you are," said the crewman laconically. "Even if we gotta carry you out, he says."

Alex hid Mote quickly in his nightshirt, and took the rest of the soup and drank it quickly as the cook stomped back down to the galley, and the crewman departed.

hungry

Berating himself for forgetting, Alex scooped her out of his shirt and put her in the empty soup mug and felt her

satisfaction

as she licked the inside. He got dressed quickly, and then took the mug with him out onto the deck. He didn't need to be carried, but he did need to lean heavily on the passage walls as he made his way along.

He emerged into the sunshine of late afternoon, and leaned back against the main mast, blinking in the light and keeping the mug covered with the palm of his hand, despite that Mote had had enough of the soup and wanted out.

annoyance

Trying to ignore the insistent muzzle pushing against his palm, Alex started to slide down into a sitting position, then stopped himself. He didn't need to meditate anymore, did he? He had an Anim! He tried prompting her mentally . . .

He got a strong impression of darkness, close and hot and full of the smell of soup. And annoyance, and stubbornness. He concentrated more fully, bringing up prompting images as he'd been taught, but all he could get was the inside of the mug.

He sighed, looked around, and made sure the crew was doing other things and not paying him any attention. He also looked to see if Jeena was around, but didn't see her. Then he quickly picked Mote out of the cup, and tucked her into his shirt pocket. Tiny footprint soup-stains marked the fabric.

happy

Then suddenly the world was overlaid with the shimmering lights of the Oether. He stared around in wonder.

The sky was a whirling haze of small spirits, dancing in mad chaos, crackling like sparks from each to each. In wild confusion they twisted and shimmered, and he thought he saw something like a flock of birds made of light swirling the sky from horizon to horizon. There was a flavor of tension, and anger, in its motions. Alex glanced about wildly, and to duskward he saw it, the thickening, swirling mass of ethereal light that was blowing the spirits before it like leaves on the wind—

He came back to his senses as he thudded painfully to his knees on the deck. A crewman came to help him, but he staggered back to his feet before he reached him.

"Storm!" he shouted, and the effort made him cough again. The crew took note, however, and someone ran to get the captain. "Duskward, just over the horizon and coming this way," Alex added, when he gulped another breath.

"How big is it? What kind would ye say?" demanded Prang, from the higher deck where he manned the wheel.

"Lots of lightning, lots of wind," Alex replied. "Other than that I don't know. I—" He stopped himself before he revealed that he'd never seen a storm through the Oether before, only through theory and description.

"A storm? You're certain, boy?" demanded the captain, striding forward. "The sky's clear as—"

"I'm sure, sir."

"Miraposa's not far duskward, think we can make it?" the captain asked Prang, who shook his furry head.

"If it's a blower, and he says it is, then we'd just run right into the teeth of it."

The captain seemed to be reminded of something, and asked, "Could this be some hostile magic, boy?" he demanded. Alex's brow wrinkled.

"Storms *are* magical, sir," he began, surprised. "The weather spirits—"

"I *know* that, any fool knows *that*," snapped the captain. "I mean, could someone be calling down the weather spirits against us? There's been talk of pirates who—"

Alex thought of the swirling shape he'd seen, and frowned.

"I don't know for certain, sir," Alex responded, wincing as Mote's claws scratched at his skin, under his shirt. "But it could be." Perhaps that was the presence he'd sensed . . .

"Whether it be or not, we'll end up in the trench if we aren't ready for the bugger," Prang commented tersely.

Alex was superfluous to events then, as the crew scrambled

around him to ready the ship. He found a place to sit, out of the way, and held Mote in one hand, stroking her fur with a fingertip. As the first hour dragged on and no sign came of the storm, some of the crew cast suspicious glances his way. Alex ignored them. His prediction was vindicated soon enough. Grey swirls of cloud appeared over the horizon, rolling forward with slow power. The setting sun stained them blood-red and purple. Alex stared at them in tense fear as they expanded, slowly made invisible by the coming darkness.

THREE

The storm seemed to wait until the light had bled from the sky. Alex kept Mote cupped against his chest, trying to stay out of the way of the sailors as they fought with the sails in the increasing wind. Lightning crackled from the clouds overhead, and Alex watched in wonder through Mote's Oetherwise eyes as the Visi flashed in unison with the lightning. Each flash rang with the backblast of magic, the ire of the nature spirits, that made Alex flinch with pain as the explosion occurred in the Oether and the sky both at once. He could feel Mote, hidden in his shirt, jerk in response as well. The rest of the crew were not so bothered; only Alex, now a sensing Animist, could feel the magical wrath of the spirits. It was certainly more of a curse than a blessing, and Alex, not for the first or last time, regretted the paths of his life that had brought him here. As the wind increased and the waves grew larger and wilder, he abandoned all such musings and concentrated instead upon hanging on.

He stayed out of the way as best he could, but eventually the work of the crew pressed him up near the aft deck, toward the railing. He kept his eyes turned away from the water, but a very Humani-sounding whistle made him look over.

Pacing the ship below was the large purple Delphin that had carried him. It was rolled sideways as it swam, so its dark brown eye could peer up at him.

"Sorr-rr-ry," it creaked mournfully at him, like a rusty hinge. Even awkwardly spoken as it was, the apology sounded sincere. Alex dipped his head in a nod of acknowledgment.

"That's all right. Not your fault I can't swim," he said to the Delphin, which clicked in pity.

"Ts-k-k-kk! T-t-teeeach-ch you? C-c'mere?" it suggested hopefully. Alex leaned back away from the rail in horror at the thought.

"No! I mean, no thank you. I think I'd better stay out of the water for awhile." *Like forever,* he added mentally. Mote sent a flicker of
  comfort
in response.

"You Aaaa'ex-x-x," commented the Delphin, the twin blowhole puffing shards of spray on the last letter of his name. "I am Rei-Kri-Ree-Cha-Kee-Kwa-Kir," she added, the long name indicating she was a female by denoting her lineage. Males had only short names; Delphini lines were matrilineal. Due to the Delphini habits, it was almost impossible to tell who the father of a calf might be.

"Um, pleasure to meet you," Alex managed, although it really had been anything but, the first time.

"S-s-storm s-s-oon. Sea angry. Sh-should know how t-to swim!" reprimanded the Delphin, but before Alex could reply she'd vanished below the waves. He got back away from the edge of the railing.

The wind had struck first, warm and wet, out of the dim red line that marked the duskward horizon, setting the sails flexing and the wood of the ship creaking. The crew had to shout to be heard over the wind, and then swiftly came the rain, hard and stinging and cold. Alex tucked up his collar and tied it, making a snug place for Mote at the base of his neck. She didn't like the wind and the cold, and sent flickers of unhappiness at them into his mind. She also urinated on him, but Alex didn't feel this was a good time to try training her. The wind alone could scoop her into the water if he encouraged her to leave his person for such business.

He knew he should probably go below, but the feel of the power of the storm was intoxicating. Mote seemed as nervous about the storm as he was, and kept overlapping her Oetherwise sense on his vision. If he glanced into the Oether, Mote peeking from the end of his collar, the air was full of twisting, whirling Visi, like a sandstorm of light and smoke. Mote was trembling against his skin. This feeling of heady excitement, he knew, was part of the lure of the Oether, the seduction of magic, of power. He felt very small, under the huge sky, above the huge sea, surrounded by the Oether; a tiny speck of mortal life, held up by a fragile chip of wood, tossed in what seemed like an infinity of eternal power. It frightened him, and yet it held him, too; part of him wanted to go into his cabin and hide and be seasick, but that part of him that wanted to stay out here and feel the fury of the storm (and be seasick) won out.

In addition, his fear of the sea below had only increased, and he wanted to be where he could see it. His imagination could only too easily picture the ship sinking, water pouring in through every timber, and himself, trapped in that tiny cabin, with no escape as the waters rose and crushed him. The thought made him start coughing again, with Mote flinching in sympathy at his rasping barks.

Wind and rain now came lashing together as the sea swelled beneath them. The timbers creaked and the sails flapped and pulled, and then tore with a screaming sound. Rodeni and Humani scrambled about the ship, hauling ropes, shouting orders. It was pitch black save for the dim greenish glow of emergency phosphor lights hastily hung around the ship. The *Charmed* rose and fell, in great heaving swoops; it reminded him of how Mote felt when he would lift or lower her too suddenly. Up and down and sway and turn and up and down and Alex grabbed a rail for support while he threw up his soup.

sympathy worry concern

It was as he was leaning over the rail, wheezing for breath, that he felt Mote's sudden tension. She gave a sound, the first sound he'd ever heard her make, a kind of high, angry squeal. He turned, and saw Jeena there, clutching a rope, staring at him, at his shoulder, at Mote, who was bristling with fear. Alex's vision was suddenly overlaid with the Oether-sight then, and Jeena, and the very air around her, was glowing like the light from a phosphor lamp. Magic. Something she'd tried had finally worked. Alex was suddenly reminded of the hostile spirit that had attacked him.

"You've done it," he managed to say. "What . . . how? Is it worth it?"

"I tried to show you the way, Alex," Jeena said, her voice calm but firm. "They wanted you. They liked you. Wanted me to convince you. But you made them angry. You wouldn't listen. You chose a *rat* instead. That was wrong. You're the enemy now."

"No, Jeena," Alex stammered, as she advanced on him, slowly along the pitching deck. Mote's teeth were chittering in fear.

"Power has a price. You said that, too. You're right . . . pity it's you who'll have to pay it." She looked up at the swirling storm, and Alex realized she must see it as intoxicating as he did; that she might even have summoned it, to hide what she was about to do . . .

He leapt back a moment before the flash of lightning seared the sky, Mote's premonition of
    terror!
warning him, but he was sick and weak and slow, and before he could recover, Jeena's fist slammed into his face, knocking him backward, sprawling against the railing, pain blurring everything. Mote screamed again, and then Jeena had grabbed his legs and heaved; he went over backward, and fell. The shock of the water hit him twice, once when he hit, and again as Mote splashed into the thrashing water beside him.
    cold wet panic fear panic
Mote! He had to find her! He flailed at the water, gasping, choking, blood pouring from his nose. A flash of intuition hit him and he grabbed desperately, and was rewarded with a handful of soggy, wriggling fur that scrambled for a foothold. He couldn't keep himself afloat with only one hand, and instead tried to hold Mote aloft, out of the water, as his head went under.
    panic fear panic!
His head broke the surface and he gasped for breath, flailing at the water, rain slashing around him; Mote was a sodden, terrified presence. The sea pulled him up the side of a wave with ease and speed, before losing interest and sucking him under again. He clawed for the surface with his free hand, and gulped air and water. He stared around frantically and thought he saw the lights of the *Charmed*, already far off as the heaving waves pulled apart the distance. Then another wave reared up, torn by the wind, and pulled him under.

fear!

The water smothered his ears, but in the ringing numbness underwater he could hear a rapid, rhythmic clicking, growing louder and faster—

Rei-Kri-Ree-Cha-Kee-Cra-Kir pushed him to the surface, and floated there as he lay draped over her back, coughing and gasping. The water bucked and heaved around her, but she bobbed like a cork. She sank again, and Alex churned at the water, but she rose again quickly, this time carrying him astride. He couldn't see a thing, but the slick shape was familiar. Mote scrambled up his arm and hid under his collar at the back of his neck.

worry panic fear

"Take me back to the ship!" Alex gasped, pleadingly. Rei emitted a low, sad whistle.

"You sure?" she squeaked through her blowhole. "You not-t-t fall. Push-d. Ss-saw it."

"I . . . you're right," Alex wheezed, realizing that if he did go back to the ship, Jeena would just find some other way to kill him; and sick, and newly bonded with a helpless baby rat as his Anim, he didn't stand a chance. "But then what . . ."

"Island not far-r-r. Will go there," chirped the blowhole, as a wave swooped them along its rising crest. Alex clung tight, and the Delph squeaked a little as his fingernails dug into its rubbery hide. "Ee!"

Alex relaxed his grip a little, since his strength was dwindling anyway. He lay helplessly across the Delph's back as she forged carefully through the water, sliding over the waves, the water and rain beating at them. Luckily, the sea was tropical; not warm, but not cold enough to kill. Some warmth seemed to seep through Rei's rubbery hide as well, but the wet and wind still left him numb. Mote drifted into nightmare-ridden fitful naps, and the images and emotions turned Alex's half-conscious perceptions into a confusing, hellish blur.

The waves grew smaller and smaller, and the rain turned from a pounding pain into a light mist, then faded. The Delphin slid on across a flat sea, still black as obsidian. Alex's arms and legs hung limp, dragging along in the current on either side of the Delphin, but he managed to look up, and thought he saw a faint glow in the sky. Then there was only darkness, and water.

Alex got the impression of greyness, then of brighter light, slowly increasing. The air was full of mist, but now he could see the large purple shape that carried him. His clothes were torn, the pocket that had held his lucky rock now a ripped hole. *Must not have been that lucky anyway,* he thought glumly. Rei swam on in silence, but gave a whistle of greeting as she felt him move. In the distance Alex thought he could see a shape, a dark mass that might be land. Mote climbed out onto his head, shaking her fur and blinking in the light, and tried miserably to groom herself before giving up and taking shelter back in his collar. Alex shut his eyes again.

He opened them some time later, he could not tell how long. The yellowed cliffs were close now, visible through the rising mist. Alex heaved a sigh of relief, thinking of dry sand and firm ground. Then the support beneath him sank like a stone, leaving him floundering and flailing at the water yet again.

"Hey!" he shouted, as he struggled to keep afloat. "What are you doing?!" Mote clawed her way up to the top of his head, her own anger ringing in Alex's mind. To be so close to safety, and have it suddenly snatched away, made him as angry and frustrated as it made him afraid.

Rei's head appeared some ten feet from him. The mouth gaped in what was probably meant to be an imitation of a Humani smile, but instead just showed the rows of sharp, white teeth, all the same shape, all pointy. Not very reassuring. *Sure they push sailors to land,* Alex thought suddenly. *But maybe you just never hear about the ones they push the other way. Or when they get hungry on the trip.* "You s-swim!" she commanded in Trade. "Neeeed tt-to k-k-know!" This was almost worse.

"Abyssians eat you, you—" Alex screamed, as his head went under. A gentle push from below brought him back into the air again before he could inhale water, and then pushed him into a somewhat horizontal position. His face went in the water. Mote fell off his head, but he felt only

annoyance

from her, as she paddled briskly in the calm water around him.

"You sh-should swim!" he heard, though his ears were underwater. "K-k-k-ickkk feet-t!" The blunt tip of her muzzle banged into his chin; he bit his tongue, but his face was brought up into the air again. He tried to grab the Delphin, but she was underwater at right angles to himself. He knew—well, he was pretty sure that the Delphin wouldn't let him drown, not after so much effort, but his only goal was to get out of this water and never go near it again. *I'll live on a mountain, or in a desert. A mountain* in *a desert.* The Delph relented, floating a little so he could use her for support.

"Please, no," he gasped. "I know you're born for this, but I'm not. And I'm sick. I'm tired. I can't swim, not now. It'll kill me." He pulled Mote out of the water and set her atop his head, where she clung, her small claws scratching his scalp.

annoyance wet fear

"You will n-n-eed to swim," chirped Rei, rolling in the water so one small dark eye could watch him. "Mayb-b-be not now. But s-s-some time. S-swim, or s-sink. You l-learn!"

"Right, I will, I promise," Alex lied earnestly. "Thank you, thank you for saving me, thank you for the advice, please, let me get to shore."

"Should s-swim," the Delph muttered to herself, but she towed him toward the beach.

At last his flailing feet scuffed up sand, and he stood gratefully, slogging through chest-deep water toward the wonderful, wonderful shore. It was pale yellow-tan sand, rather than the glistening midnight black sands of Highjade, or the pebbly gravel of Drylast, but it was land all the same, and he headed toward it thankfully.

"C-cittty there," Rei said, and Alex could blearily see the white shapes of buildings against the curvature of a wide bay formed by sheer cliffs, at the farther point of whose crescent he found himself. "Not-t-t fffar-r, you sw-wim?" The bay was some distance away, and the cliffs looked daunting. The flat, sloping shore was much closer.

"I'm walking," Alex growled weakly, and slowly slogged out of the water, Mote still clinging to his head. He glanced back, and could see Rei's purple dorsal fin moving back and forth in the shallows, and sometimes the V of her breath. He remembered something.

"Wait! What island is this?" he shouted.

"Mi-rrraposa!" came the reply. Miraposa. An island much larger than Highjade, with Humani cities; that was all Alex knew of it.

The waters slowly fell away, and Alex was struck by how heavy his own limbs were, how strong the pull of the earth was. At last his bare, sore feet were scuffing up the dry, scratchy sand at the tide line, and the morning sun was warm on his skin. He turned back to look at the water.

Rei leapt up from the waves once in a strong parabola, and whistled what might have been a farewell. She vanished, and Alex sank down to the soft sand under the weight of his own body. He fell asleep where he dropped, on his back, amid the litter of seaweed, bits of shell, and other debris rejected by the ocean.

When Alex woke, the sun was sinking, he ached all over, and his chest felt thick and clogged again. Mote's tiny tracks were all around him in the sand; he could see where she had caught, battled, killed, and eaten the legs off of a small crab, about the size of his thumb. The body of the crab was sitting on his chest, as was Mote.

inquiry? love concern

"Thanks, but no thanks," Alex groaned, gingerly picking up the crab and handing it to her. She took it daintily in her mouth and scrambled up to his shoulder as he sat up. His throat was thick with phlegm. He coughed and coughed, hacked and spat, and finally got unsteadily to his feet and tried to reconnoiter. The beach stretched in one direction away into the distance, while to the other it had an abrupt, cut-off look. That must be the point of the bay, Alex thought, and he headed toward it. His pangs of hunger had faded into a cold ache and weariness, but over it all was something far more demanding.

thirst

"Me, too," Alex agreed. "All that salt." Again, he knew, Mote didn't need to hear the words, in fact she couldn't understand them, but it made him feel better to talk to someone.

He rounded the point of the bay, scrambling over rough rocks bigger than houses, pitted and scored with sharp cutting edges by the sea. The bay was nestled in the valley between two stretches of rocky hills that reached to the sea; Alex was clambering over one of these now. The city did not sit on level with the bay, however; there was a sheer cliff-drop, like a terrace, above which was the main city. Below this, a few small buildings were perched like swallows' nests closer to the water. He'd have to climb up to the level of the main city to reach it. His head was throbbing with dehydration and weariness. Mote, who he realized had kept watch for predators while he slept on the beach, had stopped broadcasting her small complaints of thirst and discomfort, and fallen asleep on his shoulder again.

At last he ran out of things to climb, and stood panting at the top of a foothill of stone. The city was visible around the curve of the bay, Humani in size and structure. A wide river ran down the center of it. Lights showed, gold and red and orange, in arched windows caught in the shadow of sunset. They swam in his vision, and he shivered, though the air seemed warm.

Below him, the rocks dropped away into a series of lethal falls. Farther inland, though, the terrain seemed softer and more forgiving. And higher up, directly inland from him, he could see a small structure, with a light, friendly and warm. He headed toward it, even though it meant climbing again.

The rock soon became overlaid with dry, gritty soil, and scraggly plants that painfully pricked his bare feet. It was true night now, black save for stars. Several times he stumbled in the darkness, the jolts waking Mote and causing her to complain softly in his mind.

The lighted structure, when he reached it, proved to be a tall round tower. Arched windows ranged around its walls at eye level; Alex staggered up to one of these, unwilling now to go through the extra effort of walking around the building to find the door.

He stuck his head in one window, badly frightening the two Humani men who were sitting inside at a small table, playing some kind of game with cards and ceramic tiles and sharing a jug of something. The jug dropped on the table, scattering the tiles, as the bedraggled, disembodied head appeared in the window. Alex tried to ask for help, but his throat was too dry and hoarse.

"Aarrughn," he croaked at them.

The men, soldiers by the look of them, grabbed for their spears which leaned against the walls, and went to the window warily.

"Who are you? What are you doing here?" one of them asked. He spoke Trade, with a faint accent, but then everyone speaks Trade with an accent. Both men wore simple uniforms of tunics and sandals, and were darkly tanned of skin; one had black hair, the other's was a sun-faded bronze.

"Ship. Storm," Alex managed to say. "Thirsty."

"You look like the walking dead," said the first speaker, the black-haired one, but the other said, "Ship? Where? Where's the ship?" He spoke a dialect of Humani, close enough to Highjade's that Alex could follow him without trouble and respond in kind.

"At sea, storm . . . Delphini brought me . . ." Alex leaned on the windowsill like a drunk at a serving-stand hatch. One of the men turned away to grab a dipper gourd from a bucket in the corner, while the other frowned more closely at Alex.

"Hey, you have a rat on—"

"My pet, don't hurt her," Alex said.

"Strange pet," frowned the guard.

The other man came back with the gourd, half full of flat water. Alex held it up to his shoulder, and let Mote lap greedily at it, then took a swig himself, then let her lap again. Meanwhile, the guards hammered him with questions: were there any others with him, where had the ship been bound, what had it carried, and the like. The black-haired one, whose name turned out to be Karvin, picked him up under the shoulders and hauled him, rat and all, through the window, since he showed no indication of being able to walk any farther. The other guard, Luken, gave him more water and a piece of flat bread made from maize, then left to fetch someone.

Weak and dizzy, Alex gathered that these guards were suspicious of him, and didn't believe his story. The storm that had been so devastating had apparently never reached this island, and no sign of any ship had been seen. In growing delirium, Alex wasn't sure he believed the whole thing himself.

Luken came back after awhile, with another man who seemed to be an officer of some kind. Alex had not had much experience with the military. He recognized the type, though, from his days in the slave-holds. This officer type asked more questions of Alex, and seemed to be trying to intimidate him; but Alex was too weary, and, he gradually realized, too ill, to care or to respond except in short answers. Mote hid in his hair at the base of his neck; the officer did not see her, and Alex decided not to mention her; the original two guards seemed to have forgotten about her. In some places, being known as an Animist would grant respect; in others, and especially if your Anim was small and vulnerable, it was sometimes better to keep silent, or your enemies would use the knowledge against you. She did peek out at one point, though, and overlaid the glitter of the Oether across his vision; but none of the men showed any sign of magical influence. That relaxed Alex somewhat. He was still troubled by what he'd seen on the ship, right before his abrupt departure from it.

"I need to see a doctor, an allopathist," Alex coughed. He hadn't been recovered from his near-drowning the first time, he realized, before the storm had made him suffer again. Exposure and exertion had done the rest, and he now had a full-blown case of aspiration pneumonia, which was rapidly worsening.

"We could take him to the shrine of Aescula," Karvin suggested.

"No!" Alex protested weakly. "No shrines, no priests, no spirits, no gods. No magic!" His recent experience with Jeena was making him realize that he, as an Animist, could only expect trouble from true magists. Again he regretted his choice of profession. The fact that it hadn't been a choice wasn't much of a comfort.

The two guards looked at each other, and one made a holy sign invoking protection from madmen.

"Doctors cost, boy. You have tilecoin?" the officer asked him sternly. The word was unfamiliar to Alex, but judging from context, it probably meant "trade trinkets." Alex reached to feel for his trinket pouch, and realized that he'd left it safe under his pillow in his cabin aboard the *Charmed*.

"No . . . I left it . . ." he began, then fell to coughing again.

concern worry

"The king may want him for questioning," the officer told his soldiers, who attempted to look competent and alert. "We'll get him fixed up and bring him to the barracks in the morning. And bind him, you idiots. Now! You should have done that when he came in."

"He doesn't look much like a Deridal spy, sir," grumbled Luken under his breath, as he tied Alex's weakly protesting wrists behind his back with thick leather straps.

"I'm not!" Alex coughed.

"If they looked like spies, there wouldn't be much point, would there?" snapped the officer. "Afraid of magic, that's suspicious, too. No, we'll take him to . . . to the Temple of Jenju, that should help. I want to know what he's hiding."

Alex felt a stab of fear, and felt Mote tense on his shoulder, ready to leap to his defense, but he cautioned her to keep still and hidden.

Luken and the officer, whom Alex thought of now as Sir, not out of respect but because he'd never heard him addressed any other way, half-escorted and half-dragged Alex down the steep hill. Tethered at its base were three large striches. Alex was dropped onto the back of one, and his legs tied beneath its feathery belly. Luken and Sir mounted the others, and took the reins of the one carrying Alex.

"No tricks, now," Sir warned him, "or you'll fall off right in front of its feet. You don't want that, do you?"

"No, sir," Alex responded weakly, and gripped two handfuls of feathers with his tied-back hands as they started down toward the lights of town.

At the merest mental nudge, Mote skittered quickly down his shirt, and alighted on the back of the strich. Unseen by his captors, the Anim scuffled through the feathers to Alex's wrists, and the straps restraining them. Sharp nibbling teeth went to work.

satisfaction smugness happy

The city was of stone, adobe, and white stucco construction, with molded terra-cotta roof tiles on most of the larger houses, and wooden shingles, or palm and grass thatch, on others. There was a dry riverbed, Alex noted, going around the edges of the town; it was steep, with very regular sides, spanned here and there with bridges. A pair of guards on duty at the gateway to one bridge saluted them as they passed through. A few Humani were about in the streets, and stopped their socializing and business to stare at the small procession as it rode past. A number of Rodeni, ubiquitous in any city where they could maintain a foothold, peered suspiciously from the shadows and alleys.

The Rodeni on board ships were the lucky ones; most of the race lived like this, on the borders and edges of cities, especially Humani cities. They lived like the rats they resembled, thieving, scavenging, sometimes holding small jobs that would be beneath the dignity of any Human. Sometimes they were forbidden, sometimes tolerated, but always persecuted and always present. Judging by the way they ducked and hid from the direct sight of the guards, they were not welcome here.

Alex sat slumped on the strich, being jogged painfully with each thud of its two large scaly feet. His chest was congested and heavy, and every breath was a rasping wheeze. Through eyes blurred by fever he saw a small plaza with vendors with small grills offering broiled delicacies for sale. They passed over a gracefully arching bridge spanning the river, and from it Alex got a glimpse of the small harbor on the bay. *I probably* could *have swum it more easily than walking, found some ladder or something up the cliffs, and I wouldn't have gotten into this mess,* Alex thought glumly. The mere thought of water and the sea made him ache, however, and he shook his head and looked away from that dark glittering expanse.

Upriver, he could see a darkness that was interrupted at periodic points by arches of light, high up; the city's walls. Beyond that, the high cliffs on either side of the valley offered further protection. Near the river, on a raised hill, Alex saw a much grander place; a castle of stone, tall and turreted, with many windows blazing light. A wide plaza area spread before it.

Alex felt the leather straps on his wrists go slack.

pride happy

Good! Good girl! he thought, wishing he had a treat to give her. She seemed to be reinforced enough by his praise, though, and he felt a pang of love and pride that made him wonder how he could have ever thought of allowing her to be euthanized by the College. *Now, the ones on my ankles, please,* he thought to Mote, with a mental image, frowning in concentration. But Mote seemed to understand him quite well, and he felt the tiny claws scuttle down his leg. He thought then about the student with the pig, and thought that maybe it wasn't so much the teasing that had driven her to take her own life, but the forced separation from such a true and loyal friend as any Anim was. His musings were abruptly interrupted. Mote hadn't had a chance to do more than begin to fray the tough leather binding him to the strich.

"Here we are," announced Sir, the strich hopping to a halt. Alex jerked his head up in panic, and saw they had stopped in front of a compact stucco building, decorated with tile mosaics in wild colors. A single firepit blazed directly in front of it. Fragrant smoke wafted from this, and from the pipe that was being shared by a group of five priests, men and women in red and yellow robes.

Luken dismounted and went to untie Alex, reaching for his ankle—

Hide! Alex prompted quickly.

Alex winced as pinprick feet scrambled up the inside of his pants leg. Mote halted at the space provided for his knee, claws now gripping the fabric instead of his flesh, but her twitching whiskers tickling.

Luken untied his ankles, and hauled him off the strich, while Sir talked to the priests. Alex kept his hands clasped behind him so as not to reveal his freedom. He landed stiff-legged and awkward, afraid of hurting Mote, and almost fell over. Luken caught him and steadied him.

"Don't worry, boy, we really are good people," Luken assured him in a low voice, so as not to be overheard by his commander. "If you don't mean any harm you don't have anything to fear from us, or from Jenju. Jenju's our city patron. I don't think you're a spy, so he shouldn't have any objection to you."

"Ughm," groaned Alex. He was trying not to breathe the scented smoke.

His forearm in the firm grip of Sir, Alex was escorted past the chattering priests and into the shrine. Within was warm red light and more scented smoke, and swirling paintings on the walls, which competed for space with niches holding small holy items: crystals, bells, and chalices, decorated icons of strange origin, little statues and candles, bundles of feathers and herbs, fetishes and carvings, long swathes of colored fabric draped from walls to ceiling. The ceiling, Alex realized, as he was half-dropped and half-collapsed onto the carpet-covered floor, was painted to try to capture the sense of the Oether: midnight blue and black, with swirling half-seen shapes and stars forming impossible constellations. A large wooden circular chandelier hung from the domed ceiling, its seven points lit with large candles, each ringed with seven smaller ones. Around the walls were designs of grapevines and festivals, lovemaking and plentiful crops and smiling faces. There seemed to be a lot of bulls involved as well. From his classes at the College Alex vaguely remembered that Jenju was a Dei, a god, of prosperity and plenty in his more common male aspect, fertility and love in his—her—female aspect. Jenju was a well-known deity in this part of the Archipelago.

"Please wait outside," one of the priestesses was telling Sir. "We shall attend to the boy."

"Very well," Sir grumbled, and stomped to the doorway, where he stood, watching, arms folded. This seemed to satisfy the woman, and she came back to where the others were gathering together drums. Alex felt Mote creeping cautiously up the loose fabric of his pants leg, and lifted the leg slightly to give her slack to move in. She was aiming for the hole where his pocket had been torn out, he realized, and he dropped his arm next to that.

The high priest, or one of them—a dark, skinny, balding man with a necklace of silk grape leaves around his neck, and a sheet-dress of particularly psychedelic intricacy—approached Alex and smiled down at him with an array of white teeth. The drums began to pound a low, rapid beat. Unseen, Mote slipped out of his pants leg and ducked quickly up his sleeve.

"Sick and mysterious, the boy is," the priest said, patting Alex's cheek, and frowning in concern at the fever he felt there. "But trust in Jenju, child, and all will be well." The women began to sing with the beat of the drums, a chanting melody reciting the name of Jenju over and over again, the double syllables pounding. Alex found the song compelling, and attempted to ignore it.

"It's just a cold. I don't want to waste your time," Alex replied, trying to hide his fear. He glanced around; there, a fold in the many layers of carpet. "Please don't trouble Jenju on my account," he added, waving one hand while stretching out his inhabited arm. Mote scuttled from his sleeve into the tunnel formed by the rise in the carpet, following his mental suggestion.

"The decision will be his," the priest said, with a chuckle, and began to chant and move his arms in mystical patterns. Alex tried not to watch; difficult enough as he was also trying not to breathe the scented air or hear the song and drums. He concentrated instead on Mote, and the impression of her senses; everything smelled of old and new smoke, but here was the end of the carpet, and here the wall, covered in things to climb. Climb! Overlaid in his vision was a swelling glow, and a crackling sound, the sound of magic building in the Oether.

eagerness worry caution

The priest chanted out a phrase, breathing quickly, his eyes closing tight with the effort. The drums grew louder, faster. The music and chant reached a fever pitch, and a crescendo; Mote accidentally knocked over a small idol on one shelf, but the small clatter went unheard in the din. The light of magic was growing brighter in Alex and Mote's shared vision.

The priest stumbled, throwing his head back with a long exhalation. Alex and Mote both froze in panic. Alex's vision shifted into a strange double-view: both his own, from here on the ground, and from the wall about five feet away, the priest as a crackling outline of power. With a shock, Alex realized it was very similar to how he'd last seen Jeena.

I know! I know! It's all right, you're all right, Alex thought frantically to Mote, trying to soothe her, and his vision dropped back to normal.

fear

As the wild things of the real world had learned to fear their predators, the Animulae feared the greater spirits, including the Lares and the Dei. Those spirits generally despised the Animulae, and would destroy them if they could. Yet another reason, if any were needed, for Dei and their priests to hate the Animists.

It's all right, you're all right, Alex thought to her. The phrase was one often used at the College to soothe frightened beasts; it worked because of the high, wheedling sounds it made, rather than the sense of the words, but Mote could capture the intent behind the words in his thoughts, and they worked even there to reassure and comfort.

You're all right, I won't let him hurt you, Mote, I promise. Alex hoped he could keep that promise, but he could feel Mote's

    love confidence

in him, and she jumped to the next shelf.

The eyes of the priest opened, fever bright now, alive with another sapience. The mouth smiled, in a totally different smirk from the man's original expression. He gave a snort and a rumble, and tossed his head. Alex stared in horror to see that the man's flickering shadow on the wall was now that of a bipedal bull, vine leaves twined and twisted around its sweeping horns; then it flickered, and was human again. Flickered back to the bull, and back again; the sudden changes made him dizzy.

"Jenju! Jenju!" shouted the assembled musicians and priests, and they dropped in worshipful awe. No doubt Jenju was much loved and respected here, to bless the fields and the citizens, solve conflicts and give wise advice, to heal and defend and bring the rains with mighty magic. Even so, any Dei was liable to resent the existence of an Animist. Alex tensed as the ridden priest jumped over his prone from, and stopped, leaning over him with a grin. Alex shut his eyes. His teeth seemed to sense fibers, taste salt and dry hemp.

"Hmph! Ho! What is—" began the priest's mouth, speaking Trade with cheerful rolling tones, but it was not the man's voice, and it was not him. It was Jenju who stopped, and frowned at Alex.

"One of *you?*" he said, his voice now cold, and he snorted in anger and distaste. "A spy!"

"I knew it," Alex thought he heard Sir's voice say from the doorway, but no one else responded. Alex and Jenju both knew that the god meant something different; an Animist was, indeed, an Oetherwise spy, who could see the spirits without paying them homage.

"Thief of the sight and consort with vermin!" Jenju bellowed, shaking his head at Alex. Alex couldn't really argue with this; the Dei certainly did consider the Animulae to be the vermin of the Oether, to say nothing of Mote's particular species form. The assembled priests made noises of shock and horror.

"We shall soon remedy this, indeed!" announced Jenju, frowning angrily at him, as the shadows flickered madly behind him.

Alex wasn't sure what the Dei planned to do, and didn't care to find out. All his training had told him *not* to get into this position, but had stressed, *Don't breathe their smoke, don't eat their food, don't listen to them; we don't know how they do what they do, but they can do worse things than kill you—*

"And where is—" Jenju began, looking around rapidly.

—and never let them catch your Anim!

Mote's teeth chomped through the last cable. The rope snapped just as Alex kicked out wildly, and rolled to the side. The chandelier, its rope severed at its restraining hook on the wall, plummeted, crashing down onto Jenju; part of it smashed against Alex's bare foot, and he screamed; but there were plenty of other screams; the priests leapt to their feet, and Jenju stood, seemingly unharmed but attempting to throw off the chandelier that entangled him. As Alex scrambled to his feet, Mote jumped from the wall sconce to his shoulder. A priest grabbed at him; he tried to dodge and came down hard on his wounded ankle, and fell heavily. Mote tumbled from his shoulder, and landed on the carpet surrounded by stamping, running feet. She froze in

fear!

Alex grabbed her up and stuffed her down his shirtfront.

Jenju, in his fury, was wearing the chandelier like a yoke and bellowing like a bull; as he stood, the few still-burning candles came in contact with the draping cloth around the room. Flames blossomed. They caught alight the robes the ridden priest was wearing, but he ignored them; the Dei's magic protected their priests from physical harm. Other fires erupted from where spilled candles had landed. Priests attempted to smother the blazes, or free their incarnated deity. The smoke of a dozen drugs filled the air.

Alex crawled for the door; Jenju tried to grab at him, but the chandelier he wore smacked into the floor and kept him at arm's length, and his enraged attempts only succeeded in knocking over another priest who was trying to grab Alex. Alex only hoped Jenju wouldn't dare risk blasting him with magic here, because of the risk of hitting one of his own priests.

A pair of boots blocked his path; Sir, guarding the door, who bent with a roar to grab him. Alex reared up, and his head smacked hard into Sir's crotch. Sir's bellow turned into a strangled noise and he fell over Alex, who ducked between his legs and scrambled out, into the darkness of the night.

Luken stood by the firepit, obviously concerned about the noises within but afraid to risk the wrath of his commander, or his patron god, by going inside. As Alex crawled and stumbled out, he ran forward.

"What's going on?" he shouted.

"Fire! Your commander's hurt! He needs help!" Alex shouted back, and Luken dived into the smoke and confusion with a curse. Judging by the sound, he'd managed to smack right into someone coming out, and knocked them into a wall of bells and crystals.

The striches were still tethered there. Alex yanked loose their quick-release ties, and climbed up onto the nearest one with the aid of one of the log-chairs by the firepit, hobbling on his one ankle. Mote was a fuzzy

fearful excited

weight in his shirt, against his chest.

He concentrated, trying to remember old lessons, then gave a piercing double-whistle. The striches, flightless riding birds with hairy grey-brown plumage, long necks and strong feet, jerked their heads up, stubby wings wide. As Alex gave the alarm call again, they bolted, running madly off in all directions. Alex clung tightly to the feathers as his own mount followed them.

FOUR

Alex's strich ran uphill, through the narrow streets, away from the shrine. Alex lost the reins, managed to recover them, but did not attempt to slow the strich. He'd ridden them enough at the College; they were not ever Animulae, of course, being birds, but were used in rounding up and tracking, and any Animist was expected to know how to work and train such a common species. He whistled again as the bird started to slow, and it kicked into high speed again. It turned and began weaving through the shadowy streets of the city, and Alex began to lose his balance; he half-fell off, hanging on to the side of the strich by a handful of saddleblanket and one wing. This unbalanced the strich and made it wheel in a tight circle; it bucked, and kicked out at Alex with one foot. Luckily he wasn't in front of the kick, and so wasn't disemboweled, or behind it, so didn't have any bones broken; it just tore open his shirt and made him let go. He landed with a jarring thud on the cobbled street, and scrambled into a maze of alleys as the strich ran off in another direction.

He could hear the sounds of voices not far distant, but here there was only a lone Rodeni beggar at the edge of an alley, who looked surprised and suspicious at Alex's sudden appearance.

"Scrap of food for poor soul, sir?" wheedled the Roden in Trade, remembering his role. One hand stretched out beseechingly. His black fur was sparse and patchy, and he wore a cloth sack, the draw-string cinched at his waist and holes torn for his legs and tail.

"I haven't a thing, friend," Alex apologized, standing and hop-ping awkwardly on one foot. "You saw my elegant arrival."

"Ah well, ah well," the Roden grumbled, hunkering down on his haunches again. "Things always hard, so indeed."

"I need to find a doctor," Alex said, hopping over to where he could lean against the wall near the Roden. The Roden blinked suspi-ciously at him.

"Don't know," the Roden replied sullenly. "Hungry. Hard to think."

Alex sighed, and started to limp down the alley, leaning on the wall for support. Cautiously, the Roden followed him.

"Might be you know doctor?" the Roden asked him cautiously. "He might help who helps you, sir?"

"I wish, but no," grunted Alex, too tired to lie. The effort of speech was too much, and Alex started to cough, his mouth filling with mucus as he spat and wheezed.

warning!

Alex didn't see the motion, but felt the Roden's hands grab his sore ankle and jerk, while a heavy blow whistled past his ear and smashed into the side of his head. He fell with a cry of pain and sur-prise, the world fracturing into stars.

The Roden who'd spoken had sharp teeth bared, and another, a brown and white female that must have been waiting in ambush, drew back the short cudgel she carried for another blow. He could hear them squealing to one another in Rodeni, too high and fast to make out any words.

anger concern defend!

Mote scrambled up onto his head and squealed back; not in words, but in sheer defiance. The Rodeni froze in surprise. They looked at her, fluffing and trembling with fear and fury atop her mas-ter's swaying head, then looked at one another, chattering teeth and squeaking. The female cuffed the male sharply across the nose, and the male cheeped and jumped back, and began nervously grooming himself.

The female squealed in Rodeni at her mate, and the Roden

blinked, and addressed, not Alex, but the small grey shape on his head.

"We are sorry!" He then peered at Alex, who tried to focus on him. "Yes we are, sir, did not know you had a *mookchee* with you, very sorry—"

"We help!" added the female, in broken Trade, slipping her cudgel back into a harness around her torso.

"Doctor," Alex managed. His head was ringing.

They helped him stand, pushing him upright, as Mote watched imperiously from the top of Alex's head. Then they led him, as he staggered from wall to wall, through the city. They kept to the alleyways. At the ends of the alleys, Alex could see Humani citizens going about evening business, but the two Rodeni kept to the shadows and dragged him along with them.

They brought him to a back door, smelly with a stench of sewage from an open gutter and a harsh chemical smell. Then the male pounded rapidly on the door, and both the Rodeni ran, vanishing into the shadows. Alex slumped against the doorframe, coughing again, as Mote hid in his shirt.

The door opened, revealing a man with white hair that seemed out of place over the look of childlike surprise in his blue eyes. The man stared after the sounds of fleeing Rodeni feet, then looked at Alex. He wore a simple white suit of what were probably pajamas, and one hand held a kind of thin walking staff, warily.

"Eh? What?" the man demanded. "Who're you?"

"I need a doctor," Alex coughed, and fell forward into the doorway.

The man looked down at him, frowning. "I would suppose you do. Do you have any tilecoin?"

There's that word again, Alex thought. He shook his head. The man, probably the doctor himself, sighed, and leaned the staff next to the door.

"I suspected as much. Look, the Temple of Aescula is only a dozen blocks away. If you can't walk it, I'll help you there. They'll take charity cases . . ."

"No, no temple. You've got to help me. You. I need antibiotics. Mikano Blue is probably best if you have it, and ten rills of greater ephedra, eycalypt, arnica—" He groaned, trying to get back to his feet. Mote wriggled nervously down in his shirt, but he cautioned her mentally. After the trouble with the priests, he was leery of revealing himself again.

"I can't—" began the doctor, then he looked puzzled. "Why are you prescribing for yourself, anyway? Where did you . . . never mind, it's not my concern. Look, no money, no medicine. Understand?"

Alex wheezed, and drew himself up to his full height, such as it was, and glared at the doctor. In as steady a tone as he could manage, he said, "I hereby invoke your Oath of Hianacrete, Allopathist."

Thus reminded of the oath he would have taken upon graduation from his own College, the doctor grumpily acquiesced.

"All right, all right," he said, with another sigh. "I know. I wouldn't have hesitated, you know, except that His Lordship's laws are so . . . anyway, come in. I'm Temith."

"I'm Alex," said Alex, stumbling gladly into the acrid-smelling warmth of a small room with banks of cabinets on all sides, and a low narrow bed in the center, on which he sat. Temith lit a couple of lamps.

"So what seems to be the trouble?" the doctor recited, looking at him as though he wouldn't have a clue where to start.

"Aspiration pneumonia from salt water, a sprained ankle, and someone hit me over the head," replied Alex, wincing at the memory.

"I see. And . . ." Temith stopped, and then said, slowly, "Now, I don't want to alarm you, but there seems to be something moving in your shirt."

"Oh, that, it's a pet. A pet rat," Alex answered quickly, reaching in and producing Mote, who sat up in his palm. Temith leaned closer to get a good look at her. Alex took advantage of the moment to take a quick Oetherwise peek through her eyes; there was no presence of magic anywhere, and he let himself relax.

"They spread disease, you know," Temith pointed out, drawing back. "You ought to get rid of it. Especially here, especially since you're sick . . ."

"No, no she's all right, she's a pet," Alex stammered, cupping her to his chest defensively.

love

"Well, at least let me get a cage for it, put it in another room while you—" Temith began, but Alex shook his head vehemently. "All right, but don't blame me if it bites you. I have rats for my research. They always bite me." Temith shook his head, and went to a cupboard and pulled out a few bottles, and set them down on the table next to Alex while he looked for a spoon. Alex looked at the labels, and pushed one bottle aside firmly.

"I'm not taking any of that," he said, pointing to it.

"All right, have it your way, stay up all night tossing and turning," retorted Temith, handing him a spoonful of antibiotic powder. "You can read, I take it? And you know some herb medicine . . ." He arranged a battery of pills on a tray next to Alex, and poured a cup of water.

"Yes," said Alex, hoisting the spoon. "If there's some chores or something I could do for you, to help pay you back . . ." He tasted the powder cautiously, recognized the moldy flavor, and poured the rest on his tongue.

"Oh, don't worry about it. I've always wanted to meet an Animist," said Temith happily.

Alex choked on the powder and Temith had to pound him on the back to get him to stop coughing.

"Wha—"

"Well, the rat was part of it," Temith admitted. "Plus you invoked a Collegiate oath. Plus what you seem to know. Plus refusing to take sedatives. Mainly, though, it's your necklace."

Alex touched the clay beads, embarrassed, and muttered, "Oh."

"Don't worry. As I said, I've always wanted to meet one of you. But how did an Animist end up here? And in such a mess?" Temith asked, going to a cask on the other side of the room and drawing himself a mug of dark beer, while Alex finished taking the medicines. "I thought your College took better care of you."

Glad to be rid of the pretense, and too tired and sick anymore to care, Alex quickly summed up his story thus far, to his arrival on the beach.

"You must have come up the cliffs? Through the guards?" Temith shook his head glumly. "I'm surprised you're alive."

"They took me to a priest. Priests and Animists don't get along. I got into a bit of trouble there." Alex sighed, and explained what had happened.

"So, penniless, sick, and on the run," the doctor summed up, looking at him while he rubbed his chin thoughtfully. "Well, I'll do my best. Just don't die on me." He sighed, and had another drink of his beer. "That was my worry, you see. Here, if a doctor kills a patient, or at least, if the patient dies in the doctor's care . . . then the doctor is tried for murder, and probably executed." He shook his head.

"That's awful!" Alex said, shocked. "Why do you stay here?"

"Oh, various reasons, you know," Temith said, looking away. "Mostly what I do these days is research, anyway. The medicine's just a way to pay the bills. I've wanted to study an Animist for a long time, you know. I'd love to visit your College, but I gather you don't much approve of tourists."

"No," Alex agreed. "That's the Lemyri influence there, you know. But I'll help you if I can." He wasn't sure he liked the idea of being studied, but it was probably less dangerous than the alternative, of going back out into the streets, sick and hunted.

"We might as well help each other; the priests don't think much of either of our Colleges," said Temith wearily. "I mean, I know medicine isn't as powerful as magic, but it's all I can do. Everything I know, and it's still not enough . . . story of my life."

A large shape slunk out from under the bed just then, long tongue flickering, sniffing the new arrival. It was another monitor lizard, this one desert brown. Mote scrambled up Alex's shirt and hid in his hair, and Alex gingerly lifted his foot up away from the flicking tongue. From Mote he got a strong impression of a musky, frightening reptilian scent, although his own stuffed nose couldn't smell anything.

fear

"Oh, whoops," said Temith, quickly stooping to scoop up the lizard. It sat in his grasp like a large placid sausage. "You probably hate these things, don't you?"

"Hate what? Lizards?" Alex asked, puzzled. The doctor nodded. Alex looked shocked.

"Why should I hate lizards? They're animals, too."

"Well, they eat rats, like your little pet there. That's why I keep this one around." He hefted the lizard for emphasis. "We've a bit of a

problem with wild rats here in Belthas. It's the way the place is constructed: a lot of old pipes and tunnels, that kind of thing. A cat
would probably be better, but they make me sneeze," Temith
explained. "But I imagine that you'd hate anything that would eat
rats . . ."

Alex shook his head. "There's no reason to hate any animal. They
don't do things out of malice, they just do them because . . . that's
what they are. It'd make as much sense to get angry at a chair you stub
your toe on, as to hate an animal for doing what it does."

"Of course, people do—get angry at chairs, and hate animals,"
Temith commented, still holding the lizard, which was now moving
its legs in a slow, determined sort of way, wanting to be put down.
"Snakes, for example," Temith said with a shudder. "Sharks, too."

"I know . . . believe me, you try walking around with a rat on
your shoulder and you'll soon see how people feel about certain animals. But there's no reason for hate."

"Well, I imagine if a cat or a snake or something ate your rat,
you'd probably hate it," Temith suggested. He had picked up his beer,
and was drinking it with one hand while holding the lizard with the
other, tucked under his arm like a parcel. Alex gave him a wry look.

"Well, no, I probably wouldn't, because I'd be dead," he said.
"But even if not . . . I'd be angry, and I might feel all kinds of things,
including hate. But it would still be misdirected; I should hate myself,
for letting her be killed, not the cat or whatever for doing it. It would
be my fault, not hers."

"You'd really die if the rat died?" Temith asked in horror. "I
thought that was just a myth! How can you take that kind of a risk?"

Alex shrugged. "A bad wound to my throat will kill me, too, and
my throat's a bigger target than Mote is. There's risks in everything."
He didn't bother to mention the whole of it: that if he'd been properly trained, with a proper Anim, he would know the way of Separation, and wouldn't suffer the fatal brain-shock on the death of his
Anim. That recurring fear hit him again, though: How *was* he going
to be able to get back there, and learn that vital information? Mote
wouldn't live very long, rats never did; his days were numbered unless
he could find some way back.

"Still, your jugular doesn't run around on the floor by itself,"

Temith muttered, turning away. "We'll just keep your door shut," he said, as he carried the monitor outside. "I'd love to stay up all night prying into the mysteries of your College, but I'm tired, it's late, and besides, you're sick and need rest. Good night!" he added, closing the door behind him.

Alex crawled into the antiseptic-smelling covers of the bed, and slowly relaxed as the medicines cleared away the blurring in his head and replaced it with simple weariness. He fell asleep, with Mote curled up under his chin.

The days passed slowly, in a gradual recovery. Under the influence of the doctor's medicines Alex's chest slowly cleared, and the bump on his head and the pain in his ankle slowly subsided. He spent some of his time working with Mote; training her to not pee on him, getting used to the Oetherwise insight she provided, and just talking to her, playing with her. At times he felt he probably shouldn't be doing all this, that he was supposed to try to retain a certain amount of detachment. He was supposed to inhibit the bonding process to a certain extent, as a prerequisite to learning Separation upon his return to the College. But at the moment, that time seemed distant, even unlikely. If he was ever going to even last that long, he felt, given all the inherent danger of having such a vulnerable Anim to begin with, he'd need all the help and cooperation Mote could give him.

Temith did give him chores: pounding herbs with mortar and pestle, writing labels, rolling medicines into pills or measuring and wrapping them into twists of paper. As Alex grew stronger, he would sometimes be stationed in the alchemical lab, a maze of glasswork and ceramic, where potions distilled themselves drop by drop; here he would watch for change of color of the boiling fluids or, tongue in teeth in concentration, perform careful titration of mixtures with pipettes. The doctor saw a number of customers, for one thing or another; sometimes he would leave, on house calls or other business, and he would put up a sign indicating so, in order that Alex not cause questions by having to answer the door to the customers that came. Many of the doctor's patients were just seeking maintenance drugs for long-standing conditions; a few showed up with broken bones or wounds. Any that looked serious, the doctor would always refer to the temple of Aescula, the goddess of healing.

Magic had the power to heal; for many problems, a potion or a talisman or a prayer would work. And spirits could work greater magic of healing if they could aid the afflicted directly for a time. A person ridden by a Dei, of course, could withstand any pain and even perform amazing feats of endurance and athletics, as well as working stranger miracles.

Allopathists and herbalists were still used by some people, but they were rare. Their methods weren't always as effective as magic, but they still did a good business.

"It's a good living," Temith said at one point, on the subject. "People think, well, do I want to take my headache to a shrine, have to pay a lot, and risk angering a god for calling him down for my trivial complaint, or do I just want to go and pick up a couple of pills from the allopathist on the corner?" He shrugged. "I'm happy I made a sale, the patient's happy because his headache's gone, the Dei's happy because people aren't bothering him, the priests are happy because they can keep to their worship. It all works out."

In the off-hours, Temith asked Alex for information on rats, their behavior and habits, for use in his research. Alex asked about this, and learned that the doctor was working on the problem of tumors and growths that sometimes afflicted the flesh. Rats who aged into their later years often developed these tumors. At present, the only treatment for these in Humani and other races was surgery—but even then, the growths would often return. Spirits could sometimes force the growths into remission, but only if they felt the patient was "worthy"; and not many were.

Alex saw Temith's laboratory, ranks of large ceramic bins like olive presses, their sides glazed to prevent the albino rats inside from escaping. The rats seemed happy enough; Mote glanced at them, but seemed otherwise uninterested in them as they scampered about and nibbled the bread and seeds the doctor fed them. The bins were open on the bottom, and the grooves in the floor allowed them to be cleaned by sluicing the area down with water. Other smaller square cages made of ceramic sat on shelves, and were filled with clean straw, daily replaced.

The doctor was working in this room, some days later, when Alex heard a yelp and a loud crash. He hurried to the room and saw Temith, looking embarrassed and trying to wrap his shirttail around his thumb, with an explosion of shattered pottery shards at his feet.

"One of them bit me through the holes," explained the doctor, waving his bleeding thumb. "Made me drop the damn cage and now the damn things are scattered everywhere—" Alex saw a white body scuttle behind a basket of clean straw.

"I'll help you catch them," Alex offered, pulling aside the basket, but the small shape darted away and hid under a wooden pallet before he could grab it.

"The whole building's riddled with cracks and rat holes," said the doctor with a sigh, squeezing his finger so that it bled more. The bite had gone right through the ball of his thumb. Alex winced in sympathy, having been on the receiving end of bites from many things at the College. "I've got the lizard, of course, but that doesn't stop them in here, they just smell food and other rats, you know how they are. Well, of course you do. Holes everywhere. They'll be into the walls already. The next I see of them will be in the lizard's mouth."

"I wonder . . ." Alex began slowly, looking around. "I wonder if maybe I can get them back."

He ran to his room; the ankle was fully healed now. He returned, holding Mote. Temith was sweeping up the shards of the cage.

"What's your idea?" he asked, looking puzzled. "Send her down to fetch them?"

"No, I don't dare, she might catch something from them," Alex said. "But we were taught . . . Well, you see, animals of the same species tend to respond to one another. And Anims can sometimes call to others of the same species. It's worth a try, anyway . . ." A small wooden stool was near the center of the room; Alex gently set Mote onto this, and then frowned at her in concentration. Mote looked *puzzled?*

then she sat up, sniffing at him. Alex furrowed his brow, thinking hard, trying to visualize what he wanted. Just as an Animist could Call through the Oether to an Anim, so Anims could "call" through the

Oether to others of their kind. He tried to convey that to Mote, whistling to her softly, in a come-along kind of tone.

Mote stared at him in

bafflement

for a long moment, then tentatively tried to reach for him, stretching out a paw. He stepped back, and whistled again. She looked around, trying to find some way off the edge of the stool; Alex quickly tried to prompt her with other images, images of white rats, white rats coming to him.

uncertainty?

Mote washed her face, a displacement activity that showed her

frustration

Alex sighed, cleared his mind, and tried again. Mote skittered a little, distractedly, as though running in place, but her thoughts were busy. She seemed to respond best when he whistled, so he kept it up, though he felt foolish. Temith shook his head, and went back to sweeping.

At first Alex was sure he was wasting his time and breath, as he whistled aimlessly, then, feeling foolish, just improvised little tunes. Then he saw, in the rat bins nearest him, the white rats were scrabbling eagerly at the side of their pen nearest himself and Mote, and jumping and skipping into the air at the sound of him whistling.

"Great stars! Look at that!" exclaimed Temith, staring at them.

And out from under the shelves and pallets came the escaped white rats, jumping and scampering; they collected in a group, five of them, frisking like Delphini around the legs of the stool. The doctor, overcoming his surprise, lunged for them; they didn't even dodge as he grabbed them, one by one, by their tails. This was not painful for them, Alex knew, and the rats didn't even struggle as the doctor dropped them into another empty cage.

Alex showered Mote with praise and mental reinforcement, and she, encouraged, was whirling in little tight circles on the stool, her eyes shut tight in concentration, making all the rats in their cages scramble.

"Amazing!" the doctor said, and was about to say something else, when he was interrupted.

From the walls now came rats of a different color, the brown-black, heavy shapes of the wild rats, forgetting their normal caution and fear as they leapt merrily out into the open. The monitor lizard, who had wandered into the room, stopped and looked around, head turning, tongue flicking, unsure of which tasty morsel to lunge for first.

"Erm, I think that's enough!" Temith said, and Alex blinked at the rats, having horrible visions of them swarming over little dainty Mote and killing her. His fear and shock must have been broadcast, because Mote stopped, and reared up on her haunches to blink at him

query happy love

and with that, the wild rats froze for an instant, then scattered, ducking back to the cover of their holes.

The sudden motion

startled!

Mote, and Alex scooped her up in his hands as she leapt for him. "Good! Good girl, yes you are," Alex enthused, fussing over her. The monitor lunged for one of the retreating rats, but missed; the rat, a young one not much bigger than Mote herself, ducked into a hole in the baseboard. The lizard began clawing at the hole, calmly, as though prepared to spend all day excavating the morsel, if that was what it would take. Temith gently caught hold of it before it could do much damage to the stucco wall.

happy proud smug

"I never knew there were so many!" said the doctor, looking at the walls where the rats had vanished, then he stared at the white rats in their new cage, then at Mote and Alex. "That was amazing! Utterly amazing! Can you all do that? Animists, I mean?" he asked.

"I don't know . . . we can sometimes call animals the same species as our Anim, as I said, but it's not usually this effective," Alex admitted. He was rather surprised himself, and a little worried. "Maybe the whistling hit some frequency that affects them?" he wondered aloud.

"Pitch, a high sound, yes, hmm . . ." the doctor muttered, staring at the cages in thought. "There may be something in the sound which attracts . . ."

The doctor, with nervous glances at the walls, had Alex and Mote work with some of the white rats; by trial and error they figured out that Mote could make contact with the other rats, in some fashion, and could inspire them with her emotions. They made a series of pitch pipes out of some of Temith's glass tubing, and the whistling, high-pitched sounds, seemed to trigger some response in the rodents' brains and amplified Mote's ability to communicate with them.

"It makes sense, they're a social creature, they have some form of collective social structure," Temith was muttering, jotting down notes in a thick leather-bound book. Before long, though, Mote grew bored with the testing, and Alex called a halt to the study.

"Amazing, really amazing," Temith kept saying, scribbling notes in his book. "You know, this could be a really useful skill, Alex."

"I don't know," Alex said doubtfully. "Animist Preshkin had a pack of wolves that traveled with her and would perform for an audience, all because her Anim, Storm-wolf, was the alpha male of the pack, but no one's going to be interested in a mob of dancing rats."

In addition to his studies of rats, Temith showed an interest in Alex's magical talent. Alex, recalling his recent experience with Jeena, was suspicious at first, but it soon became plain that the allopathist had only curiosity, not longing, for the subject. Temith was a man driven to find the explanations, the whys, the science behind everything: a desire not just to cure tumors, but to find why they happened in the first place. He knew what medicines to prescribe for certain conditions, but he also knew why: that one drug would dilate the branches of the lungs and make breathing easier, that another would act on the blood vessels and allow them to conduct blood more freely. Not content with knowing Alex and Mote could influence the rats, he wanted to know why, what it was that allowed them to do so. From that came a long study into what an Animist could do, which Alex was happy to help with, but Temith also wanted to know how, and why, and Alex had never asked that. It was magic, that's all; it was how things were done. You performed in a certain way, and certain things happened. What sense was there in going beyond that? Temith was particularly interested in the Animists' ability to recognize and warn of magical activity.

"So you can . . . *see* magic, before it happens?" Temith asked.

Alex nodded. "It's like a light, sort of . . . and a sound. A kind of . . . humming, or buzzing," Alex said, trying to find the right words. "But it's not like you hear it in your ears, more like . . . you can sort of feel it in your soul." He paused, while Temith took notes. "But I mean, that's only the way it seems to me. It's different for everyone. Most of the Lemyri Animists, for example, they say magic has a smell, a very distinctive smell. One of my teachers used to have sneezing fits if something strongly magical happened."

"Can you tell a magist, or an Animist, just by . . . looking at them, in this way?"

"Well . . . you can tell an Animist, a bonded one, because there's this . . . glow, between them and the Anim. And a pulse. But a magist . . . sometimes, if they're very powerful, you can see it. But a lot of the time, you won't notice anything until they start casting a spell. Then the glow comes, and the sound."

"How about magical items?" Temith asked, glancing up. "Potions, and talismae, and that kind of thing."

Alex shook his head. "No . . . we're limited that way. We can only see active magic, and only in living things. Sometimes, if, say, a person drinks a potion, we can then see the effect of the potion as active magic . . . but when it's just sitting in a bottle, no."

"Is there any difference in the way you see these things?" Temith asked. "Is the glow stronger, softer, a different color, anything?"

Alex looked embarrassed. "Um . . . well, I guess I should mention, I'm pretty new at this myself. I haven't actually *seen* very many different magical effects myself. What I've been telling you is what teachers told me. As I said, it's different for everyone, so I don't know what I'd see."

Temith thought a moment, then brightened. "Would you have any objection to doing some observations?"

Alex looked frightened. "What, of a magist? I told you, they don't like Animists. And I told you what happened with the priests of Jenju."

"I agree, they can be temperamental, but they aren't all bad. I know one personally, as a matter of fact. He's . . . well, he's pretty close with his secrets, you might say. He refused to talk to me because

I wasn't 'initiated,' and then said that I didn't have the proper talent to be initiated in the first place. Said I was too close-minded, too clinical, to even try to understand the nature of metaphysics." Temith shook his head sadly. "I try to be a good person, I really do. But I always had a problem with reverence, with faith; I always had to question everything. I guess that lack of faith was what Chernan saw."

"Chernan is this magist you were talking about?" Alex asked. Temith nodded.

"He's actually what they call a thaumaturgist," Temith began, and Alex interrupted him in astonishment.

"What?! You're friends with . . . with . . . one of those?" Alex said, half in awe, half in horror. "They . . . they're powerful—they can—" Actually he didn't know much about them, other than the College's brief instruction of *avoid*. "People *born* into magic! They say there's only maybe fifty true thaumaturgists in all the Archipelago! How did you happen to meet one?" Alex was torn between terror at the thought of meeting one of these legendary magists, and fascination and curiosity to actually see one, Oetherwise or otherwise.

"We used to work for the same employer, you might say. Both ended up falling out of favor about the same time, both ended up coming here, although we live on opposite sides of the city. We don't see each other that often, though sometimes we'll go in together on bulk deals of things . . . herbs and such—spell components for him, medicines for me. Odd now that I mention it, that we use the same things, for different purposes. Anyway, he was always very interested in my researches, and I would tell him some of the scientific uses of plants and whatnot, and sometimes he'd tell me the magical uses of them. The two were always very different."

"Discouraging, wasn't it?" said Alex, noting Temith's expression and tone. "You're trying to find a scientific explanation for magic, and there just isn't one. Magic is magic, it just *happens*. You might as well ask why the stars shine or why people fall in love, or where we go when we die. Magic doesn't have to have a reason or an explanation. Magic has servants, but no masters."

"Very philosophical," Temith snorted, making a note in his book. "You're sounding just like Chernan. I don't think you need worry about him as regards your profession. I think he'd like talking to you. Who knows, he might even talk to you about things he wouldn't tell me about. And you might understand them, too. We'll pay him a visit."

They waited until dusk to make the trek across town, when the crowds had thinned out a bit. As they went, Temith kept up a running patter of information, pointing out the various styles of architecture, and various sites of interest, including the river channels that went through and around the city, and a fine clock tower which chimed the hours on big bronze bells. Alex pretended to be interested in these and in the systems of drains and channels, the high stone bridges, and the examples of statuary, archways, and buttresses. In the gloaming, he could see rats about—scurrying along the tops of walls, bustling at the edges of drainpipes, foraging along the gutters—and he kept a close hold on Mote, worried about wild rat diseases. From time to time, too, he would see Rodeni peering from alleyways and watching them from tumbledown buildings, but Temith had brought along his thin walking staff. The allopathist strolled along, from time to time using this stick to point out a particularly fine example of stonework, and idly spinning the stick in an apparently nonchalant but very practiced way, and none of the Rodeni approached him. Alex wondered about the safety of this city, when average Humani needed to carry weapons to feel safe in the streets.

At one point the crowds grew thick, around some kind of amphitheater. There were the shouts and calls of people placing bets, and having an entertaining time. Temith tried to lead Alex away from this, but Alex heard, above the noise of the crowd, the bellow of some kind of animal. At once he turned to investigate, and Temith could only follow after him as he pushed gingerly through the crowd to see what had caused the sound. At last he was able to peer down into the amphitheater itself.

It was a deep arena, with barred gates to allow entry at the level of the sand-covered floor. The source of the bellow was there; it was a bull, of some species Alex didn't recognize. It had horns as long and as lethal as old Bos, back at the College, but this bull was not old and placid, but long, wiry, and gleaming black. The horns were white and sharp, and a garland of flowers was around the bull's neck. It was trotting about, tossing its head and snorting.

"Alex, come away, you won't want to see this," Temith muttered, grabbing his arm, but Alex wriggled loose.

"No, I've heard about this," Alex insisted. "I know, they have a man with a spear and a cloak come in, and he dances with the bull, and then kills it bravely. It's all right, Temith. We butchered animals for meat at the College, after all." He craned around, looking to see where the bull-dancer might appear. "I've heard this is a very interesting and beautiful ritual."

"You're thinking of the bull-dancers of Santonia," Temith's voice said, behind him. "This is Miraposa, and these are the bulls of Belthas, blessed of Jenju."

Only now did Alex notice the vinework murals along the rim of the arena, and the group of priests on a balcony overlooking the arena. He stiffened, but they didn't notice him. Mote's quick Oetherwise inspection showed only the standard ambient traces of magic around them.

Now one of the gates down in the arena opened, and from the darkness there came not a nimble bull-dancer, but a screaming, furry mess, stumbling out even as they struggled to go back. As the crowd roared and the flickering torchlight flared, Alex saw it was a group of seven Rodeni, of various ages and sexes, eyes bulging with terror, fur streaked and spattered with blood. They were shoved out into the open by a sort of movable wall of spikes, which Alex assumed must be pushed by guards from behind. Once the Rodeni were out in the arena, the barred gate slammed down once again. The Rodeni stood shivering in a cluster, clawing at the gate, as the bull snorted and slowly trotted toward them.

Alex took a breath, and stared around at the walls of the arena. They were slick, and high, but not high enough; Prang had jumped that high, at least, back on the *Charmed* . . .

"They can make it, if they run, and jump," Alex whispered, clenching his hands on the stone, staring at the shaking mass of Rodeni, willing them to run, to move. The crowd shouted and roared, and the bull's head swung down as it leapt forward.

Temith sighed.

The Rodeni scattered; not in leaping, hopping speed, but in a stumbling, hopeless stagger, tripping and scrambling. One, a small one, couldn't decide which way to run. She crouched, squealing, scrambling at the barred gate as the bull came plunging. The bull pounced like a cat and the horns swung like claws, and the Roden was hooked through, screaming, then tossed high in the air, flung off the impaling horns at the apex of the flight. She landed on the sand, blood bubbling over her cream-colored fur. The bull ran over her without another glance, leaving her still kicking and screaming as it chased after the other Rodeni, who could not, it seemed, move faster than their lurching stumble.

"Their hind-leg tendons are cut, you see, before they're sent in," Temith's voice explained sadly. The bull had chased down another Roden and was rolling him, screaming, along the sand, as the horns swung back and forth like scythes. The other Rodeni were scrambling at the walls, clawing at the other gates, and one was even reaching up a paw to the audience, pleading. It was being showered with spit.

"But . . . sacrificing people," Alex stammered. "Well, Rodeni . . ."

"Oh, but only condemned criminals," Temith said, his voice bitter with sarcasm. Alex glanced at him, saw that the allopathist wasn't looking at the arena, was only staring at his shoes, his knuckles white on his staff. "Of course, in Belthas, being Rodeni is against the law."

A shout from the crowd and a shrill gurgling scream from below indicated another serving of justice, but Alex didn't look around. "What? Why?"

"His Lordship thinks that the Rodeni are causing the current plague of rats. He thinks it's some kind of a plot against him. So he's trying to exterminate them, or at least drive them out. Jenju's the patron deity of the city, so of course His Lordship is asking Jenju for help. So . . ." He waved a hand, and shook his head.

"But . . . that's not right, is it? The Rodeni aren't—"

"No. If anything, driving the Rodeni into hiding means they can't scavenge the garbage, which means the rats get it instead. And the more the Rodeni hide, the more tunnels they make that the rats can use, too . . ."

"Can't you do something?" Alex asked, pleadingly. "I mean, you know about rats, couldn't you talk to him, His Lordship . . . ?"

"His Lordship? The king?" Temith's face twisted into a sour expression, out of place on his gentle features. "And be accused of treason? Of being disrespectful enough to question King Belthar's wisdom? After this little warm-up, you know, they have another ceremony, if any Humani have been sentenced to die. They tie a strap around the bull, tight enough to really enrage it, and then they let you try and ride the bull, with only this strap to hang on to. If you can hang on until the bull gives up, you can go free. That's the theory. But the most anyone's ever lasted is ten seconds." There was another cheer from the crowd around them, and a Rodeni scream, cut short by a terrible ripping sound and a triumphant bellow from the bull. Temith was pale. "That's not the way I want to die."

"Not the way for anyone to die," Alex murmured. The air was thick with the smell of smoke and sweat and blood. Mote was trembling against his neck.

"I agree, but what can we do? Come on. Come away. We'll want to meet Chernan before midnight. He won't see anyone after then." Temith sighed, and led Alex away from the scene.

At last they came to a stone tower near the rocky walls of the city. There were several levels, apparently, each occupied by different individuals. Alex and Temith negotiated the winding staircase that ran up the interior, past a ceramicist on the ground floor, up past a paperworks, then a painter, and finally up to a room with the sevenfold seal of a thaumaturgist upon the wooden door. The horror of the execution was slowly being overshadowed in Alex's mind by fear, fear of the thaumaturgist. Temith seemed able to keep a professional detachment, and had to keep reminding Alex that this meeting was, in a way, research.

"Now, you probably won't want to tell me everything that you can sense while we're there, so just remember, as best you can, all right?" Temith whispered, and Alex nodded.

Alex and Temith both knew better than to knock on the seal, but Temith rapped cautiously on the wooden floor with his walking staff, and called out, "Chernan? It's me, Temith, and a friend. Can we speak with you?"

There was a pause, and Alex suddenly felt Mote stiffen.

fear!

"Mote's scared," he whispered to Temith, as he reached up to his shoulder to take her into his hands. She trembled, and suddenly through Oetherwise, his view of the seal was overlaid with a matching pattern of glowing lines, which then faded.

A voice came from the other side of the door. "I assume you know what your 'friend' is, Temith?" it said.

"Yes, I do. He did say that magists tend to be uneasy around his kind, but I told him that you weren't like all the others."

"The spirits have told me there was a sight-thief on the island . . . apparently he caused some trouble for the temple of Jenju." Alex felt a stab of fear, but he wasn't sure now if it was his or Mote's. There were shuffling sounds behind the door.

"Yes, Chernan. That's him." Alex darted a shocked look at the doctor, but Temith shook his head and made a placating gesture to Alex.

"Well then, you are welcome," intoned the voice, with what might have been a trace of dry humor, and the door rolled slowly aside.

Revealed was a single large round room at the top of the tower, with a lot of small windows around the circumference. A fire smoldered in a large fireplace at one end, sharing a chimney with the other dwellings below. Perhaps because of this, the room was uncomfortably warm after the coastal chill of outside. Though the center of the room was open, things—bookshelves, and workdesks, and piles of things, and barrels and crates of things—extended out from the walls, reminding Alex of a picture he'd seen in one of Temith's books on mathematics. Other things—stuffed creatures, bundles of herbs, all the paraphernalia of magic—hung from the ceiling.

Standing in the middle of this, far enough away from the door that there was no way he could have opened it, was Chernan. Alex, who had been expecting to see a more mystical version of Temith, grey-haired and wise, was surprised to see that Chernan was less than twice his own age—tall, though, and with piercing black eyes set in his pale face, and long dark hair in a thick braid down his back. He wore a robe that shaded from midnight blue to purple and black, like the sky outside, embroidered with what were probably supposed to be Visi, although Alex usually saw them as more swirly and less rounded than that. Chernan had his arms folded and looked imperious.

"No need to put on the show for us, Chernan," grumbled Temith. "Look, he's just a boy. He's no threat to you."

"I never implied that he was," retorted Chernan, looking at Alex scornfully. "The very idea is insulting. I merely find it a waste of my own time to deal with fools and dabblers."

"If I'm a fool and a dabbler it's only because I've never been taught any other way, sir," said Alex respectfully. Overlaid in his vision was Mote's Oether-impression: Chernan glowed faintly, with a steady hum, but Mote's fear was quieting.

"That's what we're here for," Temith put in. "Just seeking information."

"Coming to pry into things you shouldn't meddle with, again," said Chernan with a sigh, as he unfolded his arms and relaxed. Alex noted the magical aura around the magist dimmed itself, and the humming dropped in pitch, but neither vanished altogether. The magist walked to a table, where Alex now noticed a half-eaten dinner. "Still, anyone who can put those grape-stomping, bull-baiting priests in their place can't be all bad. What's your name, boy?"

"Alex, sir," said Alex, and cautiously he displayed Mote. "And this is Mote." There was no point in hiding her; surely Chernan could see into the Oether with ease that Alex would never know.

Chernan looked at him quickly, looking to see what Alex was referring to; it took him a moment to notice Mote, small and huddled and grey in Alex's hands. Then he blinked.

"That's a rat?"

"Yes, sir," Alex said, trying to urge Mote out into view, but she was still
scared
and wasn't having any of it. "She's a little nervous about . . ."

"A rat!?" Chernan looked incredulous. "You chose a rat?!"

"I didn't choose her, she chose me," Alex said, nettled.

Temith, having found a chair and settled into it, said, "It gets better, Chern." Chernan, meanwhile, was laughing. Not a booming, wizardly laugh, but a laugh like someone who's heard a good joke; it made him less threatening, and Alex, despite his annoyance at being laughed at, began to relax.

"I don't see how it could . . ." chuckled the magist. "Unless . . . no, wait. Let me see . . ." He glanced up, narrowing his eyes and raising his hand, and Alex suddenly took a step back on his heels, and Mote bristled and chattered. For the magical aura around Chernan suddenly flared, and the crackle became a roar in his head as the light engulfed him.

Temith, of course, didn't see any of this, only Chernan's gesture and Alex's step and sudden painful flinch, as though he'd been struck in the face by a bucket full of ice water. A moment later Chernan lowered his hand, grinning, and Alex uncringed, blinking and panting. Mote squealed, apparently at Chernan, but the thaumaturgist ignored her, instead picking up his half-eaten chicken leg and resuming it.

"Totally untrained, though surprisingly talented. Unfortunately for him, in this case that means he's over-bonded with that beast of his, poor fool," he said in between bites. "Impulsive, uncertain, susceptible, and currently scared, and probably very horrified that I just riffled through his mind like a soft book. You want to use him to study me."

"Not you specifically," Temith said mildly. "Just magic in general. You know, what you always refer to as my 'irreverent quest to know the unknowable.' " Alex slowly sank to the floor, his head throbbing. He felt as though his mind had been filleted.

"Which is going to get you cursed, slain, and damned one of these days, probably soon, possibly even by me," Chernan replied, with his mouth full.

"I still don't see why you object, if your secrets are so unknowable, what harm in my beating myself to death with frustration trying to know them?" Temith asked.

"It's not that, really, it's more that I resent my life and my life's calling being reduced to the level of a pithed frog for you to dissect. You'll find out no more about magic from outside, Animist or no, than you'll be able to tell how the frog thinks and dreams and feels from looking at its intestines." He tossed the bone into the fireplace, and then glanced at Alex, who was sitting on the floor, holding his head. "Oh, blast it, boy. Have a chair, have a drink if you like, though I'm sure you'll refuse it because you don't trust me. I probably shouldn't have hit you so hard, but . . ." and he paused, and seemed to deliberate a moment, then shook his head.

Alex slowly got to his feet, and made his way to a cushion near the chair Temith had selected. "Well, if we're talking drinks, I did bring this along as a peace offering," Temith commented, pulling out a bottle of amber fluid. "Not like the good stuff back home, but a year old if it's a day, promised."

"You old poisoner!" Chernan exclaimed. "I knew you'd find enough copper for another still someplace." He jumped up and started rummaging for glasses.

"Oh come now, every physician needs to be able to distill," Temith protested. "It was one of the few things I took with me."

"Medicine?" Alex asked.

"No, alcohol. It's a bit stronger. It's a good disinfectant, too."

Alex would have welcomed a drink to soothe his nerves, but didn't dare. He shook his head. "I think I'll have to pass."

"Of course," said Temith understandingly.

"More for us," agreed Chernan.

Alex spotted a cat, calico and fat, lounging in a basket by the fireplace. Making sure Mote was back snuggled under his collar, he crawled over to it, stretching out a hand to pet it. The cat purred and butted its head against him. Alex always felt much happier with animals than with people, and soon had the cat in his lap, while reassuring Mote, who was sulking, but trusting in him to protect her from the feline.

"Ah, I see you still have Alopecia," Temith commented, seeing the cat. "Wondered why my eyes were itching."

Chernan nodded. "Keeps the wretched rodents out of my tower . . . no offense, Animist," he added, with a mocking smile.

Alex glanced up at him but was afraid to say anything, for fear of having his brain shuffled again. Instead he glanced at Temith and said, "Alopecia?"

"Yes, when he found her she had mange, no fur at all. Looked horrible. I gave Chernan a salve that cured it, as you see—"

"She was a great prop for awhile, though," Chernan added, pouring himself another glass of whiskey. "A mottled, hairless cat—she looked like a demon herself." Alopecia purred contentedly, treading Alex with pinprick claws. Cats were always a bit magical.

The two men drank and talked about other things, mostly about daily life in Belthas, and traded amusing stories about their respective clientele. Temith did tell him Alex's story, Alex himself having lapsed into a rather sullen silence, trying to comfort Mote, who was still trembling, so upset about Chernan that she scarcely noticed the cat. Chernan's glow remained at the same dim level in their vision.

"And so you're stuck with the rat, and vulnerable, until you can get back?" Chernan said, looking at Alex. "You'd better hurry, lad. You don't know what you're doing with that thing, and you're getting too . . . attached to it, I suppose."

"I know, I should have been meditating, and refining the connection," said Alex. He gently turfed Alopecia off his lap; the cat wandered away across the room to investigate the remains of Chernan's dinner. "But I just haven't had much time. It's supposed to take up to a year to refine the bond, but she's not going to live very long." He bit his knuckles thoughtfully, turning his head to look at Mote, who looked up at him from his shoulder,

happy

that she was being talked about. "I think that's part of it; I think it's accelerated because of her metabolism, or something."

Chernan poured himself another glass. His voice was already more mellow, more human. "Partly why I hit you so hard, you know . . . Partly why we don't much like Animists. You tend to be resistant to magic, when you're over-bonded like that."

Alex blinked. He hadn't heard this before; the College hadn't mentioned it. "I always thought it was just because of the Lemyri, and how they feel about it—"

"That's part of it, I grant you," Chernan said, nodding. "Well, wouldn't you, if those bouncing furballs would stuff you in a hollow tree and set you on fire, given half a chance?" Alex shuddered, but he too recalled the horrible, gloating stories of Lemyri executions of magists, and suspected magists. "And they're hypocrites, too . . . because Animism *is* magic, lad. It is, no matter if they tell you differently."

"I could hardly say," said Alex. "It's the only kind I've ever done."

Chernan set his glass down carefully. "Nothing like this?"

He put his fingertips together, and seemed to concentrate. Alex cringed as the glow flared again, but this time it didn't pounce on him; instead, it expanded out to encompass the entire room. The light from the fire dimmed. Alex saw Temith slowly get to his feet, staring in amazement. Then the light flared, and made them shut their eyes. A crackling roar filled Alex's mind, then faded.

When they opened their eyes again they looked around, surprised, and Alex almost cried out, because they were standing on top of the high bamboo watchtower at the College of Animists on Highjade.

Below them the wicker and stone of the buildings stretched away, dimly lit in the night with some few lamps. In the starlight Alex could see the pens and cages ranging around the College, and most powerful of all was the smell, the sweat and stink of beasts and the yeasty smell of Lemyri and the lush green decaying smell of the rainforest of Highjade. Chernan stood with his arms folded, still glowing, near the edge of the platform, and Temith looked around, and tapped nervously on the bamboo platform beneath his feet.

puzzlement?

A great wave of wonder filled Alex's soul, and he took a step for the ladder that would lead down to the College proper—when Chernan snapped his fingers.

Instantly the College vanished, and Alex found himself in the magist's rooms once more, the air stifling hot after the cool night of Highjade. Temith, caught off-balance by the transfer, tumbled over his chair and fell, but Chernan dropped lightly into his seat, and smiled.

Alex stared at him. "You . . . how did you . . . never mind! Send me back! Please!" he begged. Even though he resented his slavery, the College was the only thing that could save his life from the daily risk of Mote's death.

Temith stared at his old friend. "What . . . teleportation?! By the gods, Chern, why didn't you tell His Highness that you could do that?! We could have settled this stupid conflict once and for all, years ago!"

"I am sorry, friends," Chernan said, to both of them. "Even magic is bound by some laws; I could send myself wherever I chose, but can only pull you along for a short time, before your own inertia causes you to snap back. Especially yours, Animist," he added, glancing at Alex. "Even space can modulate, but it takes some doing." Indeed, the magist looked drained and a bit weary, and the glow around him was dimmer still now.

"Th . . ." Alex stuttered a bit, and was lost for words. "What . . . what else can you do?"

Chernan poured himself another drink. "Temith has either coached you well, or you're just a nosy boy to begin with. No more demonstrations."

Alex sat down, stunned. The College had only spoken of magists as devious, malicious beings who tried to cheat and harm others; there had been little said, and little understood, about what they were really like, what they could really do. Alex felt as though he'd been blind and suddenly opened his eyes to see; a world of strength and power and potential that made his fate to limit himself to the life of a rat seem stupid in the extreme.

"Why did I ever have to become an Animist?" Alex groaned, hiding his head in his hands.

"Don't be discouraged, boy," Chernan said. "Maybe instead of looking at it as a destination, you can look at it as the first step on a path. Instead of just doing what everyone else has been doing— following what your Lemyri teachers keep telling you—you should try to find things out for yourself. Keep an open mind, and don't be afraid to try new things."

"That's what I always say," Temith put in.

"But what can I do?" Alex protested. "Especially if I don't learn Separation?"

"There you do have a tricky problem," admitted Chernan. "Obviously you've got to finish that part of your training, at least."

"Isn't there anything you can do for him, Chernan?" Temith asked. "After all, Jenju's priests were trying to do something—"

"It's not that simple," Chernan said, shaking his head. "If he'll let me, I might be able to kill the rat without killing him, but there's a good chance I couldn't separate him from the rat without leaving him a babbling idiot. Jenju's priests were probably trying for that approach . . . Gods know you'd have fitted right in with them, after-ward," he added, swigging whiskey. "Priests have someone else to do their thinking for them."

"Priests," snorted Temith.

"Blast their damn rafters," concurred Chernan, and they both drank a toast to that.

"But once you've learned, that," Chernan added, to Alex, "what did you call it, Separation? Yes. So. You learn that, and then come on back here. I'll teach you, if you like."

"You would?" Alex gasped. Chernan waved a hand magnani-mously.

"Certainly. You do have talent, as I said. Are you sure you don't want me to try killing the rat for you?"

"No! . . . I can't." Alex looked at Mote. "Risk or no risk. I owe her my life. It's hard to explain, but . . . But if I can get enough money, to pay off my College debt, then they can teach me Separa-tion, and when she . . . she dies, of old age, in a few years, then . . . ?"

"You need money? How much?" Chernan asked. Alex tried to calculate.

"I think it would be about two hundred rills of silver," he said, and Chernan choked on his drink, and even Temith looked stunned.

"Of silver?! For a Humani slave boy?" demanded Chernan. "That's outrageous!"

"Not just a slave," retorted Alex. "An Animist. Training and everything considered, that's not a bad price."

"I wonder how much allopathists go for these days," mused Temith, and Chernan scoffed.

"If they price by training, no one could afford you except the Viveri. No one sells magists," he added proudly. "Nor even priests. Magic is power, and power assures freedom. Magic is free, and so are we."

"I'm not," said Alex.

"Only because you're not using your power, then. Come on, there's got to be some way you can use your Animism to buy or break your way out of this bind in which your College has you. Think.

What can you do? Help us out here, Temith," he added. "Surely your overstuffed mind has already come up with some ideas from what this boy's been telling you."

"So far, he seems very good at working with rats," Temith said.

"And that's about it," Alex added ruefully.

"Then that will have to do," Chernan said, thoughtfully.

FIVE

D o you think this will work?" Alex asked doubtfully.

"Don't ask me, it's Chernan's idea, not mine," said Temith. "The principle is sound, but . . ."

"Haha." Alex laughed dutifully, though the doctor's pun was unintentional.

". . . but I think you're taking a big risk."

"You should be encouraging me," grumbled Alex. "This is the only way I'll be able to pay you back for taking care of me, anyway. And it's my only chance to get enough metal to buy my way free from the College."

"I don't see why you can't just go back—"

"I told you, they'll kill Mote! I can't let that happen!"

"But you admit that she's not going to live that long anyway. Where's the sense in that?" demanded Temith. The subject under discussion sat on her owner's shoulder and groomed herself contentedly.

"That's the thing. I don't have a lot of time," replied Alex. "And I'm stuck here. With the priests of Jenju and the soldiers after me, I can't risk doing some long-term employment. This is better. One quick exposure, one big payoff, and I'll have enough to bribe my way onto a ship heading back to Highjade and enough to pay for myself when I get there."

Temith paced back and forth a moment, thinking hard. "But there's other ports, in other cities. Can't you try and sneak aboard a ship, somewhere else, and forget this whole thing?"

"Aboard another ship, and then what? I still won't have anything to pay my College debts with. And I can't try this in some other city, you know that. The king's *here*. Besides," Alex added, "maybe if I can do this, it will take some of the pressure off the Rodeni. Maybe the king will forget about them." The horror of the sacrificial arena was still strong in his memory. True, it was no worse than you'd find on many an island, but it still rang wrong in Alex's mind.

"Well, if you're determined, I suppose I'm no one to stop you. Your ankle's healed, your cough's cleared up, as your doctor I pronounce you better, but still being a damn fool." Temith shook his head. "It's trickery, and manipulative, and, and—"

"Your professional opinion is noted," Alex said frostily. "Did you finish my disguise?"

Temith handed him a bundle of cloth with bad grace. The allopathist had turned out to be quite skilled with a needle and thread—probably practice from surgery. Alex's original clothing, bleached white by wear and torn by the sea and stone, had been mended with large irregular black patches. The llama-wool coat had fared better, but the leather patches, once stained and faded, had also been dyed a blue-black. The result was a motley pattern that reminded Alex of a bamboo bear, or a Lemyr.

"Subtle," Alex commented, pulling his hair (still short, but growing out) back into a brush at the back of his neck and tying it with a leather strip. His days recovering in the doctor's house had returned him to his native pale complexion, and he'd darkened his brows and lined his eyes with kohl. He inspected himself carefully in a mirror, and decided that, odd as he looked, he at least looked different from the sunburned, sick, and scruffy character that the guards had dragged to the Temple of Jenju.

"You look foreign, at least, and like an entertainer. A clown, at least," sighed the doctor, handing him a pair of boots. "And here are your boots, expensive as they were. I don't see why you can't just wear sandals like most people."

"With what I'll be walking through? I want a good thickness of leather over my feet, thank you very much." Alex pulled the boots on and found they were a perfect fit.

"Got you this, too, as you requested." Temith handed him a hat.

It was a broad-brimmed thing, white with a black band, and with a long crimson strich feather in the band. Alex frowned. "I'll look like a mushroom," he complained.

"It's big and roomy, as you asked for. And the hole won't show under the feather."

Alex picked up one of the doctor's scalpels, and carefully cut a small hole in the side of the hat, where the crown joined the brim, and held it up for Mote's inspection. She sniffed at it, then put up her front paws and wriggled through the hole, her tail lashing for balance. Alex scooped her out of the hat and enlarged the hole a little; this time she slipped through it easily. Alex folded up and pinned that side of the brim, to further hide the hole, then cut another one through the brim itself. He stood, and put the hat on his head; Mote hopped easily from his shoulder to the hole in the hat, and seemed satisfied.

"Ready?" asked Temith.

"Ready," Alex replied, squaring his shoulders. He picked up the result of a night's hard work, by Temith, under protest. It was a delicate musical pipe of glass and copper tubing.

The stranger strode through the town. His bright contrasting garb made him glitter like a magpie among the sparrow-colors of the townsfolk. On his strange pipe he played a melody exotic and haunting. (It was, in fact, awkward variations on the refrain of "Oene Summer's Daye," with half the notes in the ultrasonic, but no one knew this.) People stopped their work, housewives hanging out clothing and mending rat-nibbled garments, merchants calling their wares and cursing their rat-spoiled stock, chefs cooking and chasing thieving rats from the dishes, artisans crafting and cursing rat-nipped fingers, all looked up in surprise as the young man in his strange clothing marched past. (He'd tried skipping, back in the alley where he wasn't seen, but the new boots were too stiff and he'd almost ended up falling and ramming the flute through the back of his throat, so he'd stopped that quickly and stuck to marching.)

The people of Belthas did not have much imagination, but they knew a performance when they saw it. First a few, then several, then a crowd of people, led by curious children, followed the stranger as he strode through the streets, toward the palace of the king. The children laughed and skipped. (Well, some of them. Many, children being children, shouted names and threw things.) The adults murmured and gossiped among themselves.

The notes of the pipe shivering in the morning air, he walked over the King's Bridge, followed by his chattering entourage. Below, the waters of the river, muddied by rains in the mountains but prevented from their full force by the upstream waterdam, rumbled and hissed. The flags of the king's castle snapped in the breeze.

He reached the castle gate, with its mosaic murals, and high walls topped with sharp shards. Here the guards blocked his way with their pikes and frowns. "Who are you, and what business have you here?" they demanded.

The stranger grinned, and put a hand to his hatbrim as though he would doff it, but he did not. "My name is of little matter, but I have a greater matter for His Lordship's attention," announced the stranger in Trade, in a loud, clear voice. His accent was strange.

The guards looked at each other, and then held a quick conversation with some of their fellows, who had come over to see what was happening. After a few muttered words with the stranger, and a messenger sent into the castle and returned, four royal guards with narrow bronze short swords drawn came to escort the stranger. The crowd gasped and muttered at the sight of the swords, rich bronze turned into lethal weapon, and knew that the stranger was likely to be executed for his audacity. This would indeed be worth watching. But the stranger only smiled as the guards surrounded him and checked him for weapons, and he seemed delighted to be led in their midst. Some of the crowd tried to follow, but the guards stopped them; they had to be content with peering through the archways into the castle gardens beyond.

The king, with his family, was taking his breakfast in the garden. The table was set on a high veranda surrounded by manicured lawns of flatmint and bushes of wild rose and climbing melons. Lemon trees, pruned into neat ball shapes, cast some small shade on the smooth stone veranda, roofed over with grapevines, where the polished table was set. Flags hung on either side, showing the symbol of the king and kingdom, a stylized design of a red bull on a white field.

The stranger, watched warily by the king's personal bodyguards, was allowed to approach no closer than ten feet from the raised porch. Apparently unconcerned by his visitor, the king was sectioning his grapefruit. The mysterious stranger swept off his hat and bowed low (Mote having retreated to his collar), but did not drop to one knee as was customary; the crowd outside, craning to see, rumbled in amazement.

In the crowd, Temith winced and clapped his hand over his eyes. "I knew it," he muttered to himself. He and Chernan had done their best to coach Alex in manners of protocol, but obviously it hadn't all sunk in.

The king's wife, a plump woman in rich brocade, and their son, a fat sullen child of about seven still in his pajamas, peered haughtily down at the intruder from their secure porch, but the king himself, resplendent in his robe of purple wool, merely put down his spoon and frowned.

"So. What's the meaning of this?" he asked, coldly. The word from the messenger had been vague, but intriguing.

"Your Most Noble Highness," recited Alex, "I have come to rid your fair city of the rats that plague it." He stood again, replacing his hat and giving a winning smile.

"Really," said the king, buttering his toast. "Guards, have this impertinent clown sent to the bull-pits."

Alex stepped back as the guards stepped forward.

Help! he thought frantically.

He caught the echo of a wordless command.

There was a rustling in the grapevines, and a huge brown rat fell out of the vines with a shower of leaves. It landed in the middle of a large pile of sticky rolls, sending them rolling as it dived off the plate. The queen screamed and ran from the table, knocking over her chair in the process. The prince began to cry. The king stood up in horror, and one of his bodyguards lunged forward, sword smashing down into the middle of the table, a moment too late as the rat leapt from the table; the prince jumped onto a chair as it dropped, and shrieked. The rat dived into the safety of the shrubbery, just ahead of another strike from the guard. The blow instead struck the stone of the veranda and bent the guard's bronze sword badly.

The king looked hard at Alex, and held up a hand, and the soldiers who'd grabbed him relaxed their grip slightly. Alex shut his eyes gratefully.

Thank you thank you thank you . . .

love happy proud

The king's expression became thoughtful, as he slowly sat back down. He was still holding his toast, but now dropped it with distaste into the ruined breakfast, and looked again at Alex. "Perhaps we might have some use for you. Please explain."

"I want more sticky rolls!" whined the prince, jumping down from his chair and kicking one of the servants in the shins. The man limped to obey. The king smiled lovingly at his son, and then turned his attention back to Alex.

"Sire, you can be rid of all such rats in your city before lunchtime," Alex promised. "For three hundred rills of silver, and with the help of your watercourse men, I shall lift this plague of vermin."

"Lunchtime, eh?" The king's fingers scratched at his chin as he looked thoughtfully at Alex. "Very well, let us see what you can do," he said with a dismissive wave. "If you fail, though, of course, I'll have you sent to die in the bull-pits."

"Your Majesty is just, as he is wise," Alex said, with another bow. The crowd outside the gates began chattering.

A short time later, after a brief conference with the king's men (the king himself having gone into the castle to console his wife and son) the strange musician jumped to the steps of the palace with a flourish, and lifted his pipe to his lips. He blew a ringing trill of three high notes, and then the music danced into a rapid rain of trills and squeals, squeaks and shrieks, half of them beyond the range of Humani hearing. The stranger cut a merry caper on the marble steps (he'd tripped, but recovered well); even his hat seemed to vibrate with the music.

And then rats poured from the palace, from the kitchens, from the walls, from the roof tiles, from the ornamental palms, from stable and drain and nook and cranny. They swarmed to the piper as he danced lithely down the steps and set off at a quick march, the rats tumbling and frolicking at his heels.

The crowd spread and scattered in awe and revulsion as he came through the gates, riding at the head of the low furry tide. As they stepped back they almost stepped on more rats, who came flocking out of the surrounding houses, from the alleys and the stalls of the marketplace. As he walked across the square, rats rushed forth to meet him and join the crowd swirling around and over his boots. The Rodeni in their hovels and holes, wincing at the noise of the pipe, stared in shock and wonder as their pestilent competitors leapt from walls and piles of rubbish, to flow like water toward the gaily dressed figure of the musician. He strode through the streets, the sharp shrill notes of the pipe echoing off the walls; people threw open their shutters and leaned out to stare in amazement. People in the streets leapt to the safety of stools and stairs and stalls as the rats came tumbling past. Cats and terriers, eyes agleam, crept forward then froze in horror at the sheer enormity of the prey before them; they ran in fear rather than face that milling mob. Monitor lizards struck and snapped, but were sated and bloated long before the racing feast was past.

Big rats, little rats, black rats from the roofs and brown rats from the cellars, big bristling males nearly dragging their balls in the dust, females waddling and heavy with young. Lithe young ones, bright eyed, scuffling and leaping in play as they ran, and small fuzzy ones, staring wide with newly opened eyes as they moved with rapid leaps and jumps alongside their kin. Rats upon rats upon rats, scaly tails thrashing, their thousands and thousands of tiny feet pattering like raindrops on the cobblestones, the street behind them scattered with their droppings.

Alex couldn't look behind him—didn't dare turn, at the pace he was moving. It was difficult enough to pick his footing on the uneven cobblestones, and now, if he slowed, rats would come pouring and scampering over his boots and around and in front of him, and make progress even more hazardous. Under his hat, Mote scampered and danced in circles on his head, her thoughts abuzz with the channeling of power.

Chernan had shown him around the city in the cover of evening, and Alex had planned out the route yesterday, making himself memorize it. They'd worked out the effective range of the sound of the pipe, and argued the route back and forth, with Temith adding helpful advice from time to time. There was a limit, Alex knew, to how long the rats would even be able to run; they were creatures not built for long marches. Luckily, the town was generally circular, or rather oval, and several main roads went from end to end, with a single highway round it, skirting the side rivers. "You won't get them all," Temith had acknowledged. "You wouldn't anyway; some of them will be too far underground or out of hearing, and some you just won't be getting close enough to."

"No matter," Chernan had said. "The king won't be going out into the slums to count each and every rat. Even if you just get a few, it'll still look like magic."

"Well, it is," Alex had said, frowning.

"Mostly," Temith had added.

Alex had been doubtful about the concept at first, unsure of the ethics of it, but wild rats were, after all, vermin; he'd certainly killed enough of them in his time at the College. His main concern with the plan was that he and Mote might be exposed to diseases the rats might carry; so he went through every effort to avoid allowing them to come into contact with him. He would not waste time with the alleys and side streets, where in the narrow and uneven footing the rats might catch up to him. The main streets should do well enough, and now through these main streets Alex marched, the furry throng behind him growing steadily.

After a time, Mote began to send little signals of

confusion overwhelmed

as the mass of rats the little Anim communicated with grew almost too much for such a simple spirit; but then the sheer number and size of the pack began to work for her. The rats overcame their normal fears and instincts and simply joined with the massive mind of the swarm of rodents. Soon Alex sensed she was working more on stopping the rats from simply swarming in a frenzy of joyous feeding and merry nibbling destruction over everything they came across. He felt the thrill, the strength of command, the mastery over other creatures, as the animals did what he commanded, followed his will. He realized this success was his own power, his own talent, channeled and amplified through his Anim. *What would my teachers think, if they saw this?* he wondered. *Is this why they thought I was worth buying? Would this make them proud?* He pushed his thoughts away quickly, and made himself concentrate on Mote's instead.

Alex quartered the town and crossed the river again, where he noted that the flood of water had slowed to a trickle, the sides of the river muddy below their stone-sided embankments. The rats ran along the bridge behind him, so thick now that they were tumbling over and running along each others' backs as the narrow bridge pressed the mass into a thick column. He set off down the next street, and now the word had spread and people leaned from windows as he approached, cheering and shouting and then jumping back as rats poured from the eves and trees and rafters and ricks, from within stables and from under tables. And the pipe played on, and the piper strode, full of confidence and music and magic and power, without a glance to the side or behind him.

The pestilential parade reached the seaward bridge-gate, but instead of crossing the bridge the piper stepped down, jumping over the water-smoothed stone of the diminished river's banks and alighting on the weed-slick stones there. The rats followed, a rush of tiny moving bodies pouring into the channel, down the high slick sides, hopping from stone to stone as still more came pouring out from long-forgotten drains and nooks beneath the bridges. Others, weary and dry from their long march, lapped eagerly at the water running in a trickle down the center of the riverbed, shaking the droplets from their whiskers. Some nibbled on scraps of waterweed or grabbed up stranded polliwogs in their paws, snatching a bite or two. Then, leaping atop a moss-covered statue pushed from the bridge centuries ago, the piper gave a last piercing whistle, and turned.

And he stopped, and he stared.

Before him stretched a massive, heaving carpet, patchwork brown and black, the heat of their packed bodies making the cool air of morning steam above them. A crowd of rats, a mob of rats, an ocean of rats; they could have sunk the *Charmed* with their weight. He could smell their musky-ammonia funk in the air. His breath stopped, the flute stopped, and in the sudden silence he could hear the shaking rasping rustling of hundreds of thousands of whiffling noses, rasping teeth, scuffling feet and sliding tails, shaking fur and grooming claws. Eyes glittered in the unaccustomed sunlight, a sparkling of onyx and ruby through the pelts of mink and sable, all fixed upon him.

Alex stood, shaking, staring back at them. Suddenly he felt very young, very foolish; he was reminded of the storm at sea, the strange weakness man feels when confronted with something unimaginably older and stronger and greater than himself, something he cannot understand and can only fear and respect. Here was a life and strength and vitality of nature elevated to her purest form; survive and multiply, incarnate. The beating of a million hearts seemed to throb inside his own. You could never destroy this, could not conquer it, could not defeat it. You could beat it down and force it back but there was an unthinking will here, stronger than trap or poison or fire or flood, and it would return again and again, stronger and smarter, surviving, long after you and all your descendants were gone to dust. The power flowing through the hand and mind of Animist; magic. Power to command . . . power to destroy.

There was a roaring in his ears, and a rope ladder smacked into his face. The rats burst from their stunned immobility into milling panic, but too late. Alex wanted to scream to the rats to jump, to flee, to run, but his throat was tight with anguish and he couldn't speak. He grabbed the ladder reflexively, and felt himself hauled upward.

The river came surging down the channel; the floodgates at the inland wall had been opened. No longer diverted into twin streams around the city walls, the flood-swollen waters leapt forward like muddy beasts; pouncing watercats and surging waterweasels that tore into the mass of rats. The rats were lifted high on the waves, struggling and swimming, climbing and clinging to one another in great sodden rafts that were tumbled past. Rats clung desperately to the stones of the bank, to the pilings of the bridge, but the water surged higher, faster than they could climb, and tiny claws were torn loose and the rats were pulled into the froth. Some clung to branches and boards torn loose in the sudden flood; so many tried to climb aboard this precarious safety that the floats spun and tumbled anyway, or sank beneath the heaving weight. Alex saw one clinging to a piling of the bridge as he was hauled upward, stared down into beady eyes full of terror and remembered the Roden reaching up from the pit, as the bull closed in. Then the rushing waters flexed, and the rat was gone.

In memory Alex suddenly felt the pull of water, the splash and heaviness of it, the way it filled your mouth and throat and lungs with cold fire as you tried to scream. The choking need for air, when none came. The blindness and confusion as the foam filled your ears and blurred your eyes and burned in your sinuses. The cruel waves that smashed you down and pulled you into the suffocating depths of agony, the sky an impossibly faraway gleaming dream, the water an inescapable nightmare on every side.

Hands pulled Alex over the wall of the bridge, but he could not stop staring into the surging water as the last stragglers were swept from the rocks and vanished under the bridge. He ran across the bridge, pushing through crowds, to look over the other side, and saw the current swollen with small shapes pouring out the swift channel beyond the city walls, over the cliff's edge to the jagged rocks and surf pounding against sea-slick rocks below. In the ear of imagination he could hear millions of tiny screams beyond the range of hearing. On the bridge, the two palace guards who had thrown him the ladder, and Temith, who'd managed to meet him here, stared at him.

shock

Alex reached up to his head, and found his hat in the way, and so he just patted the top of his hat helplessly.

regret

He gulped, and nodded. *Regret. Sorrow. Guilt. Shame. Misery.*

A voice shouted, and another, and another. The sound swelled, a roaring of voices. Cheering.

"Don't just stand there, idiot!" the voice of Temith hissed in his ear. "Go get your reward! That's what this was all about, right?"

Alex turned like a clockwork toy, and started to walk off the bridge, his legs now weak and heavy. He might have just staggered off aimlessly and ended up who knew where, but the cheering, shouting crowd swept him up in their midst, as the river had caught the rats, and half-shoved, half-carried him back to the palace.

Supported by the chattering crowd, Alex could not clear his mind of the memory of ranks of shining eyes that had followed—helplessly? trusting? merrily? He knew they were not like Mote, really, that they were, in fact, pests and vermin and dangerous to people, and even to Mote and himself. Yet he could not help but feel tainted, as though he had committed some act of betrayal, some abuse of his power. The rush, the thrill of dominance, had faded rapidly and left only a sick feeling. Judging from the uncomfortable sadness on the top of his head, even Mote's simple soul felt much the same. Soon enough, he knew, the rat population would rebuild itself, and the town would be no better off; it was really all a trick, as Temith had pointed out. The only brightness was the thought of the reward, which could set him free, free to live his own life, where he'd never have to do anything like this again. And maybe now the king would not look on the Rodeni so harshly . . . But Alex could not console himself.

They reached the palace, coming now to the front gates. The king had taken the opportunity to change his clothes, into a more formal garment of indigo and gold, and he came out onto a balcony not far above Alex and the crowd. Alex was pushed forward, and stumbled; he managed to turn it into a bow, this time remembering to drop to one knee.

"Hat!" someone hissed from the crowd. It sounded like Temith. Alex, glancing up at the king's angry frown, grabbed for his hat.

startled!

Mote clung to the inside of the crown as the hat was swept down; Alex clasped the thing to his chest hurriedly, and felt Mote crawl into his shirt pocket as the royal frown changed into a more tolerant expression. *That's twice I've offended the king,* Alex thought nervously. *Chernan said he gets very upset when people are disrespectful; and he's already threatened me.*

"Well, it seems you have done what you said, boy," the king commented, and the crowd cheered again.

"Yes sir, Your Highness," Alex managed, still in something of a daze.

"Three hundred rills of silver, however," the king said with a chuckle. "An extravagant sum. Here is one hundred; take it with our blessing."

The king tossed a bag to Alex, who was feeling a slow, sick sensation at the sudden drop in his imagined finances. He'd promised shares to Temith and to Chernan, for their help . . . The feeling grew colder as the bag hit the stone beside him with a clinking sound, instead of the ring of rare and precious metal.

Alex took the bag and pulled out a handful of small square ceramic tiles, each stamped with an ornate seal that looked like a profile portrait of the king's head. "What—this isn't silver," he said, in his emotion forgetting once again the respectful address. Staring at the tile, he did not see the king's angry frown.

"It is a coin of the realm, boy, inscribed with my seal and guaranteed in my name as the worth of ten rills of silver."

"But it's not silver, it's just ceramic!" Alex protested, shaking the "coin." "An apprentice potter could make a pile of these! What good are they?" The Archipelago depended on barter, and that was the only financial custom Alex knew. Living as he had, in secrecy in the doctor's house, Alex did not know that the king kept all real things of value in his vaults, and issued instead this "currency," the tilecoin, to take the place of trade.

"Those coins are backed up by our royal honor!" growled the king. Something snapped inside Alex, the thousands of little screams and the crashing down of expectations, and he threw the coin to the ground, where it shattered. The crowd gasped in horror.

"They're worthless!" Alex shouted.

For an instant, king and Animist glared at each other, and then the king screamed for his guards.

Alex turned and fled, the crowd jumping back from him as he did so; the guards hot on his heels had drawn short-bladed bronze swords and were not careful where the points went as they ran. Alex thought he saw Temith, and threw the bag of tilecoins in the man's direction, in hopes that at least he could repay the doctor who had shown him kindness and been right all along. He didn't see what happened to it.

He ran back over the King's Bridge, above the waters of the river that still gurgled and chugged to itself. For a moment he thought about diving into that swift current and following the rats downstream, but his thoughts rebelled at the idea of the cold and drowning water, and he ran on.

He did not know where he was heading, only that he aimed for where the crowd of the populace seemed thinnest. The guards behind him had called up others, and Alex risked a glance behind him to see that a couple of them had gotten striches, the birds bouncing swiftly in pursuit of him. He turned a corner, not looking where he was going, and knocked over a cart of eggs and chickens. The air filled with chaos and feathers behind him as he ran on.

Something tripped him, and he fell forward hard. He heard a crunching sound in his coat pocket, and screamed in mortal terror, but then felt Mote's unhurt

confusion?

in his collar, and realized that it was his musical pipe that had broken. *Good riddance,* he thought bitterly. He had time to realize that the guards quickly approaching would be likely to break everything else that could possibly break on his person, then something grabbed his ankles and hauled him backward through a mud puddle, and dragged him through a narrow opening.

From the top of his tower, Chernan had watched the scene. The thaumaturgist only shook his head, though, and started down the stairs. He walked slowly, as though strange new thoughts were unfolding in his mind like flowers. Watching the boy lead the rats . . . it had reminded him of something, woken thoughts long dormant. Yes. Why not?

When he reached the plaza the crowd was being dispersed. Out of theater more than any fear he carried a staff, which tocked gently on the cobblestones, and people would glance up at him, in his embroidered robes, and give way quickly, avoiding his gaze. He saw a couple of guards half-dragging, half-escorting a figure between them, toward the lower gates of the castle. He stopped and seemed to think for a moment, then shook his head and walked on.

The guards would have moved to block his path, but Chernan didn't let them; with a glance of his power the thaumaturgist walked right past them. The guards looked puzzled, right through him, and sniffed the air in a puzzled fashion, exchanging glances and shrugging.

It was the same way indoors, walking quietly through the halls; he'd done this before, on an idle lark, and knew his way about. Softly now, his staff held in hand rather than tapping along, he passed unseen through the castle, finally finding and following King Belthar, as he stormed through his rooms, grumbling at the impudence of the Animist. Chernan listened to his rants and smiled to himself.

He waited until at last the king had dismissed all his advisors and soldiers, and sat down, alone at last, in a small library. It was dark and ugly and cold, like most of this castle. The windows were little arrow-slits, fine for defense, unpleasant for living. The walls had a few tapestries draped over the rough-hewn stone, but this close to the sea, there was an ever-present damp, and the tinge of mildew was attacking the worked thread. He watched in amusement as the king unrolled a map of Miraposa on the desk, trying to read it with the help of a few sputtering candles. From time to time he would sniff, and look around, sniffing at the candles suspiciously, and then at the map, and then his own hands.

Chernan waited until the king was looking behind himself, searching for the source of the strong smell of mint that was a side effect of this spell of invisibility, before dropping that spell with an accompanying flash. The reaction was most gratifying; the king jerked back in panic as the robed figure suddenly appeared before him, back-lit by the narrow window. He stared, and opened his mouth to scream for the guards, but no sound came out. His look of shock changed to one of horror.

"There's no need for that, Your Highness," Chernan said, his voice soothingly speaking in Trade. "Besides, I assure you, you'll only be calling them here to die." He watched the slow change of expression over the man's face, then let go his magical hold on the man's vocal cords.

"Death's what you came for, is it?" the king finally said, when he was able. He did not sound fearful, though, only defiant. "I know you. You're Deridal's wizard."

"Late of Deridal, perhaps. I've been a citizen of yours, sir, for the past three years. And I do pay my taxes, I assure you," Chernan said, with a smile, moving away from the window so that the king could see his expression. "One might even say I am a subject of yours, sir." He gave a little bow.

"What do you want?" asked King Belthar, frowning. "What brings you here?"

"I saw the . . . entertainment today, sir," Chernan answered. The king's mouth twitched in remembered anger. "It occurred to me that my lord—" and he gave me a little bow, "—deserves better than the services of a second-rate pseudo-magist. I thought you might be interested in hiring someone worthy of your coins."

King Belthas looked surprised, but under the pressure of the flattery his ruffled emotions were calming. "You, you mean?"

Chernan bowed again. "None other. I apologize for startling Your Lordship, but I thought some demonstration of my powers might convince you to look most favorably upon me. I was, after all, a King's Wizard. It is my calling. I should be honored with the chance at last to serve with a lord worthy of my talents."

"But you served King Carawan," protested the king. "How can I trust you?"

"I assure you, Your Majesty . . . as long as you refrain from going mad as a stoat, and from having a demon-born brat of a daughter who will oust me . . . I assure you, you've nothing to fear from me." Chernan smiled again. King Belthar looked thoughtful.

"And . . . you'd consider such a king, with such a daughter, an enemy, then?" he asked, rubbing his chin in thought.

"If that was such as my new lord wished," Chernan answered sweetly, with another small bow. "I confess it would give me no small pleasure to see some harm come to those who drove me from my previous position."

"You are a scheming, devious man," the king declared, leaning back in his chair and looking at him. Chernan didn't bother to reply, and King Belthar thought a long moment, and then nodded slowly. "Yes, I could use such."

"Excellent," Chernan said, with a bow, adding, "my lord."

Alex tumbled a few feet, and landed sitting in a pile of loose, wet, moldy straw. Bits of glass and copper fell out of his pocket. Two large eyes glinted in the darkness of a cellar, the roof only a foot or two above his head.

"You quick! Follow!" whispered a voice. Alex stood, banged his head, dropped to a crawl, and followed. Outside he heard the shouts of the guards, and the stamp of feet.

He shuffled on hands and knees through stinking slurry, away from the small square of fitful light high above. In a moment, he was deep in darkness. Mote stuck her head out of his collar, sniffing, looking around; then knowledge and hazy vision dawned.

He was in a low cellar still, the roof of which sagged dangerously. Ahead of him a crack led into deeper but dryer darkness, and a large moving shape beckoned there.

The shape stepped forward, put out a hand, and Alex reached out to clasp the knobby, clawed hand of a Roden. He tensed in fear, but the hand gripped gently.

"Strange one, magic one, I not harm you and the *mookchee*," whispered the voice in Trade. There was the sound of teeth rasping in a chuckle. "The small ones eat *our* food, too."

"Where are we going?" Alex whispered, as the Roden led him down tight and twisting passageways. It was hard to tell, but Alex was pretty sure they were making progress upward back to street level. From time to time light fell in cracks and splashes from above. Sometimes the roof was tall enough for him to stand in a waddling crouch, other times he went back to his knees. Underfoot was sometimes dry, sometimes wet, all with a faint smell of fungus and organic decay. The Roden hopped along easily on all fours.

"Someplace safe for now."

Now the passages opened up, into side-chambers and crossing tunnels, and now and then they would step for brief periods out into the open air, across narrow alleys blocked and strewn with shattered barrels and boards, piles of trash and fallen fences. Rodeni were all around, hopping and scuffling and bounding on four legs and two, eating and talking and fighting and playing, but all stopped as the black Roden led him past.

Some of them just stared, some slowly swayed their heads to see him fully. Some jumped back in fear, others held their ground, hairs bristling in anger. Young ones blinked wide-eyed, or ran to their mothers to hide their heads in the maternal fur. Some tried to crowd close, noses whiffling, some dropped to all fours and pressed their ears flat in submission. Some of the angry ones snarled and squittered and cheeped at his guide. They drew back and silenced, however, when they saw Mote riding boldly on his shoulder.

"Won't the king send his people in here to look for me?" worried Alex. "I don't want you to come to harm because of me . . ."

"They will come. But we can hide. They give up soon. Know as we do that His Lordship angers quickly but soon loses interest. There may come a price on your head, and watchmen will watch for you, and search, but he picks his wars carefully, does His Lordship. And we have much practice in hiding from him."

They ducked back into tight darkness again, a darkness that smelled of grape and vinegar. Crystals of tartar crunched underfoot. Then the darkness was lit by thin bars of light, high up: uneven cracks in the plaster wall.

"This my home," his guide told him.

It was just a space between the walls of, judging by the smell, a winery. The walls were thick enough to keep the winery cool, but barely thick enough to allow for this room to have been made in the hollow between the layers. Alex could extend his arms, bent at right angles at the elbows, and touch the crumbling walls. The room was longer than wide, however, by some ten feet. Beyond that, an incomplete wall of bricks showed other small Rodeni faces peering through the holes—another home like this one.

The floor was covered with chips of wood and boards that had been gnawed. In the far end the smallest chips, and bits of rag and leaves and small clean dry trash had been gathered into a pile. Lying curled up on this pile was the brown-and-white female Roden Alex remembered seeing his first day in this town; now he recognized his guide as the same beggar who'd attempted to mug him.

His guide dropped his hand and hopped across the room to the side of the female, patting her brow gently with one hand until her eyes opened, as Alex stood uncomfortably in the doorway. Through the cracks in the far wall, bright eyes watched him.

The two Rodeni here exchanged whispered cheeping in their own language, then his guide turned, and beckoned Alex forward eagerly.

Alex approached cautiously, squeezing in the narrow space, and knelt so as to be on a level with his hosts.

As he got close, he could see there was something wrong with the female; her fur was mussed and stiff, her eyes bleary. Her limbs trembled slightly. A long gash marred the fur over her shoulders, and though it was not fresh and not bleeding, it still looked very painful. There was the smell of ammonia, and of blood. It was too dim to see clearly.

"This is Nuck," his guide told him, and the female passed a shaking hand over her whiskers, as though attempting to groom herself. "I am Flip," he added.

"I'm Alex," said Alex, and added, "And this is Mote," as he took her from his shoulder.

The eyes of the Rodeni widened. There was a scuffle and whispered chatter behind the wall. Nuck blinked, and reached out a hand. "The *mookchee* . . ." she whispered.

Alex let Mote jump down to the nest, and the tiny rat sniffed at the Roden's muzzle. Nuck gingerly extended one fingertip to touch the Anim gently.

"Pretty," Nuck murmured, in Trade. "Soft. Small."

"The last small one in the city," Flip said, with a note of respect and awe.

"Oh, no, I think a lot of them got away," Alex stammered, blushing in shame.

"You rest here now, stay some time. Then we get you away from His Lordship," Flip told him.

Nuck spoke to her mate, and Flip turned to Alex. "Nuck asks if the *mookchee* can bless the pup," he translated, looking hopeful.

"Uhm . . . what's a *mookchee?*" Alex asked, unable to wonder any longer.

"Oh! Your small one . . . the color and the star. In legend we have, those ones that look so, are lucky? Magic? Friendly? What do Humani say . . ." Flip thought, and looked around.

"Fay-rees!" squeaked a voice from the wall, and Flip nodded rapidly at the wall.

"Yes, Trit! Fay-rees." He nodded to Alex, and then gently reached behind the recumbent form of Nuck.

"Fay—you mean fairies?" Alex asked. It was another name for the minor spirits, but also the related, mythical creatures that were thought to be able to manifest as tiny persons.

There was a high squeaking, and Flip hauled out a fat, wriggling shape from the bedding beside Nuck. It was a Rodeni pup, about the size of a Humani newborn. Alex didn't know how old it could be; the eyes were still tightly shut, the ears still folded flaps at the side of the head. Little arms paddled at the air, little hind feet kicked weakly, as Flip picked it up around the waist. It was covered in short, soft brown fur, like a puppy, and tiny whiskers fine as Alex's own hair bristled at its muzzle.

"What's its name?" Alex asked. The pup squeaked but settled down as Flip set it beside its mother's head. Mote came forward and sniffed at it, then hopped up on its head, to Nuck's apparent happiness.

"He has none yet," Flip explained. "We, they . . . sometimes, it tempts fate to name them yet," he said. "There were two. Now there is one. When he can see, he will be named." Flip tried to sound calm, but cast a worried glance at Nuck, whose eyes had shut again.

"What's wrong with her?" Alex whispered to him. Flip heaved a small sigh.

"Soldiers caught her. Tried to kill. She got away, but is hurt . . ." His voice stopped, but one paw silently slashed the air in the Trade gesture for "bad."

"That's terrible!"

"But she got away. Most times, if watchmen catch us, they kill us. She escaped." He looked at his mate again, who seemed to have fallen back into her stupor. Mote was sitting on the pup's head, grooming behind its ears, while the pup nosed blindly about for food in the warmth of its mother. "But I worry . . ." Flip added softly. "I ask Reat, our shaman, he prays, but can do no more."

"I can help," Alex said urgently, shedding his patched coat. "I've been trained, I know medicine for some species of rodents, and no offense, but you can't be that much different. Let me help her."

"You are doctor?" Flip seemed taken aback.

"I've had some training. But we'll need medicines."

"You can help? Please?" Flip grabbed his hand, looking from his mate to the pup and back to Alex.

"Yes, yes, I will, but we have to get—" Alex leaned closer to Nuck, and gently brushed the fur back from the wound. It was fairly deep, but seemed to have gone through muscle and bone rather than punching deeper. One arm seemed to be broken, and so did a couple of ribs. He pictured boots kicking, and spears slashing. He didn't like the tense hot feel of her skin, or the way her belly lay so limp, but he'd have to do the best he could.

"Herbs, and molds, and bandages and stitches and draughts," Alex muttered to himself. "Can you take me back to the doctor's house? Where you took me before?"

"You ask doctor to help? To give medicines?" Flip queried.

Alex sighed. "I don't think he'll want anything more to do with me. But if I have to, I'll steal them."

They hurried back through the Rodeni passageways. Then they came back to the squalid, chemical-smelling alleyway that backed on to Temith's rooms. The back door was latched. Alex debated inwardly about knocking, but then Flip gently shouldered past him, and reached into the latch-hole with careful claws. A moment later he'd snagged the string through, and with a careful clunk the door pushed open.

Alex motioned to Flip to stay outside, as he carefully edged into the hallway. He stopped to listen, and then moved down to the doctor's study.

There was no one there. The doctor's piles of paper and clay tablets, a chalkboard filled with scribbling that looked like a cross between mathematics and music, an arrangement of copper pipes, and all the other miscellany of the scientific mind were there, but no Temith. Alex crept down the hall to the rodent room; this too was empty save for cage upon cage of white rats, now all sleeping. Alex wondered if they had heard his playing, and clung to and chewed the bars of their cages, or scrabbled at the sides of their bins, attempting to get out and follow him to death.

Alex completed his careful search of the place, ending up in the pharmacy, but no one was here. The doctor was out. *Perhaps,* Alex thought with a sudden pang of guilt, *the guards captured him after I threw the coins to him. Perhaps he's in trouble, or even dead.*

Alex shook his head. One rescue at a time. He grabbed down bottles and jars from the shelves, and packs of bandage and suture and fine needles from the drawers, and threw it all into a bag.

He went looking for anything else that might be helpful, even entering Temith's room. There was his bed, and a desk with some letters which Alex left alone. There were some wooden chests, latched but unlocked, and Alex heaved them open.

What was inside was cloth—robes, red robes. Obviously Temith's graduation robes from the College of Allopathists; the robes were red as blood and embroidered with the ring-shaped cells found in blood. He lifted up the rich silk to see if anything useful was underneath. What was underneath was more silk—green, and embroidered with leaves. College of Botanists. Alex, puzzled, tossed it aside; below was black silk, speckled with patterns in silver: College of Astronomists. He pulled it out, and below that, the yellow silk and equations of Mathematists.

In the next chest, the similar robe in purple from the College of Physicists, the blue one embroidered with microscopic animalcules of the Biologists, the grey of the Alchemists, sky blue of Philosophists . . . The room took on a carnival air of colorful silk as Alex rummaged through the chests, throwing the robes every which way. Then he stepped back, not knowing what to think.

These couldn't be fairly won. Each was a lifetime's achievement, and Temith wasn't even that old. Maybe Temith was a collector of collegiate tokens? Alex checked on an impulse to make sure his necklace was still there. It was; that wasn't the answer.

No . . . Temith must be a fraud, all this time, with costumes to prove it, to pretend to be whatever he needed to be. Currently pretending to be a doctor, but if there was any trouble, such as Alex had surely just brought down on him, he could flee, change his name, put on a different robe and pretend to be something else. Clever, and cunning. Alex thought for a moment about stealing one, trying to think of what he could pose as, but abandoned the idea; for one thing, Temith was quite tall and none of the robes would fit Alex. Shaking his head, and thanking his stars that the charlatan hadn't managed to hurt him with some incorrect medication, Alex completed his foraging by taking one of Temith's pillowcases to carry things. Then he fled with Flip back to the room behind the winery.

The pup had fallen asleep beside its mother, feet twitching in infant dreams. Nuck woke up again as Alex knelt nearby, and Flip nuzzled her and explained.

"Ask her where she hurts, and how," Alex said, mixing a small bowl of solution to clean the wound.

Flip held a long conversation with his mate, then turned to Alex. "She says she feels dizzy, and sick. She does not want food. The men kicked her, and beat her on all sides, and now she feels cold and hurting inside, but the cut burns."

"I'll give her this medicine, but the pup shouldn't nurse for a while after I do, because it will go into the milk, too, do you see?" Alex explained, taking out another bottle and trying to guess the Roden's weight. "Will he be all right for a bit?"

"He will be hungry, but he has been many times before already," Flip sighed, picking up the sleeping pup. Nuck watched her pup go, with sadness in the dark eyes.

She lay very still as Alex bathed the wound, then sewed it closed. The thick Rodeni hide was like working lamb leather. He gently touched her flank and side, and winced as she cringed in tension, limbs shaking. If not for the fur, he thought to himself, she'd have bruises upon bruises. He splinted her arm, but he could do nothing for the broken ribs. He gave her a dose of the antibiotic powder he himself had taken, and a sip of a draught to control bleeding. None of Temith's medicines for control of fever could be used, however, because they were all for Humani and could be dangerous to other species. Flip watched him carefully, from time to time reaching out and touching his mate's paw or muzzle.

Alex gave her a drink of a pain-draught, and after a time the tension of agony slowly slipped from the muscles, and Nuck relaxed a little, breathing more easily. Flip chattered his teeth happily, and she squeaked softly in response.

"She says she feels better," Flip told Alex. Alex sat back, and winced at a stabbing in his shoulder blades; he hadn't realized how tense he'd been, working over the Roden.

"Good, good," Alex said with a sigh. "I hope that helps. I know you said I should leave town soon, but I'll stay and help. I know she's strong, anyway . . . I remember the thump she gave me." He smiled to show he was joking, though the Rodeni looked abashed anyway.

"We are sorry, sorry for that," Flip said, looking down.

"Oh, don't worry, that's all in the past," Alex said with a smile.

"Thank you, kind one," Flip said. Nuck squeaked again, and Flip translated, "She wants to know, can she have the pup back, please?"

"If we can put a blanket round her so he can't nurse, I suppose," Alex replied. Flip rummaged about until he found a large piece of cloth, that he tucked gently in around the female, covering the teats that showed pink through the brown and white fur, then placed the pup next to her. Nuck draped one paw over the wiggling shape, and sighed, drifting into sleep again.

"He is our first," Flip whispered proudly. "Nuck worries about him much. He was still pink when we met you the first time, and we were hungry, so hungry . . . we would not have attempted to rob you otherwise, magic sir," he said, looking for forgiveness from Alex.

"Don't worry about it . . . and you don't have to call me sir. I owe you, if anything, for saving my life." Alex yawned, in spite of himself.

Flip went out to forage for food, and came back some while later. Alex had fallen asleep, sitting against the wall, his knees drawn up in the cramped space, next to Nuck, who also slept on. Flip had brought a number of fresh rolls, baked into the shape of rats; obviously some enterprising baker had taken advantage of the day's festivities. Alex wondered, as he ate his rolls, whether today would become a tradition, with rat-rolls and music every year, and the ritual drowning of some poor rats, or even Rodeni, in the river. He shuddered.

Nuck did not wake, and Flip and Alex decided to let her sleep rather than disturb her. There was nothing to drink, except the diluted pain-draught Alex had made, so they drank that. It tasted of anise. Alex found it welcome, for easing the cramp in his legs and back. Mote explored the room, and then sat in a hole in the partial wall and smugly endured the adulation and exclamation of the neighboring Rodeni. Alex was introduced to them; it was a single female named Leep, and her two sons, Len and Trit; the young Rodeni were about ten years old, but that made them about the equivalent to Alex's own age in comparable maturity; Rodeni aged faster than Humani. Len and Trit spoke Trade well, and chirped all kinds of questions and stories back and forth through the wall with Alex, their voices pitched low to allow Nuck to sleep. Finally even Alex began to nod off, and the young Rodeni were reluctantly shooed away by their mother.

Flip curled up nearby, and Alex stretched out a little on the lumpy floor. Through the wall he could dimly hear the occasional mumbled voices from the winery. Mote came back and curled up under his chin, and he drifted into deep slumber.

The sound that woke him some time later was the peevish, high cry of the pup, bewailing the cooling stiffness of his mother's body.

Flip jumped to his feet, touched his mate's cheek, her nose, and then slumped beside her, trembling with grief. A few faces appeared for a moment at the far wall, then withdrew, without a word or a squeak. Alex stared in shock and sorrow, and then put his face in his hands. The pup squealed on, hungry and cold, until at last Flip gathered it against his chest, where its cries were muffled by his fur.

"I'm sorry . . . I'm so sorry . . . I thought . . ." Alex gulped.

"I know it was not your medicines," Flip whispered. "You drank them yourself. So did I."

"I think . . . bleeding inside but I couldn't be sure . . ." He couldn't speak anymore, as his throat closed up and tears started. Mote, on his shoulder, whufffled in his ear, leaning against him, trying to console him.

love concern comfort

"They never taught us surgery for . . . no one knows surgery for rodents because no one's supposed to have one for an Anim, no one cares—" Alex looked up, and saw, in a small line of sunlight on the floor, a puddle of urine that had leaked from the corpse in death. Dark with blood and proteins.

"Internal hemorrhage," Alex whispered. "Those bastards . . . they beat her insides bloody and—"

"She had blood from inside, yes," Flip sighed. "I worried then that there would be no hope, but I did not want to trouble her. And I did not mention, for fear you would not help; such blood is a plague sign as well as that of wounds within."

"I know you don't have any plague," Alex said, "except those Humani bastards that think cruelty doesn't count if it's to someone other than themselves."

Flip sighed in sadness, and held the pup out to Alex. "Will you hold him?" he asked. "I must . . . tend to what remains behind when others leave us."

Alex took the pup in his arms. It was heavy and warm and soft as fine velvet. Mote leaned down and sniffed at it. The pup's paws pushed at him as it wriggled. He touched one paw with his fingertip, but unlike a primate infant it did not grasp him. "You—you'd trust me?" Alex said, rubbing the tears from his face.

Flip had bound Nuck's body up in the cloth blanket, and was preparing to drag it outside. He turned at Alex's question. Alex had never thought eyes that were just black beads could show emotion, but it was there; the sorrow and love and loss as real as any. "I trust you, as I trusted you with her. Beyond your magic, beyond the *mookchee,* I know you are a good soul." He gently touched his burden. "You did what you could, and all that could be done. You ended the pain, and though she died, it was in peace, and in love and hope. Very few of Rodeni have that blessing." Flip turned, and walked out, dragging the sad shape.

Alex sat with the pup cuddled awkwardly against his chest. Mote sent loving thoughts to him, and lapped at his tears with her tiny tongue. The pup nuzzled him blindly for awhile, but quickly realized there was no nutrition here. It pushed away, trying to find its way back to the fount of warmth and food that was all its blind life had known. Alex had to keep turning it around to keep it from crawling away.

What would happen to it? he wondered suddenly. Now there was no mother, no food. It was surely too young to eat solids yet; he tried to offer it a scrap of bread, but the pup pushed it away and latched on to one of Alex's fingers instead, sucking hard. Alex sighed, and let it; the tiny new teeth scraped lightly on his knuckles, and the paws paddled at him. The pup seemed to quiet a bit from this, though it still squeaked in annoyance that there was no milk. Its hind feet kicked at him with feeble rabbit-like thumps.

Flip returned after a time, and Alex saw him flinch with pain again at the sight of the empty nest. He motioned to Alex with one weak paw. "Come, please . . . bring the pup," he requested, and Alex stood in a half-crouch, and followed.

Down a few passages, and up a narrow ladder in a crawlspace between buildings, into a small space below the roof tiles. Here it was warm, with the sun on the tiles above, and here were more Rodeni, a beige male and two females, one black and one brown. Flip greeted them solemnly, and introduced them to Alex, but they did not speak Trade and only managed to cheep and chitter at him, dipping their heads and flattening their ears in respect. Alex caught a word here and there and responded as best he could. Mote was brought out, and regarded with amazement by all.

Flip took the pup from Alex, and handed it over to the brown female, who, he could see, had two pups of her own, about the same age. The brown female took the pup eagerly, and cuddled it close, then tucking it into her bed of palm leaves with the other two, as the other female came over to stroke and fuss over the pup as well. Flip and the other male stood away, talking in low squeaks, then Flip returned to Alex, and they climbed back down.

"Is he a . . . relative? A friend of yours?" Alex asked, referring to the male of the family above. Flip clicked his teeth. He was sorrowing, Alex could see, but not allowing it to cripple him; not yet. First, there were things that must be done; Alex got the impression that getting rid of him was one of these.

"No . . . I know him. We all know everyone. Jook and Clip's pups are the same age as Nuck's, and with two wives Chet will not have to run raw to feed him." Flip led Alex into a small courtyard between windowless walls, where a Rodeni marketplace was going on, cramped with Rodeni with boxes and cloths spread with small things, and cheeping cries ringing in the air. At the sight of Alex, many stopped, and stared, then the cries rang out again tenfold in gossip and surprise.

"The king does not like trade, but we cannot use his coins," Flip explained, leading him to a vendor. Flip turned suddenly, and looked at him. "I was told the story . . . why did you not take the coins, and exchange them in the Humani markets for what you wanted?"

"I . . . I didn't think of that at the time," Alex said, embarrassed. "We don't use 'coins' either, where I come from. And he was cheating me anyway, so I was angry, and . . . I didn't think." Flip made a sound with his teeth that seemed to be the Rodeni equivalent of "tsk-tsk."

"You want to get away from His Lordship, yes?" Flip asked, and Alex nodded. "Then you must go to Deridal."

"Can't I just sneak aboard a ship here?" Alex asked hopefully. "You're Rodeni, ships have Rodeni, you must have connections . . ."

"But *you* are Humani, and His Lordship will have men watching for you, everywhere. Even in other towns, now," Flip said. "He owns them, he does. Deridal is not his, and you may find someone there who can help you gain passage to a ship."

"I'm going to go back to Temith's, first," Alex said. "He knows something about having to move on the sly, I know that now. I can't impose on your kindness any more, Flip. I just wish I could have . . . could have . . ." His voice choked off.

Flip patted Alex's hand gently. "So do I. But wishes only work for wizards, as they say." In silence Flip led him back to the doctor's, and Alex slipped through the back door. Flip gave him a final bow, and another to Mote, watching from his shoulder, and vanished into the shadows.

Alex crept carefully in, then stopped in remembering. He'd left the place a mess in his frantic search for medications earlier. If he wanted to ask Temith for help, he'd better clean the place up before the doctor returned . . .

He rounded the corner to the allopathist's bedroom, and stopped. Temith was standing in the middle of the room, looking around at the chaos. He looked up when he saw Alex, and his face broke into a glad smile. Alex, however, stared in horror; the doctor's clothing was torn and filthy, his left eye blackened, and he held one hand awkwardly against his chest, obviously injured.

"Alex! You did get away! Thank goodness, I was worried. They decided to detain me for questioning, but I pretended ignorance and they released me. Came home and passed out in the sickroom, after trying to treat myself, only just now got around to . . . well, you can see. They must've suspected something; they went through all my things while I was gone, looking for you I suppose." He started to rummage on the shelves. "They stole a few things, though, and here I am with two sprained fingers. Always seems to be my fingers . . . Where did I put those plasters? I thought for sure they were in the sickroom, but . . ."

"I . . . I took them," Alex managed, in a whisper. "I'm the one who made all this mess."

Temith turned, wide-eyed (though one was still swollen almost shut) in surprise. "You did? Whatever for?"

Alex quickly rambled out the story of his rescue by the Rodeni, his attempt to help them, and his failure. "I didn't mean to leave it such a mess, I was just in a hurry, and I wasn't thinking . . ." he stammered.

"Alex!" exclaimed Temith, flinging his hands up in exasperation, then wincing and curling his sprained fingers to his chest again. "Why didn't you just *ask* me?"

"You weren't here!" Alex protested. "I guess you were being beaten by the guards!"

"The guards probably would have passed me by if you hadn't chucked that bag of coins at me," Temith replied. "Pity you didn't cinch it first. Coins went everywhere, and in the middle of a mob, too. I thought I was going to be trampled to death. That's how I ended up looking like this. The guards saved me, pulled me out, took me to the palace for questioning and detained me awhile. They wanted to know if I knew you." Temith shook his head sadly. "I guess I wasn't lying when I said I didn't know you."

"You're one to talk!" Alex protested, pointing at the colored robes that still lay scattered around. "You're no doctor! You're just a quack, who's good at sewing and putting on a show!"

Temith looked around at the robes. "They're pretty, aren't they?" he said, as if he hadn't seen them before. "I always thought I should sell them, or get rid of them, but they *are* pretty. Seemed foolish, really. All the knowledge was more precious than anything, but they decide they have to give you a pretty robe, too."

"They can't be real," insisted Alex. "Unless you stole them. That's years of work! Years and years and years!"

"I was a quick student," Temith said quietly, as he began to pick up the robes and pile them back in the chests haphazardly. "Always trying to find the truth. I jumped ahead in levels here and there, because I couldn't rest for wanting to know what was next. And after all that knowledge, I came out staring at a vast, endless sea of ignorance . . . and there were no more books to read, nothing more the teachers could give me—and I was old, and I still hadn't found the truth."

He let the black Astronomist's robe pour through his hands like oil into the chest. "I came home. I was born here on Miraposa, you know. Found a place to retire, a simple job in a simple land, with good people who let me continue my work, studying from experiments. I lost that job and came here with what I could. Still wondering, still searching."

"I don't believe it!" Alex insisted, but doubt was dawning. "You can't prove that you're a graduate of all those Colleges! Come on, tell me something that only a graduate Alchemist would know."

"And how would you, an Animist, know if what I said was correct?" asked Temith, with a sad smile.

"What are three plants with anti-inflammatory properties?" demanded Alex. "What's sugar made of? What causes swelling plague? How do you treat diarrhea in capianas?"

"Chimgan, souweed, and green kelp. Carbon, hydrogen, and oxygen. Bacteria, the species *Ersinia pestis*. And there's no such thing as a capiana," said Temith with annoyance. "Really, this is juvenile. I don't give a damn whether you believe me or not. You take advantage of my hospitality, ignore my advice and go off on a fool's romp, incriminate me and nearly get me killed by a greedy mob, steal from me, wreck my home, and then come barging back in here and insult me. All I can say is I pity poor Mote for getting stuck with you." Temith shook his head. Mote looked up and gave a faint squeak at the sound of her name.

Alex leaned heavily against the wall. "I don't know what to kick myself more for," he said, "for my ingratitude toward you, or that you probably could have saved Nuck if I'd gone to find you. I'm sorry. I'll leave."

"Where are you planning to go?" Temith asked.

"I've been told Deridal would be a good choice," said Alex. "Being as it's away from His Lordship, as they call him."

"You'll never make it out of the city," Temith told him. "Not without money, without help." He sighed. "I'll help you."

"What? Why?" asked Alex in surprise.

"I still haven't finished my experiments and research on Animism," Temith said. "I don't know when I'll get another chance. I can't force you to stay, and it's not safe anyway, but I can at least ask you questions along the road."

"I . . . I'd be honored. Thank you."

Temith just shook his head and said nothing.

SIX

Temith arranged the loan of a small strich-cart full of straw, and concealed Alex and Mote under the hay, along with packed provisions for the short journey to Deridal; no more than a day's travel, he'd told Alex.

"Who'll take care of your monitor lizard while you're gone?" Alex had asked, because an Animist tended to worry about such things.

"It was on loan from a neighbor anyway," Temith had explained; "I just gave it back."

Alex, buried under the hay, tried not to itch. Mote had cleared away a small space in front of his face, and was nibbling happily on a seed head. Alex tried to distract himself from the bumpy ride by talking to her, inside his head.

"I wish I knew what to do, Mote."

query?

"You know, about whether to go back to Highjade or not. I wish I'd kept that money. I was an idiot." But who would have thought that pieces of pottery could be made valuable, just because someone said they were?

comfort

"I know, you love me. But what do you think? It's not just my life anymore, it's yours now, too. What do you think I should do?"

love

"You don't think, that's right. I keep forgetting. You just feel."
He sighed mentally. "That must be nice."

Temith was silent, thinking about their destination, Deridal.
Three years had passed since he'd been banished. He'd left, but he'd
settled in Belthas because it was the closest city to the place he still
thought of as home. Sometimes friends from the Deridal palace
would visit him, always in secret, because his banishment forbade it.
His pride and a sort of loyal lawfulness had kept him from ever
attempting to return himself. He wasn't sure himself if he wasn't simply using Alex as an excuse to visit Deridal now. Maybe no one would
remember him, or his banishment, or maybe they just wouldn't care.
After all, maybe he'd failed, but no one else had succeeded either. Not
even Chernan.

He was thinking these things as he drove the small cart with its
two draft-striches toward the eastern gate. He'd already watched the
guards check a few people passing out, to make sure they were not the
young lad who was the subject of the manhunt still going on in the
city. He was somewhat surprised when they barred his way.

"Greetings, officers," he said, trying to look innocent and doing it
pretty well. "What's the matter?"

"Good morning, doctor," said one of the guards respectfully.
"What's your business today?"

"Off to Belmarle to get some more glassware. Fragile, you know.
Going to have to pack it in hay for the trip back," Temith explained,
jerking a thumb at the load of hay. One hand was bound in a splint.
"And how are you doing—Shan, isn't it? That little urinary problem
cleared up fine, I take it?"

Shan flinched and looked around, but no one seemed to have
heard, and he continued, "I'm afraid His Lordship's orders are to
search any and all carts with large boxes, barrels, or casks, and particularly any piles of loose straw." He indicated the wagon with a shrug.
"Don't worry, sir, this won't take a moment," he added, as he hefted
his bronze-tipped spear to jab into the center of the hay.

Surprising how these things come back to one, Temith mused, as
he used his good hand to grab the spear's haft in mid-jab; Shan,
thrown off-balance, stumbled and fell forward as Temith twisted the

weapon out of his grip and used it to parry the lunge of the other guard. Shan, meanwhile, had fallen halfway into the cart, his hands smacking down for balance and unfortunately through the hollowed-out area under the straw and right onto Mote's tail. Mote squealed, Alex roared in fury and came up flailing madly and head-butted the guard entirely by accident. The guard fell under the wagon, cursing, and Alex staggered and sat down hard in the hay, his head ringing. He saw Temith faced off with another guard, and blinked as he recognized Luken. Luken recognized him, too.

"You!"

"You!"

"Yes, hello," added Temith, and smacked Luken neatly between the eyes with the butt end of the spear. Luken staggered and Temith helped him fall into the wagon beside Alex, before slapping the reins of the striches and letting them bolt forward at a fast clip, as the townsfolk who had seen the scuffle stared after them.

"Why'd you grab him?" Alex shouted over the creaking and rattling of the cart. Mote had climbed up on his shoulder, her tail bruised but otherwise unhurt, and was radiating

enjoyment

at the feel of the wind in her whiskers.

"Don't you know him?" Temith called back, trying to keep the striches on the level road. The two-wheeled cart was swaying madly with the speed.

"He's just a guard, one of the ones I got away from before!" shouted Alex. Luken groaned and lifted a hand weakly, trying to rub his head or find something to hang on to in the rocking cart.

"We'd better keep him, then, unless you don't care about him dying," Temith called back. "Twice letting you escape, they'll think he's treasonous and have him executed in the bull pits."

"What about the other one?"

"Did you kill him?"

"I don't think so! I heard him call me a—"

"Then we can't do anything about it!"

"But he saw us! Saw you! I heard you talking—"

"That's no reason to kill him, though!"

"I told you, I didn't kill him!"

"What?"

"What?"

"Ow," put in Luken, and winced as a jolt of the cart banged his head against its side.

Several miles out of town, they stopped briefly to get things straightened out. Temith realized, now that he knew he'd been recognized, that he couldn't go back to Belthas; he'd be put into the bull pits before he knew what was happening. The only way on was forward. Luken listened—with the preoccupied air of the nearly concussed—to their story, explanations, and reasons for taking him along, and seemed content to sit in the cart and be woozy for now. Alex buried himself back in the hay as Temith whipped the striches into motion once more, trying to make as much time as they could before any Belthasian pursuit came up behind them.

"Soon enough we'll reach the border," Temith called back to the two—three—passengers. "And they won't dare follow past that. They may want a war, but they aren't ready yet."

"What?" shouted Alex over the wind and the hay.

"Never mind!"

Alex was standing in a river that was climbing—or was it a seashore with the tide coming in, the waves rising higher? He could not move, he was looking for Mote. There she was, and there, and there, and there; a mass of small grey shapes frantically struggling in the water, and the flurry of panic in his mind gave no clue as to which might be the real one. He tried to scoop them from the water, and they climbed up him, a swarm of wet fur and tiny claws, trying to escape the water. Still there were more, and still he tried to save them, as the water rose and he was dragged slowly down under the weight of small despairing forms. Scaly tails and coarse fur slapped at his face and mouth, the rising water heated by their bodies. He felt no revulsion or fear of them, only guilt and panic and shame as his feet were swept from beneath him and he went down into the waves.

He came up gasping, scrambling up through the hay, spitting and coughing. The cart stopped with a jolt and he fell forward and tumbled out the back, where he rolled on the road, gagging and pulling hay out of his mouth with his fingers.

"The hurricane awakes," grumbled Luken, who was still sprawled in the wagon. His bull-decorated tabard had been removed and soaked with water, and he held this cooling pack to his head gingerly. A flowering bruise decorated his forehead and the color had seeped down into his eye sockets, making him look more badly injured than he really was. Temith took advantage of the stop to help himself to a jug of beer from the provisions he'd packed. He was sweating in the hot afternoon sun, and his face was showing signs of sunburn. Luken glanced over. "That smells like beer. Pass it on over, by the gods."

"No," retorted Temith, and belched. "All sedatives strictly off-limits to patients with head wounds. You might slip into a coma and die. There's water in that blue jug there."

"We don't treat prisoners this harshly where *I* come from," complained Luken, as Alex stood up and put a hand down into the hay for Mote. Then Luken thought about it. "Well, actually, we treat them worse. Never mind."

"Why'd you call me a hurricane?" Alex asked, as Mote scrambled in *welcome* up his arm.

"Because you come in, all whirling around your own self, and smash through other people's lives, and tear them up and leave them in shreds, and drag them along with you," said Luken, taking a swig of water. "Me, and your cruel friend here, and who knows who else. It's all your damn fault. You probably sunk that gods-lost boat you came in on, too."

Alex flinched. "I never meant for any of this to happen," he managed.

"Very poetic for a spearman," Temith commented to Luken, ignoring Alex's response.

"Better at poetry than at spears, anyway, when an allopathist can drop me so quickly." Actually Luken had been working on his metaphor for quite some time, having resigned himself to traveling along with these two. Going back was out of the question in the current political climate.

"I'm the one who pulled you onto the cart, anyway, not Alex," said Temith.

"So why? Why didn't you just wound me and leave me behind?"

"You want to go back? Do you like your job? Did you even want to join the army in the first place, poet?" Temith glared at him. Luken started to say a few things, and then heaved a sigh of annoyance.

"No, I don't. And no, I didn't, and you know it. I was conscripted out of Belranna and I never had the choice. But it was a job, I had a place, and now it's gone."

"Belranna, back when it was Melliranna, I'll wager," said Temith.

"Yes, gods damn you. Gods damn us, too, when we wouldn't listen to them when they told us not to fight Belthas. Didn't believe then that he was the Bull of the prophecy."

"What prophecy?" Alex asked, as he climbed carefully back aboard the cart. Mote scrambled for balance on his shoulder.

"There's a prophecy that says that a great lord will come and unite the island's kingdoms into one, and with the strength of a great bull shall pull it back into glory, though rats may try to tear it asunder," said Luken, making room for him in the cart. "You've seen the flags. And that's why His Lordship has us kill the Rodeni whenever we can, and why he was willing to pay you to get rid of the rats. He hates 'em."

"I hate him, too," said Alex, with feeling. "And you, too, if you're killing Rodeni."

"I never did," Luken protested wearily. "I was lucky, stuck out on that watchtower until you came along. Then I got demoted to gate duty. And now look at me."

"I'd rather not."

Temith clicked to the striches again, and they resumed their trotting pace. Around them on both sides stretched groves of olive trees, leaves dusty-silver in the afternoon light.

"Deridal lands," Temith commented, noticing Alex looking around. "We managed to pass the border a few hours back. A patrol came by and didn't give us a second glance."

"Pathetic," snorted Luken. "We should have conquered this rock months ago."

It was full night by the time the odd group rattled into the small city of Deridal, the striches plodding along slowly, mouths open and panting. The city was built on a large flat-topped hill, with a range of higher hills beyond it; Deridal was inland, and farther dawnward, in relation to Belthas. A strange white structure twisted down from the hills, gleaming in the moonlight; Temith said it was the city's aqueduct. The city itself was surrounded by a high wall; as they came up to it, a couple of guards, dressed much less formally than those in Belthas, gave them a casual glance and let them through. Alex noted that Temith looked away from them and was careful to not meet their gaze, though Luken gave them a devil-may-care cheery salute from his sprawled position. They'd laughed and half-saluted back, though they didn't seem to recognize him, and stepped aside to let the cart pass.

Alex had donned a torn beggar's robe the doctor had given him as a disguise, with his coat underneath it. He did not like having to keep such a distinctive garment, but the stiff collar and numerous pockets were important; they provided shelter and concealment for Mote. At the moment she was in his collar once again, sniffing the air from her perch just below his ear.

Deridal was, now that he came to look at it, built on very different lines than Belthas. Belthas was tight and narrow, with tall buildings, lots of walls, lots of alleys, lots of bridges and low arches that didn't seem to go much of anywhere. It was packed and huddled within confining cliffs, and the king's citadel at the center was on a hill, further walled, with small windows and thick gates. It was an ugly, half-buried city, a city built for shelter and defense.

Deridal, on the other hand, sprawled. Its buildings were like blocks scattered haphazardly on the table of the hilltop by giant children. Deridal had wide spaces and small gardens and open courtyards. The aqueduct brought in water from the mountains, and Temith informed them that there were a few springs in the city itself. The palace here seemed to be the collection of airy buildings and domes and towers near the middle of the city—more like the finest of the villas than any place for defense. The city walls, and the guards, seemed an afterthought.

"Well, we're here," Temith said, looking around, trying to be cheerful. He seemed nervous, though excited—like a child venturing somewhere forbidden yet fascinating. He glanced about constantly, and from time to time would duck his head and turn away, seeing someone he thought might recognize him.

"So, now what?" Luken asked. Both of them looked at Alex, who blinked.

"What? I mean, I don't know," he stammered. "I was thinking of finding a boat home."

"Deridal doesn't have a coast, as you can see," commented Luken. "But maybe you could find a smuggler to take you to a seaport."

"Then back to the College?" Temith asked. Alex nodded.

"I don't want to . . . I don't want to lose Mote," he said, slowly, taking her in his hands and stroking the soft fur with a fingertip. "But if I don't have any way to pay off my debts . . ."

"Maybe you can do the same trick with the rats here," suggested Luken. "And this time, don't act like a damn hick when they pay you." Temith shook his head.

"Deridal still trades, but even the king doesn't have bronze to spare for something like that, much less silver. Besides, you'll notice, nowhere near so many rats here." Indeed, they didn't see any— although Alex did see a number of Rodeni, out in the open and apparently unafraid, as they went about their business.

"I wouldn't do it anyway," said Alex, "but still, maybe there's something? I hate to say it, but anything I could steal, even?"

"No! This is a city that works well; people have enough to eat, a place to live, a say in their government, leisure time for themselves and their gods. It is not a city that gathers a lot of easily pocketable treasures." Temith was steering the cart carefully toward the open marketplace near the city's center.

"Having a lunatic for a king probably has something to do with it," Luken commented dryly.

"Maybe I could go to the College with you?" Temith suggested to

Alex. "Much as I appreciate the information you've given me already, I'd love a chance to cross-examine your teachers. Maybe even take a course or two."

"Thinking of adding a necklace to those robes?" the Animist responded. "I think you'll find six years of shoveling feces far different than your academic pursuits."

"You've obviously never followed academic pursuits," chuckled Temith.

They stopped the cart in the market, where Temith, growing bolder now that it seemed no one had recognized him, began the process of bartering the vehicle and animals away for more versatile items. His home, his equipment, probably even his lab rats would be confiscated and sold; he'd have to make every deal count from now on. Luken and Alex disembarked and went to sit in the shade of a grape arbor at the edge of a small cafe.

"To hells with the doctor's orders," snorted Luken, when a server came out to ask what they wanted, and he ordered a pitcher of wine. The server brought it, along with two glasses, and Luken tossed a Belthasian tile on the table. The server picked it up, inspected it, and gave an apologetic smile.

"I'm sorry, sir, but currency is considered at half-value," he said. Luken looked like he might argue, then heaved a heavy sigh and handed over another tile, and the server bowed and departed.

"I don't even know why His Lordship bothers to make it illegal, at those rates," he grumbled, and poured wine for himself, without offering Alex any. Alex didn't want any, however, and instead asked for, and got, a cup of water, and fed Mote some of the grapes from the arbor. They watched Temith dicker for awhile, then look around for them; Alex waved and Temith waved back, adding a patting motion to indicate that they should wait there. Alex nodded and the scientist walked off, in discussion with some other merchant, leading the striches by their reins. Alex and Luken sat in silence for awhile, each lost in his own thoughts, until a disturbance in the crowd caught their attention.

On the main road to the palace there appeared to be some form of procession, a group of fine large striches bobbing along at a brisk pace. There were two that carried military-looking men, with spears held ready and bows at their sides.

"Only two?" Luken said to himself, surprised.

Behind them came a man Alex assumed must be the "mad king" of Deridal. He was wearing a fairly simple pair of pants and a very large loose green shirt-like garment that billowed extravagantly. His hair was matted into thick ropes, grey and uneven, but woven tight through a band of gold that was a simple crown. On one wrist, on a falconer's glove, the king held a large blue and red macaw that screamed loudly.

Riding nearby, Alex and Luken saw a couple of other men and women who were dressed more richly, and had more typical falcons on their gloves. They seemed to be leading something as well, a large hunting animal something like a strich and something like a lizard, but it was pacing behind the king's strich and Alex couldn't see clearly what it was. He was trying to make it out when suddenly one of the other falconers urged her mount forward to pace the king's, and Alex's breath caught in his throat. Luken let out a low whistle of appreciation.

She was tall and proud, and sat on the trotting strich as calmly as a swan on a pond. Her hair was tossed and gilded by the breeze, its color that of the bubbles on fresh coffee. It was long, and thick, and not braided, but gently bound in a wrap of ribbon, and it went down her back and then up around her shoulders in a thick coil, like a pet python; restrained, yet all the more sensuous for that. Her skin was like the coffee with cream, and looked soft as the inquisitive Mote-fur moving at the back of his neck. The lady shone with a radiance, perhaps from the shimmering white embroidered blouse she wore that the wind blew close against her slim—

jealous!

A sharp pain on his earlobe interrupted Alex's gawking, and he yelped and rubbed at the nipped spot. Mote grabbed his hand and clung to it, chittering angrily at him as she was brought around to his face.

"Mote, there's no need to be like that," Alex protested, trying to get another glimpse of the princess—for he was sure the beautiful girl could be nothing less.

"Shut up, Alex," Luken said, craning to see the procession. "They're coming this way!"

The crowd stepped by to let them pass; many whooped and cheered and waved as the nobles went by, and a few ducked their heads in a brief token of respect, but there was none of the deep and true reverence and bowing that had been shown to the king of Belthas.

Mote's scolding suddenly ceased and she froze, still hanging onto his fingers, staring upward at something behind him. Her

anger

turned into

fear defiance fear

and her teeth bared, chattering. Alex turned quickly as her mental image forced its way into his mind.

The sudden sharp Oether-ness of a power more than mortal shone from a window in the building behind him, its attention fixed elsewhere. The humming, crackling light was increasing, rearing back to strike; indistinctly, through the magical haze of Mote's perception, Alex could just make out a human shape, hand raised, finger pointing, tracking the procession . . .

Mote jumped to grab onto his shoulder as Alex leapt from his chair, running into the building, shoving past the people inside, racing for the stairs and up them. Now he could hear the chant of the shadowy figure, and the words were those of death, swift and final, calling down the spirits for the magic of a lethal spell. Within the sparse room, the shadowed figure concentrated out the window, too intent on his spellcasting to notice Alex's arrival. Alex himself was caught strongly, too strongly in Mote's perception; had he been trained to work with his Anim, he would have known the dangers of this deep linkage, but he didn't know. All he could see was the theurgist, humming with power as the spirits came to him. All he could sense was Mote's combination of fear, and her instincts to flight or fight, turning more and more into the latter as her master brought her too close to the source of her panic. Which is probably how best to explain that Alex blindly threw himself at the shaman in a flailing tackle.

He hit solidly, and the spell spattered and exploded around them like black powder going off; Alex felt it smack into his brain and shat-

ter his world like glass, there was a feeling of falling, and then everything went black.

Luken was surprised enough when the Animist leapt from his chair
and went racing into the bar itself, but was even more surprised when,
a moment later, there were shouts and screams and Alex, locked in
struggle with another man, crashed down and through the grape
arbor. Blue lights were flashing around them, and Luken gave a strangled scream as pain shot through his much-abused forehead, sending
little blue flashes across his vision as he curled himself into a ball.
Around him he heard similar screams. Suddenly, the pain stopped.

Running feet pounded around him as people came up, from the
crowd, from the guards around the mad king's party. Alex was lying in a
friendly manner, out cold on top of a strange man who wore a long-
tailed coat of the embroidered fashion of a shaman, similarly unmoving.

Alex looked around himself in bemusement; everything was blurry
and grey, like the dreams he'd had from time to time since leaving the
Charmed. There were low sounds, too low to hear, and in his mind
was ringing with

fear confusion fear guilt fear

loud, strong, and . . . close. Too close. He tried to glance around, and
down, and saw his hands were like the Rodeni's, only more primitive,
in fact . . .

Mote? he thought.

fear

He felt and saw this body, Mote's body, Mote, jump up and land
on something, and stare at something large, which, he suddenly realized, was his own face. And in his mind came clearly the source of the
fear: the fact that no breath, no familiar breeze, blew from his body's
nostrils.

Alex's consciousness was stunned to see his own limp body there,
while someone else was horrified at the sight of her master's unmoving form, and was going bug-eyed in fear, fur bristling.

worry worry panic fear

Mote, it's me, I'm here . . . ?
wrongness worry fear fear
He sensed a brief acknowledgment of his sending, and realized that she knew he seemed to be sharing her consciousness, having lost his own, and wasn't concerned with that phenomenon. Rather, the reason for her panic was that his body was not breathing. This caused him some concern as well. He noted, now, a fuzziness to his thoughts, and wondered if, in a moment, his consciousness would be snuffed out again, this time for good.

A moment later, a blurred shape with a familiar smell of hay and wine (Alex hadn't noticed before how poor Mote's eyesight really was—but how keen were her sense of smell, and recognition of smells!) leaned over, and pounded his body hard on the chest. Mote, exploding with
fury defensiveness!
leapt as the impact made her bounce, and lunged squealing to bite. But the rough treatment seemed to work, for he heard a whooping gasp, and—

Pain hit him like a brick—no, like a lot of bricks, like a whole patio full of bricks, and smashed wooden trellises, and grapes. He stared up, gasping for breath, and saw Mote spinning madly in midair, being held by the tail from Luken's hand, which was bleeding from a nasty bite on the knuckles.
fury rage struggle dizzy
"Tell your stupid pet rat if it bites me again I'm going to smack it against the wall, and you can both go to hell," snapped Luken, and dropped her. Mote landed on Alex's chest, full of
joy love relief
and Alex tried to put up a hand to pat her, felt the joint of his shoulder try to move in a way that was blatantly wrong, and decided to pass out for awhile instead.

Alex woke slowly this time, feeling bruises and stiffness, seeing light on closed eyelids. His head pounded in dull pain. Memory was hazy, but . . . He blinked, and his vision swam, and cleared.

He was in a bed that was built into a wall. A window was putting a square of light on his face. His shoulder ached, but seemed to move again. It had been dislocated in the fall, probably, but seemed to have been reset. Alex stopped, and then began frantically searching through the pillows.

dark scared smelly hard loud annoyed

Another person, an older man in a flowing caftan, came up carrying a large ceramic vase. "I think this is what you're looking for," he said, and upended it. Mote tumbled out onto the bedspread, along with a couple of rancid olives. Alex scooped her up and held her gratefully, while she groomed her fur and

sulked

"Thank you. Um . . . who am I thanking? What's happened?" Alex looked around.

"You saved the king from an assassination attempt. He's very pleased. We saw you were an Animist by your necklace, and the rat dancing on your chest, of course."

This damn necklace, Alex thought to himself. It was a token of pride, if one was a true Animist with a powerful familiar, but in his own situation it was like wearing an archery target. *Hello, I'm an Animist with a rat. Strike here to kill me.* Still, it didn't seem to have done him any harm in this situation . . .

"The king . . . and the princess . . . is everyone all right?" Alex asked.

"A few headaches and blisters here and there, from the spell. Your friend—I assume he's your friend, he keeps saying he knows you—was hit particularly hard by it. He's badly bruised."

"No, no . . . Temith did that to him," Alex said. "I mean, if it's the same . . . friend I'm thinking of."

The man raised an eyebrow. "Temith? That explains everything, of course. Only Temith would decide, not only to come back, but with a Belthasian guard and an Animist in tow. This is either a very poor conspiracy, or a very amusing story."

"What happened to the magist?" Alex asked. "Is he . . ."

"He's dead, I'm afraid. I think he must have been killed in the fall. Your friend, your Belthasian spy, is in the cells. Where is Temith?"

"I don't know, and if I did know, I wouldn't tell you," retorted Alex.

"Come now, he and I are old friends. He never mentioned me, I suppose? I'm called Valence, King's Talker."

"I'm Alex, the rat is Mote. King's Talker? You talk for him?" Alex asked.

"Well, more that I talk to people he can't talk to at the moment, or doesn't want to talk to, or has to talk to but doesn't know what to talk about with. Or sometimes I talk to him, if he feels lonely. It's a flexible office." Valence gave a shrug and a smile. He appeared to be about forty, with deep chocolate skin and eyes that twinkled. He was bald, and probably about the same age as Temith. His voice was beautiful, deep and rolling and with perfect diction and authority: a very kingly voice, in fact. "But he does want to talk to you, he just didn't want to stay around while we waited for you to come back to consciousness."

"Neither did I," said a new voice. It, too, was a low, deep voice, but nowhere near as pleasant; growling with hidden resonance. "You mammals make the most disgusting sounds when you sleep."

Striding into the room came the thing that Alex had thought was some form of hunting beast. Bipedal, it was the size of a small strich as it walked, the long tail held out behind for balance. When it reached the side of the bed, however, it tilted upright, and then the head crest nearly brushed the beams of the ceiling. The front limbs ended in long-fingered hands, two fingers and a thumb, the digits interlaced in a surprisingly Humani-looking posture. The hind legs were built like those of a strich, for running speed, two toes tipped with large curved claws that were not civilized-looking at all. The inner third toe on each foot was deformed, a scarred lump on the inside of the ankle. At first Alex thought the creature was covered in overlapping scales, but then he realized they were feathers; tawny brown, edged with black. A crest of feathers capped the head with a flash of bright orange and crimson. On face and hands and feet the feathers faded out into black, leathery skin. The muzzle was long and narrow, more reptile than bird. Red eyes the size of Alex's palm watched him closely. One of the . . . Theropi, Alex's memory supplied.

"I always thought you things were smaller," Alex said weakly. "Everything looks smaller in books."

"I am large for my kind," the Therop replied. "I am known here

as General Rhhuunn, of His Majesty's military and personal guard."
When he talked, his mouth opened slightly, but the sounds in Trade
seemed to come from deep in the long gullet. His name was a rolling
chord that would be easier to sound from a bass lute than from a
Humani throat.

"We usually just call him the General," Valence supplied helpfully.

"Why—no offense, but . . . what is a Therop doing here?"

The head dropped on the neck to come closer. Alex got a glimpse
of sharp teeth and a whiff of hot carnivore breath. The headcrest
raised a bit, and the tail waved slowly from side to side. "One might
ask the same question of an Animist. And indeed, this one does. I do
not recall that we requested one." Mote was full of
fear
at the smells of the Therop, and hid behind Alex's neck.

"But you obviously need one," Alex shot back. "That shaman was
going to kill your king, and you wouldn't have known anything about
it until he'd dropped dead."

The head drew back a bit. "An interesting point, and one which I
have given some thought to quite recently. Would you be interested
in the position?"

"Wha—? As the King's Animist, you mean?" Alex asked, startled.
The General and Valence nodded.

"The king likes you, and that's half the battle right there,"
Valence sighed. "Normally we can't get him to accept half the people
we'd like to have around."

"His Majesty is fond of the . . . unusual. I myself was ordered
through a slave broker, for example," the General said. Alex looked at
the seven-foot-tall Therop, taking in the sharp teeth, long claws,
swells of muscle beneath the smoothed feathers, and said, "I wouldn't
have liked to meet that slaver."

"He had little to do with it. When Thunder-Stalks-Before-the-
Storm died, our enemies captured my tribe and sold us. That was
when my claws were cut." He lifted one foot, and Alex realized the
deformed toe had once held a lethal curved talon. "We were to be sold
to the Viveri. But instead, the king paid my price, and that of the rest
of my clan. He then set us all free, requesting only that one of us come
to work for him. I chose to." The eyes blinked slowly.

"Thunder-Stalks—was he the tribe leader, or something?" Alex asked. The General glanced at him.

"He was our life," he answered coldly. "Now, will you accept the position? I must return to my duties."

"What do I—" Alex began.

"Food and board and expenses, of course," Valance rattled off, "plus a *trel* of bronze per month, and the positions of Central Table Member, Close Guard, Head Caretaker of Beasts, Wearer of Big Hat with Feathers, and Extra Cake Bimonthly." He saw Alex's stare, and looked helpless. "The king's titles, you see. And you'll attend the king, with the General and his other advisors, on all state and public occasions plus whenever else the General feels it would be prudent."

"You're in charge of a lot, aren't you?" Alex asked the General, who merely blinked at him.

"The king's safety is my utmost concern, and secondarily that of his family. It is my sworn and honorable duty," he said. "And I must go back to it now, with your answer."

Alex thought quickly. He wasn't that interested in staying in this isolated, strange city; he wanted, he *needed,* to get back to Highjade. He was obviously doing something wrong; that moment when he'd found himself in Mote's mind . . . He needed training, perhaps even Separation. He didn't want to die, or lose his mind. But perhaps he could get some wealth, even a royal bonus if the king felt like being generous (and he seemed capricious enough to be). Enough, maybe, to pay himself off, at least enough that he would be allowed to keep Mote, and fine-tune his training with her. A permanent position would mean, too, no more worrying about sleeping on the streets and finding enough food; it would mean respect and shelter and no one attempting to crush Mote when she ran around off his person. With this permanent position, maybe the College would have to accept him as a viable student, and teach him Separation, as though he'd gotten everything right from the beginning! Then, too, memory returning in a rush, there was that shimmering vision of the princess, beautiful as a star, somewhere, perhaps, in this very castle!

"Will you let my friend go?" Alex asked, warily. "And . . . and let Temith come back, if he wants to?"

The General and Valence exchanged glances, and then Valence said, "Temith's banishment was decreed by another, but if the king agrees to pardon him, I suppose he can return, or, failing that, he can remain banished, but we don't want to harm him." He sighed. "And as for your Belthasian friend, we'll need to see some proof of his trustworthiness before we release him . . ."

"You probably have Belthasians in and out of this city all the time," said Alex. "Your patrols ignored us, your guards joked with us, your citizens accept tilecoins. What's one more Belthasian going to do?" he asked, thinking, but not adding, *and if that's what you call security, then you're on someone else's payroll,* as he looked at the impassive, inhuman face of the General.

"He does have a point," Valence said to the Therop, who tossed his head and gave a puffing hiss, his throat flexing. Alex was reminded of the annoyed monitor lizard on the *Charmed*.

"Fine, fine. Let them go, let them all go. Give them the keys to the palace, too," he hissed, waving his clawed hands in a gesture of annoyance. Fringes of red feathers decorated his forearms as well. "Gods know my honored lord will probably give them all titles anyway." He hissed again, and looked at Alex in disgust. "We concede to your requests."

"When do I start?" Alex asked with a cheerful smile. The General bared his teeth briefly. It might have been a smile. Or it might not.

"You will be expected at dinner tonight," he rumbled, causing Alex to wonder briefly if he was intended to be the main course.

At that point they were interrupted by a soldier, one of Deridal's, who came hastily into the room and saluted the General. He looked worried.

"Sir, you recall the assassin, the shaman that he killed—" the soldier began, indicating Alex. Alex was startled, but the General nodded. "Yes? What?"

"Sir, he . . . he escaped." The soldier looked straight ahead.

"What?" snarled the Therop. "What do you mean he escaped? The man was dead, Sergeant. No pulse, no breathing. A corpse doesn't get up and run away."

"I know, sir. But this one did, sir."

"The body vanished, is that what you mean?"

"No, sir. Like you said, sir. He got up and ran away."

"I see. And this dead man managed to outrun all of you?" The General was definitely angry now. His tail, which had been gently waving, was now stuck out straight behind him like a balancing rod. The soldier was looking terrified. Alex watched all this in horror. Valence seemed to be showing mild interest.

"We . . . we didn't try, sir. Sir, he *was* dead. I helped carry him, he was *dead!* And when he ran off . . . we were scared. It's magic, sir, spirits. Ghosts. We're not trained for that."

"Maybe you should be. At least someone should be," growled the General, with a glance at Alex. "Come along, Sergeant. Where did you last see him?" The General and the soldier stalked from the room. Valence shook Alex's hand, carefully, because it was still sore.

"Well, welcome, Alex. Really, don't mind the General, he's really a very decent soul, underneath."

Alex looked dubious, wondering how good the Therop's hearing might be. "I don't know . . . he seems awfully . . . predatory."

"He can't help that, you know, I think it's just how they're made. He's devoted to His Majesty, never lets any harm come to him. Especially since the accident."

"Accident?"

"About four years ago, well, the queen happened to drink a little too heavily one night, and climbed up on the parapets of the High Tower. The king tried to pull her down, and ended up getting yanked down with her. At least, that's what we think happened; we found him on a balcony twenty feet down, and her, well, all the way in the courtyard. She was dead, of course, and the king must have landed on his head. He's never been right since then. Admittedly, he was a little eccentric before, but not this bad. Temith was here then. He tried to help the king recover . . . and failed. So did the King's Magician, Chernan. He also failed."

Alex's head jerked up. "Chernan? He was here, too?"

"Oh, you've met him, then? Oh well, I suppose he and Temith probably kept in touch . . . anyway, yes, they both tried. And so did others. The princess was having a hard time of it, you know, and she got furious with all these people unable to help her father. She ordered banishment for everyone who tried and failed." Valence sighed. "We were sorry to see Temith and Chernan go, I don't mind telling you. But she was insistent."

"And the General was around then?" Alex asked.

"Oh yes, he was very upset. He wasn't there, of course, or he'd have stopped the queen from climbing up there in the first place. He thought it was a Belthasian plot of some kind, but we could never figure out what had happened, exactly."

Alex made a small noncommittal noise, but kept his thoughts to himself.

Dinner was held in the banquet hall, a multi-domed room near the center of the palace. Under the center dome was the king's table, on a raised dais; smaller round tables, seating ten each, were arranged around the rest of the room. At these sat a wide variety of people, from some dressed like minor nobles (friends and relatives of the king and officials, as well as Parliament members, Alex was later to learn). At the king's table proper sat King Carawan, on an ornate carved chair; Valence and the General sat or, rather, stood, in the General's case, to either side of him. Next to Valence sat a middle-aged woman with a slightly dreamy, smug manner; this was Meridian, the court's poet and entertainer. Alex learned later that she was as capable of as wild leaps of logic as the mad king himself. This seemed to allow her, often, to understand him when no one else did. She also claimed to have magical ability to predict the future from dreams and spirit guidance, but Alex watched her warily through the entire meal and noticed nothing Oetherwise about her.

Beside her, on a wooden perch fixed in a chair, was the blue and red parrot, who seemed to be named Coocoo and who spent the mealtime picking up bits of food from the plate and dropping them onto the floor. Valence had explained to Alex that while the king liked the pomp and entertainment of falconry, he hated killing things, and so would carry a parrot instead of a hawk. Since then, the parrot had gradually become something of a favorite, though it knew only a few words and would bite when it could. Next to the parrot, and occasional reprimander of it as it attempted to climb down onto the table, was the current visiting representative from

Parliament. He was one of the priests of an obscure god devoted to the safety of fishermen—rather useless since the few fishermen of Deridal spent their days in a calm, shallow lake on the edge of the Deridal lands, dealing with nothing more aggressive than freshwater clams. Alex was at first suspicious of this priest, who was seated next to him. The chubby old man, however, wearing rather stained and faded garments of blue-green ticked with fraying silver, put Alex in mind of a frightened cavy as he looked worriedly about. Alex got the impression he probably trusted the spirits about as much as Alex himself did, and was glad that his services were not often called on. He was called Turvel, and was blatantly frightened of Mote, leaning so far away from Alex that occasionally Coocoo would attempt to bite his arm. Mote had been given a bath to wash the olive oil off her, and was now wearing a tiny copper collar around her neck. "To prevent misunderstandings, hopefully," Valence had said when he'd given it to Alex. Mote didn't like it much, but was quickly getting used to it. Alex himself was dressed in fine new clothes of wool and linen, and surreptitiously had cut a few strategic holes in the garments to allow Mote shelter.

Next to Alex on the other side sat a tall, elegant, but somehow hard woman of older middle age, wearing a simple, close-fitting garment. She smelled of garlic and woodsmoke, and was introduced as Serra, the chef. She kept a stern eye on the servants as they brought forth the food, and watched closely the reactions of the diners as each course was brought out. Next to her was a scruffy-looking older man, who concentrated mainly on the food but from time to time would interrupt with an opinionated diatribe against whatever was being discussed; this done, he would then go back to eating, ignoring any discussion his comment might have sparked. This was Wender, and he didn't seem to have an official occupation. Alex paid all these fascinating people little attention, however, because sitting between Wender and the General was Princess Celine.

Mote's jealousy stopped his thoughts from dwelling too long on the princess, or his gaze from fixing her too closely, which was probably for the best as otherwise he would have stared throughout the meal. She now wore a dress of dove grey, edged with copper-colored silk imported from the Lemyri lands to the south. She had smiled graciously when introduced to Alex, he sweeping a low bow and Mote glaring in

dislike jealousy

at her. The princess didn't notice Mote's opinion, but she seemed troubled by something, though, and Alex noted how she seemed to resent the close presence of the General.

King Carawan had peered at Alex from behind his tangles of salt-and-pepper hair and, on being introduced, had gripped Alex's hand and asked, in a voice that was cheerful but intense, whether Alex knew anything about what the wild waves might be saying. Alex had professed ignorance on this topic, and the king had shrugged, patted him on the shoulder, and told him to keep his ears clean. Now he was concentrating on his dinner and seemed oblivious to everyone else around him.

Most of the meal seemed to consist of stuffed things: stuffed peppers, stuffed mushrooms, tiny larks stuffed with their own eggs, a lobster stuffed with clams and scallops, and a suckling pig stuffed with pigeons stuffed with dormice stuffed with pork. There were soups and salads, too, but anything that could be stuffed, was. Alex was looking in puzzlement at his multilayered food when Serra leaned over and whispered, not unkindly, "I'm afraid the king has this fear of hollow food. He was startled by a meringue once and ever since I've had to make everything stuffed. There's cold slices in the pantry if you get tired of it."

"It's really very good," Alex said, and it was delicious, although the little fried dormice inside his pigeon rather troubled him.

The General didn't seem to chew, just took up chunks on his fork and swallowed them, gullet flexing. The action was so hawklike that Alex wanted to hide Mote from him, though the Therop seemed to be ignoring them both.

The general air in the dining hall reminded him more of the formal meals at the College than what he'd expected a real royal dinner would be like. At the tables there was conversation, and laughter, and a generally relaxed air. It was like a large family gathering, where everyone knew everyone else, and while respectful to the king and princess, no one was hiding their faces or kneeling or bowing. It seemed very odd.

At his own table, the conversation was mostly directed toward Alex, asking about where he'd come from, what the College was like, and what he'd been doing. Alex carefully avoided mentioning the incident in Belthas, for fear he'd be asked to perform the same stunt of extermination here. He never wanted to go through that again. Of the group, the king and the princess did the least talking. The king was interested only in packing away as much of the meal as he could, casting suspicious glances to either side to see if anyone was trying to take his plate. The princess was listening intently to the conversations, and her dark blue eyes watched Alex's face carefully as he gave his replies, making him stammer and stutter. She spoke very little, only to ask such things as, "And where was this? And why did that happen?" and other requests for elaboration.

Alex tried to impress her as best he could, telling wild stories about his travels and his life at the College, but truth kept making him stumble; he didn't want to mention he was a slave, for example. He had to invent wildly to cover these stumbles, blushing madly as he heard the nonsense he was saying and found himself unable to stop. The others at his table, though, as though sensing his discomfort, quickly changed the subject to domestic matters they discussed among themselves. Alex was left to try to collect his wits over the cups of coffee, and the dishes of dumplings stuffed with plums stuffed with grapes stuffed with cream. Alex felt rather stuffed himself.

With the coffee, Serra and Wender and Valence all lit up pipes, and the king let out a hearty belch and put his feet up on the table. "Hello! It's a new ally! Drink deeply from the field," he said cheerfully, bright eyes blinking through his matted bangs at Alex as he offered a wineglass. "There's an animal. An omnivore related to Humani . . . ?"

"Well, inasmuch as we're all lobe-finned fish," Alex replied, quoting something a teacher of his had liked to say, as Mote hopped down his arm onto the table, and ran into the center of it, where she bowed very prettily before the king. Alex was impressed; he hadn't asked her to do any of that, but she'd probably picked it out of his mind.

"Wonderful! You're the most dangerous animal to the big baity fellow. In a wineglass!" said the king happily, extending one hand to Mote. She hopped up onto it, and the king carefully put her into his own empty wineglass, where she sat, looking

puzzled?

over the rim. "Hmm, well, maybe a conclusion is simply the place where you can be in a glass," the king amended, holding up his rat-filled glass to the light, then passing it over to Valence. The glass was passed back to Alex, who took Mote back out of it.

"Hello to you and me," said the king, smiling at Alex. "Animist! The sight whose imagery is sometimes that of fear!"

"I suppose that's a way to think of it, sir," Alex said, rather taken aback.

"Good, good. One brown mouse sitting in a battle," said the king, rubbing his hands. "Valence!"

The Talker blinked at the king over the smoke of his pipe. "Yes, sir?"

"Could we make it idiotproof, and someone will make a suit of armor for the rat?" Alex was lost, but Valence and the other advisors seemed able to stitch the king's fractured ideas into some interpretation.

"I don't think we could, sir," Valence replied, looking doubtful. "Not even leather."

"Pity we can't grab your rat and ring the bell, when the person comes, could make a suit of armor for the final solution. What was his name? Scientist. He put forward the theory that the inhabitants have to have liquor when you are only one flaw!" the king said, frowning at Valence. "Who was that?"

"I'm sure I don't recall, sir," Valence said, catching the look from the princess. But Alex's curiosity made him say,

"Scientist? You mean Temith, don't you? I mean, sir?"

"Yes! The pioneer of the people, a literate. The greatest." The king beamed happily. "Send for him!"

"He's not available, sir," Valence began, when a servant stepped up to the table and, bowing to apologize for his interruption, stooped to whisper something in the General's ear, or rather, the unseen hole in the side of his head that passed for an ear. The General glared (or didn't change expression, it was hard to tell) and glanced from the king, to the princess, to Valence. He blinked slowly, then said, "Fate knocks, but coincidence breaks down the door. Have them come in."

The servant retreated, and the diners looked askance as, a moment later, a pair of soldiers came into the hall, shoving a filthy, wet figure before them. A final shove drove the figure to his knees on the stone floor, in proper bringing-prisoner-before-the-king fashion. Alex heard Serra gasp.

"We caught him trying to break in and free the Belthasian prisoner, sir," reported one of the guards, with a quick salute to the General after a bow to the king. "He fell in the midden while we were trying to catch him."

Temith, for it was he, slowly raised his head, trying not to meet the gaze of the king he'd served, and failed, so long ago; trying to raise his head from the weight of shame, if only to get the pain of humiliation over quicker. He saw Alex sitting there at the table, and did a double take; here he'd climbed over walls and through ditches, trying to break into the prison cells where he knew that Luken, and suspected that Alex, were being kept, and here was the Animist—!

Alex stood hastily, and was about to protest Temith's innocence, but the king was quicker, and jumped down from the dais with surprising spryness.

"Hello! I happen to be disconnected, but welcome to see you again!" he said, beaming happily. "Make some rat armor."

Temith blinked, trying to hide a smile at the old king. The General had moved to stand nearby, and the guards shifted their grips on their toksticks and exchanged glances.

"Um. For rats to wear, or to protect against them?" Temith asked, respectfully.

"Look at you! Still brilliant!" said the king, waving his hands happily. "Doesn't matter." He seemed to notice something, and his eyes changed again—like clouds passing over the landscape, drifting, never sure. "It . . . is good to see you again," the king said, sounding puzzled, and patted him on one shoulder. "Even if you are shorter."

"I'm kneeling down, sir," Temith explained gently. The king looked startled, and then seemed to recover. He looked around, and could be visibly seen to try to concentrate. Alex was reminded of the times, drunk with his friends, he would have to exert such concentration to perform such tasks as walking. The king frowned again, and then drew himself up.

"Of course you are kneeling. Only proper. Now, where were we? Oh yes, um, I hereby knight you Sir Temith, with all the ... all the ..." He glanced frantically over at Valence, who was looking stunned.

Alex nudged Valence, and hissed, " 'All the titles of your previous station!' Remember?"

"Titles of your previous station, sir," said Valence, smoothly, ignoring exclamations from the others at the table.

"Yes! With all the titles of your ... of whatever you do. Did. Previous. Sir," said the king, and patted Temith once on each shoulder. "Rise to claim ring and sky."

"Yes sir," said Temith, his voice a little shaky, as he stood, and looked around.

"To Sir Temith," said Valence, raising his coffee mug, and there was a confused raising of mugs, and a few cheers here and there from those who remembered the scientist from years past. Serra was looking stunned, but a smile was creeping across her features.

"Sir Temith!" was stammered, and a general slurping followed. Mote stuck her face in a coffee mug and sneezed.

Temith stared around the room, dripping sewer water, as the General shook his head slowly. Princess Celine did not join in the toast, but looked less than pleased. She shot a look of venom at Alex, and he felt like he'd been punched in the gut.

query? comfort console

"Very well, Father," the princess said abruptly, getting to her feet. "Keep your doctor, and your rat-boy. Much good they'll do you, I'm sure," she added, with a glance that took in the other advisors as well. She turned haughtily and swept from the room without another word. Alex watched her go. So did the king, who then shook his head sadly.

SEVEN

Alex's room was down a hallway open on one side to a central courtyard. There were no names or numbers on the doors, just individual colorful mosaics set into the wood. Many of the rooms in this area were empty, the population of the palace having dwindled since the decline of the king.

The suite was built on the pattern of two half-circles with their rounded sides touching. In one half was a sitting room, with a fireplace set into the stone of the straight wall, along with shelves and a hanging rug of vibrant colors. A large circular mosaic on the floor depicted twelve red Delphini symmetrically entangled in a swarm of yellow kelp in a blue sea. This pattern was repeated in smaller scale on the outside of the door. An arched opening in the curved side of the room led through a bead curtain to the bedroom. The wall that formed the join of the two half-circles was riddled with niches and cut-outs of circles and crescents. The ceilings were half-domes matching the half-circles, and were painted in swirling murals of Delphini and other sea life. The whole palace, as a matter of fact, was much more aesthetically pleasing than anything Alex had seen in Belthas. Every room and wall and floor was decorated with these elaborate mosaics and paintings, and the rounded arches and cupolas and domes were soothing to the eye, and allowed sun and air into the rooms; pleasantly cool in the heat of the day, warm and comforting in the evenings.

The bedroom had an identical mosaic on the floor, and the flat wall had two more sub-rooms scooped into it. One held what Alex first thought was a bathtub, but proved to be a bed once a servant came and filled it with sacks of sage hay, spread it with a featherbed, then added sheets, wool blankets, and pillows stuffed with wool and feathers. Niches were set into the walls of this little nook, and Alex fixed the largest one up for Mote, with a small lined basket to sleep in, a bowl of water to drink, and a tray of sand for her eliminations. There was no furniture in either room save that built into the walls, but Alex later went down to one of the storerooms and had a small couch and a chair and a writing table brought in. These, too, were quite fine, carved of hard wood polished well, and padded with embroidered seats.

The larger niche also had a curtain, and proved to be the bathroom. There was a tub, a sink, and a toilet, and running water; the water ran from a pipe in the wall, and could be directed with a flexible hose into sink or tub or toilet tank as one chose. The water was clean but not heated, though there was a small ceramic stove beside the sink, with a basket for heating stones, and a place to tuck the heated stones under the tub. Alex tried a bath and still found it much colder than the hot springs on Highjade, while Mote explored the rim of the tub, tasted the soap, and then fell into the tub and clawed her way up Alex's naked chest in her effort to escape the water.

In the bedroom was a window, and in the sitting room, a pair of doors set with glass in matching patterns of bull's-eye squares of crimson, yellow, and indigo. Window and doors opened out onto a small walled half-circle of a garden, constantly watered by two splashing Delphin-shaped fountains that trickled off when the bathroom water was used. Alex learned later that the palace got water from an underground spring, but the aqueduct was necessary to supply enough water for the rest of the city.

In the little private garden there were small stone benches to sit on, and shade from pepper trees that draped over the walls from outside. The garden might once have been quite intricate; but it had been overrun by mint. Mint grew thickly in the moist and partial shade, higher than Alex's waist in places. He had to trample it down to get to the wooden gate set in the wall, and the scent rose like mist.

Beyond the gate was a larger garden, and to either side he could see the curved walls of the other private gardens. Beyond the larger garden rose a trio of towers in the center of the palace: older structures, and apparently little used now. In the large garden were gravel paths, twining through ground cover plants that were sprinkled by mosaic-studded fountains. Beds of flowers, bright squashes, and ornamental peppers erupted from these and from every nook between walls. Vines of climbing flowers—jasmine and honeysuckle and unfamiliar things—grew over the walls. Pepper trees draped long fronds, while lemon and orange trees were trimmed into neat globes. Here and there, a cypress stuck up like a dark column into the sky. A number of blackbirds were bathing in one of the fountains. Shady ponds held ornamental axolotls.

The king's private gardens had suffered in his madness and now resembled an inventor's desk overgrown by exotic plants, some of them half-destroyed as punishment for being rude to the king. The princess avoided that garden and instead could be found sometimes, like a rare flower, in this one. Alex spotted her the first day, as she read a book in the shade of a small arbor. At the time, he was being called for a summons to the king, but he filed the information, and plans, away for later.

Alex was told to report for weapons training the next day at dawn. Blinking and sleepy, he staggered into the long wood-floored hall, to find General Rhhuunn glaring at him.

"Late," he gruffed.

"Sorry, sir." Alex stifled a yawn. "I couldn't find the room." The palace was like a maze.

"Do you have your familiar?"

Alex pulled Mote out from his tangled hair. The General nodded. "Put it aside. We do not wish it hurt."

"Um, right," Alex agreed, and set Mote on the window sill. She sat up on her haunches and watched warily.

The General sorted carefully through a bundle of sticks, from time to time glancing at Alex. "Any previous training?"

"No sir."

"As part of security, all retinue are expected to be familiar with at least one form of unarmed and one form of armed combat and defense."

"Is this the king's rule?" Alex asked.

"No, it is mine," the General replied. "Come here."

Alex did so, cautiously. The General stood watching him, hands still folded demurely across his chest, tail waving slowly. Alex expected now the Therop would attack him and humiliate him to assert dominance, and he was prepared to not let it be so easy. He cautioned Mote not to come to his defense, in case she was hurt in the struggle. He'd had enough experience dodging animal bites and claws, it shouldn't be too hard. It would be deeply satisfying to grab a handful of those stupid feathers, and yank. He watched those clawed hands, ready for the first sign of move—

The foot slashed out in a sweep that spun him around and dropped him on the floor, and the other foot was suddenly pressing on his chest. Alex stared at the two toes and the scarred stump behind them. High above, the red eyes stared down impassively. Alex thought about the missing sickle claw, and how it could have gutted him from chin to groin in a single sweep. The foot lifted.

"Traditional, as even you knew. Very well, now that is done, let us begin."

Every day at dawn, the General put him through routines, sometimes calling in one of the soldiers to practice throws with Alex, since the Theropi anatomy was incompatible with the techniques he was teaching. Alex couldn't help thinking that, while a person trained by the General could defend himself against another person of similar training, he could do nothing against a Therop. Despite many attempts, he never did manage to land a solid blow on the feathery tyrant. Weapons training was interesting. There were long fencing spears, and shorter spears, and short spears. There were the toksticks, in pairs, and spinsticks, and flails and triflails, and hooksticks and fangsticks and others. There were clubs and smakjabs and thups, many the inspiration of the Lemyri, whose use of wood for hurting people was legendary. Some of the weapons had points of stone or ceramic, but Alex knew how quickly these tended to blunt and shatter. He'd spent many hours chipping obsidian for the blades used at the College. He thought again to the bronze swords used by Belthas's royal guards, and was amazed that anyone would spend that kind of wealth on a weapon.

Alex finally chose a stick that felt pleasant enough in his grip, one about three feet long and tapered. It was a smakjab, made of hard, polished wood. A leather loop allowed it to be spun and caught, to shift from the heavy, blunt end, to the small, pointed end. Alex practiced sweeps, strikes, blocks, and jabs with it, while being attacked by everything else in the pile, wielded by the General or whomever else he was sparring with.

"Does everyone have to learn all this?" he asked one day, during a particularly painful workout. The General nodded.

"Even the princess?" Alex asked. The Therop turned to him sharply.

"A word of wisdom, boy. Stay away from the princess."

Alex was taken aback by the harshness of the Therop's voice, and looked at him closely.

"Why?"

"For one thing, yes, she is trained." The eyes blinked, a cloudy nictitating membrane sliding slowly across the crimson. "I should not like to see you hurt."

"And another?" Alex asked.

"Practice. Don't talk," rumbled the General, swinging at him.

Mote awoke, stretched, yawned. She sat up and groomed herself; wash hands, wash face. Wash behind ears. Wash back, wash flanks, wash tummy. Wash toes, scratch scratch, wash toes. Grab tail and wash. Wash hands again. Shake briskly, look around.

bored

Alex was still asleep. They'd been here in this new place for many days now, and every day was busy. Alex didn't have as much time to talk to her or play with her, even though she came along with him wherever he went. Mote jumped lightly onto his head and whiffled in his ear, but he just made low complaining sounds and rolled over, pulling the pillow around his head. Giving up, Mote jumped down to the tile floor and began to investigate.

There seemed to be nothing tasty on this floor. She trundled out into the other room, and found nothing of interest here either, but her search led her to the door. The door was shut, but there was plenty of room underneath it.

Mote hesitated. She knew Alex didn't like her to go far. She knew it was a big and dangerous world out there. But she didn't know what might be in that hallway, and the wanting-to-know, the curiosity, quickly overcame caution. She pushed her way under the door.

The hallway held strange and interesting smells. Leery of the huge open space overhead, Mote stayed close to the wall and scurried along, nose to the ground and whiskers going like mad. After a time, she came to another door, with another space under it. Glad to see shelter again, she ducked beneath it.

This room smelled funny, and the echoes told her ears that it had many more things in it than Alex's room. There were papers and wood and things on the floors. Mote stopped and chewed one of these, delighting in the crisp texture and crackling tearing sounds, and gleefully shredded the thing into small bits. Alex wouldn't allow her to tear his papers, but these things were fair game as far as she was concerned. They were no good to eat, though, and she was hungry, so she set off again, looking for something tasty.

She could smell other rats. Earlier, the first night in the new place, she'd found a hole in the plaster of the walls and gone investigating. A large brown male had attempted to attack her and drive her away, her strange smell of Humani making him hostile. Mote would have none of that, and instead tore into the male with teeth and claws. Rearing up and kicking him back with her hind legs when he attempted to pounce on her, and biting him sharply in paws and face and anywhere else she could reach, she was a small grey fury which reeked of Humani—a fearsome thing. The male retreated in bewilderment, and Mote had emerged triumphant. She'd found one of Alex's dirty socks and dragged it back into the hole, running it all around the inside walls and finally leaving it at the edge of "her" territory. The stink of

Humani was strong down there now, and no more rats had come to challenge her.

This was not her territory, but the rats that lived here were all hiding now. There was a smell of a person thing, but it was a sleeping-smell. (Of course a sleeping person smells different than an awake one.) It was a familiar smell, too, a smell that was linked in her mind with Alex's feelings of friend. There was a different rat smell, also familiar. She continued her explorations in complete confidence. At last she found something, half-hidden in a corner behind a large thing, which smelled like it might be tasty. There was a nut stuck to a piece of wood and metal. The smell of nut-fat-tasty was strong, and she took an exploratory nibble, trying to jerk the nut loose.

WHACK!!

Something had grabbed her! Something had hold of that nasty hard collar around her neck, and was pinning her down! She struggled, and the board the tasty thing was on lifted up, held under her chin. It was heavy and awkward, and a little scary, and she shook her head to try to free herself, clattering the wood against the stone.

Footsteps! Vibrations! Mote froze, and cried out in mental

fear! panic! confusion! terror!

Something pulled away the big thing she was under, and there was a dim moving shape, and a voice, and a hand came down. Unable to move because of the weight of the wood that had grabbed her, Mote cowered in the corner and let herself be picked up gently, wood thing and all, by a hand.

Alex came pelting down the hall, shouting "Mote! Mote!" and whistling.

"In here!" Temith called, and Alex burst through the door, panting. The scientist was holding Mote in one hand, and supporting a small plank of wood that seemed somehow to be stuck to the Anim.

"What happened?! What did you do?" Alex cried. At the sound of his voice, Mote wriggled again and sent

relief warmth love apology

"I thought I'd picked them all up, but trust her to find one I missed," Temith said, shaking his head. "Beating a path to my door, indeed." His careful fingers gently lifted a metal bar, and Mote was free. She leapt onto Alex and ran up to his shoulder as he leaned to see what it was.

Temith looked abashed, and showed Alex the simple design; a small catch, attached to a hazelnut, that held back a spring-driven copper bar. "Thank the gods it landed on her collar," he commented to Alex, and drew back the bar and released it. The SNAP! made Alex and Mote jump. Shaking a little, Alex retrieved Mote and inspected her, seeing the bend and dent in the collar she wore.

"You *are* a lucky *mookchee,*" he told her, and Mote bruxed her teeth, grinding happily, at the compliment.

Alex looked at Temith, who had picked up a set of pliers and was trying to pull the trap apart. He tugged on the spring bar, and then the pliers slipped, and the trap went, not SNAP! this time, but *snib*, on Temith's splinted fingers. Temith yelped and flailed, and Alex had to help him pry the trap off. Temith then cut the spring to bits with the bronze-tipped pliers. The scientist looked apologetic. "I'm very sorry," he said, dropping the bits of metal back onto the cluttered workbench. "I really did think I'd gotten them all."

Temith's room was built along the same lines as Alex's, but in shades of blue, green, and yellow. Benches, tables, and hand-carts were covered with—stuff. Paper made up a large component, and the niches in the walls were full of books, but there was also glassware, things in jars, devices, plants, rocks, and a vast miscellany. It reminded Alex a bit of Chernan's tower room, but instead of mystical runes, things were labeled in Temith's neat spidery handwriting. It was in a cramped order, of a sort, but looked as though a museum of every College in the world had been crammed into these two small rooms. There was dust all over, but a spirited attempt had been made to clean it off.

"They left my room just like I left it," Temith said, happily, waving at the mess. "Well, no, not really. That was a joke. It used to be quite organized. I suppose people went through looking for books and whatnot from time to time. Still, everything seems to be here."

"Including your rat-killing traps," Alex said.

"Yes, and those. I'd almost forgotten about them . . . I couldn't make them in Belthas, you know, I couldn't afford the metal. And when I came back, of course, Serra mentioned that we ought to find them all, because of Mote . . ."

"You knew Serra from before, too?" Alex asked, looking around at the mess.

"Oh, well, yes," Temith said, looking away and smiling to himself. Alex took note of his expression, and grinned.

"You mean, you and she . . ."

"Well. Nothing formal, you understand," Temith said, looking rather shy now. "I mean, well, there might have been, but when I had to leave, we thought, well, it would probably be better for her to stay here."

"Because you couldn't provide for her on an allopathist's practice?" Alex suggested. It was funny to him, young as he was, to think of the grey-haired scientist romantically involved with anyone. Temith looked rather surprised.

"What? No no . . . she's more than capable of looking after herself, I assure you! She is one of the king's advisors, after all. No . . . actually it was for *his* sake that she stayed."

"The king's?" Alex asked. Temith nodded.

"I don't suppose you'd quite understand . . . not yet, anyway. We're more like a family here, you see. King Carawan is . . . Well, he may be mad, but we still honor him, look out for him. He's the symbol of everything we have here. That's why it's so important to protect him, you see. If he should die . . . everything would change."

"He's not going to live forever," Alex said doubtfully. "And then the princess . . . ?"

"Will become queen, yes. I'm sure she'll do quite well at it, but . . . it will be better for all if she's a bit older before it happens, do you see? I mean, she's not much older than you, Alex, and, no offense, but sometimes there are lessons that need to be learned through living long enough, gaining wisdom, experience—"

"Spoken like a know-it-all old scientist," Alex said, jokingly.

"Spoken like an arrogant young brat," Temith countered cheerfully. He dropped the pieces of the rat-trap onto the workbench, and frowned at them. "I was sure I got them all. I counted them." He shook his head. "I must be getting old. Mind going. Soon I'll be able to carry on a conversation with His Highness and understand it."

There was a familiar smell and scuffling sound in the room; Alex saw a couple of the scientist's cages on one workbench. He peered in at a number of albino rats. One or two of the older ones had misshapen swellings on them.

"I managed to sneak back to my place in Belthas, to see if there was anything left," Temith said. "The place was a mess . . . thieves, I suppose. Everything of value gone, and those poor things starving. So I brought them along."

"I always wondered where you found white ones," Alex commented, tapping at them; a group of young healthy rats, grown from the litter of one of the tumor-afflicted females, sniffed at him.

"Well, it's a fairly common mutation, albinism," Temith said. "Like the axolotls in the pond. And they've been bred that way for a long time. The Colleges of Allopathists and of Biologists use them for research. I brought some with me when I graduated."

"Axolotls or rats?"

"Both, actually, but we were discussing rats."

"I was thinking about trying to train some rats, with Mote's help," Alex said, looking at them. "Could I borrow some?"

"Certainly! They breed like anything. I've plenty." A thought struck him. "Speaking of . . . I mean, pardon if this is, well, embarrassing, but do you have any plans to breed Mote? If you Animists even do that sort of thing?"

Alex looked embarrassed but not offended. "No, I mean, we do, certainly. Most of the species at the College were bred from Anims. But it's always a risk for an animal, parturition. Since at the moment my life's in her paws, I don't want to risk losing her." He rubbed Mote behind her ears; she had hopped down to land on the young rats' cage, and was trying to play with them.

Alex selected six of the young female rats and worked on training them. He frankly doubted anyone would care to have rats running loose at the dinner table, but he could put on small performances with them to entertain the king. It was pleasant to be working with animals again. Dealing with people and politics was confusing and bothersome, but working with animals was fun.

Alex's duties didn't leave him a lot of free time, but these projects fell under his job description. The king spent most of his days in the safety of the palace's walls, in his chambers filled with books, toys, and paintings, and the gardens where he could often be found talking to the shrubs, playing on the strange swings and slides he'd built, and attempting to pat the ornamental axolotls in the pools. From time to time the king would summon him, and would talk for awhile on matters not only out of context but out of reality, and Alex would do his best to respond. The king seemed disappointed when Alex didn't wear the Big Hat with Feathers, so Alex had finally relented, and modified the strange thing. It was a sort of indescribable thing with a wide curving brim and a large bunch of feathers on each side, like wings. Alex had seen some of the usefulness of a hat in his previous, mercifully brief job, and so he'd modified this one accordingly: removing some of the feathers and cutting holes in the bottom of the crown and the brim, pinning up one side and adding a "hurricane strip" under the chin. He did these alterations a few at a time, and if King Carawan noticed the Big Hat was slowly growing slightly less flamboyant he didn't seem to care.

The king was also fond of Mote, and would sometimes construct mazes and obstacle courses for her from wooden blocks and clay and various parts of his toys, and then summon Alex to run her through them while the king timed her with a large expensive clock. Alex wasn't certain if this sort of thing would be approved of by the College, but Mote genuinely enjoyed the challenge and exercise. The king wanted to appoint her to a Parliament seat, but Alex quickly prompted Mote to shake her head in response to his query, and the king graciously accepted her refusal. All in all it was a fairly pleasant time for Alex. His duties were simple, if strange. He was adopted into the small ring of advisors to the king, a group of men and women who shared a common, almost parental fondness for their mad ruler, and more important, the easygoing city he ruled.

"It shouldn't work," Temith had explained to him, at one of the earliest orientation meetings. "We have very little crime, no one goes hungry, and people seem happy. Half the laws are totally frivolous—"

"The other half we couldn't enforce if we wanted to," Valence added. "It's as though people realize they can't trust the king to be infallible, not when he keeps claiming to be a rosebush . . . so they've learned to sort things out for themselves."

"It's totally against human nature," added Serra, who, it turned out, was chef only as a hobby, and was actually the minister of trade and finance. "But it works, somehow. Still, I think we could be better served if we regulated things a bit more, aiming funds toward a more expansionist—"

"You're sounding like you-know-who again," grumbled Valence under his breath, and Serra quickly shut her mouth, and shook her head.

"I know, sorry. And it probably would mess everything up; change one thing and you can end up changing everything. It's like— like—" She glanced at Meridian for help. "Metaphor for me, Meri?"

"Like cutting one strand of a spider's web—the entire pattern changes?" suggested the poet.

"Yes, or like . . . one of Temith's paper flying toys. They work fine when they stay small and simple, but when you tried to make that big complicated one, and jumped off the—" Valence began, with a smile.

"That would have worked if my fingers hadn't gotten caught in the steering mechanism," Temith replied sharply.

Meridian had been hired since Temith's banishment, and so neither he nor Alex had ever met her before; in the interests of getting acquainted, the three of them went out to a cafe in the town—the same one where Alex had stopped the assassination. Alex drank orange juice, Temith had beer, and Meri had several glasses of wine. There was a bowl on their table of fruits and nuts.

Meridian was probably quite striking when she had been younger; now her best feature was her smile, wide and honest. She was the palest person Alex had ever seen, with fair skin and blue eyes and hair of a golden color, lightening now with white. She wrote poetry and told stories and she could play several different musical instruments. She kept up a merry prattle of anecdotes and jokes throughout the meal. Temith found her rather wearying, but Alex was reminded of one of his teachers at the College, the Humani woman who taught oratory. Usually whoever had the best bartering skills would pick up the tab; since Alex and Temith had invited Meri for this outing, one of them would do it, but neither of them considered himself to be skilled barterers. Meri had an idea.

"Here," she said, picking up a small walnut from the fruit bowl. She put her hands together around the shell, then closed them into separate pudgy fists. "You each choose; whoever finds the walnut has to pay for the drinks."

Alex shrugged and deferred to Temith to choose first. The scientist good-naturedly indicated the left hand. Meri turned it over and opened: palm empty.

"Oh well. I suppose . . ." Temith began.

"Not so quickly . . . the Animist must choose as well." Still the smile.

Alex frowned and pointed to the remaining closed hand. Meri opened her hand, and showed the empty palm. She smiled; Alex's frown deepened, Temith's eyes widened.

"Both wrong . . . or perhaps you're both right," she said, reaching forward. She pulled half a walnut out of Temith's ear and the other half out of Alex's ear. She put her hands together, then showed the walnut whole, and bounced it on the table to prove its solidity. Then she picked it up again, and it rolled across and through her fingers of her own accord, and when her hand opened, the nut was gone again.

"Magic?" said Temith, and glanced at Alex.

Alex was frowning, and shaking his head. "No. It's not magic." There was no sign in the Oether at all . . . unless it was a magic walnut. Inanimate enchantments were undetectable. But who would bother to make a magic walnut? And even so, using the magic in this way would surely show in the Oether. Mote was sitting on the table, unperturbed by the actions of the Humani around her.

"Is it what you know, or is it what other people don't know?" She smiled. "What is known, or what is believed? What is believed, or what is seen?" Meri raised her hands and said, "What you see—" and then turned them, to show the broken walnut and a separate, whole walnut concealed in the hollow of her palms. "Or what is hidden, unknown? Preparation and misdirection, my fellow advisors, nothing more."

"I shouldn't have just assumed it was magic," Temith said

thoughtfully. "If I had, and you'd agreed, and I didn't have Alex to tell me otherwise, I might have thought there was no other explanation . . . and I would not have just learned something right now."

"Just because you can't see it, doesn't mean it isn't there," agreed Meri. "But then, just because you can see it, doesn't mean it is."

Meridian looked serious for a moment, and Alex frowned in thought. Temith only smiled politely and shook his head at Meri. "You speak in riddles, but very insightful ones. That's fair enough pay for a few drinks." He got up to barter with the cafe owner. Meri laughed and handed one of the broken nuts to Mote, who took it happily. Then, at Alex's insistence, she started showing him how the trick was done.

Alex kept his eyes out for any actual magical activity in the scope of his duties, and did some checking in his spare time as to the presence of any magical groups in Deridal that might have had some reason to threaten the king.

There were a few temples, mainly small shrines to the local gods. Most of them seemed quite harmless. He found information about a group of shamans that seemed to wear similar robes to the mysterious would-be assassin. These were the followers of the cult of Yeg-Sha. But Yeg-Sha was a cult that involved the worship of the spirits of chance and luck and gambling; murder wasn't really their style. The shaman involved might have been talked into the attempt for payment, of course; gamblers often needed money. Alex kept an eye on them, off and on, for a time, but didn't see anyone who looked like the assassin, though admittedly his memory was rather fuzzy on the subject. He didn't dare interrupt their infrequent meetings (always in a different location) to question them directly, but instead decided just to keep to his guard duties and be wary of any further attempts. Beyond this, most other groups and single shamans and other theurgists didn't seem opposed to the king; most quite approved of his tolerance. King Belthar was rather more oppressive—not of faiths, per se, but of people in general, fond of taxation and legislation and punishments. Most magists seemed to prefer life in Deridal. It rather limited the choices of people who'd want to kill the king with magic. Yet it wasn't long before Alex suspected something else suspicious was going on.

Temith's snap-trap was written off in Alex's mind as coincidence. Then came the day Alex woke up in the middle of the night and wandered into the bathroom and back out, when he noticed a motion on the tiled floor.

It wasn't Mote, who was sound asleep, her dreaming mind sending little faint flutters. Alex frowned at it, fumbled for a match, and lit a lamp.

The bright green snake stopped as the light struck it, looking absurdly colorful on the mosaic tiles. Its tongue flickered, and the wedge-shaped head cast about cautiously. Its eyes were bright yellow. White musk and urates marred part of its scales, as though it had defecated and then crawled back through it. It was beautiful, nonetheless.

"Pretty little thing," Alex told it, though it couldn't understand him, of course. With the aid of a broom, Alex carefully pinned its head, and then caught it up gently, keeping a careful grip behind its head. It wriggled a bit, then wrapped securely around his arm. He inspected it carefully, then gently decanted it into a large vase, which he corked with a spare shirt, then placed the whole thing into the wood-bin, and shut the lid on it. Then he went back to bed.

In the morning he rummaged through the library, then brought the matter up to Valence.

"The thing that bothers me is that it's a palm snake," Alex said. "You don't usually get them this far inland."

"Maybe it came in with some trade goods?" Valence suggested.

"And it had musked on itself. It wouldn't do that unless it was frightened, and it wouldn't have gotten any on itself unless it was confined," Alex said, personally pleased that he'd deduced all this. Valence didn't seem to give it much credit, however.

"I think you're grasping at straws, Alex. Who, besides you, is capable of catching a lethal serpent?" he asked. "Where is it, anyway?"

"Right here," said Alex, pulling up his sleeve; the snake was wrapped around his arm like a gleaming bracer, and it lifted its head to look at Valence, who leapt back.

"Aigh! What are you doing?!" he screamed. Alex looked surprised.

"But it's just a species of tree boa, Valence, nonvenomous. It mimics the tree-vipers to scare off predators, you see, but you can tell by the rostral pits and the keeling on the—" Alex began, but Valence interrupted him.

"Why didn't you kill it?" he demanded.

Alex looked annoyed. "Why should I have? It's just a snake. Mote's safe in my room, until I figure out what to do with it. Huh, little thing?" he said, talking to the snake. It crawled back up his sleeve, as Valence shuddered.

Alex eventually made a special trip down to a palm swamp near the coast, and set the snake loose there. But the place was some distance away, confirming that the snake must have been brought into Deridal somehow. He cast around for where the snake might have come from, perhaps in a shipment of trade goods, as Valence had said. Alex kept his doors and windows shut tight at night, and a fire lit, because Miraposa's nights got rather colder than the warmth of Highjade. Finally he asked Mote to search around for holes, and she eagerly darted into one near the base of his bed. Alex put his head down to it and saw one of his socks in there, and tugged it out, but couldn't see Mote beyond. He could sense her

eager curious

thoughts as she rummaged about in the darkness, though, and tried to concentrate on them, as he lay prone on the floor. He knew Animists weren't supposed to do this, it was over-bonding, but . . .

Slowly he began to get a sense of enclosed darkness, and cool stone, and a faint breeze blowing. Then, as Mote sensed his thoughts, the impressions became stronger; and with them came the smells, strong and sharp, of rat, and dust, and a breeze that smelled of many things. There was a very faint smell, too, of snake musk. Normally snakes had almost no smell, but the faint smell of snake-fear left a trail through these passages. He half-felt, half-saw the shifting darkness around Mote as she scuttled along through the gaps in the stucco walls. It was like the times he was almost asleep, almost dreaming, and the dreams would flicker around the corners of his vision, slowly growing stronger, more real.

At last Mote emerged into an open space, though still sheltered by something, a piece of furniture perhaps. This room was cool and dim, curtains drawn to shut out the heat. The smell trail of snake musk ended here, in a small woven basket. Mote sniffed the basket, but the smell of snake permeated it. Alex urged her out into the room itself to find the door, and then, frowning, got up and walked down the hall outside. The worn floors of the palace meant there was a gap below all the doors, most of them large enough to allow Mote passage.

She was half-under one of these doors, peeping out, and came scuttling out when he approached,

happy

to see him. She clambered up his pant leg as Alex stared at the door. It was locked, but there was the mural on the door, and Alex had been instructed as to who lived where, so as to know where to find them in an emergency. This was the pattern of red, yellow, and orange Viveri that marked Valence's room.

That evening, a sound broke the stillness of the night. To Alex, asleep, it came into his dreams as hyena whoops, but then, as he woke up, blinking, he realized it was different. It swelled out of the night, out of the darkness, more felt than heard. It was a sound sonorous and deep, like a low thrum, but within the tone was a cadence, a musical throbbing like the heartbeat of the night. Alex stared around, and quickly stepped outside into the gardens, looking all over, trying to see where it could be coming from, but the sound seemed to come from everywhere, from the night sky and the stars themselves. Mote had heard it, too, and had clambered onto Alex and was sheltering behind his neck, feeling

fearful

He saw Temith, who'd come out to his own garden's gateway and was looking up with an expression of sadness on his kind face. He followed the scientist's gaze, and then saw a motion against the stars.

On top of the highest dome of the palace towers, a shadow, and a slow motion that moved like a wave on the sea to the pulse of the song. Alex couldn't tell if the noise sounded beautiful or terrifying, or both. He backed up to the scientist's doorway.

"What—what is it?" he whispered. Temith glanced at him.

"It's the General. He does this every year." Temith smiled. "You get used to it."

"I don't understand." Now that Alex knew what to look for, the shadowy motion was revealed as a long neck, slowly moving from a tucked position on the chest to full extension, and back as the long rolling thrumses sounded. The Therop was also turning in a slow circle on the broad top of the dome, like a huge ugly bird doing a noisy and awkward courtship dance.

"It's the Theropi solstice. I was there, once, on Theropios for it. Darkness, and the Night Sun rises, and suddenly, the whole island began to ring. Every Therop on Archipelago, right now, is singing. In their homeland, with hundreds of thousands of voices, the song is like—" Temith lifted a hand and then dropped it. "Well, impressive. But loud."

Alex tried to imagine it, to imagine hearing the song echoed in thousands of throats, a great sounding of life and affirmation against the long night.

"He sounds sad," Alex ventured.

"I imagine he gets homesick sometimes," Temith said. Alex looked around.

"Did Valence tell you about the snake?" he asked cautiously. Temith looked shocked.

"Snake!? Where?!" He stared around in horror.

"Not here. One crawled into my room the other night," Alex said.

"Oh gods," shuddered the scientist, looking around at his feet. "Do you think there are more? I . . . I know it's irrational, I just . . . I can't stand them. They terrify me. Is it gone? Did you kill it?" Above them, the Therop's song rang on like the tolling of a huge bell.

"I got rid of it," Alex reassured him. Temith relaxed a little, but still looked warily around.

"Thank gods it was you who found it," he said. "I wouldn't know what to do . . . I can't move when I see them, I don't even think I could kill one or run away from it . . ."

Alex was about to tell him about the basket he'd found—or rather, that Mote had found—in Valence's room, but stopped himself.

"Ugh! Snakes!" Temith was muttering to himself, and went quickly back into his room, bolting the door behind him. A moment later his window shut as well.

Alex found, now that he was awake, the night air was invigorating, and there wasn't much point in trying to get to sleep with all the noise the General was making. He wandered out into the gardens; everything was tinted slightly with the ruddy light of the Night Sun, the great red star. It was larger than the other stars, brighter, and deeply red. The Night Sun didn't always show itself, and in many cultures to see it this bright and full was a sign of dangerous times, but apparently the Theropi found something worshipful in its bloody luminance. Typical, Alex thought, glaring up at the figure on the dome. *How long is he going to keep making that noise?* he wondered, as he swatted at the mosquitoes that burred up, disturbed by his footsteps in the damp grass. As if in answer to his thoughts, then, the last peal fell silent, and then there was a sort of hissing bark, and the indistinct figure dropped down from the dome. Relieved, Alex went back inside as well.

On the balcony below the dome, the General stilled himself, trying to keep his tail from wagging in anger and tension. He had been shocked out of his ritual meditations by a sudden explosion of pain. He dipped his neck, fingers carefully feeling. . . . there, yes—he tried to clench his massive jaw against the pain, but the contraction only hurt worse. He let his jaw go slack as he gripped the shaft of the bolt and yanked it out. He glanced at it, and dropped it with disdain. It was a crossbow bolt from his—from the king's own armory, fletched with bright blue feathers. It had been aimed at his head, and had hit it; but instead of punching through his skull, it had gone too high, too steep, and had instead gone through the thick lump of muscle above and behind his cranium. It had come out the other side and stopped halfway. The General worked his jaw; weaker, yes. He could keep it closed, but only barely. His plumage would hide the wound, but . . .

No one was coming to see if he was really dead, no sounds of footsteps. With a snarl, the Therop rose to his feet; he wasn't sure what upset him more, that someone had tried to kill him, or that someone had interrupted his Solstice. He leapt off the balcony into the room beyond, tail swinging for balance. He bounced down the stairs to ground level, and then raced in quick strides toward the king's chambers. His tail smashed against a vase of flowers and broke it; when calm he could keep his tail gently flexing out of the way, but when he was angry or hunting, the stiffening tendons would tense and leave it like this, swinging out behind him.

Blood-spattered, he kicked open the door to the king's room. When Carawan didn't stir at the sound he almost gave a roar of despair, but then the king yawned, and rolled over in his sleep. A thick pair of earmuffs, probably donned when the General had begun his song, explained that. Panting, the General searched, striding quickly through the rich chambers, the wide curving rooms with their pillars and archways, all thickly decorated with murals of glass and stone, shells and semiprecious gems—these days, too, with paint and colored wax marring many of the pictures. He searched beneath all the richly carved furnishings, and in all the side chambers and closets. There was no one.

The General was in a foul mood the next morning at practice; apparently one of the earlier students had managed to land a lucky blow on his head. In any case, the feathers there were mussed, and a bit bloody. Alex knew that some of the other residents of the palace took their lessons earlier, and he suspected it must have been one of these. He tried to drop hints, but mention of his fellow advisors only earned him snarls in response, and the mention of Princess Celine only got him disarmed and crushed to the floor under a heavy foot, and a low "I told you, you will stay *away* from the princess. She is none of your concern." Alex dropped the subject then, but the fires of suspicion and rebellion burned.

Alex didn't have much of a chance to do anything other than stay away from Celine as it was. His part in getting Temith reinstated had obviously biased her against him from the beginning. Alex felt bad about this, but honesty compelled him to admit to himself that he hadn't really had any chance anyway. Celine was beautiful and royal, and proud and wonderful, and what chance would a scruffy, penniless Animist have with someone like that? By asking around he'd learned that Celine had been eagerly courted by many young men of rich families in Deridal and the other cities as well, but between the General and her mad father, they had all been frightened away. Alex felt pity for her, but held out some small hope in thinking that someone as strong-willed as Celine would have found a way around this if she'd chosen one of her suitors. Perhaps she didn't care for that type—perhaps someone different, someone . . . like himself?

The evening after the General had been singing, Alex was sitting in his room working with his "other" rats, the white lab rats he'd borrowed from Temith. He usually worked them in the evenings, as their natural inclinations made them more active and curious then. Spread out on the table were a few props he had arranged. He had used harmless dyes to color the albino rats in order to tell them apart, and to further their difference from any "vermin" rats. Right now, he had a bright green one sitting up on the table. He worked them only one at a time, though Alex was also working on getting them to perform together. He had planned to set up a little circus of them, for the entertainment of the king. Some Animists would entertain their lord with leaping lions or dancing bears; Alex had rats. Alex held a clicker Temith had made for him, a flexible disk of copper.

The green rat, whiffling excitedly, ran up to the base of a little ladder. "Climb it!" Alex said, and as the rat put its paws up on the slope, Alex clicked, and the rat looked around expectantly for its reward. Alex gave it a tiny piece of pasta sauce on the tip of his finger. When it had swallowed the mouthful, Alex restarted the exercise, this time rewarding the rat only when it put its paws on a higher rung of the ladder. Mote watched from his shoulder with an indulgent eye, demanding her own share of the cheesy pasta sauce as a reward for not interfering. She could have speeded the process considerably, Alex knew. Sometimes, when the normal rat was feeling particularly confused and frustrated, Alex would relent, and allow Mote to help. She'd run down onto the table, greet the rat (she played with all of them and treated them like sisters) and then perform the task, with the other rat following along close behind her, mirroring her every move. Alex was sure the other rats were not learning on any conscious level, as one Human might teach another. Rather, Mote would force the other rat, just as she'd forced the wild rats, to do what she wanted; after a few repetitions, the movements seemed to "sink in," and the rat was more able to perform the task on its own. It was rather, Alex reflected, like the process of "baiting": leading an animal through a sequence of behaviors by holding food in front of its nose as it walked. Baiting wasn't considered in as high regard as the training by successive approximation Alex was using now, so he tried not to ask Mote for help unless the normal rat seemed to be getting upset by its own failure. When they were successful, the rats seemed to really enjoy performing; they worked for their treats, but also seemed to show excitement at performing the quick, simple tasks Alex would set them. It was play as well as work.

So intent was he on watching the rat that the knock at the door, faint and tentative as it was, rather startled him. "Just a moment!" he called, and cursed himself mentally as he saw the green rat look up and around, puzzled, not sure if that was a command or not. He quickly scooped up the green rat and put it back into its cage, a sawdust-filled bin with sides too high for the rats to jump or climb. Then he called, "Come in!"

The door opened, and Alex's eyes widened to see Princess Celine herself, standing in the doorway, holding a guttering candle and looking terrified. She wore a silk nightgown and a woolen robe over it; her beautiful hair was bound up in cloth rolls for bed, but she looked far from asleep; her eyes were wide and her face pale in fear. Mote, sensing Alex's reaction, gave a flare of

jealousy!

"Y-Your Highness," Alex stammered, trying to remember if he was supposed to bow or nod or what, and blushing in shame to realize he was wearing a shirt with rat-urine stain on it. (Mote never stained his clothing anymore, but the new rats occasionally forgot, or would "mark" him in this way to show affection.)

"Animist, I don't have much time," Celine whispered, stepping in and quickly shutting the door. "Please, tell me . . . is there a magic on me?"

Alex stopped his gawking and quickly concentrated. "Uh . . . no. Nothing," he reported, though Mote was sulky at having to pay any attention, even Oetherwise, to the princess. Alex berated himself mentally; it would have been an excellent opportunity for some line like "Your beauty is certainly enchanting" or "Only the spell you have cast over me, my lady," but he never seemed to think of these things until later.

Celine seemed to give a sigh of relief, and then, as though the tension that had driven her down here had cut some vital support, she sagged, trembling. Alex lunged to his feet and shoved a chair over to her.

"What's wrong?" Alex asked her, as she sank gratefully into the chair. "Is someone following you?"

"No . . . yes . . . I don't know," she whispered, her hands clenched around the candle she carried, staring into its flame. "All the time, I'm being watched. Followed."

"The General?" Alex guessed, whispering, too.

Celine's hands clenched on the candle. "He's insane. He can't stand that anyone could be closer to the king, my father, than himself. He's jealous of me. I think he thinks *he's* the . . . the *prince,* or something! He controls everything." Her voice faded. "But that's not what brought me down here. I don't think he'd . . . try anything, not while my father's still alive." Alex found himself kneeling beside her chair, hanging on every word. Mote,

disgusted,

had burrowed down under his collar.

"What is it, Your Highness?" Alex asked. "You asked if there was magic . . ."

Celine gave a shudder, one of horror and fear. She was fighting back tears, Alex could see; only her royal courage and spirit held her steady.

"I've been having dreams," she whispered. "I can never quite remember them, but . . . shadows, and faces, and I'm helpless. Mocking laughter . . ." She caught her breath, controlled herself. "Last night I woke up, from dreams of shadows, and there was a shadow on the wall. A shadow I remembered." She shut her eyes tight in recollection. "Then it vanished . . . but . . . I think it was . . . Chernan."

"Chernan!?" Alex forgot to whisper, but the repetition of the name seemed to hurt Celine, and he instantly regretted saying it.

"When he was here . . . he thought he loved me, I think. I was young, and foolish. I teased him, led him on." She shuddered. "How horrible it seems now! And when he started to get too insistent, I put my foot down. And he got angry. He never spoke of it again, but . . ."—her eyes closed tightly, and this time two tears escaped—". . . less than a month later, my parents had their . . . accident."

"Oh no," Alex breathed. Celine nodded slowly.

"I was willing to give him a chance to fix what he'd done. If he *had* done it . . . I had no proof. But he wouldn't. The other advisors . . . they don't listen to me, Alex! They won't hear what I have to say, they treat me like I'm just a girl, a silly girl who can't think or cope or do anything other than look pretty. Even then, they wouldn't listen to me." She sighed. "I knew I had to get Chernan away from me. But I didn't want to risk angering him further. I had him banished, along with every other shaman and allopathist and herbalist and charlatan that tried to treat my father . . . Temith, too." She opened her eyes. "I know he's your friend, I suppose he didn't mean any harm, but at the time, I was seeing Chernan's influence everywhere. It seemed like everyone would listen to him, no one would listen to me. Temith was his friend, so I was afraid of him. I was afraid of everything."

Alex's personal experience with Chernan was limited, but now, seeing the princess's fear, he was reminded of his own fear of the thaumaturgist, of the way the wizard had pillaged his mind, and coaxed him into abusing his own talent. Chernan, he decided, must be more evil than he'd realized. "You were right to be concerned," Alex told her, trying to comfort her. "But Ch—that magist doesn't have any spells over you right now. And he doesn't have any over me. And I'd know, instantly, if he appeared and tried to put a spell on anyone here."

Celine nodded. "You saved us from the magical assassin. I don't think it was him, but . . . it might have been someone he hired. But it might *have* been him, in a magical disguise!" she added, the possibility suddenly dawning. "Could that be done? I don't know much about magic . . ."

"I suppose it could be," Alex said. "I didn't get a chance to see the face clearly, when it happened, and I don't really remember." It occurred to him that the General would have known, and said something, if he'd recognized the magist. Unless the princess's suspicions were correct.

"And now, these dreams . . . I think it's him, Alex. I think he's trying to get to me, somehow. Before, when he was here, sometimes I would dream . . ." She shook her head fiercely, dispelling a thought. "Or he's somehow traveling here, by magic. Is that possible?"

Alex hated to tell her, to cause her more fear, but he nodded.

She was very afraid, Alex could see; the wax from the candle had run over her hand but she didn't even flinch from the heat. "I think he could be coming here, doing things . . . I worry that he might have spoken to the General, worked out some kind of secret alliance. Or maybe he hides his face behind a magic disguise, and what we think is our friend, really isn't, it's him." She reached out a cautious hand, and rested it on Alex's shoulder. Despite his concern for her, he almost melted under that soft palm. "Alex . . . you're the only one who would know the truth. You're the only one who can know who to trust." Her eyes, dark and deep and fearful as the space between the stars, gazed at him. They were a very deep blue, almost indigo.

"You can trust me, my lady," Alex gulped. "I will protect you—from Chernan, from any threat that dares to challenge you."

jealous! defensive!

Alex ducked his shoulder away from under Celine's hand just in time to avoid Mote's angry lunge that would have nipped the princess's dainty fingers. Mote obviously felt that Alex's person and his attention was her territory and she bitterly resented Celine taking liberties or stealing his affection. Alex had heard of this sort of thing happening to other Animists. He turned the motion into an awkward bow. One nice thing he'd noticed, with her sitting and him kneeling, was that it wasn't quite so obvious that she was taller than he.

"Thank you, Alex, Royal Animist," Celine said. She gave him a grateful smile as she slowly rose to her feet; she didn't seem to notice Mote glowering at her from Alex's shoulder. Mote was scrubbing herself thoroughly against the fabric of his shirt, trying to cover over any scent of the princess with her own. "I'd better get back to my own room, now, before someone sees me—" Her face took on that hunted look again. "But my room is the one across the garden. I'll leave my windows open. At night, could you . . . check, and see, and make sure there is nothing . . . unusual? You would see it if there were, correct?"

"Yes, milady," Alex said, awed. Certainly he'd noticed that window, and knew to whom it belonged, and he had to admit he'd glanced that way more than necessary anyway, hoping to catch a glimpse of the radiant princess—but the curtains were always drawn. But now . . . He gave another deep bow. "And whenever I can, I shall be there to make sure that no magic threatens you, known or unknown."

Celine smiled, and gave a gracious nod of her head, and allowed Alex to open the door for her. "Alex . . . before you arrived, I didn't know what to do. I . . . apologize if I seem sometimes haughty, or cold. It is the mask I wear, to hide from *them,* the ones who don't understand. But you . . . you are special. I am very glad you are here." And she gave him another soft smile and turned and drifted down the hallway. Her hair had come loose from one of its rolls, and the tip of it trailed the tiles behind her. Alex leaned heavily on the doorway as he watched her go. Mote stuck her nose in his ear, whiffling in

indignation!

but he ignored her.

EIGHT

Alex learned that the princess was a member of Parliament, and he went to watch a session of this strange new form of government. He went primarily to fulfill his promise to Celine, to watch for any Otherwise threats, but he was also curious about the system. He'd come to gather that the king was not, in any real sense, in charge of the city anymore; he couldn't be. His advisors and officials ran it as it had always been, keeping it in his memory out of genuine fondness for a kind and just ruler fallen on strange times.

"Sometimes he does come up with good ideas, though," Valence told Alex once. "And some ideas seemed like madness, long before he ever had the accident. Striches, for example. There were none on the island eight years ago, but he heard about them and insisted we get some. Traded to the Lemyri for them, wouldn't go anywhere else. Now you'll find them everywhere; we made quite a lot selling them to other cities. Of course, the General thought we should keep them to ourselves."

The king would put ideas up before Parliament, twelve members of which were elected by vote from the general populace. Six more were appointed by the king, and six others, the Traditionals, had their origins lost in the mists of time, but appointed their own successors after a term of seven years. The six appointed by the king were a rather mixed bunch; they were the princess, Coocoo, a Rodeni merchant named Gleet, a seven-year-old boy named Echal who spent most of the time playing with a yo-yo, Garri the innkeeper, and, surprisingly, Luken.

Luken came up to Alex and smilingly shook his hand, as he spotted him in the ranks of the audience. "We've both done well!" he told Alex. "I gather since Temith explained who I was to the king, he figured we were all friends, and he gave me a Parliament chair, and I guess I really owe it to you. Here, let me find you a better seat."

Parliament was held in an open forum, with ranks of stone benches cut into the hillside around the stage where chairs had been set up for the Parliament members. On other days, the stage was used by actors and musicians; even Parliament sometimes had to dodge flying vegetables if they were debating an unpopular ruling. Alex was shown to a seat right up front, looking up at the members, as Luken climbed back onto the stage to take his place.

The chairman of the electoral group opened the meeting by clearing his throat and standing. "We have a number of issues up before us today—" he began.

"Louder!" shouted someone from the audience. The chairman glared, and Coocoo screamed.

"That's better!" shouted someone else, and there was a smattering of laughter and applause.

"If we could get back to the matters at hand," grumbled the chairman. "First off, the issue of immigration, Rodeni in particular—"

"They've nowhere else to go!" said Gleet, jumping to his feet and running claws quickly through the cream-colored fur of his face, a nervous gesture. "Belthar's stopping every one who goes to any city of his rule!"

"That's never stopped you people before," said one of the other electorals, and Gleet glared.

"Aye, but if Belthar's men catch you, it's death!"

"I don't see what the problem is," put in Princess Celine. "They've always been welcome as good and equal citizens here in Deridal, and I don't see that we should turn them away now." Alex was surprised to see how much more relaxed and confident she seemed here, and then he realized that the General was nowhere around. She had already spotted him in the audience before the session had opened; she'd met his gaze and he'd given her a confident smile and the universal Trade nonverbal signal for "good proper correct"(the appendages—fingers, flippers, toes, whatever—shape a circle) and she'd smiled and relaxed. Alex felt a warm pleasure at having helped her, and Mote grumbled mentally to herself from under the Big Hat with Feathers.

"Still, what are they going to do? How will they live?" protested one of the Traditionals. "Our borders are fixed by the wall, we can't keep expanding our population without—"

"Tear down the wall!" shouted someone from the crowd, and it quickly became a chant until a couple of guards stepped forward from the edges of the crowd, and then the noise settled into a few hoots and laughter, then silence. Alex gathered it was more of a traditional in-joke than anything else.

"None of that," snapped the chairman. "Why do they all come here anyway? That's what I'd like to know."

"Public forum has been the way of things since—" began the Traditional, whom Alex recognized now as the city's Ceramicist, one of the most highly respected men in the city, a gentle, bearlike fellow.

"Not *them*," snapped the chairman, waving a hand at the crowd, some of whom waved back. "I mean the Rodeni!"

"It's the Screaming Towers," Gleet answered, who had retaken his seat. There was a small chorus of squeaking agreement from a number of Rodeni in the audience. "King Belthar put 'em up, he says, to keep all the rats away, but they work on the Rodeni, too. Screaming all the time! Makes it so you can't think or sleep or anything!"

Alex tried to look inconspicuous but felt a twinge of dread and guilt. He wondered what pitches the "screams" played at, and thought he could guess. Temith's laboratory, his notes and his research, would have been raided and searched and seized by Belthas's men after the scientist's violent departure.

"We've got to have some control over this immigration," said the chairman. "The king's suggestion, as I have it, is—" He adjusted his spectacles, and opened a folded letter. "Ahem . . . 'Hooray, I like a fuzzy, why not have armor and tea?' " He looked up. "All those in favor?" he asked. A few embarrassed glances were exchanged and some hands in the audience were raised, but none on the stage. "Right, then . . ."

The debate wandered on, eventually resulting in a motion to count and take names and descriptions of all Rodeni entering by the front gates, and word issued reminding all inhabitants of Deridal that begging and theft were not considered legitimate occupations and would result in harsh punishments. There was a recess for lunch, then, and Alex wandered away with the rest of the crowd, thinking.

He spotted Gleet sitting at a cafe table, moodily gnawing on a corn muffin, and approached him. The Roden blinked up at him, and pushed out a chair with his feet, which were shod with Rodeni strap-sandals. "Ah, it's the fellow with the *mookchee* from up the palace. Have a seat."

"Thanks," Alex said, settling into it. "Actually, I came to ask you a question."

"Ask away," Gleet responded, crumbs decking his wide whiskers. "Don't even matter if you listen to my answer, no one else ever does." His tufted tail twitched in resignation.

"Do you know a lot of the Rodeni around here? And the new ones, just arriving?"

"A lot of them come to me, ask can I do something, seeing as I'm in Parliament," Gleet answered. "I tell them, you come and see sometime, you'll see how much good I am."

"I'm looking for someone named Flip, he's all black furred, kind of poor looking—"

"Furrfu, that narrows it down a bit," Gleet said sarcastically. "But I can keep word and watch out. What's the matter?"

"Nothing, he's, well, he's a friend of mine. If he shows up here I'd want to help him out." The waiter came by then, and Alex ordered the first thing on the menu, *parichos*. "The Screaming Towers you mentioned," Alex said, when the man had gone again. "Could you tell me about them?"

Gleet replied, "I haven't seen them myself. The Belthasian Rodeni say they were just put up a few days ago, all along the river through the middle. Big upright tubes, they tell me, with holes; big as some of the palace towers. They make a noise by magic; I don't think you folks can hear it. It's a shriek that gets into your brain. It doesn't travel too well, if you hide deep under something you get away from it, but even we can't live that way forever; got to eat sometime. It's a shame. The bones of that city were Rodeni-built, you know, long time past."

"I didn't know you built cities," Alex said, surprised. "All the literature—"

"Well, not high things, towers, no. We don't have quite the muscle for it," Gleet responded, flexing one of his scrawny arms for emphasis. "But when Belthas was built, generations ago, Humani built their buildings and we—well, not we, but the Rodeni back then, our ancestors, you know—they did the trenches and the drains and the cellars and the watercourses. Leveled it, channeled it. That place'd be a rocky waterfall if not for us. But time passed and the Humani got more and more of the good stuff and pushed us aside, and kept pushing, and now they're pushing us right out."

Alex's food arrived; he hadn't quite mastered the local dialect yet, and was rather disconcerted to find himself presented with a bowl of small crispy fried lizards. He picked one up by its stiff tail, but the look in its shrunken eye sockets seemed so accusing he put it down again hurriedly, and said, "What will the Rodeni that come here do?"

Mote hopped down to the table, briefly investigated the *parichos,* and sneezed. Gleet bruxed at her, grinding his long teeth together in a Rodeni laugh. He held out a piece of muffin, which she took cheerfully.

"Eh, they'll find ways to manage. Anywhere there's a job a Human won't do, you can find a Roden that'll do it. There's always work to be done here, cleanin' the aqueduct and maintaining the sewers. They'll find work. Not all, I grant you; plenty'd rather live lazy by theft and the like, rather than work, but that's true of most any folk."

"All the Archipelago over," Alex agreed.

"Just hope that Belthar doesn't start to export his new noise-maker. Heh, the new Rodeni coming in said he had a fellow in, some person what made music and called all the rats to get washed away in the river, then ran the bugger out of town." One bright black eye seemed to be looking closely at Alex; you never could be sure, since you couldn't see the pupils, but he felt the gaze on him. "Fool's tales, whrr?"

"The things people come up with," Alex stammered, trying to sound dismissive, while feeling the heat of his ears. Gleet bruxed quietly, and changed the subject, to Alex's relief.

"Here, are you going to eat those?" he asked, pointing to the lizards.

The conversation bore fruit a few days later, when a servant came to where Alex was being thrown around the room in his morning training, to tell him he had a visitor.

"You should finish your session," the General told him, as Alex quickly stripped off his practice tunic and pulled on his shirt.

"You can beat me up double tomorrow," Alex retorted. "At least, I don't doubt that you'll try."

He escaped that growling disapproval and hurried out to the courtyard, where Flip was standing and blinking nervously at the bright sunshine.

"Flip!" Alex exclaimed, as Flip jumped in surprise at the sound of his voice. Alex dropped to his knees to be on level with the Roden. "You made it, and you found me. Please, what do you need? A place to stay? Food? Trinkets? You helped me, let me return the favor."

"You did well, then," Flip responded, with whiskers forward in a friendly gesture. He himself looked awful, Alex now realized; his fur and eyes were dull, and his spine showed plainly down the arch of his back. The fur had all fallen off his tail; he looked more ratlike than ever, hardly like a Trading being at all. He saw Alex's expression at his condition, and he clawed weakly at his protruding ribs.

"After Nuck . . ." he said with a sigh. "Not wanting to . . . forage, eat. But Leep and Len and Trit brought food. And when screams started, brought me with them."

"Come on," Alex urged, getting to his feet. "We can find you a place to stay, and some food . . . and for Leep and the boys, too."

Alex brought the subject up to the other advisors first. Though he might have been able to manipulate the king into agreeing to most any plan, he didn't want to risk upsetting the people on his side who really *did* know what they were doing. After some discussion, an old outbuilding of the palace, long fallen into disuse, was turned over to "Alex's" Rodeni. Leep and her family, along with Flip, moved in happily. Their affluence seemed to grant them some kind of social status within the Rodeni community; Alex would sometimes go to visit them, and there were always new Rodeni visiting as well. Alex was introduced to a vast number of new faces, most all of them recent arrivals from Belthas and other cities under the control of King Belthar. They all wanted to meet Mote, and she grew quite spoiled by all the attention. Despite their friendly manner, the news they brought was troubling. All the cities and lands of Belthar were forcing out the Rodeni, by force of persecution in most places, and aided by the magical "Screaming Towers" erected in Belthas itself. Word had it, too, that similar towers were being built in Belthamial, which was the next nearest city to Deridal after Belthas. The Rodeni also brought word of troop movements; new troops trained in other cities, exercising their training by catching and killing Rodeni, were gathering in Belthas and Belthamial, in numbers that seemed a little too great for mere racial suppression.

Alex mentioned this to the General, but the Therop only gave a cynical hiss. "Tell me something I am *unaware* of, Human," he said. "Of course they prepare for war. You have only to look at a map of this island and see. A dozen cities, with names recently changed to add the prefix of the one who calls himself the Bull of the Prophecy. A dozen more small towns, wiped from the map entirely. All that remains is this small city, with its walls, its mad king, and myself."

"Well, we've lasted this long," Alex said bravely. The General shook his head.

"Bold words . . . sometimes I take comfort in them. I think, however, that it was only because we were no threat that they took no action before now."

"So . . . war is inevitable? Why not just surrender?" Alex suggested. The General glared, and Alex stepped back from the red eyes.

"If we surrender, King Carawan will be killed. I swore to defend his life, and his kingdom. And I will not back down, not surrender. I will not fall into dishonor again."

Alex stared at the Therop; it was hard to read any emotion or thought behind those red eyes, set on either side of that massive fanged maw . . . but he thought he could feel, somehow, the flicker of madness in the alien depths.

"Everyone's crazy," Alex muttered later, as he was walking back to his room. "Temith's trying to grow tumors on rats, Parliament's a stage show, the General's planning to have us all die going down with the ship, Celine thinks she can stand up to a thaumaturgist, the other advisors are plotting around behind one another's backs, snakes, the Rodeni are trying to hide behind us as though we can protect them, the king's brain keeps leaping madly off in all directions and the other advisors go running after it. They're all lunatics, aren't they, Mote? Oooh yes! Yes! Yes they are! Yes they are!" he cooed to her, as she sat up *happy!*
in his hands. A servant watched in befuddlement as they wandered past, the Animist carrying on a one-sided conversation with the rat in his hands.

With the Rodeni came other problems. One of these was brought to Alex's attention by Flip. The black Roden had pulled Alex aside on one of the Animist's visits. Alex made a point of stopping by Flip's dwelling often, to make sure he was doing well. His condition seemed improved, outwardly at least; he'd lost the starved and desperate air he'd had, and his coat was glossing up. But today his look and manner was one of concern, and, after quickly looking around to be sure there were none to overhear, he let Alex know what, or rather who, was troubling him.

"He is called Clak. He is a shaman, from a city miles away. He says Belthar killed all the other Rodeni there," Flip explained. The Rodeni tended to follow a more diverse religion, worshiping minor spirits rather than major deities. Shamans were the ones selected and trained to channel and interpret the spirits for the community. "He said his people would not listen to him, so they died. He wants to save us from dying, too. He is strong, and wise, but . . . he frightens me."

"Frightens you?" asked Alex cautiously. Flip looked uneasy.

"He . . . he says . . . you know, how when one is cornered, one fights?" Flip asked. Alex nodded. "He says we are cornered here, that we should take over the city before Belthar does, or before Deridal wants us out as well. That only if we are in control, will we be safe."

"He's crazy . . . for one thing, we've no intention of harming you; we've got enough problems outside the wall without having to go after ones within. And, I mean no offense, but you aren't that skilled at fighting, and there's not very many of you—"

"There are . . . enough. More than enough. Too many," Flip said quietly. "Too many brings problems. Crowding, anger—" He stopped, and sighed. "Many listen to Clak."

"Well, don't you have other shamans?" Alex asked. "What do they say?"

"There were two," Flip said, quietly. "Reat from Belthas, and Kerrit of Deridal. Clak killed them."

Alex looked horrified. "What?"

"Sometime happens. There is ritual, tradition. But it seemed . . . wrong. Clak didn't seem to care about tradition—got too serious, too angry. He said he was fighting for us, and the other shamans were only servants of the Humani." He grabbed Alex's hand, looking up at him with pleading black eyes. "I don't want us to fight Humani. But if Clak succeeds there will be no choice."

"But what am I supposed to do about it? I mean, I could tell the king—well, the advisors, at any rate, and they could go and find Clak and arrest him, or something . . ."

"But that would only prove that he spoke true, and that the Humani are seeking to destroy us," Flip said. "But you, you are almost a shaman yourself. You call the small ones, you carry a *mookchee*, you allowed us to shelter in the city. Maybe you can—"

"I don't want to even try to kill anyone!" Alex protested. "I don't think I could, no matter how much the General teaches me."

"You not have to kill him, just talk. All the Rodeni, they only hear Clak, only hear what he says. You can tell them another way, that the Humani will not hurt them, that it is better to fight alongside the soldiers than against them."

"Can I bring someone along?" Alex asked, thinking he didn't want to go into a den of angry Rodeni by himself.

"Yes, one. Bring a fighter," Flip suggested. "But quickly! Before dark!"

"What's this all about, anyway?" Luken protested, as Alex led him along the streets.

"I might run into trouble—"

"Oh, that would be a new surprise," Luken scoffed, tapping along with his spear as they went. In addition to his parliamentary duties, Luken had joined the Deridal military; he and Alex had found a sort of friendship in their mutual hatred of the General and his training regimen. Despite this, Luken was now getting very good with staves and spears, as well as the powerful, deadly Deridal crossbow.

"Well, I want you along as backup. In case things get ugly."

"Very flattering. Of course your old allopathist can still fight better than I can, and I still get the headaches to prove it."

"Yes, but I couldn't find him. I found you instead, so you'll have to do." He'd also stopped to grab something else, just in case.

"Thanks for the vote of confidence," grumbled Luken.

They caught up to Flip at the end of an alleyway. It occurred to Alex that almost all his contacts with Rodeni had been in alleys or cellars or other sheltered places; only a few of the native Deridal Rodeni seemed to feel comfortable out in the open spaces.

Flip looked up at Luken, and seemed to find him acceptable. He led them into an old storehouse, from wherein Alex could hear the chittering murmur of Rodeni voices. It reminded him of the cavy pens back at the College, and he had to fight down a pang of homesickness.

Flip had explained to Alex, "You will have to fight him—"

"You said I didn't have to!" Alex protested, and Flip waved his hands hurriedly.

"No no. Not *kill*. You not have to kill him. But you need to challenge his right to speak as a leader. You need to . . . scuffle." The Roden tapped his finger-scuffling hands together to demonstrate, and blinked, trying hard to think of words in Trade for exclusively Rodeni concepts. "Is like . . . you show all, you are tough enough to mean what you say."

"Dominance assertion," Alex sighed.

"One of you loses, one wins. Both speak, but, well, we may not listen as well to loser. Still, if his wisdom is more than the other's strength, he may be followed after all."

"But you said Clak killed the other shamans," Alex said, doubtfully.

"That was . . . not right. But impressive. Even I thought, perhaps he is right." Flip sighed. "You see. That is why you bring along a Humani fighter; Clak will not want to fight you both to death."

That had been another reason Alex had brought Luken instead of one of his fellow advisors; Luken was young and very tall, impressive-looking, broad of chest and arm. The only one Alex could have grabbed who looked more capable of combat was the General himself, and Alex was too frightened of the Therop to even think of asking. Luken had to duck his head as they entered the narrow warehouse door and went down a small passage into its crowded cellar space.

Alex didn't know what he was expecting from a Rodeni shaman. Something, someone, fairly small, probably lost under a riot of colored scarves and beaded necklaces laced with talismae. Sort of a smaller, furry priest of Jenju, perhaps. What was addressing a small crowd of Rodeni, standing in the middle of them on a stage made from barrels and boards, behind a podium made from a wooden crate, was not quite what he had pictured.

Clak was taller than Alex. Alex was used to Humani being that tall, but a Roden, when the long yellow teeth were in a perfect position to bite his eyes out, was somehow far more unpleasant. Of course, it made sense; probably Clak's magical talent had allowed him to get a good share of the food early in life, and he'd thrived and grown.

The crowd erupted in murring whispers when the Humani entered, and Clak stopped in the middle of his oration. He'd been speaking in Trade, Alex realized; perhaps the Rodeni of different cities had dialects different enough that Trade was the best compromise. The crowd seemed to be composed about half and half of the scruffier, smaller Belthasian Rodeni, and Deridal's own slightly better-kept population.

Clak did not wear scarves and necklaces; in fact, he was naked. His fur was the most unusual color Alex had ever seen on a Roden: a pale cream, marked at his muzzle, hands, feet, and the tufted tip of his tail with dark brown. His eyes were like pale rubies, and burned with feverish intensity. His nakedness made him look more animal than the normal Roden, but while this should have comforted Alex (for he was much more experienced with beasts than with any Trading race, even his own), instead it frightened him. As he turned to face the Human, too, Alex saw another reason he seemed so tall; he stood up on his toes, balancing with his tail behind him and a short staff beside him. It was a strange, awkward pose, and increased his aura of exotic menace. He did have a staff, at least, as was expected of a magist; it was carved with the wedge-shaped Rodeni runes. Alex himself had taken the time to throw on a fancy embroidered tunic and to grab the Big Hat with Feathers, cinched up tight under his chin, in order to show his official status. He felt silly and overdressed next to the Roden.

Alex could feel Mote trembling, and he could see overlaid the patterns of glowing magic, strong around the shaman. The education he'd gotten at the College was wrong; they'd said that shamans were not very powerful, and would not show as strongly in the Oether, but Clak glowed almost as brightly as Chernan had. Perhaps no one at the College had ever met a shaman as powerful as this; not lived to tell about it, at any rate. Alex sent a wordless plea to Mote. He was remembering Chernan's comment: that sometimes an Animist could be resistant to magic, through the bond with the Anim. He sensed her compliance, felt the warmth and presence of her intensify as he stepped forward, and climbed up onto the stage.

"So. It is you, Human, lackey to the king, slayer of small ones," Clak said. He spoke Trade well, with hardly any of the Rodeni accent. Alex answered in the same language, but knew his voice would have the sloppy, round tones of Humani corrupting it.

"I am Alex, friend of *mookchees*—" and he extended an arm so that the mystical grey rat on his shoulder could run up into his palm and sit up before the crowd before running back again. There was an appreciative murmur from the crowd at this. "—friend to the king, who is friend to all, save the one, Belthar, who drove you all from your homes. You would do better, accomplish more, if you join with myself and Deridal to fight against Belthar for your freedom."

"There can be no alliance with Humani," growled Clak, raising his carved staff to a ready stance. Alex noted it was about the same length and heft as his own smakjab. "Every time we trust Humani it ends in death, destruction, despair. The spirits have spoken . . . they have *shouted;* any who go to ally themselves with Humani will be cursed. Cursed, with sickness and death!" He banged his staff loudly on the stage. Alex felt Mote jump at the noise, and his own features flinched; but less at the noise than at the words. Nuck had died when Alex had tried to help her . . . and when the Rodeni had helped Alex, hadn't King Belthas decided to turn on them with greater ingenuity and fury? What if the shaman had a point?

No, he couldn't allow himself to think that. He was trying to think of a good response when the Roden took the opportunity away.

"Do you come to challenge my words, Human?" he shouted.

"I do so challenge!" Alex shouted back, remembering the response Flip had taught him. He sent a final plea to Mote for help in deflecting any spells the shaman might throw at him, but knew his best chance lay in keeping the shaman distracted enough with physical problems that he wouldn't be able to maintain the concentration for a spell. He lunged with the smakjab.

Clak brought his own staff down in a parry, then counterstruck back along the line of Alex's weapon with a jab. Alex was ready for this, though, and stepped out of the way, and brought his free hand down on the staff, knocking it aside. Clak spun the staff back again and for a moment they traded parries and conterstrikes, the sounds of wood on wood ringing; at one point they clinched, and Alex cringed at the sight of the horrible sharp teeth inches from his face. Clak gave a quick snap, but Alex was ready for it and ducking, so Clak kicked as well.

Alex stumbled back; the Roden's teeth had just torn a thin slice along his forehead. Clak stepped forward, swinging, but Alex recovered and kicked. The Roden grabbed his foot and threw him, with surprising strength in his knobbly hands. Alex rolled, protecting his shoulder and the clinging rodent presence there, and then jumped back to his feet. Blood from his forehead was running into his eyes.

Clak was already coming at him at an awkward run, not the leaping bounce typical of Rodeni, with staff swinging in an overhand blow; Alex ducked under it and grabbed the Roden's tail, jerking him backward; Clak thudded to the stage but rolled back to his feet.

Clak wasn't that good a fighter, Alex realized; while his skill with the smakjab was better than Alex's own, he wasn't using his teeth or his jumping ability to full advantage. It must be some rule of this ritual combat, Alex realized, and thanked his luck for it. Clak slowly approached him, staff ready; they feinted and parried a few blows, watching each other warily. For a moment Alex got the podium between them, and they circled around it until, with a shrill curse, Clak vaulted over it, Alex leaping back. The crowd of watching Rodeni was silent. Luken, pressed back against the wall by the furry crowd, bit his nails in trepidation, as the two combatants traded blows and parries in lightning scuffle, then broke apart again. Alex was panting hard, but Clak seemed unchanged. Even his fur was flat and calm.

"You speak boldly, boy," snarled Clak, "and you fight well. But I cannot allow you to harm my race, my people. Do you hear me?" He raised his voice, and his gaze seemed to take in the wide watching eyes of the Rodeni in the room. Alex stood ready, panting, trying to blink the blood out of his eyes. Clak stepped forward. "Yes. Even the boldest fighter has a vulnerable spot."

He jabbed then, Alex tried to parry, but the blow was a feint, and twisted at the last instant to smack into his gut, and the breath whuffed out of him. As he doubled over, Clak's hand moved.

The watching Rodeni gasped, echoing the boy's strangled cry. Clak had yanked the small grey rat from the Animist's shoulder, and even now held her aloft by the tail. She was struggling, trying to bite, but Clak waved her gently, setting her spinning frantically. The Rodeni watching whispered and meeped, their own tails twitching in sympathy.

"No . . . please, put her down," wheezed the Animist, staring, dropping to one knee. "You're fighting with me, not her . . ."

"You are *all* our enemies, and must *die,*" hissed Clak, as he swung the tiny grey body overarm with all his might, against the edge of the podium.

The rat gave a single squeal, then her head smacked against the wood, a thudding, crunching sound. There were cries from the audience, and Flip buried his face in his paws. Luken bit through his fingertip.

Alex didn't even get a chance to cry out.

His eyes rolled back in his head, and he slumped limply to the floor. His smakjab rolled away and fell off the stage, its clatter sounding unbearably loud in the suddenly silent room.

Clak held up the small, limp grey body by the tail, watching blood drip from the mouth and nose. The hind legs twitched once, then fell still. Clak tossed the corpse contemptuously onto that of her master.

The crowd of Rodeni watching did not make a sound. Luken, gripping his spear and desperately hoping he could make it out of the place alive, thought the lack of sound was worse than the chattering noises of teeth. He'd heard stories, from the other soldiers in Belthas, when they would come back from raids on the Rodeni dens . . . when they were squealing and panicking, then all was well, but when they fell silent . . . that was time to withdraw. You'd chase one screaming into an alley, then suddenly, it would be quiet, and all these eyes would appear from the shadows, in the silence . . .

The only one not affected by the silence was Clak himself. He stalked over to the dead Animist in his curious, high-stepping stance. "So must perish all our enemies," he said. "You see how easy it is? All we need to do is strike, strike at their weakness. Take them asleep if you like, take them in the darkness. One by one, strike them down, take what is theirs, what is rightfully ours. We must—"

Alex grabbed the tiptoed ankle in front of his face, and yanked. Clak tumbled down in mid-sentence with a shriek, and the silence was broken by the sudden clamor of voices. Luken stared.

As the Roden fell, Alex rolled on top of him, fingers grabbing for his throat. The shaman's claws scrabbled at Alex, his hind feet kicking and clawing. He tried to bite, but Alex had a grip on his neck and was using it to hold down the Roden's head, keeping his face away from the snapping yellow teeth. Clak's tail lashed, and his claws reached up to tear at the Human's face. Alex, kneeling over the Roden, stretched one knee back and brought it down hard on the Roden's large scrotum, mashing it down, pinning it against the hard wood stage.

A wheep of sympathy resounded around the room again, and

Luken cringed, his eyes watering. But Clak didn't seem to notice, or even care; he didn't even bother try to draw his testicles up into his body, as Rodeni could do when so attacked.

Alex noticed this, too, even through his fury, and he changed his grip to a choke, ducking his head and shoving it into the fur of the Roden's chest to shield his eyes from the scrambling claws. His hands gripped tight, constricting the Roden's windpipe, feeling the pounding of the arteries under the fur. Clak writhed and struggled and kicked beneath him, but Alex outweighed him just slightly, due to the dense Humani bones, and had better leverage from his position. Slowly Clak's struggling weakened, and then slackened, and stopped. Alex hung on for a little bit longer, but when he finally loosened his grip he saw the furry chest continue to move.

"Rope," Alex wheezed, slowly getting to his feet. His face was torn and bleeding from the marks of Clak's claws and teeth. "He'll come around soon, and I don't want to have to fight him again. No wonder he didn't use any spells on me . . . he was using them all on himself, to make him strong, immune to pain . . ." He shook his head.

"Alex?" Luken asked, stepping forward through the Rodeni. Someone handed him a coil of rope, and he passed it up to the Animist. "I thought . . . aren't you supposed to be dead?"

For an answer Alex untied the hurricane strip and took off the Big Hat. The crowd gasped as Mote stood up on his head, sniffing the air gladly after the stuffy, sweaty confines of the hat. She tilted, gracefully balancing, as Alex scooped up the small dead rat.

"I spent hours training her," he said, to no one in particular, as Luken quickly bound up the prostrate Clak. "She was the smartest one. She knew how to sit up, circle, wave, kiss . . . I even taught her to fetch. I started carrying her around after I found the snake in my room; I thought, just to be safe."

"Is very bad for to kill a *mookchee*," said one of the Rodeni, firmly. "Clak was wrong."

"She wasn't really a *mookchee*, though," said Alex, stroking the fur. Mote had run down his arm and was sniffing

sadness

at the body. "She was one of Temith's white rats. I dyed her fur.

Couldn't do anything about the red eyes, but no one ever looks that closely. I called her Fleck."

"What are we going to do with him?" Luken asked, meaning Clak.

"That's not up to us." He stood up, and addressed the crowd of Rodeni. He still held the dead rat in his hands, and Mote was sitting next to it. Alex recalled how the two had played together after Fleck's training sessions, and would often sleep curled up in a grey furry ball together. The differences were obvious when you saw them side by side. "Clak's fate, that's up to you. I won't kill him, I refuse to. He's a true shaman, and he's been blessed by the spirits; that's why I couldn't cause him pain, why he wouldn't yield. But that doesn't mean he was right. Clak has told you his side . . . let me tell you my side. Not as Humani, not as Rodeni, just a person, a person who cares about the persons in this room." He paused; he wasn't good at public speaking, despite the training he'd had on Giving Entertaining Educational Lectures at the College. "Deridal and Rodeni, we have a common enemy—King Belthar. He wants the Rodeni dead . . . he wants Deridal dead. He wants *us* dead, you see? You aren't just Rodeni, you're citizens of Deridal. We're glad to have you. We need your help."

After Alex's speech, some of the younger and bolder Rodeni decided to join the Deridal military. Alex was already talking to the General about it. The General at first was dubious, but after thinking about it for a time, decided to give it a try. Len and Trit, emboldened by their past friendship with Alex and urged on by their peers, went to meet with the General for a training session. The Therop proceeded to wipe the walls with the small, light fellows. Standing with one clawed foot on the back of each panting, bruised Roden, the General had blinked thoughtfully, and said, "Some potential. Very well. Let your fellows know that they can be employed at two-thirds the pay of a Humani soldier."

Alex had expected to hear no more from the Rodeni on the subject after seeing Len and Trit so abused, but the next day they were back, and with them a goodly number of others, males and females.

The General worked with them and a couple of Humani officers to schedule a training regimen, and then turned their training over to the Humani officers. The Rodeni were glad; the Humani were much kinder and less intimidating than the massive predator. With this change, even more began to join, including the older ones; even Flip signed up, and later mentioned to Alex that it was good to have something else to occupy his time. He had learned how to fire a bow; he couldn't see very well to aim, but in large-scale battles that was seldom a real problem, as long as you were pointing in the right direction. Still, the Rodeni didn't bother to attend archery with the Humani soldiers, but practiced on their own in the fields around Deridal, where a stray shot couldn't do much damage.

Soon Alex was given a respite from the General as well; his basic training was complete. Now he only had to practice with some of the soldiers daily, and meet with the General only once a week to learn new techniques. He often sparred with Luken and sometimes some of the other advisors; he even faced off with Temith once, who did his best to cheerfully pound Alex into a pulp and came close to succeeding. The doctor's knowledge of vulnerable pressure points was almost as good as any Lemyr's.

The Rodeni loved to spar with Alex, and would gleefully set upon him in groups, waving a wide variety of sticks. Alex did his best, and for a while was able to hold his own against them. They learned quickly, however, and Alex suspected they practiced a lot more than he did; he soon began to be overwhelmed by the leaping, lightning attacks and was frequently dragged to the mat and sat on by bruxing, squeaking opponents.

But interest seemed to fall off after awhile, and Alex was disappointed as fewer and fewer Rodeni showed up to training sessions. Some of the Humani soldiers were out sick with a flu that was going around, and Alex suspected that the Rodeni had taken their absence to mean that if you didn't want to show up for practice, you just didn't. The General, when informed of this desertion, was disappointed in the Rodeni lack of responsibility, but claimed he knew that the Rodeni had no experience as soldiers and probably would never be able to master the concepts of discipline. Len and Trit still came to training, however. They, too, seemed to miss their fellows, becoming more reserved and serious in their training, and less liable to chatter and talk.

Alex came down to practice one day, and found the two Rodeni brothers sparring with Luken. They did quite well, working as a team to encircle and outflank the Human. Trit used a smakjab like Alex's, although it was a bit larger for him, and Len was awkwardly holding a pair of toksticks. Alex frowned, and walked over to them.

They stopped their wary circling as he approached, and Luken waved. Len and Trit whistled a greeting. Alex frowned more deeply.

"All right, you two, where's Len and Trit?" he demanded.

Luken looked surprised, and the two Rodeni exchanged glances. "This *is* them, Alex, are you blind?" said Luken, wiping his brow.

"No, and they're not. I don't know who they are, but *he* doesn't even know how to hold toksticks—"

"Hurt my hand, I did!" said the Roden defensively, shaking a wrist and wincing, but Alex ignored him and continued, "And *she's* a female," he said, pointing. The Rodeni glanced down at themselves while Luken stared. Both Rodeni wore loose-tied pants.

"What? Are you sure?" he asked.

"You can tell! You are, aren't you? Who are you?" he demanded. The Rodeni flinched back from him.

"Pleep, sir," said the female, nervously gnawing on the end of her smakjab. The other one threw down his toksticks in disgust. They clattered.

"Furrfu, Pleep! We're not supposed to say! Now there'll be big trouble because of us!" He was almost in tears, or rather, the uncontrollable trembling that served the same meaning for the Rodeni.

"Chis, he knows! No more lies!" Pleep insisted.

"Come on! Where are Len and Trit?" Alex demanded. "And why did they send you to pretend to be them?" The two Rodeni did look very like the missing ones, in color and age.

The Rodeni exchanged glances again, and finally Pleep said, in a whisper, "Out sick?" She squealed as Chis tried to cuff her, and swung her smakjab at the Roden in retaliation. Alex blocked the blow with his own weapon and fixed her with a look. He couldn't help but feel betrayed by his Rodeni friends. He'd gone through so much to try to get them to accept and be accepted by Deridal, and now they were throwing it all away, and lying about it as well.

"Sick? Out sick? You mean they just didn't want to show up!" he snapped. Pleep shook her head as Chis growled to himself and picked up his sticks.

"No!" she said, and then unexpectedly grabbed his hand. "Please! Say nothing! We'll go, won't lie to you anymore, very sorry. Forget we were here!"

"Is the something to do with Clak?" He'd been told that the shaman had vanished, in disgrace at being beaten by a Human. Clak left with curses and dire threats and prophecies; perhaps these had frightened off the Rodeni. But then why would these two impostors be here at all?

Alex took her hand in his, gently. "Please. Take me to them," he said. "They've got some explaining to do."

The two glum Rodeni led Alex through the ruined remains of an old, burned-out building. A few Rodeni were about, working at sewing or carving or other small crafts in the sunlight, sitting on pieces of masonry or small scraps of cloth. One of them, an albino as large as Alex himself, was shaping a wooden table leg with careful nibbles of his great teeth. He slowly turned the leg in his mouth as a Human would eat cobbed maize, while comparing it with two finished legs set out before him. He glared at Alex through pale garnet eyes, and took a particularly vicious chomp from the wood. Alex looked away, not seeking trouble.

They went down a short flight of steps into the darkness of an old cellar. Alex was careful of his footing as the small hand tugged at his, down a low-roofed hall . . .

The hand was jerked away with a squeal, and suddenly it seemed as though the passage had fallen in on all sides. Rodeni shouts echoed as Alex was pummeled by stones and sticks.

He swore, slammed his back to the wall, and swept out with the smakjab he'd been absentmindedly carrying along. Thuds of contact and squeals rewarded his action. He switched into a defensive spin, whirling the short length of stick blindly about him. A smakjab wasn't much good for this, you really needed something longer. This was brought home painfully as darting blows lashed through and hammered him on legs and chest and gut. Pain and fear swirled around him as he fought to maintain his concentration and his defense. The squeaking squeals of the Rodeni surrounding him seemed to grow shriller, more like animals than any Trading race.

As loudly as he could above the cries of the Rodeni, Alex shouted, "Dammit, I'm the King's Animist! If you kill me the General will have you all burned out of here! He knows I'm here!" Not exactly true, but Alex was not in a mood to debate.

There was more squeaking and squealing, but no apparent change. Alex stopped his spin to attempt to start sweeping his way out, and what felt like a carved table leg crashed down on his head. He dropped to his knees, stars of flame exploding in his vision.

Mote ran down the hall and under the door to Temith's study, skittering into the room with her nose a blur. She spun and ran out again, nose to the floor, and tore frantically down the hallway.

Temith was in one of the sunlit breakfast halls, wearing his pajamas and dressing gown. He was idly buttering a muffin when claws sunk into his leg and raced up the outside of his pants. He yelped and jerked up his leg, and Mote, squeaking in panic, landed in his lap. She jumped up and down, her cries shrill and fearful.

"You scared me, Mote! Blastrafters, if you'd wanted some muffin you could just ask nicely," Temith said, breaking off a piece. "Is it all right if she has some muffin, Alex?" He looked around. "Alex?"

Mote climbed up the scientist's nightshirt and grabbed onto his collar, squealing and tugging at the fabric.

"What?! Where's Alex?" he demanded, looking at her. Mote yanked on his collar and squealed again, her voice muffled by the fabric.

"What? What is it, girl? Is he in trouble?" Temith asked, as he tried to pull her off. She clamped her jaws tight and kept squeaking.

"Let's see, about now he'd be . . . what, at fighting practice, shouldn't he?" said Temith, standing up, with Mote hanging from his shirt like a large brooch. "I guess we'd better go find him."

.   .   .

After a confused period of shouting and dragging, Alex found his head clearing. He was lying on a filthy floor, with dim light provided by a number of light-wells along a high wall. He raised his head weakly, and saw Flip standing next to him. The black Roden had his shortbow, and a flint-headed arrow nocked. He was speaking Rodeni and looking past Alex. Alex's translation skills were not the best at the moment. He could, however, gather that Flip was informing the large albino, named Erk, that unless Erk wanted to be on intimate terms with the Oether, Erk would drop his club and back off. Erk, out of Alex's vision, retorted that Flip wouldn't dare and couldn't anyway, and Flip informed him that he certainly would, and that hitting a fat white something-or-other at this distance would be both easy and enjoyable.

This seemed to be a large underground room, with pillars supporting parts of the ceiling and chunks of masonry scattering along the dirty floor. It was huge, and unfamiliar. There was a large number of Rodeni who seemed to be on Flip's side, and a smaller group who seemed to be with Erk, seen as Alex painfully turned his head. Also prone on the floor nearby were Pleep and Chis, unconscious and their tails held fast by some of Erk's companions.

Erk protested that he'd been appointed to guard the something entry and that everyone knew no Humani somethings were allowed inside. Flip said that yes, that was true, but Alex was not a Humani something, but a friend, and anyone but a certain red-eyed something should know that. Erk retorted that the opinions of a something outsider should not be allowed to jeopardize the lives of others; no exceptions should be made to keep secrecy.

"Apologies, please, won't tell secrets, just am want for to help," Alex managed to speak up, in Rodeni. "Came seek Len, Trit. Worried about." Rodeni was a surprisingly complex language, hard to learn and even harder to speak. Even at his best, Alex could only manage a few words.

"We don't need your poison help, you stupid brat Human!" snarled Erk, in accented Trade. "You're the king's lackey and a spy! Clak was right, we should have listened to him, and now we're paying for it! We should kill you while we have the chance!"

"If you kill me down here, you'll all suffer. Now, you can let me go peacefully and I won't tell anyone about this. Or you can accept my help," said Alex in the same language, pushing himself up and wincing.

There was a long pause. The Rodeni on all sides seemed to be trembling, as they faced each other, ignoring the Human for the moment. Despite the pain and his anger and fear, Alex could feel the tension in the air, strung tight with emotion. He suddenly wished he had Mote with him; it felt almost like magic, but without his Anim, he couldn't be sure. Then suddenly the tension snapped, falling limp; the Rodeni seemed to give a faint slump in unison, falling into wary trepidation rather than continued fury.

"Let him see, then!" Erk growled. "And on your heads be it! We could do with less of you Belthas cretins anyway." He turned and left, his fellows lingering a bit and casting nervous glances back before following. There was muttered chittering. Alex hadn't seen this kind of hostility within a Rodeni community before. The sense of a family race was missing.

Flip unstrung his bow carefully as Alex stood. "Must ask that you promise not to say anything," Flip explained, and the other Rodeni nodded in agreement. Some were helping Pleep and Chis to stand up. "But maybe you can help." His eyes, little more than dark gleams in the light, still managed to convey desperate pleading, and Alex winced inside as he recalled the last time Flip had asked him for help.

"I promise," Alex said. "I'll try."

"You go down that way." Flip pointed down a passageway. "Down to the farthest end." Another Roden handed him an oil lamp.

"Aren't you coming with me?" Alex asked, and all the Rodeni drew back.

"No, no. Cannot. Sorry," Flip apologized. He seemed to remember something. "Where is your *mookchee?*"

"I left her in my room, because she doesn't like to watch me at practice," Alex explained. "Why?"

"Good, is good. Shouldn't take the *mookchee* there." Flip nodded, and then jerked his muzzle toward the hallway. "You go and see."

Curious, but wary of another sneak attack, Alex set off down the hallway. He looked at the walls as he went; they seemed to be partly old cellars and stone walls, but some seemed more recent; bits of brick and stone drywalled up for support. The passage was low and cramped, and dipped and turned. Alex couldn't think what building this might have been; then it occurred to him that the Rodeni themselves had dug it. And the room he'd left, and the passages from it. All Rodeni construction, burrowing away under the streets of Deridal, trying to make room for all the newcomers. No wonder there hadn't seemed to be as many as there should have been. They'd all been working down here.

It was very dark and quiet, and smelly; unusual, since normally the Rodeni were very good about keeping their quarters clean. The smell increased as he went farther down the hallway, sloping downward as he went.

The smell grew to a powerful stink of ammonia and smoke and decay, and as he turned a corner at the end of the hall, he saw why.

The floors and corners and wall niches of the catacombs here were filled with Rodeni, lying huddled, their fur matted and disordered. The air was full of the sounds of wheezing, whimpering breaths. In between the prone forms, other Rodeni walked slowly, carrying food or jugs of water, or trying to clean up spills of urine or piles of runny feces with crude brooms. They looked up as he entered, but seemed too weak to care about his presence.

Alex looked around in horror. Two Rodeni, obviously ill, were carefully rolling a third, stiff in death, onto a simple stretcher. They dragged the corpse away; but Alex could tell, just by a look around the walls, that their work was far from over. The air was thick with the stink of pestilence and death.

A movement at his elbow caught his eye. He looked and saw Len, holding a broom, looking up at him. Alex almost cried out in shock and horror when he saw the young Roden's eyes were filmed with fever.

"You found out anyway, then," Len said, glumly. "I told Trit it wouldn't work."

"Len! What's going on? Where's Trit?"

"Sick. All sick have to come here, can't leave. I couldn't let him go alone," Len explained. "I thought, well, I'm not sick yet, maybe I can stay with him but not get sick." He rubbed his whiskers ruefully. "I was wrong."

"What—how long has this been happening?" demanded Alex, walking into the room, carefully stepping over the feeble forms on the floor. "What's happening?"

"The elders say we put too many of us in a small space," Len explained, walking with him and trying to clear a path for Alex with his broom. "Not supposed to do that. Makes us fight, but we're trying not to, because we know our kin have nowhere else to go. And the crowding makes a sickness. It happens. Has happened before. There are rats about, too. They are dying, too. It may be one of their plagues. You didn't bring Mote, did you?" he asked in sudden concern.

"No, she's at home—Len! Isn't there a cure? Haven't you tried to get help?"

"Some are saying it's our fault, for ignoring Clak, for ignoring what the spirits said." Len blinked at Alex. "We were crowded when he came, and though he warned us, we did nothing. And we began to get sick. The worse it got, the more Clak urged us to fight, as our ancestors do in crowding times. But . . . then you came, and stopped him." Len paused, to take a wheezing, rattling breath. "But before Clak left, he gave us a last warning, a plea. He said everyone who was in league with the Humani would suffer and die. We didn't want to believe him. We thought we could contain it, down here. But now . . . it's among everyone who went to join the army. The spirits are angry, and it's our fault . . ."

"We've got to do something, find another shaman who can help—"

"Clak killed the others, remember?" Len shook his head. "And everyone thinks that if Humani know there is a sickness, if we ask them for help, they will drive us out and kill us in case it might spread to Humani. It has happened before." He looked up. "And they may be right. I remember all the Humani soldiers who were too sick to come to practice."

"But that's just a flu!" Alex protested. "Len, that has nothing to do with it! If Humani were dying like ra—like flies, like this, I'd know about it!"

"You think so. But we know how Humani think, too," Len said, and gently touched one of the huddled shapes. "Trit? Wake up?"

Alex knelt as Trit rolled over, wrapped in filthy blankets. His nostrils and the corners of his eyes were stained with blood-colored porphyrin discharge. "Alex?" he whispered.

"They should have said something, should have told me, we

might have been able to do something before it went this far," Alex muttered under his breath, and took Trit's clawed little hand. It was hot with fever. "Trit, how do you feel? What's happening?"

"Weak. Tired. Cold," Trit said, and Len nodded weakly.

"I've been sick about three days," Len said. "He's had it about a week." He offered a jug of water to his brother, who took a gulp, then winced and lay back down again. In a low voice, Len added, "Lisk lasted two weeks sick. He was the longest. You slip under . . . and never wake up. You drown in your own lungs."

"This is terrible! Please, you have to let me get help for you, tell someone—"

"Not up to us, Alex," Len said, with a rueful twitch of his whiskers. "You'd have to convince the . . . everybody."

"Who do I talk to? Do you have a council of elders or something?"

Len slowly lashed his tail, gnawing on his broom. "Things just . . . happen. Can't really explain it in Humani terms."

"I'll try. I'll do my best," Alex told them. "And if I can't, I'll keep my promise, but I'll do what I can to find some way to help you myself."

Len nodded slowly, not looking at Alex.

Alex walked out of the primitive plague-hospital, and back up the long hallway. As he reached the top, the waiting Rodeni drew back from him, keeping a wary distance for fear of contagion. Erk was back, holding a short club and with his teeth bared, but maintaining a safe distance.

"A one-wide tunnel," Erk told him gruffly. It was a Rodeni term for a standoff. "You know our secret, but we can't kill you without risking the same danger we'd have if our secret was known."

"I won't tell your secret," Alex replied, "I promised not to. But if you will release me from that, let me tell people, I'm sure they'd be willing to help—"

"No! It was your 'help' that brought us to this!" snapped Erk. "We were fine, and then you, you angered Belthar and gave him the idea for those Towers!"

"I never—!" Alex began, but Erk out-shouted him.

"You forced all these immigrants in here! Crowded them in, crowded us out, angered the spirits—"

"A lot of these 'immigrants' are friends and family, Erk!" shouted a fawn female Alex didn't recognize. "We can't turn them away!"

Erk squealed back something in Rodeni, and the discussion erupted in shouting. Alex could only catch a word here and there. From nearby, Flip caught his eye. "Always on the brink of fight," he said. "Very hard."

The noise was interrupted then by the panicky arrival of three Rodeni from one of the other passageways, squealing a warning; one of them was hopping along on three legs, dragging one hind foot, and another was bleeding profusely from his nose. From behind them came the distinctive pound of Humani tread. As the assembled Rodeni drew back and gripped makeshift weapons, Temith rounded the corner, still wearing a dressing gown, with Mote clinging to his head.

"Alex! There you are!" he cried, upon seeing him. "Your rat's been frantic, I thought you were in some danger!"

"No, no, everything's fine," Alex said pointedly, with a glance around at the Rodeni, who squeaked and chittered among themselves, exchanging glances. "Just a misunderstanding, I'm sure."

"Why did they decide to attack me, then, I wonder?" said Temith, looking at the wounded Rodeni who'd preceded him. They avoided his gaze, and looked instead at the other Rodeni, who quickly explained things in their own chittering language.

"Probably just another misunderstanding," replied Alex. "Now, I'm sure everything's understood and everything's all right, and we'll just be going, shall we?"

"Yes, perfectly fine, everything is," gritted Erk through his long teeth, ruby eyes narrowed in a calculating stare into Alex's. "You might as well leave."

Mote wanted to jump to her master, but Alex warned her to stay away for the moment. Sulking, she clung to Temith's head as they made their way out of the catacombs and back into the fresh morning sunlight. The Rodeni watched them go.

Back at the palace, Alex washed and scrubbed himself all over with harsh soap, and set his clothes in hot soapy water to boil in a pot on top of the small bathroom stove. Then, dressed in fresh clothing, he went down the hall to Temith's workroom and found Mote busily exploring one of the cluttered workbenches, as the scientist was going through his shelves of books, selecting volumes and stacking them on a table.

"Alex," Temith said, as the Animist entered and crossed to where Mote sat up on her hind legs, eager to be picked up. "What's all this about a plague down there?"

Mote leapt onto Alex's shirtfront and clambered up to his shoulder, as Alex's expression carefully froze.

"What, sir?" he asked, trying to sound innocent.

Temith shut the book he was looking through, and sighed. "I figured they'd done something like this; sworn you to secrecy, probably? They mentioned something like that. Wondering if they could trust you. I'm sure they can. But they were talking about a plague, and death, and fear of Humani retribution, and I don't like the sound of that. Now, you can either explain, which, I think I should mention, is part of your duty to the king, or I can get the General and a lot of troops to go down there and see for ourselves what's what."

"You speak Rodeni," Alex guessed flatly.

Temith shrugged. "I can read and write it better than I can speak it, and now that I'm older, I can't hear all the high words as well, but—" He shook his head. "Still, the phrase, 'we should kill them now!' was repeated often enough for me to grasp the concept."

"They aren't like that!" Alex protested. "You people always seem to think they're evil and vicious. They're just like us, only they've gotten the short end of the stick for so many years that they—"

"I didn't say they were evil, Alex, and if we really thought they were so horrible, would we have let them move in? You've got the king's ear in many ways, but believe me, if we'd objected to them, they wouldn't be there. Now tell me about this plague."

"I can't. I promised I wouldn't. And it's none of our business anyway. It's killing them, not us." Alex folded his arms on his chest.

"You know about the sickness going around up here?" Temith demanded. "No, probably not, you don't get out of the palace much. I'm the only actual doctor this town has, and when the priests throw up their hands and the soldiers throw up their lunch, *I'm* the one that gets called in, when it's too late to do anything. Lots of people are sick, Alex. *People,* Humani like you and me. A sizeable portion of the *army* is on *sick leave.* That's got to stop, at any cost!"

"We're not dying, though!" Alex protested. "They're sick and dying, and we're just having a case of flu! We can't blame that on them!"

"No one has actually recovered yet, Alex. It may just take longer to kill Humani. We *are* larger, after all."

Alex fell silent at that, chewing on his knuckle in frantic thought. Temith picked up a book, opened it, sniffed the pages, and put it away with a shake of his head.

"Alex," Temith said, "what if they're right? What if it is the same plague? The Rodeni *have* suffered a population explosion, and they're crowded together in an enclosed area. It's the perfect situation for a disease to crop up. I'm not saying we should blame them, I'm saying we can't ignore facts. If this is the same plague that's affecting Humani . . ."

"It's not, it can't be," Alex explained. "You said the soldiers are throwing up. The Rodeni aren't. They die of fluid in their lungs. Different, see? If it was the same thing, then the Rodeni would be—" He trailed off, as half-remembered lessons surfaced.

"Rodeni can't vomit, Alex," Temith said, voicing Alex's realization. "Their physiology—"

"Still. Still. It doesn't mean it's the same," Alex protested. "Maybe it isn't a Rodeni plague. It's killing them and leaving no survivors, so not likely that it's something they harbor in their population. If it is the same as this flu, then maybe it's a Humani disease. Maybe we can catch and carry it and survive, at least long enough to spread it around. But it puts Rodeni flat out within a couple of days, and dead in about a week." He thought of Len and Trit, shut away in the dark stink, waiting, doomed to die, and his eyes stung.

"If we can find some way to help our people, we can help the Rodeni, too," Temith insisted. "But we need to find out everything we can about this disease, or diseases, in order to do anything." He hauled out a microscope from under a canvas hood, and cleared a space on his desk with a sweep of his arm. Books clattered, and Alex jumped back. Temith was never so abrupt.

"I'll need to get samples, of blood and discharges," Temith muttered, rummaging for slides. "And you've been exposed, now. So if it is a Humani sickness . . . Let me know, instantly, if you start feeling sick."

"Mote," stammered Alex. "They said rats are dying of it . . . I washed, and my clothes—but if I'm actually infected, contagious . . ."

Temith sighed, looking at Mote who was worriedly grooming her master's cheek. "You'd better hope I find a cure, then."

A knock came at the door then, and Temith answered it, and took the scroll that one of the palace messengers handed to him. Alex watched, cold with fear, as he unrolled and read it.

"Well," he said, rolling it back up again. "Duty calls. Best to keep this to ourselves for now, I think. We've got more pressing problems."

"More pressing than dying of a horrible disease?" demanded Alex.

"Dinner," said Temith, crumpling the scroll.

"Dinner?!"

"Or you could think of it as a polite prelude to a declaration of war, with refreshments," the doctor said. "King Belthar has requested a formal meeting with Deridal. You and I will have to be part of the retinue. We leave as soon as possible, to meet the Belthasian procession at the border."

NINE

It was afternoon when the two processions met, on a widening in the road that traveled between Deridal and Belthas. The last of the outlying farms had passed some time ago, and now there were only scrub weeds. Here, on either side of the road, were heaps of tumbled stones, the remnant of some long-destroyed fortification. Whatever significance this area had, Alex wasn't sure; many of the more formal royal protocols still baffled him. More than once, on hearing of some bizarre particular of etiquette or procedure that had to be followed, he'd been startled to learn that these weren't in fact ideas from the mind of mad King Carawan, but instead were deeply significant and important traditions passed down centuries ago. As they'd traveled, Temith had tried to coach him on formal table manners, but Alex was too distracted with his fears for the Rodeni, and for his own health, to pay much attention.

The Belthasian procession was much more impressive than the one he was accompanying. The Deridal procession consisted of himself and the other members of the Close Guard advisors mounted on striches. A group of soldiers and guards, with weapons ready, marched alongside. They wore only the minimum of their leather armor: breastplates and shields, so as not to become fatigued on the long walk. The General, wearing a blue silken tabard that dropped to his

back-bent knees, paced alongside. King Carawan himself rode in an
ornate cart, with arched canvas to shield him from the sun. It was
drawn by four draft striches. He was eating pickles out of a jar.
Valence sat beside him, in robes of blue and copper, steering the
birds. Celine had remained behind, in accordance with custom, and
Alex hoped she would be all right in his absence.

King Belthar traveled in a sedan chair draped with flags and pen-
nants and the stylized red bull design of Belthas. The chair was carried
by twelve strong men in elegant uniforms of white and crimson. They
looked sunburnt and tried, but their faces tried not to show it. Other
ministers and officials rode in small three-wheeled carts pulled by
other servants, and with them all marched twenty soldiers: the king's
personal Guards. They were wearing the colors of the king, with—
and Alex couldn't help but stare—not only shining bronze tips to
their spears, and wide blades of bronze hilted with copper at their
sides, but actual *plates* of that rare alloy on their bodies, like the scales
of a reptile, and bronze shields, painted with the bull design.

Metal of any kind was rare, and while bronze was the best known
alloy for common use, it was still very costly. The soldiers' gear
emphasized not only Belthar's wealth, but the loyalty of these particular troops. Any lesser men could have deserted and bought themselves
their own little kingdom elsewhere, simply by selling their kit.

Alex was staring in awe at this, when suddenly, in the carts of officials, he saw a familiar face.

Chernan, now wearing a robe-coat of fine blue wool embellished
with white trim and embroidery, had seen him, too. Temith looked
startled, and was about to say something, but stopped himself, and
shot Alex a warning glance. The three exchanged looks of surprise in
silence as the processions halted.

"Greetings and well met, my friend and neighbor," announced
King Belthar, from his chair. "I thank you for coming."

"Hello!" cried King Carawan, blinking at the gleam of bronze.
"And welcome to the lifestyle of the seventh day!" he added, to the air
in general. If he recognized his former wizard in the ranks of the
enemy, he didn't seem to care. Valence did notice Chernan, but gave
no sign either, occupied as he was with his role as King's Talker.

"King Carawan bids you welcome and is pleased to meet with our neighbor and friend," Valence translated smoothly. His white teeth flashed against his ebony skin as he smiled warmly.

"A friend is someone else's idea of movement," the king commented to Meridian, who was riding alongside the cart. She smiled, and tried not to giggle.

"I see we have a mutual acquaintance," commented King Belthar, with a cold glance to Alex. "A wanted young man, in more ways than one."

"Warm weather, if it's just another brick in the butter," complained King Carawan. "Besides, I know the darkness. When power narrows the areas of man's vision, the past reminds him of his neck."

"His Majesty knows that past problems are not of our concern now, and will not taint this meeting," Valence replied with another smile, and a seemingly casual glance at Chernan as he spoke. The magist arched an eyebrow and smiled like a cat. "Let us continue our journey without further delay. The token, please," Valence added.

One of Belthar's retinue stepped forward, bearing a disk of carved wood about a foot across. He held it up; on one side it was red, the other, white. At a nod from Valence, the token was heaved into the air, turning end over end as it flew.

"Seven!" shouted King Carawan, at a nudge from the General, and Valence substituted, "White."

The token thudded to the dusty road, red as a splash of blood.

"Splendid," said King Belthar, settling back in his sedan chair. "You will be our guests tonight." He drew the curtain back against the dust. Alex shook his head. Even the bizarre intricacies of animal behavior were nothing compared to the reaches the Humani mind could achieve when it wanted to complicate matters.

There was complicated shuffling in the ranks as the equivalent members of the parties moved to flank one another, before moving down the road toward Belthas. The two kings' transports went side by side near the front; though the curtains on the sedan chair remained closed, King Carawan leaned out of his cart and offered pickles to the bearers as they stumped along, and seemed disappointed when they refused.

Alex steered his strich until it was paralleling Chernan's cart, and the magist turned in his seat to give Alex a cool smile.

"Well, you seem to have done all right for yourself," he said, as Alex drew near and reined the strich in to keep pace with the cart. "I see they make you wear the Big Hat. Still, the pay's good. I trust the princess is as beautiful as ever?" He gave an oily smile.

Alex felt himself flush with rage and almost cause an incident right there. He was about to leap off his strich and try to strangle this smirking bastard who would threaten and mock the woman of Alex's admiration, when Temith interceded.

"Are you doing well in your new profession, old friend?" asked Temith coldly, whose strich paced along on the other side of the cart. He shook his head in hurt amazement. "I don't understand! What's gotten into you? Why are you serving Belthar, and why are you doing it with my ideas? Is your own power not enough anymore?"

"I'm sure I don't know what you mean, old friend," Chernan said with a confident smile. Alex's anger over the princess was replaced with the memory of the Rodeni.

"He means the Towers!" hissed Alex, mindful of the listening servants. "Temith's design! When we were working out the thing with the rats! What are you doing?"

"Perhaps I was . . . inspired?" Chernan said with a shrug. "But I assure you, I'm not infringing on your . . . field, or fields, Temith. The fulfilling of prophecy is, I'm sure you'll agree, a matter for magic, fate, and gods, not for scientists."

" 'The Bull drives all before him, like rats they flee his roar,' " Temith quoted softly. "Ha! My work is 'impious meddling' until you think you can use it, then you steal it, turn it around, and use it against us. And you call it magic!" He stared at his old friend. "Have you gone mad? Turning against Carawan?"

"He turned against us first, Temith," Chernan snapped suddenly. "Or rather, his daughter did. Maybe you can go crawling back like a lap dog, but I have more pride than that." Temith drew back, blinking, horrified. Chernan gave a dismissive toss of his head, and then looked at Alex. "You place too much importance on the Towers. It's a simple matter of pest control, I assure you," Chernan said airily. "It shouldn't trouble you so . . . unless, are *you* having some troubles with the Rodeni now, too?"

"What? What do you know about—" Alex began indignantly, and Temith shot him a glare that warned him to keep his voice down. Alex subsided.

"Of course, I must thank you for the concept, Temith. You always did leave such thorough instructions, I had no trouble translating them. I thought of giving you partial credit, a plaque at the base, perhaps, but, well, certain opinions . . ." Chernan gestured toward the sedan chair with its puffing porters.

"Why didn't you just use magic?" Alex hissed. "If you're so powerful—"

"I like to use my magic for *important* things," Chernan said, "though I'd be happy to make an exception for you . . ." He pointed a finger at Alex, who jerked back in sudden terror, all his bravado gone. At the movement, his strich leapt into the air, flapping as though it thought it could fly. Chernan just smiled and shook his head.

"That's not the important thing; the Rodeni are crowded into our city now, with nowhere else to go. You can't get us to kill them all for you, just because your king has a grudge," Temith stammered, still not sure what to make of all this. "This isn't like you, Chernan! Whatever happened to being too powerful to interfere in the affairs of mortals?"

"Perhaps I've converted. Become a . . . humanitarian, you might say. I'm sure you'll find we're willing to negotiate, once things are settled. I suppose we could make a Tower or two for Deridal, if the price was right," Chernan suggested. "We're working on ones in all the cities in the kingdom, anyway."

"But what about the Rodeni?"

"I've nothing against Rodeni," Chernan replied sincerely. "But we have to put our own interests first. Rodeni don't even pay taxes, most of them. We need to consider the welfare of the citizens that do." A thought seemed to strike him. "Did you bring your rat with you, Animist?" Alex had controlled his mount, but was still keeping a safe distance from the wizard.

Not that it will do me any good, he thought.

"Why?" Alex asked, suspiciously.

"Well, if you bring it into the city, it will be affected by the Towers. I borrowed some of your test subjects along with your notes, Temith, you know," he commented aside to the scientist. "They went simply mad, breaking their little teeth chewing at their cages, clawing their own little ears off . . . and poor Alopecia's eardrums ruptured, of course, when I was testing the large model . . ."

Temith was speechless, and could only stare in shock, but Chernan saw his expression.

"What's the matter? Isn't that part of being a good scientist? Torturing small animals?" Chernan asked innocently. "I was just trying to follow in your footsteps, really, old friend . . ."

Temith looked on the verge of an Incident himself, this time; Alex had never seen him so taken aback, or so angry.

"I left Mote at home," Alex broke in quickly, glowering, "but thank you for the warning." He pulled back and let the cart roll past him, dropping back in the procession behind the Deridal wagon. Temith and Chernan continued snarling at each other in hushed tones. Alex saw Valence watching them carefully.

Alex's mind raced. Why hadn't he thought of that before? But then, he'd become so used to thinking of Mote as something different, special, totally unlike the rough vermin that made up the majority of the rats of the world. He'd forgotten that she was, in the flesh if not the spirit, no different than they, and subject to the same problems. The Screaming Towers . . . What to do? Send her home? Trust her to someone for the long journey—but no, he couldn't; couldn't see Oetherwise without his Anim at his side and therefore could not do his duty to keep the king safe. He'd already thought of that, as he was wondering if he could quarantine her somehow, in case he did fall sick with the Rodeni's plague. But this was a more immediate problem.

He rummaged through his pockets, acutely conscious of Mote's touch on his neck, until he found what he'd been looking for: the beeswax seal from the scroll summoning him to this meeting. The scroll had been waiting in his room when he'd returned from Temith's study, and he'd folded it and stuffed it in a pocket and forgotten about it. In the heat of his pocket the beeswax had become soft and stuck with a fine layer of wool fluff. He picked as much of it off as he could, and brought Mote down, holding her cupped in one hand as he dropped the reins to the let the strich follow the procession as it might. Temith and Chernan were far ahead, and didn't seem to see him.

He rubbed the wax into soft beads, and carefully pressed them deep into the fine-skinned ears, trying to block the opening as best he could without letting the wax be pressed so far down it would be impossible to remove later. Mote didn't like it at all, but bore it patiently, her small twinges of

discomfort dislike reproach

flickering in his mind. From time to time he would share her senses, listening carefully to the sounds getting dimmer and dimmer, until at last the clicking of wheel and claw on stone was silent. He made doubly sure, with a swatch of gauze padded and wrapped down tight and secure to her collar, pinning the ears flat. Mote's

disgruntlement! discomfort!

was strong at this. Alex apologized profusely but silently, and fed her sunflower seeds, discovered in another pocket, until she stopped trying to claw the bandage off and fell asleep in his lap.

She woke again as they approached the city, and Alex tucked her quickly under the Big Hat. And then, through her ears, he could hear something: a muffled ringing, like that which Humani ears sometimes hear for no apparent reason. It was muffled, but persistent, and he could feel her

annoyance

at it.

The procession passed through the gates, and Alex saw the Towers. He counted five of them, though they were getting difficult to see in the darkness of night. Set up along the river at intervals, they were brick and cylindrical, with a stout wooden door in the base. A waterwheel jutted from the side, rolling along with the pace of the swift-flowing river. In arrangements up about fifteen feet from the base, and extending up like clumps of rushes from the tower to high overhead, were long thin pipes of ceramic and thick green glass. An overhang just below the pipes, studded with sharp chips, kept thieves and vandals from climbing up to reach the pipes. With the pipes were also conical funnels that amplified the sounds and spread it out in all directions. To Alex's ears, however, there *was* no sound; a faint sighing, like wind in the tops of pine trees, almost pleasant. Alex was impressed by the Towers, and wondered at how quickly they'd been constructed. The king had obviously thrown a lot of money and effort into the project.

Closer to the Towers, now, the ringing in Mote's ears was louder, and he could feel her discomfort and nervousness at it. It seemed to touch some chord of fear and repulsion that had nothing to do with any predator or coherent anger. She gnawed fitfully at the inside of the Hat, and broadcast her anxiety and dislike of the noise so that Alex, too, began to feel jittery and upset.

The procession wound its way to the castle; crowds in the streets were kept back by many carefully placed guards. While there was no bronze for the common soldiers, their armor shone of lacquered and polished leather, and the tips of their spears were the red of the hard strong stone quarried in the Phombei lands. He saw the General glancing around as well, and noting the show of military force. The hard reptilian face could not show much expression, but the feathered crest kept raising and lowering, a wary gesture.

Within the castle courtyard the procession halted, the riders dismounting and the porters carefully setting down their distinguished burdens. Here were more soldiers, not threatening, merely on display, along the walls of the courtyard and the battlements of the castle. As the guests were led through into the vast dining hall within the castle, still more soldiers lined the corridors like living statues on either side. In the hall, too, lit by chandeliers and high windows full of the gold of the setting sun, there was more sheen of bronze from soldiers standing ornamental guard on all sides. Despite all this, Alex was struck again by how dreary and ugly the Belthas castle was, especially now after seeing the airy, colorful comfort of the palace at Deridal. Alex wondered if King Belthar, too, had noticed this discrepancy, and was looking forward to the possibility of moving into the palace, once his troops had conquered Deridal.

Unlike the Deridal hall, this dining room had only a single long table, with benches for the soldiers with the party, and chairs for the officials, and fine carved wood and ceramic-tiled seats for the two Their Majesties. The queen and prince were not present; each member of the party was paired up across from his opposite in the other city. King Belthar not having an Animist, and King Carawan having never seen the need to hire a foreign minister, the order broke down somewhat at this end of the table and Temith found himself across from the pinched features of Minister Lespin, and Alex was once again facing Chernan.

The food was served: rolls of bread, and a thick chili of beef, spicy and warm. It was served out of communal bowls, as was all the rest of the food, but still by tradition the two kings ate nothing and drank nothing. This annoyed King Carawan, who complained peevishly at first until soothed with the promise that there would be stuffed apples on the way home. Valence and the General did not eat, either, partly out of caution and partly because it would have been unkind to King Carawan, who was sitting between them. Alex and the other lesser members of the party were under no such restrictions, and ate heartily. Musicians in an alcove played upon drums and bowed lyre and wood-flute.

Alex's duty was to watch Oetherwise, and he did so, scanning the room as he chewed, but there was no sign of any interference from the spirits. A few presences flitted about, drawn perhaps by the tension in the air, but they were distant and unmanifested, representing no danger. Chernan still had that faint glow about him, but nothing more. He watched Alex in mild amusement. Alex knew that Chernan knew Alex was watching him Oetherwise, and Alex could tell, too, that Chernan wasn't bothering to watch Alex in similar fashion; after all, an Animist couldn't do spells, couldn't do much of anything. There was nothing he needed to watch for. So, out of subtle contempt, he allowed Alex to watch him, without returning scrutiny. It irked Alex, but he kept up his glare, with Mote peeking unseen through a hole in the Hat, behind a feather. Chernan didn't notice her. Alex wondered if the magist had ever once had any need to feel afraid, once he'd mastered his powers.

"Do you still work from your old quarters?" he asked Chernan casually. The discussion at the other end of the table was muted by distance and music, too much to make out any details, but King Belthar seemed calm and confident, while the General's rumbling tones implied stubbornness and caution.

"No, I simply don't have the time," the thaumaturgist replied, with a dismissive gesture of his fork. "I always felt I was at my best as

a royal wizard . . . and my new employer is, I must say, far more worthy of my time than the last one." He glanced up the table, to where
King Carawan was trying to tie his matted locks under his own nose,
and then glanced back to Alex with a pitying expression.

"You've probably moved in up here, then?" Alex guessed. "I've
got a place myself, at the palace; nothing fancy, but it's certainly better than I'm used to."

"You probably got my old room, I shouldn't wonder. Red Delphini, correct?"

"Uh, yes, actually. I didn't notice anything of yours . . ."

"I took most of it with me," Chernan replied, "although there's
probably a few talismae lying about. Yours, if you'd like them," he
added magnanimously. "Of course, you can't use them, can you? Not
yet, anyway . . ."

"Uh, thank you," Alex said, in surprise. He hadn't noticed any
such talismae: charms, with minor spells for good luck or health or
protection, that sort of thing. But then again, enchanted objects
didn't glow in the Oether seen by an Animist, only living things did.
Odd that the magist would even mention it. It made Alex feel
uneasy, too, to know that Chernan now knew where he slept. Perhaps this, too, was some kind of ploy, or trap . . . Alex stared at his
plate. There were too many questions these days, too many possibil-
ities and secrets. He couldn't be sure of anyone or anything. Maybe
it was time to find out some facts, instead of just listening to what
people were willing to tell him.

"I took most things with me from Deridal, and everything out of
my tower. I've a place here; has a view of the gardens, plenty of room
for my rituals, top floor and access to the library. Can't complain,
really." Chernan helped himself to more maize-bread.

They made small talk awhile about the differences of royal life in
the two cities. Despite the animosity between them all, it was
expected that while under the enemy's roof as guests, they would be
polite, and the enemy the same. This protocol must not be violated;
rudeness could lead to instant hostility, and a total breakdown of the
thin ice of diplomacy. Keeping all this in mind, and using the most
polite form of the etiquette, Alex excused himself to the privy.

There were guards in the hall, and guards outside the privy chamber, and a guard inside where the sink, water jug, and soap were as well, staring straight ahead with blank expression. Alex looked at him. "I'm not going to fall in, you know," he told the guard, but the man did not move or reply. Alex went into the stall, firmly shutting the wooden door behind him.

Here at least there were no guards; there wouldn't have been any room for them. Alex ignored for the moment the malodorous hole and the bucket of water beside it, and looked up instead, to find the small ventilation holes set high in the wall. Just about rat-size.

He lifted Mote up to one, and she skittered down into it and along, crawling quickly away from the stink of the privy. Alex put the privy to its proper use, thinking that the guard was probably listening and ready to make a full report. He came out, washed his hands and dried them, and draped the damp square of towel over the guard's arm. The guard didn't move, but Alex hurried out anyway. He got back to his seat just as the next course was served.

Now he could no longer watch the Oether, and his senses were somewhat diffused, as though he was here, but kept daydreaming about

dark crumbling stone, scuttle clamber claw mustiness, ringing in the ears—stop and smell—food and smoke—not right—farther on, scuffle climb, into the hollow spaces, the mortar and the mends

The conversation at the other end of the table became audible in a lull in the music.

"—and thus I would feel safer, my good friends, if you were under my protection," King Belthar was saying. "Especially as you are somewhat isolated, with the threat of bandits and Rodeni and . . . who can say? Possible invasion from offshore? I am sure you realize I have more than adequate military forces to assure your defense."

"You will be pleased to know, then, that we are more than capable of providing our own defense, should the need arise. You need not worry your kind heart on our account," replied Valence, just as smoothly.

"Still, I gather you've been faced with some problems of late. Just . . . rumors, I've heard. I should make some recompense, for I fear it may be result of the Rodeni we have decided to suffer no further.

When they were driven from our cities, I gather they came to lodge in yours, bringing, as such vermin do, all manner of troubles. These things my foreign minister so tells me. I would be glad to help steer your noble kingdom through this time of trouble," said King Belthar, and the General's response was lost in the renewed vigor of the musicians.

climb and turn and the stone warm, up and up, ringing in the ears—sign and smell of rats, males and females, weeks stale now—smell of flowers and soap—a crack showing light—dimness and space beyond, the smell of a stranger—no—farther on and in and up . . .

"Alex?" a voice said, as someone tapped him on the shoulder. Alex jumped, and turned to see Temith looking worried at him. "Are you all right?"

"Oh, sorry, I'm fine," Alex stammered. Temith frowned, but not at him, and glanced down to the other end of the table.

"Better stay awake, this doesn't look good," he said, watching the royal figures. Alex peered down that way, but saw only smiles and the imminent arrival of a large casserole.

"Looks fine to me," he said, puzzled. Temith shook his head.

"King Belthar's trying to goad them into insulting him, wanting to know why we won't trust him to help run Deridal. Valence is doing well at dodging it, but if Belthar doesn't stop subtly insulting His Lordship I think the General might say something we'll all regret."

"How can you tell all that?" asked Alex, straining to hear. "I can't hea—"

can't hear anything, anything but the ringing, the horrible high scream that never stops—here is the smell, the burning sharp smell of the smelly-man—here there is another smell, a bad smell, a meat and fur smell, the hole beneath the wood and the tile below

fear panic!

"Alex? Are you sure you're all right?" Temith shook him back to awareness again, and gave his food a suspicious look. "I wouldn't put it past them to put something in the food to skew our Animist. I know you said you tend to be susceptible—"

"No, no, I'm fine—what were you saying?"

"I was saying, I can make out what they're saying by their mouths. The way their lips move. Well, not the General's. But Alex, are you sure—"

Alex glanced over at Chernan, who was watching them carefully, and gave the man a friendly smile, then turned back to Temith. "I'm fine. Please, how did you manage to learn that? I'd be interested to know—"

"I just picked it up somewhere," Temith replied, glancing worriedly back to the kings, but Alex tapped his arm and caught his attention again.

Lowering his voice, he said, "I'd appreciate it if you'd explain something absolutely fascinating and lengthy, and not mind if I stare absently past you."

Temith was taken aback a moment, then thought quickly, and launched into, "Well, it's very curious that you should ask that, Alex. In fact, the explosive black powder was originally invented almost a century ago, by the Viveri, who use it in mining, of course. It wasn't until Makoka the alchemist rediscovered it at his College, thirty years ago, that its use became widespread. Of course, it's such a simple compound it's a wonder no one had stumbled upon it before . . ."

Alex nodded approvingly and went back to

fear panic

Noise beating in the ears, shivering in the stone, the cold and the stink of chemical and meat and heat

Go on. You're all right, Mote. You're all right. You're fine. Careful, girl, quickly . . .

inch by inch out into the open . . .

Alex blinked and smiled and nodded at Temith, who gratefully wrapped up his impromptu lecture.

Some part of his consciousness skittered quickly across the cold tiles of a floor, searching for the smell of paper and ink, terrified by the smell of the room, the sound in the air; coming like the breeze from somewhere. An open window, Alex realized, and sent a burst of sympathy and apology and love to Mote. He looked around, wondering what direction she might be in. A view of the gardens, close to the library . . .

There, paper and ink, coming from above. Climb! Claws in the rough stone, back against the edge of this thing of wood. Surface, smooth and tile. Large thing. Paper things.

inquiry?

A blur. Mote backed up and move her head, to Alex's request, until at last the thing swam into view. A piece of paper, with words written on it: "We will be traveling to meet the Deridal delegation. Your presence is requested. You will be expected—" No, that wasn't right. This was a countertop, by the tiles of it. Letters, and a flat wood thing to slit them open, inkwood and ink. A big vase full of bay branches on it, too. A desk is what's needed. All wood. Wood and paper and a smell like he's always sitting there. A smell—

fear!

A motion, below, distantly seen. Mote froze, crouched in terror. The motion stopped, became now only a distant blur on a lighter blur. The smell was strung thickly through with terror.

Alex couldn't see, but could guess: Alopecia. Maybe that bastard Chernan deafened her with his experiments, but I bet she can still see and smell. Hasn't seen Mote yet, or she'd have moved to pounce . . . but she might have smelled . . . The way out was blocked; Mote couldn't climb down and escape from this countertop without alerting the cat. Alex wished rats had better vision so he could be sure; without sound, without sight, with the medicine smell of those damn bay leaves blown by the breeze . . .

It gave him an idea. He comforted Mote, and hoped that Alopecia was settling down for a nap. Then an image, an idea, and Mote understood.

Carefully, quietly, Mote grabbed the thick end of the letter-slitter in her sharp teeth, and pushed. It clicked; she froze again, and Alex quickly comforted her; it was her smell and sight they had to worry about, not sound. Under his guidance she shifted a little, placing herself behind the vase, behind the aromatic leaves, the wooden knife in her teeth.

The point of the slitter stuck at the base of the vase. A wait, then shift, slide; the slitter's point edged into the groove between tiles, and slid farther, and stuck again. Piece of inkwood, thick and smooth and clean, grab it in the teeth, pull, slide. Force it under the slitter, raising the fat end upward . . .

The shape was gone from the patch of lightness.

Quickly! Push down on the fat end of the slitter! Push! It does not move! Mote jumps up and down on it in panic but it does not—

An explosion of fur and stink and panic! Mote leapt up as the world was full of cat, cat that pounced, claws slashing that catch and toss, scratching but not managing to sink deep, cat with teeth and breath a-stink, cat that landed right where she had been, atop the lever. The vase toppled.

The distant crash, unheard in the dining hall, echoed in Alex's mind at that of his full, untouched wineglass going over, as he jerked back in panic, arms flailing.

Cat vanished, the air full of cat-fear-stink. Mote landed in the bay-leaf ruin, teeth chattering, eyes bulging. Clambered down, sped to the safety of the wall, and ran! The cat had gone. Here now were pillars of wood, and the smell of desk. Climb!

Thinking quickly, Alex slapped a fist down onto a peppercorn that had escaped his plate.

"Spider!" he gasped, to the shocked looks of the people around him. Luckily, the attention at the other end of the table seemed to be elsewhere. Chernan looked at him contemptuously, but Temith looked rather baffled. The servants, horrified that they had allowed an arachnid to invade the formal supper, groveled and apologized profusely.

Recovering from the shock, Alex thanked the servant who cleared away the spilled wine and squashed peppercorn, and refilled his glass. He pretended to sip at it, as his thoughts went elsewhere—

Here are papers and papers and papers, and the smell of herbs and ink, struggle up over the edge, pull, struggle, and—NOISE!

Screaming and shrieking and endless wail as the bandage slips; run in blind panic to the corner of the desk, frantic burrowing among the papers—

Alex tried to comfort her but the ears were full of the sound and panic, too much for the small and simple spirit which cowered in fear and pain, the screaming, the screaming like a dagger in the brain, and Alex in desperation shoved her mentally behind him.

And now there was screaming in *his* ears, and he pressed his paws to his ears to stop it, shoving the wax in deeper; gritting his teeth he grabbed the end of the bandage and pulled it tight again, yanking it under his collar, trying to draw it tight without thumbs—

In the banquet hall, Mote blinked, and jerked upright, dropping the funny thing in her hand. Splash! There was a—thing! Many things! So clear it must be close, but there was almost no smell! And sounds! But not the bad sound. There were nice sounds instead. Relieved, she licked her flat funny palms and groomed her—oops, no muzzle. Hmm. Hair? Groom the hair, run fingers through it.

Alex drew the band tight and blocked out the worst of the bad sound. He checked to see how Mote was doing—

groom the shoulder—No. *no?* No. Smile, nod. *?* Like this. *understanding.* Eat something, just relax and keep doing that. *concern?* No, I'll be fine.

—and then shook his head carefully, cautious of his bound ears, and padded across the papers, lifting his tail above the papers to keep it from making noise.

Mote smiled and nodded at all the moving things, and picked up something that smelled good. Holding it in her two hands, she nibbled daintily at it, while smiling and nodding at the moving things.

Alex found what he was looking for at the end of the long desk; the red-leather bound book on which Chernan's smell, and the smell of fresh ink, were strong. Among the papers Alex had noticed quite a number that smelled faintly of Temith, the herbal soap he always used, and covered with his spidery writing. Chernan's handwriting was bold and looping, and this book bore a mark on its cover that looked like a stylized C.

The binding was heavy, but he forced it open and pushed the pages back. The writing was confusing in its loops, and he couldn't seem to hold his head properly to bring it into focus. A moment's thought, then he climbed off into the rubble of things, and emerged a moment later shoving a magnifying crystal in front of him with his paws. He shoved it up onto the pages, and found that it helped; he had to keep scooting it across the page to read.

One of the moving things—people, they must be, made sounds at Mote. She smiled and nodded, as she'd been taught and told to do. A plate of things was offered. She had to bend down and sniff hard to smell them right, but they smelled tasty, so she took a handful and started to nibble on them.

It took a long time paging through the notebook; he checked back in with Mote, and found his mouth half-full of chewed cigar while the assembled company laughed and snickered. General consensus seemed to be that he was drunk, but of course he hadn't had a drop. He cautioned her again, and asked her to please just sit still and only eat what was in front of her, and she sulkily agreed. He hoped he could find out what he needed before she got bored and decided to take his body on a scamper through the dining hall.

He drummed his claws on the edge of the page. His neck hurt from having to tilt and twist his head to bring the pages into focus; and the wide angle of vision was disorienting. The air was full of smells, but so strong it was impossible for Alex to know what they all were. The high scream in his ears was almost to the point of pain, but he could force himself to ignore it, knowing it was harmless.

He found what he was looking for in the most recently written few pages of the book; the ink still had a sharp smell. He couldn't read it well, could only grasp a few sentences, and the style was more of Chernan's memos to himself than any clear journal of his activities, but it was enough. He wanted to read more, farther back, but time was pressing. He knew he couldn't find his way back through the walls alone, but he hopped off the desk to the chair, and from there leapt to the floor, and scuttled for the wall.

A tidal wave of fur came out of nowhere and smashed into him, claws on his back, teeth on his neck, crushing him, pinning him to the floor. Alopecia's stink was all around him.

A normal rat, or Mote, would likely have been frozen into squealing terror. But Alex was an Animist . . .

"Shoo! Scat!" he tried to command, but it came out as only a chittering squeal. The cat ignored him, and Alex remembered she couldn't hear, anyway; but her teeth were coming down . . .

And Alex was also Humani, and Humani are primates, with an inborn tendency to aggression.

He twisted, and sank his long yellow teeth deep into one furry paw.

Alopecia screamed, yanking her paw away, dragging Alex with it, as she tried to shake him off. He let go at the top of the arc and twisted himself as he landed, onto the cat's back. He sank his teeth again, unmindful of his scratches and the cat's frantic flailing, noting only the deep satisfaction of a good chomp. His own claws scrabbled, making little impression on the thick fur, as cat and rat spun around on the tile floor.

Alex let go, and was flung to the floor, and he landed there crouched, teeth bared and bloody, but Alopecia had had enough, and fled once again. This time Alex wasted no time in making his way to the shelter inside the walls. He stopped here, to inspect himself; a few minor scratches, but nothing more. He sighed in relief, feeling guilty, despite his brush with death, at having to hurt an animal that was only doing what it was born to do. He adjusted the earplug until the screaming of the Towers was muted deep again, then gently prompted Mote and rotated around her.

He found himself with his nose halfway down a mug of water, and brought his head up, blinking. He'd managed to attract the attention of most of this half of the table, with the exception of the small group at the end, where conversation was getting even more heated. Temith was hiding his face in his hands in embarrassment.

Alex glanced across the table, and noticed that Chernan was missing. Deciding that he might as well play along, he leaned unsteadily over to Temith and asked, in slurred tones, "Where's the wizard gone?"

Temith peeked sideways out from between his fingers at Alex, and Alex gave him a conspiratorial wink. Temith looked baffled, but brought his hands down anyway. "He threw down his napkin and left in the middle of your little . . . performance," muttered the scientist. "Went storming off. Surprised you didn't notice; he was staring at you the whole time . . ."

Alex gulped in cold fear, but at the far end of the table there was a clatter as the General stood, knocking over his chair with a lashing tail.

"This meeting can serve no further purpose, and we have far to go this night. We thank you for your hospitality, but we must leave now," his voice rumbled across the hall.

"Not staying for dessert?" King Belthar asked pleasantly.

"The dessert is just cultivated by irritation," King Carawan replied, with a cheerful wave. "Starlight and dewdrop are waiting for my appointment down at the risk of self-contempt. There is no good-bye."

With the king guided before them, Valence and the General strode briskly away, and among the rest of the Deridal embassy there was much quick dropping of forks and pushing away and standing to follow. Alex stood up, and felt a thick inner queasiness, probably from the cigars he'd eaten. He staggered weakly after the company, his mind only partly able to control his body as he searched frantically for Mote.

She was running through some nameless passage; he got the impression of cold stone and darkness. He urged her to find a way out, quickly, and felt her speed increase, the nose scenting for the smell of fresh air.

Alex lagged behind, feigning drunkenness, as the group mounted up in cart and strich. He could feel Mote trying to find them, working her way along outer walls, but it was very dark now and he could not imagine where she might be; rooms and rooms away, perhaps. He stumbled and fumbled with his strich, stalling for time, but then the General, fuming, came up behind him. Claws grabbed him under his arms, prickling sharp, and hoisted him bodily into the air and slammed him down atop the skittish bird.

"We are leaving *now*," growled the General, and Alex looked around frantically, trying to find some other distraction. Then, below the tiles of the main archway, he saw a small furry face peek out, and got an impression of fresh air and empty space.

As the procession passed beneath the archway, Mote dropped out of the crack in the wall like a failed bat, and landed neatly in Alex's outstretched hands.

From a window across the courtyard, a single figure saw this. Chernan, his feet still wet from the spilled vase in his wrecked chamber, set his jaw in anger as he watched the procession leave.

They rode off at a brisk pace, the soldiers jogging to keep up. Once they were out of the walls of the city and well into the darkness of the countryside, Alex turned to get the General's attention, just in time to catch a kick that tossed him clean off the strich and sent him tumbling into the dust fifteen feet away.

"Blasted fool of an ape-boy!" roared the General, springing after him, leaping right over the strich. All his feathers stood on end, and he looked twice as large and ten times as vicious. Mote clung to the saddle and squealed at the Therop as he went over. "Drunken idiot! You brought us humiliation! Shame! Dishonor!" The pupils of his eyes were dilated in fury.

Alex rolled over, in time to dodge being landed on, as he shouted, "They started the plague! It's a curse! It's Chernan's magic!" He scrambled to his feet as the General pivoted around his stiff-tail and struck at him again. The foot smacked into his rib cage and tore down, knocking him over and crushing the air from his lungs. If the General had still had his toe-claws, Alex would have been opened up like a banana. The foot picked him up and tossed him in to the air.

"Steady, General! Stop!" Valence yelled. The General did not hear, or pretended not to, and struck out with his hand in a slap that spun Alex around in midair and dropped him back into the dust. The clenched claws had torn three long welts across his chest.

"Deep roots are not of that! No!" admonished King Carawan, waving his half-eaten stuffed apple. The General, foot raised to stomp Alex's writhing form, glanced over at the king, and slowly lowered his foot, and his plumage. He glared down at Alex, jaws working, and then carefully lifted up his other foot. He gingerly removed Mote from where she was clinging to his ankle by her teeth, like a small but furious bull terrier. He dropped the rat onto her Animist, who was sitting up, panting for breath, with blood streaming from his nose and chest.

"Plague . . . they started . . . wizard . . . curse," Alex wheezed, as Mote tried to groom his cheek.

"What are you going on about?" Temith asked, leaning down from his strich. Alex gulped, spat blood, and got to his feet, keeping a wary eye on the General, who glowered silently.

"The sickness . . . the soldiers, the Rodeni. It's magic. It's a curse. I couldn't see it clearly but now I know. Chernan's doing it, through the Rodeni. That's why they built the Screaming Towers; they don't want any Rodeni coming back to infect them."

"Alex, you're drunk, aren't you?" Meridian said gently. "This is really very—"

"No! I'm sober! Listen, I know this is true. It makes sense. Besides, I read Chernan's notes . . . I sent Mote to look in his notebook," Alex answered, glaring at the General. "But she can't read. So I had to— trade places with her. That was her, eating those cigars, not me."

"I'm still not sure what you're getting at," Temith said, puzzled. "But then, the ways of magic have always puzzled me—"

"The magic's only a part of it, I think. Temith, you speak Rodeni. You've studied them, I know you have, you've studied everything else," insisted Alex. "What happens when you crowd them all together? Why can you only carry so many on a ship, for example?"

"They fight for more space," Temith said, slowly. "They get very aggressive. They can't seem to help themselves . . . like lemmings."

"Right! It's how they're made! Why? Why would they evolve to fight for space?" Alex asked rhetorically. "Why does anything? Because crowding . . ."

". . . makes them more susceptible to disease," finished Temith. "Population explosion leads to plague."

"Yes! You see, Belthar planned it, with Chernan's help and Temith's notes. Crowd the Rodeni into Deridal. When the Rodeni are crowded, they fight for space. They have to. If they stay crowded, then disease can start to grow and spread; any shaman can bring down a plague-curse and Chernan's more powerful than any shaman, it would have been child's play for him."

"Either way, Belthar would benefit," Valence said thoughtfully. "If the Rodeni wear down our forces fighting inside the walls, or if they breed a plague that will spread to Humani. But still, it seems rather a lot of complexity to go through . . ."

"That's Chernan's style, though," Temith said sadly. "Prophecy and symbols and irony. It's the kind of thing a wizard would think of."

"It's madness, is what it is!" cried Serra, who had taken advantage of the pause to bring out more food. "No offense meant, Your Highness," she added to King Carawan, as she handed him another apple. He was leaning back in the cart, enraptured by the night sky.

"Astronomy!" he said gleefully, taking the apple while still staring upward, and he held the apple aloft. "A star!"

"Not madness," said Temith, "just . . . perversity. A game, using the Rodeni as pawns."

Alex said, "The Rodeni tried to fight. I stopped them, stopped their shaman that was trying to save them. Somehow, I managed it, kept them from fighting. But in doing so I just made it easy for Chernan. It was easy to start the disease, and even easier to make Humani sick, too, and now the Humani will blame them for . . ."

Valence, who had been sitting quietly in thought, now spoke slowly. "Then, don't you see, there's validity for everything Belthar does to the Rodeni. If they fight their way out in Deridal, then he can say, 'See how vicious they are, they turn on their protectors.' If they don't, but stay crowded and bring disease, then Belthar can say, 'See, they're filthy, they bring plague.' And with this 'proof' behind him, he'll have the support of every Humani on the island to carry out his genocide of the Rodeni. And the destruction of Deridal will just be another step in his 'pest control' program."

"Very fascinating," growled the General, "but now that we know this, let us move on. This sickness. Do you know how we can stop it? I sense I will shortly have need of every soldier we can get."

"I don't know . . . I just know how to see magic, not how to stop it." Alex tried to wad his shirt up to staunch the wounds on his chest; though they were shallow, they still bled. "I don't think the sickness is supposed to kill Humani . . . just make us sick. But the Rodeni are smaller, and . . ."

"I suppose the Belthasians thought they were being reasonable by not killing all of Deridal's Humani," Valence commented dryly.

The General had been bobbing his head, a habit of his when thinking. Now he said, "A third of our troops are sick. In another week, it might be over half. Belthas does not like to lose citizens, even soldiers; nor do they like to damage the cities they intend to conquer. They prefer subterfuge and negotiation to direct combat. They might hesitate to attack us at our full strength . . . but so depleted, they would stand a much better chance of a swift, clean battle."

"But if we can tell the priests, maybe they can make up a counter-spell, find some way to undo the curse," began Alex.

"If we get a chance," interrupted Temith quickly. "On your guard!"

The company turned, and saw the approaching cloud of dust in the Night Sun's ruddy light.

The General barked orders, and the Deridal soldiers rushed to form a circle around the king's wagon. Valence reached into the back of the wagon and pulled out a bundle, and started throwing weapons to the others as he called them by name. Alex looked up as his name was called, just in time to catch his smakjab. Beside him, Temith was looking grim and holding a fencing spear. The other advisors had their weapons ready as well. The outer circle of soldiers also wielded weapons; Alex found himself part of an inner circle composed of his fellow advisors. In the center, the king was being held gently but firmly in his seat by the paw of the General, who stood behind him with a massive double-headed, bronze-bladed halberd that must have been ten feet long.

"What if they just want to talk to us?" he whispered to the scientist. Temith shook his head.

"At that speed? Either they found out about your discovery, or the king's managed to work up his courage to open hostilities."

"Isn't this dishonorable? I thought Belthar—"

"He'll put a good light on it for his people. Shut up now, and concentrate," said Temith, as the charging foes came closer. Alex saw they were all mounted on striches, and as they approached Alex sounded, as loud as he could, the strich alarm call.

The organized charge broke up into a chaotic scramble, but the enemy had not intended to enter into combat mounted; a strich did not have enough mass to be effective in a melee. Deridal's own striches, tethered to the cart in haste as the enemy approached, bucked and struggled with no effect. The running birds jumped and bolted, however, their riders flinging themselves off. The thirty some soldiers arrived at last in a confused muddle rather than a solid wedge.

They had hurled javelins as they closed; the front line of Deridal soldiers was quick to block these with their wooden shields. A few hit home, however; there was a scream of agony from a man, and hissing honks from the striches. The enemy had swords; the bronze flashed in the night. Alex realized these must be some of the king's elite guard, trusted to this dishonorable mission. They also had short spears ready, against the slightly longer spears of the Deridal soldiers.

The enemy employed simple jabs and thrusts—crude but effective, but the Deridal soldiers could parry these, and disarm them with their own spears, then keep the enemy from coming close enough to use their short bronze swords.

The numbers told, however, and for every Belthasian that fell there were two more to take his place, while when a Deridal soldier fell, he left a gap in the defensive ring. The Deridal soldier in front of Alex jabbed with his spear; Alex heard the crack as the tip shattered against the enemy's bronze breastplate; then a scream, and a spattering of blood. The Deridal man fell, revealing his slayer with bronze sword bloodied, facing Alex.

As the man charged, Alex struck out in pure panic with the smakjab, and missed. The man's sword raised, and Alex found himself with his back against the wood of the cart. He brought up the smakjab in defense to parry the blow and managed to knock it aside. Then from his left Temith darted in, and thrust his fencing spear into the soldier's armpit, between the plates of armor, and withdrew it again in a single smooth motion.

"Come on, Alex," Temith said, as the man tumbled, "remember your training. Defend the king. If he falls, it's over."

Behind them, a soldier had hacked his way through the rear defenses and climbed up onto the wagon. The General turned and brought the halberd around in a tearing sweep; head and body tumbled away on opposite sides of the wagon, and the king applauded. The head landed by Alex's feet; he kicked it under the wagon so as not to trip on it, and tried to concentrate on his training and not think about what he'd just done. On the other side of the cart, he thought he heard Meridian scream, and Serra curse. Valence struck out with a heavy short staff, and there was a double clunk as a soldier got first his breastplate, then his skull, bashed in.

Another soldier appeared in front of Alex, wielding a spear; he stabbed it forward. Alex ducked to the side, and the spear thudded into the wood of the wagon. Alex brought his smakjab down hard on the soldier's hands gripping the spear; there was a satisfying crunch, and the man screamed and let go. Alex brought the smakjab around in a two-handed sweep that connected hard on the soldier's head, then spun the stick in his grip and stabbed, catching his opponent in the groin. The man dropped with a gurgle; not dead, but with no intention of fighting anyone at the moment. He turned to say something to Temith, and saw the scientist stab with his spear again, catching a man through the midriff; the soldier staggered back, crying and screaming in pain. Alex stared in horror at the man's pathetic writhing and pleading.

The distraction was almost fatal; Alex looked away to meet another soldier, sword coming right for his face. A sweep of motion passed him from above, the General's halberd slicing past like a deadly pendulum, and the soldier was knocked aside and tossed away, lifted off the ground by the blade in his skull before he slid free. Blood splashed Alex's face, and stung in his eyes.

Then suddenly, it was over. Six of the Deridal guards were dead or unconscious, the rest were sorely wounded, and Valence was bleeding badly from a spear through his thigh and a sword-cut across his scalp. Meridian, the poet, had been felled by a sword in her liver and lay crying piteously; her toksticks lay in a pool of her blood. Serra, gore-spattered but unhurt, was kneeling beside her, trying to staunch the bleeding. Five of the enemy had regained their striches and were beating a rapid retreat. The remainder were scattered about the road.

"Should we chase them?" Temith asked, looking exhausted.

"No. We must get back to the safety of the walls," snapped the General, dropping his halberd into the cart. One of the draft striches was down and thrashing, crippled by a sword-gash across its leg, and two of the riding striches were speared, almost dead. The General untied one of the unharmed ones, and passed the reins to Valence. "King's Talker, come with the king. The rest, follow as you can." He dipped a quick bow to the king. "With your permission, Your Majesty?"

"Has sent us a thing licensed for the ride of your mind," said the king graciously, with a slight nod, and the General picked him up in his arms like a child. The king put one companionable arm around the feathery neck. The Therop turned and ran toward Deridal, with the king waving merrily at them from over the General's shoulder as they went.

"Undignified, but it gets him there," grunted Valence, as he climbed painfully onto his strich, and rode after them.

Alex, shaking with adrenaline, helped Temith and Serra. They bound the wounds of the injured. Meridian went unconscious as they tried to help her, and then died a few minutes later.

That was how quickly it went, Alex thought; one moment Serra crying and cursing, Temith looking miserable, head shaking. Then Meridian, plump poet and silly singer, paler than ever now in the pink starlight, slumped and stopped breathing. No last words, no heroic gestures, no scene. Just gone, and the world went on.

The Belthasian weapons of bronze left horrible open wounds and punctures, deep and bloody. Alex was used to the Lemyri weapons, blunt, meant to break bones and bruise, rather than slash and disembowel. Another soldier died before they could help him. The dead and wounded were crowded into the cart with the bronze armor and weapons of the fallen enemies. The two injured striches were beyond help, and Alex ended their suffering, quickly administering a lethal blow to the back of their skulls as he'd been taught at College. Then Alex and Temith climbed into the heavily laden cart, and Serra took the reins of the striches and led them, rubbing tears back harshly. The soldiers who were capable walked alongside, weapons ready, glancing warily back the way they'd come.

"What if another attack comes?" Alex asked, as the chef-and-minister-of-trade-and-finance clucked to the striches and they started painfully off, slow and limping.

"Then they mustn't find us," replied Serra, with a deep breath. She was pulling the cart off the road, along the stony ground. "There's another pass that goes almost to the walls, not even visible from the main road. We'll take that."

"Another attack will come, though," Temith said, still working on tending the soldiers in the cart, with Alex's help. "A big one. I think we can say the war's begun."

"A lot more work, and a lot more death, before we see the end," Serra said. She sighed. "Tem, sometimes I wish . . ."

"I know, I know," Temith said, squinting against the starlight as he tried to thread a suture needle. "But wishes only work for . . . you know."

Alex said nothing. Mote, huddled on his shoulder, sneezed.

The pass was little more than a goat-trail widened by time into something the cart could just barely scrape along. At times it crept along the canyon walls a matter of inches from a sheer plummet. Alex was sure that at any moment the edges of the road would crumble and spill them, but it did not. Serra led them with skill and ease along the safe route. It took longer, though, and it was well past dawn before they reached the border.

They reached an outpost keep of Deridal. Here they found activity and confusion, as ten guardsmen were posted here, trying to work out schedules of patrols. As they approached the city itself, the activity was increased tenfold.

Deridal was in full preparation for defense. Along the wall's battlements were soldiers running to and fro with baskets of arrows and bows. Drills were being conducted, routines practiced, plans discussed. Throughout the mess strode the General, barking orders right and left, checking defenses, inspecting troops. From time to time a soldier would double over and vomit over the wall, sick with the flu. It was apparent that already the lack of troops was showing; there were not enough men to the positions, and those remaining were having to struggle to complete their tasks.

"You'd better let me know what we can do about this curse-plague, so I can get started on treatment," Temith told Alex, as they helped the injured into the crowded hospital. The stink of bile was sharp in the air, and almost made Alex ill just at the smell. He already felt dizzy; he'd had no sleep, through the long and miserable ride back to Deridal. Another of the soldiers had died on the way. Alex was starting to feel like he had during Exams, when lack of sleep would weaken his mind and make the real world seem to flicker with half-seen shapes, and the Oether crackle with malice. They said that a weakened, exhausted mind was particularly vulnerable to hostile spirits.

"How should I know how to stop the curse? It's a thaumaturgist's spell. I'm not a wizard!"

"You're the Animist, and if this is magic, it's your field," Temith retorted. "What do you think we pay you for? It isn't to wear the Big Hat, I'll tell you."

"What can I do against magic?" Alex asked helplessly, yawning, as Temith began giving orders to the nurses. "What can anyone do against magic?"

"That's what I've been asking myself for years. Disease, I can fight that. Drought, poison, parasites, even madness, I can fight. Not always win, mind you, but fight. But magic?" He shook his head. "The only thing that works against magic is more magic. And I don't have magic. You do. We'll send for a priest. I have some of the Aesculans helping, but we need to do something now. So do something. Check for magic."

Alex started to retort, then stopped himself. Instead he took out Mote, and stood in the middle of the room, and shut his eyes tightly. Mote sat up, and looked around, and then dropped back to all fours. Alex opened his eyes and shrugged. Temith, busy with some powders, wasn't watching him but looked up as Alex spoke.

"Well, I . . . I don't see anything." The Oether was clear, and Mote sat unruffled on his shoulder. "I didn't expect to. But Chernan's book said . . ."

"What? What did it say?"

"Something about . . . 'A curse on them, on those who help them . . .' " Alex tried to remember the exact words. "And 'what holds them together will bring about their doom, in blood and hate' . . . and 'The Towers will keep us safe from the Rodeni. The curse will sicken their soldiers . . .'"

"Typical wizard prophecy," snorted Temith, but then he grew thoughtful. "But you can't see any magic? All these men—" Temith waved a hand around at the crowded hospital of groaning, puking men, "—are sick, with some kind of magical curse, according to you and Chernan, but you don't expect to see anything?"

"Animists can only see active magic, alive magic," Alex explained. "Spells, and spirits, and people. Because we see through the Anims. Mages and priests, they can see *all* magic, including enchantments on things like talismae. I can't see those in the Oether."

Temith paused, and looked at him, and then looked down at his desk. "So . . . so for example, if I picked up this pencil—" he did so, showing it to Alex, "—and I said, this is a magical pencil . . . you wouldn't know if I was lying or not?"

"Please, Temith!" Alex cried. "That's not important. Of course there's no such thing as a magical pencil. This is about curses. Curses sometimes show in the Oether, but sometimes not." He shook his head. "A curse that clings, like one that makes someone think they're a beast . . . or turns them *into* a beast . . . that does show in the Oether. But a curse that cripples someone, for example . . . that shows in the Oether at the moment it happens, like lightning. Then it vanishes, leaves the person crippled, and there's nothing to see in the Oether, not even for a magist."

"All right, all right," said Temith, throwing down the pencil. "If it clings, makes the person sick, then it's got to show on someone. Maybe the magic's on the sick Rodeni. Maybe they're the source. Did you check?"

"No," said Alex, yawning. "When I was there, in the tunnels, I didn't have Mote with me, and—"

"All right, leave that blank and go on. Maybe it's like that second kind of curse you mentioned. Hits someone, makes them sick, and then leaves, leaving them sick. How could this curse just hit the soldiers? Would Chernan have to come and point to each one—"

"No, he'd just have to find some way to curse them, with a potion or a cursed talismae, or something, some powerful item of bad magic," Alex said, trying to remember old lessons. "Rather like a disease, really. Some way to get them to come in contact with the magic. Like walking over it, or seeing it, or breathing the air around it."

"Like some kind of metaphysical poison in a well," Temith muttered, and then froze.

"What?" asked Alex, as the scientist stared into space.

"I am an idiot. Send someone down to find my robes and tear them into rags to mop up all this puke, because that's all they're good for, I am such an idiot. It's in the water. I'll bet my life that's it."

"But we all drink the water!"

"No, we don't! We drink palace water, that's from springs. But where the barracks is, where the Rodeni gather, that whole area—that's all served by one branch of the aqueduct. That's where the sickness is. I thought it was just because that's a poor section of town, open sewers, Rodeni, but . . ."

"But one of my friends is a soldier, and a Rodeni, and he's not sick."

"The black one? He lives in that palace outbuilding. He and the other Rodeni archers practice outside the walls, I've seen them. He's not sick because he's not drinking that poisoned water!"

"Cursed, you mean," Alex corrected him.

Temith made a dismissive gesture. "Cursed, then. Curse the water, spread a sickness . . ." he said.

"Probably the magic affects the Rodeni one way, and the Humani another, that would explain the different symptoms," said Alex slowly.

"Or, the curse makes the Rodeni sick, not enough to kill them, just as it isn't enough to kill Humani . . . but crowded in there, stressed *and* cursed now, their resistance to disease is gone, and they get sick with a regular Rodeni respiratory illness. They probably all feel like puking from the curse, too, just like the soldiers. But they can't."

"Oh dear bloody sunrise," Alex moaned, thinking of Len and Trit, suffering and waiting for death in the darkness.

"We'll do what we can for them, Alex. But at least we have a hypothesis to go on, now. You'd know a curse-thing if you saw it? Oh, you said you can't. Only living spirits. Damn." He drummed his fingers, frowning in disappointment.

"Well, it might not show in the Oether to me," Alex said, "but I'd know a curse-talisman if I saw one. They have to be enchanted, you see. That means carvings, and symbols, and usually something deeply evil and wrong. Like, like an effigy, stuck full of poison pins, or something like that. It would be pretty blatant, I would think."

"Then check the aqueduct," Temith told him. "Start at the barracks and work your way back. If you don't find anything on the structure, you might have to get inside it. Get some of the Rodeni to help you."

"The Rodeni, I've got to warn them, tell them to stop drinking it . . ." said Alex. "If you're right, what can they drink, then?" Alex asked. "Rainwater? Can we run a pipe from the palace springs? I know it's not a lot, but we know it's pure, we've been drinking it—"

"No! No, we can't do that." Temith paused, and seemed lost in thought. Then, without another word, he walked into his office, beckoning Alex to follow him. The Animist did, and Temith shut the door and turned to him.

"Listen. I wasn't going to tell you about this, but you are an advisor, after all, and you'll be able to better decide what's safest for the Rodeni to drink if I tell you." He looked around, as though to make sure they were alone. "You were saying, earlier, about how the Rodeni should have tried to fight their way to more space, but you stopped them, and thus maintained the crowding that helped spread the plague?"

"Yes," Alex said, looking down miserably. "When I think I'm the one that caused this . . ."

"No, no, listen. It's not your fault. I've no doubt you were influential in the Rodeni decision to maintain peace, but really, it could only happen this way here. Listen. I'm going to tell you something that not many people know. Even the king doesn't know this. I know it, a couple of the other advisors do. I don't know if Chernan does or not." Temith drummed his fingers on the desk, then took a deep breath. "All right. You've noticed, haven't you, what a . . . *nice* city this is? Not much crime, people seem to get along, that kind of thing?"

"Yes?"

"Ever wonder why? I mean, you look at Humani as a species, we're not normally this easy-going."

"I just assumed . . ." Alex shrugged. "Low taxes, plenty of food, a benevolent and entertaining ruler . . ."

"That's part of it, I'll grant you. But that's not the whole story." Temith shook his head. "I was curious about it. Did some tests. You know the palace's water is provided by the subterranean springs, right? And most of the rest of the city's water is provided by the aqueduct."

Alex nodded, not sure where the scientist was heading.

Temith stared at his desktop for a long moment, rubbing his hands together nervously, then sighed. "There's something in the water from the aqueduct. I'm sure they didn't know it when they built it, hundreds of years ago. I think the river that supplies the aqueduct filters through some odd minerals. I'm not sure. I never dared investigate too much, for fear the secret would slip out. Whatever the substance is, it acts like a calming influence. It makes people— Humani, anyway—more slow to anger. More placid. And it almost certainly works just as well on Rodeni, if not better." He sighed.

"You mean . . . the citizens are all drugged?" Alex was horrified.

"No, not really," Temith protested. "I've done some research, and I think by now as a population we're not much influenced by it. But all these Belthasian Rodeni, they've never ingested it before. It makes them much calmer than they would normally be. And, you see, if you take them off it, start giving them palace spring water, then their anti-crowding instincts are going to take over. They're going to start fighting."

"That won't be so bad, will it, if we can get them to fight Belthar's army?" Alex suggested. Temith shook his head.

"When they start going aggressive, they stop thinking. They become a mob. They'll attack anything that they can, and we'll be closest to them."

Alex shuddered. "All right, I see your point. I'll go and check the aqueduct and the cisterns, and see if I can find any magic there . . ."

"Be careful," Temith warned him. "If you get struck down by a magical curse, I can't do anything for you. And I don't think the priests will be very sympathetic toward an Animist."

Alex shuddered, but nodded. "Believe me, I'll be careful."

"And bring me back a water sample," Temith added. "If you find anything out of the ordinary, send word, and I'll see if I can find a priest to send, to try to undo the curse." He shook his head. "But right now, I need them to help me with the sick. Good luck, Alex." Temith gave a little half-salute, as one advisor to another. Alex drew himself up, and returned it, and then headed for the door.

TEN

The streets of Deridal were crowded; word of the war seemed to have spread without any need for town criers or any other messages. People were stocking up on food and drink, or just milling through the streets, trying to find out what was going on. He saw no sign of any Rodeni about; there were usually some in any crowd, but not now. It worried him, made him run faster.

The duskward side of town was on the lowest slope of the hill, hence it was where all the drains tended to terminate. It was a low-rent area; there were old warehouses, a slaughterhouse and tannery, and of course, the Rodeni. But even here Alex didn't see them; from time to time he thought he caught a glint of an eye or a vanishing tufted tail in the shadows and alleys, but he couldn't be sure. Remembering his previous experience with them, Alex didn't try to go after the Rodeni now, instead concentrating on reaching the barracks and training field, right up against the city wall.

He'd been here before, visiting Luken, and had seen then the neatly kept dirt field with its practice dummies and training equipment, and the airy, dormitory-like buildings at either end that housed some of the soldiers. Some soldiers still lived in Deridal proper, with their families or friends, coming to work each day like any other professionals, so the barracks were not as large as might have been thought. Across from that was the small infirmary where injuries were dealt with; serious cases could be stabilized here and then moved into the hospital closer to the palace grounds.

The training area right now was an organized mob of soldiers, jogging past in neat groups, many of them carrying bundles of arrows or barrels or other things Alex couldn't identify. He stepped aside quickly as a groaning team of them came by, hauling a heavy-wheeled cart.

Just outside the training area was a large open plaza, with a fountain in the center of it. The fountain's water spilled off into separate basins for washing and drinking. It was fed by a branch of the aqueduct, which passed overhead. A few soldiers stood at ease around the fountain, some of them soaking their feet in one of the basins. In front of dwellings around the plaza, Alex could see piles of wood chips, signs of the Rodeni habit of gnawing, but still not a furry face to be seen.

Alex scanned the area Oetherwise, with Mote looking around from his shoulder. Nothing seemed out of the ordinary; the Oether was quiet. He inspected the soldiers carefully, but none showed any signs of magic. Still, he realized, this meant nothing. He wished he were a true magist, a shaman or wizard, who would have been able to see any malignant magic on the inanimate fountain.

He went up to the fountain; it was of ancient stone, decorated by carvings smoothed into blobs with wear. The relaxing soldiers looked up in annoyance and surprise as Alex came cautiously up to them. He picked up a broken spear and started to poke gingerly at the water, careful not to splash any on himself. But surely, if the curse was right here, he'd see it activate. He'd have seen it strike these soldiers, too. So, he should be all right. Still, better to be careful. Cautioning Mote to stay safe and dry atop his head, and under no circumstances to drink the water, he tried to hoist himself up onto the higher pools, touching only the dry brick. His grip slipped, and he almost fell, but recovered himself. The two soldiers, exchanging glances, but recognizing and acknowledging the Hat, moved away instead of questioning him.

He finally hoisted himself up to stand on the edge of the highest pool and peered into it. It was about three feet square, with algae growing on the brick. Gingerly, Alex reached in with his broken spear and patted around on the algae, but didn't find anything that hadn't been there long enough to be growing algae. He checked the other pools as well, with the same results.

Everything seemed fine. Even a minor curse would require something, Alex knew, some kind of rune scratched into the stone or a talisman wedged into the flow of water. But there wasn't anything. Not here, anyway. He looked up at the aqueduct that fed this fountain. It was high, some ten feet above him, and covered specifically to prevent people from tossing anything into it. Still, there were cracks and gaps in the terra-cotta half-tubes that covered it, some of them quite large; big enough for a ritual bundle to be tossed through.

He had to go into the barracks area to borrow a ladder, and bumped into Luken in the process. Alex didn't dare tell Luken everything, but convinced him to come along and help look for anything suspicious in the aqueduct. He said, to cover the truth, that Temith suspected some contamination had gotten into the water and was making people sick. Luken snorted and said, "That's why I drink beer," but he came along anyway. Alex didn't like misleading his friend, but consoled himself with the thought that, if Luken should be caught by the curse, he could be restored by the priests. Alex wouldn't be given that chance.

Luken was willing to help him, and together they manhandled the ladder into position, and Alex climbed up to peer into the gurgling darkness of the water pipe. It was about two and a half feet wide, slick inside, and dark with the chuckle of water. At once Alex knew something was wrong. The water should flow silently, not this gurgling sound. And there was a smell, a smell of death and decay, noticeable here even over the stink of the nearby tannery. He peered into the darkness, into the Oether, searching, waiting, dreading what he might find, expecting at any moment the crackle of magic, but there was only a slow dull dread. That was worse. Mote nuzzled his ear, sensing his fear.

love comfort

"Luken, can you help me?" he asked, climbing down. "There *is* something there, I think, but I can't see it or reach it. I can smell it, though."

"How nice. Join the Deridal Army and get to play with dead cats in drainpipes," grunted Luken. He shifted the ladder a bit and went up it himself, and peered down through a crack in the pipe, then snaked one long arm in. Alex flinched, expecting to see a flash—Wait! Was that a sparkle, a flash of magic drawing back to strike?

"Stop! Wait!" he shouted, and Luken jerked his hand out.

"What? What?" Luken demanded, shaking his hand and flinging water down. Alex, squinting hard, Mote cheeping on his shoulder at the effort he was forcing on her, didn't notice. His attention was fixed in the Oether . . .

Come on, Mote, I know there's something there, there's got to be, help me, find it!

frustration concern fear

There were always some swirls and light visible in the Oether . . . was that a brighter patch, around Luken, around the pipe? Was there something more? He squinted, and Mote cheeped, but he couldn't be sure. Sometimes, when he'd first begun his training, trying his hardest, he'd think he was seeing things in the Oether that others claimed didn't exist. Perhaps it was only his imagination, or perhaps he could see more than most.

"I . . . I'm not sure," Alex stammered, "I thought I saw—"

"Come on, quit screwing about. It's cold up here and it stinks. Let's get this damn thing cleared and over with." Luken fished about, wrinkling his face at the smell. "There's a rope, or something. Slippery, and it's tight. Holding something in here. What the—" He felt around some more. "It must be tied up to something, but . . ." He peered up along the pipe. "There's no more holes. You'd have to tie it from the inside, somehow."

"A Roden could do that, I guess, if they didn't mind getting wet," Alex said, doubtfully. "Can we just cut the rope, do you think," he asked, "and let whatever it is wash into the fountain?"

"What if it's bigger than the outflow pipe?" Luken said, pointing to where the pipe narrowed to force the water to shoot into the fountain. "It'll stick there and then we'll never get it out without breaking the damn pipe open." He peered into the hole again, and made a face at the smell. "Yuck," he complained, as Alex stood underneath and peered up anxiously.

"Careful!" the Animist called.

"Yeah, yeah. What're you so jumpy about—oof!—anyway? Whatever this thing is, it's dead, really dead." The Oether was still quiet. Luken fussed with the unseen rope, grimacing as he tried to get a grip on it. "Really bad angle for this," he complained, as the ladder rocked. "And whatever this damn dead thing is, it's heavy," he added, as his muscular arm tensed and pulled hard on the rope. Slowly it began to move.

"Uh, really, be careful," Alex said, squinting up. "Whatever it is . . . it's probably very nasty. Don't touch it. It might, um, make you sick."

"Thanks so much for that information," Luken said, "since it's about to make me sick anyway, from this godsawful stink." And Alex could smell it, too, much stronger now, the sudden thick miasma of decay and evil. Luken, not possessed with Alex's knowledge, just gagged and cursed and got another grip on the rope, and hauled. Slowly the rope moved, then, with a horrible slurping sound, the resistance gave way. Luken, on the ladder, was taken off-balance by the sudden slack, and the ladder tottered and sideslipped, banging hard into the pipe, cracking it, and then buckled. Luken gave a shout and clung tight to the rope, but it was no longer offering any support. As Luken fell, his weight pulled out the object, shattering out through the cracked pipe like a hideous nightmare of horror. Luken tumbled to the cobbles, and the sodden thing landed on Alex, who was staring up in horror despite Mote's frantic cheeping in his ear.

Alex saw, tumbling out of the pipe in a shower of rubble and water, the rotting, cloudy-eyed face of the Rodeni shaman Clak, yellow teeth bared in a grimace of hatred from beyond the grave. Talismae of death-charms hung around his neck, the skin was peeling back from the putrescent flesh; from the expression in the gaping jaws, he'd died a horrible, agonizing death, and now the tormented corpse served as a fount of evil, twisted magic—

The corpse landed right on Alex, who was too horrified to move. It crushed him, knocking him down. The explosive prickle of evil magic that he'd been expecting, dreading, came exploding all around him. There was reeking putrescence, ice-cold and thick with the murk of evil, juices running from it. He could feel the taint of evil magic

burning on his skin, his brain screaming in panic and terror, the stink
clawing up his lungs. Mote was squealing and squealing. He could
feel the curse working its way inward, like a botfly maggot—

Luken staggered to his feet, cursing, gagging, and shouted for
help. He stared at the Animist curled up in a fetal position, spasming,
dry-heaving helplessly, the rotting corpse of a Roden beside him.
Mote stood on his head, squealing plaintively.

They brought him back to the hospital, and at his weak insistence
dropped him off in the area overseen by the allopathists. One of them
pushed a wheelbarrow with the disgusting object the Animist had
insisted they bring along with them. A few of the priests and priestesses of Aescula watched them go by, two soldiers supporting a staggering, retching boy between them, and shook their heads pityingly,
making signs for the warding off of evil. Alex collapsed into uncon-
sciousness before he reached the bed, the fires of fever and sickness
pounding through his head. Mote's frantic concern was only a dim
silver echo at the back of his mind.

He woke up some time later, and found Temith standing beside
the bed, shaking him gently. The sheets were soaked with sweat and
Alex's insides felt knotted into burning tangles. He groaned, weakly.

"How are you feeling?" Temith asked, his voice showing more
curiosity than concern.

"Bad," Alex croaked. "I think . . . I don't think I'm going to
make it. Listen, I need to tell you something, about the princess . . .
she needs help—"

"You'll make it, Alex, I promise. You didn't even drink any of the
water . . ."

"But the curse . . . it's killing me, dammit," Alex interrupted, and
grunted as a spasm gripped him.

"I gave you a treatment for the bacterial contamination from the
corpse, just in case," Temith began, but Alex interrupted him.

"But it's not working, is it? It's magic, Temith! Only one person
can stop this . . . You're going to need to find . . . Chernan . . ."
wheezed Alex. That bastard Chernan, who had killed the Rodeni
shaman to use him for his curse. Even though Alex hadn't liked Clak,

no one deserved to die like that, and to have their death used to kill the ones they'd tried to protect. No wonder the curse was so evil, so wrong.

Temith watched him in sympathy, as though debating within himself, and then sighed, and took out a small corked flask. A few runes were etched into the glass, and it was half full of a thick blue liquid. "You probably won't trust it . . . but the priests gave me this. They said it should counteract the curse. Once I told them about it, they knew what to do. Chernan may be powerful, Alex, but so are the gods. But I don't know what's in it," he added, to forestall Alex's next question. "I know it works on the normal soldiers, though."

Alex thought, feeling Mote's trembling under his chin, weighing his chances. He glanced into the Oether; of course the potion wouldn't show, but he wanted to make sure Temith wasn't under some magical influence himself. Whatever the potion might do to his Animist abilities, it still might stop the curse . . . and without that, he'd surely die. Besides, it probably couldn't be too harmful, it wasn't *designed* against Animists, surely . . . unless this was another plot . . . Another cramp crumpled him, and he grabbed the bottle.

"I don't care, I'll try it," he gasped.

"One swallow, that's all," Temith cautioned. "It's strong magic, they told me."

Alex bravely took a gulp; the liquid burned like fire, but instead of the bitterness he was expecting, it was sickly sweet, with a strong flavor. He wheezed as it coursed down his throat, and Temith took the bottle from his shaking hand. Alex could feel the burn spread down his esophagus and explode in his stomach, a warmth that seemed to be driving away the tight pain. He concentrated, looking for any sign of magic, hoping he could still even sense the Oether. He couldn't be sure, it was hard to detect magic on yourself, but . . . it did seem to be working. Slowly he relaxed.

"I think it's working," he panted, and sighed, slowly uncurling from his flinched position. Yes, he could feel himself relaxing. He burped, with the aftertaste of the magic potion, and slowly allowed himself a sigh of relief. He glanced up at Temith . . .

Who was watching him with an oddly innocent expression. "Feel better?"

"Yes . . . it works. And I can still sense Mote, and—" he checked quickly, "the Oether, too . . . no aftereffects from the potion that I can see . . ." He blinked, and nodded.

"Well, I should hope not . . . It was just herbs and sugar water, after all." Temith was smirking openly now.

Alex stared at him. "What?"

"The potion. Aniseed, peppermint, bismuth, water and sugar. Made it myself. Good for upset stomach."

"B-but . . . but the curse—"

"Luken was fine when he brought you in."

"But the other soldiers—"

"Sick, yes, but a corpse in the water supply will do that anyway. I gave them medicine for it, now that I know what it is, and they're getting better. I gave you the same stuff, while you were unconscious," he added, holding up a syringe. "You should have felt better when you woke up. But you didn't. You needed—you *thought* you needed a magical cure, for a magical illness."

Alex couldn't think of anything to say.

"And since you wouldn't be able to tell if it was magic or not, I just made one up and told you it was," Temith said, with a smile. "And it worked. I'm therefore going to conclude that this is not a magical illness, despite looking like one. Unless I've suddenly acquired the ability to magic, without noticing." He looked thoughtful then. "You know, probably a lot of people could pretend to do magic, like Meri did with the walnut. Without an Animist to say if it was real, no one would know. And if an Animist can't tell if a curse or an item is magical, then even they'd be fooled by a trick like this. Some charlatan could sell you a lucky rock or something—" Alex blinked "—and you'd never know otherwise. Only a real priest or a wizard could tell it was just an ordinary rock."

"But why would Chernan go through all that trouble?" Alex wondered. "We *know* he's a wizard, we've seen what he can do. There's no doubt of that. Why *wouldn't* he just make a magical curse?"

"Why build the Screaming Towers, when he could just wave his hands and kill all the Rodeni?" Temith asked, with a shrug. "Why is he fooling around as Belthar's wizard, when we know he could have magically transported himself into Carawan's bedroom and killed him in his sleep? I don't know! It's like he's playing some kind of game, where only he knows the rules."

"But, wait . . . the Rodeni were getting sick before this," Alex said. "While Clak was still alive, he was telling them that the sickness was caused by the fact that they were crowded . . . he can't have been doing that and been dead in the aqueduct at the same time."

"So maybe the Rodeni were getting sick from crowding," Temith said. "Or maybe the curse, Chernan's curse, is only on the Rodeni. You didn't check *them* for magic."

"I don't understand any of this," Alex wailed. "How can that thing, that talismae of Clak's body, killed in pain and draped in runes . . . how can it not be magic? When that . . . thing fell on me, I could see, I could feel—"

"You *thought* you could. But if it was magic, you'd still be sick now. The soldiers didn't know about any curse. They thought it was a flu, and when I told them I had a cure for it, and they believed me, they got better." Temith shook his head. "But you, you were convinced it was magic, and that you weren't going to get better until magic fixed it. I thought about just trying to explain, but I thought a practical experiment might be useful. The only way you could have died from this would be if you let yourself, no, if you set out to *kill* yourself, with fear and stress."

"Not magic," Alex said, trying to understand. He wasn't sure what to think. He was ravenously hungry now and couldn't deny that he seemed to be cured, but Temith's crazy idea that the malignant magic had been all a figment of Alex's own imagination was hard to swallow.

"There's no doubt magic's involved somewhere, I'm sure," Temith said. "Maybe Chernan needed to save his power for something else, something worse. That's why we need you. Now get the hell out of bed and get to work, Belthas's army's on the move and we need to get ready."

"You have an antidote for this? For the tainted water, not for—" Alex waved a hand vaguely.

"Yes, of course," answered the scientist.

"Will it work for the Rodeni?" Alex asked, getting to his feet and looking around for his boots.

"I don't know, I don't have any around to test it on," said Temith. "Besides, they've got something else, remember? They have their own plague, a real one and probably magical, if what you've told me is true."

"They've still been drinking that water, it can't have been doing them any good," insisted Alex. "I have to help them! They're dying!"

"You're coming back to the palace first," Temith told him. "We're moving everyone into the main tower, it's the most defensible place. We'll need you to check for magic, for spies, for any sign of . . . him. We know he can transport himself magically, and I know he can make himself invisible, and he can change his shape, too, or so he used to brag. He could be waiting for us, and we'll need you to spot him, if he is."

Securing the center of the palace didn't take too much work. The king, protesting vaguely, was ushered up to the topmost room of the central tower. This was a large airy room with several large windows leading out to small balconies, which the General quickly bolted. Furnishings were minimal—a few chairs, a table, and a lot of stuff piled into the corners: books and star charts, and astrolabes and telescopes. The roof was domed; it was from this roof that the General had been singing. Temith started rummaging through the telescopes and pulled out several of them, handing them to a passing soldier with orders to take them to the men watching the wall. Other soldiers were working to nail boards over the windows and collecting weapons. Alex's fellow advisors were all present. Valence had seated the king in a chair and was standing beside him, his leg bandaged, while Serra directed the bringing up of food and supplies to be stored in the small room. Alex kept a gimlet eye on all the advisors, the General in particular, and on the soldiers and servants that moved to and fro on their busy errands, but no sign showed of anything unusual in the Oether.

Princess Celine came pounding up the steps, and burst into the room, holding a short staff that was shod with bronze. Her hair was wet and unbound, falling in wild ringlets like a waterfall of tails down her back and shoulders. Alex blinked helplessly. Mote chattered her teeth in annoyance.

"Why wasn't I consulted?" she shouted, pointing her staff at the General, who jerked his head back in a birdlike motion. "What foolishness is this? You want to trap us at the top of this tower, so we'll have nowhere to run if the Belthasians break through the wall? Whose side are you on, General?" she demanded, her beautiful chest heaving with fury under her silk gown. Alex was rapt with wonder and worship that she would have the strength to defy the General so. He stepped forward, intent on taking her side in any conflict that might arise, but neither she nor the Therop seemed to notice.

"I am, as always, loyal and protective of your father, my king, Princess," said the General, his voice a soft thrum. "His safety is my primary concern."

"Then why do you trap him, doom us?" retorted the princess, pointing around at the barred windows. "Safe! As a coffin is safe! There's no way out!"

"There are ways. Ways and ways," the General said, linking his fingers. "We have to do our best to make this place defensible. I only regret we did not have time to complete the fortifications I requested. Parliament funds—"

"You and your fortifications! Your walls! What good are you? You failed your own savage kin, slave, and now you fail us." The General's jaw clenched as Celine continued, "If you'd listened to me, and we'd *attacked* Belthas, instead of hiding like chickens in a shed—"

"*You* might want us all dead, but the choice is the king's, not yours, hatchling!" roared the General, and the princess whirled her staff at him in fury, smacking him hard across the chest before he could dodge. Alex was stunned. He'd never even managed to land a blow on the Therop.

"A new error in the evening sky faded from a distant voice!" admonished King Carawan to his daughter, who rolled her eyes. He then turned to the General, and said sternly, "No fighting with your think face, you'll hurt your instep."

"I wouldn't dream of it," hissed the Therop, glaring at the princess.

"How's your head, chicken-lizard?" she retorted. She spun her staff with cold skill. Alex was openmouthed in admiration.

"Stop it!" Valence shouted, stepping between them, frowning. "General, remember yourself. Princess, please know we are doing the best we can. The wall around the city is thick and strong. We have good defenses, Temith's devices, and many of the soldiers are recovered. I am sure that will be enough, but in case some spies or assassins have infiltrated the city, it's better that we remain in these defensible towers."

"You see? We are doing the best that can be done, Princess," said the General, growling. "You and your father will be quite safe here."

"I'd sooner take my chances on the ground, outside your death trap of a tower, and outside your idiotic wall, you treasonous, treacherous *animal*," Celine spat, with anger and fear in equal tones in her voice. She turned and ran down the stairs. The General blinked the nictitating membranes of his eyes, and gave a surprisingly Humani-sounding sigh.

"Mammals," he said, in tones of exasperation.

"Teenagers," Serra corrected. "Separate species. No offense meant, Alex."

"One of us had better go after her," Temith said, with a weary sigh.

Valence gave a wry grimace. "In the mood she's in? I've already gotten wounded in this war, thank you."

The advisors turned to look at Alex.

"Would you mind?" Valence asked, hopefully. "Maybe she'll listen to you. You're closer to her age—"

"And besides, he's probably got training in handling vicious beasts," muttered Serra, and then yelped at a jab in the ribs from Temith.

Alex paid them no mind. "Me? Go talk to the princess?" he asked, wide-eyed. "I . . . I'd be honored."

jealous complain sulk

Alex pushed the rat back under his hat, as Temith added, "We're pretty much done for the moment . . . you can go and run that other errand of yours, too, if you hurry."

"But do try to find her," Valence put in, "and get her to at least come back to the palace. Then we'll need you back again—"

A soldier poked his head into the room and dipped his head in quick salute to the General. "Sir, the far scouts report the front of the Belthasian army's crossing the duskward border. He can't get a good count, he says. There's a lot of dust, but it looks like several hundred at least."

"Carry on," the General grunted, and the soldier withdrew.

"Probably should hurry," Serra told Alex, and he nodded, and took off.

He found the princess in the side gardens, sitting in the middle of a small grove of cypress. In a pool nearby, some of the ornamental albino axolotls grinned hopefully up at her, but she ignored them. Her head was bowed, but she didn't seem to be crying, just frowning. Alex stopped before she noticed him, and quickly pulled Mote out of his hat. He held her in his hands up to his face so that he could look seriously into her little black beady eyes.

"Listen, Mote. I know you don't like her, or at least, you don't like that I like her. But the advisors say we have to talk to her, all right?" he subvocalized, concentrating mentally on the words, hoping some sense of them would sink down to the Anim, even though she could not understand language. The rat's wiggling whiskers tickled his nose. "So this is part of our job. And besides, you know I'll never leave you for her. I can't. You're my Anim, you're a part of me, I couldn't even get rid of you if I wanted to; I'd die. So please, please, don't bite her, or scream at me, or something like that. All right? Will you be good?"

There was a mulling mental pause, and then Mote pinned back her ears and half-shut her eyes.

sulk agreement sulk

Her jaws worked a little; just displacement activity, but even so it looked like she was grumbling under her breath. Alex gave her a grateful cuddle and rewarded her by rubbing her behind the ears, which she enjoyed, then he let her scramble back under his hat.

Alex stopped at the edge of the encircling trees, and cleared his throat. Princess Celine glanced up sharply, then seemed to relax when she saw who it was. She had her short staff on the grass beside her, but didn't reach for it.

"Oh. It's you," she said, glumly. "I suppose they sent you?"

Alex nodded, and approached cautiously. "They wanted to be sure you were safe."

"Safe!" Celine gave a bitter laugh. "What do they know about it?" She shook her head. "We've trapped ourselves . . . but that's nothing new. We should have attacked Belthas long ago. If we'd knocked them back before they could become a threat, we wouldn't be in this situation now. But does anyone listen to me? No." She picked up a twig and began breaking it into segments.

Alex sat down across from her. "I'll listen," he said. "And I can try to help convince them, if you think it would help—"

"They won't listen to you if you listen to me," Celine replied savagely. The stick had been broken to bits. She threw them into the pool, and the axolotls investigated them thoughtfully. Alex helpfully pushed another stick toward her. She took it and began methodically destroying it as well. "We should attack Belthas. It's their capital city, it's closest to us; if we could take it, and hold it, we might be able to turn things around. It's where the treasury is, where the king's family is. Yes, Belthas has a large army, but it's mostly conscripts, from other conquered cities. I think it wouldn't take much to turn them. If we could get in there somehow . . ." She shook her head. "But no one listens to me. They only listen to the jabbering husk that used to be my father, and he only wants peace. As if peace could be achieved without war!" she scoffed, and grabbed another stick. Alex was about to point out the essential logical flaw in this, but wisely stopped himself.

"What are you going to do?" he asked, instead. "They, the other advisors, wanted to make sure you were all right—"

"I'll be all right, on my own," Celine said coldly. "I can take care of myself. They know it, too."

"But if we lose," Alex said, "if the worst happens, if the enemy breaks through . . ."

"I can take care of myself," Celine insisted. "I can run, or hide. As long as I'm not trapped in that tower with that . . . thing." She shuddered. "Besides. I know that he . . . the wizard . . . he's going to tell them to take me alive. They won't be trying to kill me, just capture me. As long as I'm alive, I'll keep fighting. Don't worry about me."

"I can't help it," said Alex. "I can't help but worry. I, I care about you." He could feel himself blushing like mad and he was suddenly apparently fascinated by the axolotls. They smiled their goofy smiles at him and flapped their gill-ears lazily. He risked a sideways glance up and saw Celine give a faint smile, too, not goofy at all, but warm and yet sad, and his heart gave a thud.

disgust annoyance sulk

"Uh . . . any more problems with . . . you know, him, the thaumaturgist?" he asked, quickly changing the subject. He didn't want to say the name any more than she did; sometimes magicians, like demons and spirits, could hear their names wherever they were spoken. He hadn't seen or sensed any Oetherwise activity around the princess since their previous talk, but he thought he would check.

Celine shook her head. "No . . . somehow I think he's concentrating on something else. On the war, I assume. He's probably got some massive spell planned."

"Did they tell you what he'd done to the water, and to the Rodeni shaman?" Alex asked. Celine shook her head, and so Alex told her about it.

"Doesn't surprise me . . . he always hated priests," she said.

"But what bothers me is, he must have gotten someone, probably another Roden, to help him," Alex said, thinking about it. "The pipe was narrow, and the way Clak's body was tied in there, someone would have had to be right in the pipe. Only a Roden could fit."

"The Rodeni helped build it, you know, and the drains here and in Belthas, too, as a matter of fact. So of course, it's big enough for a Roden, but it must have been awkward for Chernan."

"Impossible, more likely," Alex said, shaking his head. "But then, he is a wizard. I suppose nothing's impossible for him. But I don't see why he didn't just use some magic on the curse itself, then. Temith says he's wondering where Chernan is *really* expending his power."

"Temith," said the princess. "I don't trust anything he says. He hates anything he can't understand, so he makes up explanations that sound good, theories that don't really make sense; he doesn't really care about anyone, just about things, his work, his ideas. He wanted to drill a hole in my father's head, can you imagine!?"

Alex didn't want to. "I'm sure he means well," he muttered, but Celine just made a scoffing sound. Even though it was like a snort, it was still a very beautiful snort. She looked miserable, and Alex wished he could do something, anything, to distract her from her misery.

"Here," Alex said suddenly, remembering something. "Please, don't be sad. Look, wait. Watch this." He glanced up, and gave a short sharp double whistle.

After a moment, the cypress trees were full of fluttering, and the resident flock of blackbirds descended down around them, landing on the grass around Alex, some of them even landing on his hat. Alex tried to look cool and mysterious as the birds landed on him and around him, hopping curiously about. Celine stared in most gratifying awe and wonder, then reached out a hand to touch one of the glossy black birds; the bird took fright and flew, quickly followed by the rest of the flock. They retreated to the trees, whistling peevishly amongst themselves. After slowly learning that, after hearing that whistle, scatterings of seeds and crumbs could be found around the area where the Animist was, they were disappointed now to find none.

He'd been saving that trick for weeks, hoping to use it in more cheerful circumstances as a way to impress the princess. Even now, it brought a smile to her face, and it was well worth it.

"Magic!" she cried, delighted.

Alex didn't dare tell her that it wasn't.

Most of the palace was all on the ground level, and almost all the palace life went on there. The few high towers, at the center of the complex, had been abandoned since the time of the king and queen's accident. Now the dusty rooms were thrown open again, and officials, servants, and royalty swept in. The open halls and peaceful gardens of the lower levels would be useless for defense, if the Belthasian soldiers managed to enter the city.

Alex hadn't managed to convince Princess Celine to rejoin them, but she had been convinced to return to the towers themselves; she moved about from room to room, tense and nervous. Alex had tried to follow along with her, but she was still angry and frustrated and, Alex could guess, terrified of the impending battle, and she did not want company. Rather than risk her anger, Alex had gone to report back to his fellow advisors, planning then to go and find the Rodeni. But reports had come in that the Belthasian army was marching quickly, and Alex was forbidden to leave the palace grounds. He thought to protest, but instead went out to wander, and to search for a Rodeni soldier, or any Rodeni at all, that might be able to pass the word along to the rest.

One of the intermediate floors of the tower was quickly set up as a temporary home for the king. Furniture was recovered from underneath dustcovers and pressed into service. A few floors down, provisions in the form of casks of water, wine and rum, salted and smoked foods and vegetables, were arranged in one of the few rooms with a fireplace. The rest of the royal retinue was left to find quarters as best they could, once the king had been settled and went down for his nap.

Alex kept wandering, partially to get a quick look at all the servants and others who had come into the towers with them, in order to make sure none were being influenced from the Oether, and partly still searching for a handy Roden. There didn't seem to be any at all, which was unusual. Even before his discovery of the plague—or curse, or poisoning, or whatever it was—there had been a few remaining in the army, Flip among them, but now there was no one. It was suspicious, and made him more suspicious than usual in his scanning of people for any Oether influence. Mote stayed calm and unruffled on his shoulder, however, and he didn't sight any telltale glowing auras that would indicate a presence other than normal. People were working at setting up sleeping places, defenses, caches of weapons, all with the haste but confidence of the well drilled. Alex had no idea what was supposed to be done, and felt like he was getting in the way. He found Temith rummaging through some old documents and potion-pots on a dusty desk. Being on watch, up here in these towers, reminded him of something that had been troubling him for awhile, and he stopped to talk to Temith about it.

"Something's been bothering me," Alex said with a frown. He moved his hands in a constant over-and-under rolling motion, so that

Mote could run along the succession of his palms thus presented. "You remember, back in Belthas, when Che—when your friend, that magist, took us to the College of Animists with his magic?" The memory was still very strong; the smells, the warmth of the night air, the ache of familiarity.

"Yes," Temith agreed. "It looked very fascinating. Bothersome, too, now that I know he's our enemy. Homesick, are you?"

"No . . . well, yes, but that's not what's bothering me. We appeared on the tower, right? That was the central watchtower; we appeared up there, and it was just you and me and him up there." Alex paused. "That was wrong. Something was wrong at the College."

Temith looked puzzled, so Alex explained. "The College grounds are patrolled, by the students, constantly. *Constantly.* Stand in one spot, you'll have two patrols pass you per hour. No matter what time of the day or night. It's one of the main points of the teaching, it goes back to the Animist's position as a watch-keeper against the Oether." Alex's memories of the College were bound together by the long, interminable threads of daywatch duty, nightwatch duty, perimeter checks . . . Sometimes, if he was having trouble falling asleep, he would go on patrol in his head; he could see every footstep down the long dusty black-sand trails, through each gate and in and around each compound. Usually he'd fall asleep before he'd reached Hoof-stock. "Also, it's partly to make sure all the animals are all right, and nothing's escaping or escaped. And, too, we've had problems in the past, with theurgists of one sect or another trying to break in and sab-otage the College, or outright destroy it. And so we're always walking patrols, and in addition, there's the watchtowers, three of them: Front, Central, and Last. And they're always manned. Always. Every hour of the day or night, there should be two students, one Humani, one Lemyri, up on that platform we appeared on."

He'd stopped running Mote, and was rubbing her ears instead. He was thinking back to his own hours on the watchtowers; it was a good place to do schoolwork, or meditate, or read a book; usually your fellow watcher would agree to take it in turns with you, even the honorable Lemyri soon grew bored with the endless lack of anything important to watch. He recalled some of those days, sitting back-to-back with a friend, both of them basking in the sun. He'd give anything to be back there now, with friends and familiar happenings and boredom, rather than this terrible weight of fear and responsibility.

Temith cocked his head. "Well, what could have happened?"

"I don't know . . . but it must be something very wrong. Either the College has suddenly fallen away from its traditions, which I can hardly see happening . . . after all, it's mostly Lemyri. Or something else . . . maybe there suddenly aren't enough people to fill all the watches. Maybe there isn't *anyone* . . . although everything else seemed normal, I didn't smell any death, didn't hear anything unusual."

"Maybe . . ." Temith thought for a long moment, moving some little clay pots around on the desk. "Maybe Chernan needed to move the watchers out of the way, to put us there." He demonstrated with the pots, sliding one across to the other and pushing it gently out of the way. Alex flinched, and not just at Temith's idle pronunciation of the wizard's name.

"You mean he pushed them off the tower?" Alex asked, then shook his head. "No, that can't be. We'd have heard screams. And the Lemyri, anyway, would have been able to grab something before he or she fell . . ."

"Maybe he switched our places with them," Temith then suggested. "Maybe somewhere at your College now there's a couple of students who remember briefly being in a stuffy, cluttered room."

"I don't know. It's just been worrying me. I need to go back, but what if there isn't any College to go back to?" Alex gently transferred Mote back to his shoulder.

"I'm sure they're all right," Temith told him reassuringly. "If you were thinking of the College of Alchemists, maybe, I could easily see them vanishing under a cloud of poisonous gas that they weren't careful with, but you Animists are tougher than that."

Alex didn't say anything, but he sighed. *I want to go home,* he thought, sadly, but he knew it was too childish to say aloud.

The wall was the strength of the city, as the General had foreseen. Belthasian troops came marching, but the archers and catapults on the Deridal wall laid down a steady stream of fire, preventing them from getting too close. Instead, they massed in groups just outside the range of the catapults, their numbers slowly increasing as more troops arrived and dusk fell.

The soldiers on the wall watched, and waited, as darkness slowly drew in. They waited until the deepest dark, then cranked the catapults back to full power, instead of half as they had been, and launched a terrible barrage against the enemy with grapeshot and shrapnel charges. Men and striches ran and screamed as the fire rained down. A particularly large explosion, a direct hit on a Belthasian black powder store, sent a ball of crimson and gold flame into the night, visible from the high towers. King Carawan applauded the garish display and complained bitterly at not being allowed to go out onto the balcony to watch.

Within the inner towers of the palace, things had settled down. Some of the people were even asleep, if turning fitfully at the sounds of distant explosions. The General stood within close distance of the king, watching the battle with his hawk-keen eyes, and from time to time signaling commands by means of a waved flag to runners down below. Temith had drifted off to sleep in a chair, while Serra was sharpening several of her large cleavers. Valence, leaning on a cane, his leg bandaged, seemed unable to rest, wandering fitfully from room to room, checking and rechecking everything. The princess, too, was uneasy, and drifted around the rooms like the ghost of a maiden imprisoned, though few romantic maids were ever spirited enough to carry around a lethal-looking crossbow as they paced. Alex, to his calling, was watching the Oether through Mote's eyes on his shoulder, but every time the white-clad figure of the princess would breeze into the room he could not help but lose his concentration. Mote would growl softly under her breath and forcibly project the Oether over his vision, to help him keep focused on the task at hand. He tried to smile bravely to the princess, to keep her spirits up, but tight-lipped and tense, she seemed not to see him.

The fear and excitement slowly died down, as time went on and nothing seemed to be happening. Alex gathered, from listening to conversations between the General and Valence, that the wall was holding and the soldiers managing to beat back the intruders. Though their numbers were reduced, it seemed that their superior training would indeed manage to carry the day. Alex, looking through one of the spare telescopes, looked carefully for any sign of Rodeni figures among the fighters along the wall; but there were none. He grew increasingly worried, but he didn't feel he could ask permission to leave in the middle of the siege; it would look too much like cowardice. He sighed, and hoped that Belthas soon would give up and go home. The General seemed to think it was only a matter of time before they realized the futility of an open attack and would offer to negotiate, or settle in for a siege instead. Alex was desperate to begin work on finding some way to help the sick Rodeni. While time ticked by, more lives were surely being lost.

The night continued, with occasional sounds of warfare. The Oether was quiet, with nothing more than background noise. Alex had heard somewhere that warfare was long periods of waiting, followed by short periods of sudden excitement. This was the long waiting, he realized, as boredom set in and at last he dropped into a doze against a pile of rolled carpets at the top of the highest tower. The night sky was dark and peaceful. The short period of excitement came a few hours later.

The wall was holding. It was well built, well defended. Deridal's hilltop location meant that any charge would have to counter the steep incline as well as the actions of the defenders. Deridal might have been undermanned, but they had plenty of war machines and enough men to use them.

King Belthar, watching the battle from the safe distance of one of the neighboring hillsides, watched in annoyance as wave after wave of his army broke against the high smooth wall, then dropped back in defeat. He was no tactician, had no real qualifications for leading an army other than his royal prerogative, but usually force of numbers was all he'd needed. The other cities of Miraposa, for the most part small and simple, had been easily overrun and conquered, and once a few had fallen, a lot more had given in without a struggle. He'd always postponed Deridal; it was so . . . silly, with its crazy king and its people who seemed to be immune to the daily angst and rebellion of most peoples under his own rule. Time enough to take it; and he'd always intended to. While not a seaport, unfortunately, it was in an ideal location, quite centrally located on Miraposa while close to his current capital. Also to be considered were its defensible position, aqueducts, sound economic structure and lush fields, not to mention the pleasing layout of the palace itself. Yes, he'd planned, when he had a moment, to take Deridal, move into that pleasant location, and rule the entire island from that jewel of a city. Right now, though, he was viewing that jewel more as an inflamed cyst that was refusing to lance properly. While he'd been busy with other matters—other towns, plagues of rats, plans for an armada—Deridal had been quietly building this massive wall and training their soldiers to do something other than march in formation. And now he could see why. It was very frustrating.

"Wizard!" he shouted, glancing around. There was no response. Then he remembered that he had to use the fellow's actual name. "Wizard Chernan!" The wizard had stayed back at the castle, but had said that if the king required his presence—

There was the smell of mint, and Chernan shimmered into view in front of him, making him jump. "Your Highness bellows?" Chernan said politely, with a little bow. As a concession to the fact that they were at war, Chernan had wrapped his hair-braid up in leather and was wearing a sort of bronze chain-mail tabard over his robes. The king didn't remember seeing any armor like it before, but then again, a wizard was anything but normal.

"Don't do that!" snarled Belthar. "Why aren't we winning, damn it?"

Chernan slowly glanced over toward the battle, where the current wave of attackers was having boiling pitch poured on them. "Odd," he commented. "I thought you had more men than that. And didn't I see a lot of siege engines in Belthas?"

"They're on their way," grumbled Belthar. "I thought we should get started as soon as possible, so when the infantry arrived here, we—"

"So . . . when we actually will have the tools to break a hole in the wall, you won't actually have any men left to go through it?" Chernan asked, all innocence. King Belthar glared, but deep down, he was too frightened of the wizard to react to the insolence as he normally would have.

"We shouldn't even have to be doing this," he growled instead.

"You were supposed to take care of things! You said we could drive the Rodeni into Deridal and they'd take the city for us, you said—"

"It would have worked. It was working. But you got impatient, you recall," Chernan put in, mildly. The king was too caught up in his complaint to react to the insult of being interrupted.

"Then, you said, you could wipe out their army with a plague curse—"

"And I was, and that was working, too. That's the only reason you haven't lost all your men, except those who were unlucky enough to be the first ones here."

"I had to act! They discovered—it's not honorable; magic, plagues . . . I couldn't let word get back to my subjects, you know that," King Belthar muttered, frowning at the walls of Deridal. Some kind of brilliantly flaring projectiles were being fired into the ranks of his men. Most cultures had knowledge of the Lemyri invention of black powder. But Deridal seemed to have uncommon knowledge, in terms of explosive and caustic chemicals, not to mention more effective and accurate war machinery.

"Yes, they found out about us, with that Animist," shrugged Chernan. "You should have left it to me. I was working on ways to take down the palace from the inside." He gave a smile. "I could have dealt with them easily."

"Oh? Then deal with this, damn you!" shouted Belthar, his temper, never the most stable, finally snapping. "If you're so mighty, get us through this damn wall!"

"Now, sire, weren't you just now complaining that my methods are dishonorable?" Chernan began, reasonably, but Belthar cut him off.

"If you don't help us, we might *lose,*" growled the king. "And I never lose."

Chernan gave the king a patronizing look, and a slight bow. "Your wish is my command, sire," he said, and he faded from view, with a puff of mint.

From the high tower, you could see most of the way around Deridal. Standing guard atop her master's snoring head, Mote slowly turned in circles, watching, waiting, her little head tracking slowly side to side as she looked for things her weak normal eyes couldn't see, but her inner eyes could. And then, there it was, flaring, shining. She squealed as loud as she could, and Alex woke up.

Somewhere down there, at the gate. Magic, strong magic. He shouted down to a waiting messenger, who ran to carry word. Alex thought it was an odd place to attack, since even with the lack of manpower it would be the toughest to breach. He couldn't see who the glowing figure was, but he could guess.

Chernan walked briskly up to the main gates of Deridal, the ranks of burned and battered troops falling back in respect and awe. Alex didn't need to shout warnings; the wizard was perfectly visible and obvious, and while arrows splattered down around him, none could touch him. The skies roiled overhead. As he strode, he gestured, casually to either side, a sort of come-along motion.

And raising up at his command, the battered dead that littered the field stood, and slowly stumbled after him. In the Oether, dim lights of necromancy bloomed in them, fireflies following Chernan's torch. Bolts and arrows flew with renewed vigor at the corpses, sinking into flesh, with no effect.

That's how he did it, Alex realized, *how he got Clak's body into the pipe . . . he killed him, then had his corpse arise and climb up in there. He didn't need a Roden's help. And the shaman that ran away when he was dead . . . Chernan, again?*

One Deridal soldier, with a curse, shouted for a crossbow. Someone managed to throw one to him, and, with a prayer, he took careful aim and fired. The bolt whistled past Chernan's head.

Chernan stopped, and for the first time looked up at the archers on the walls. He made a single dismissive gesture.

As one, as though they were reeds blown in an invisible wind, the soldiers on the wall fell forward, eyes rolling up into their heads. They fell from the wall, already dead, splattering to the ground below. Reinforcements came running: Chernan gestured again, and the soldiers faltered, stumbled, dropping weapons, turning to flee. This time a blast of white flame seemed to erupt from the wizard, a wave of power so great and bright it made everyone, not just Alex, cry out and cringe, shielding their eyes. Within it bloomed a massive creature, a bull, made of crimson flame. It lowered its lava-horns and charged the gates.

The soldiers directly in its path fell screaming, dying, clawing at their blistering flesh. Everyone heard the explosive boom as the beast hit the massive gates and forced them slowly open, breath flaming, shoulders heaving. Alex, blinking in the Oether, only saw the pale lights of Chernan's zombie-soldiers glittering on both sides of the wall now. Then everything was lost in an explosion of light. The bull-shape roared and exploded, leaving the doors blasted wide.

It was that simple, that sudden. Alex could only gape and tremble at the might of the true thaumaturgist's power.

The Belthasians came boiling into Deridal like floodwater. They ran with one aim in mind. Shoving their way through the shouting citizens and battling through the ranks of soldiers, they headed toward the palace. While Deridal's soldiers rushed to try to beat them back, in the milling city it was not safe to use weapons of mass destruction, and numbers began to tell. Chernan seemed to have vanished.

Brought down to the tower rooms by the General's guttural shouts and the stamping stammer of panicked feet, Alex slid down a ladder and landed hard, looking around wildly. Mote clung to his shoulder. He heard shouts and the sounds of fighting, and looked out a window to see milling figures below, and some decked in the red tunics of Belthas running toward this tower.

He ducked back inside and grabbed his smakjab. All around, others were running, a frenzy of panic and motion. He intended to run up to the top room, where his fellow advisors and the king were probably located, but first he ran across the way to Princess Celine's chambers. The door to the princess's room was wide open; she was nowhere to be seen. Quickly he checked the other rooms on this level, and glanced out the window into the gardens; there was no sign of her. Though it was hard to tell, in the milling confusion outside; the enemy was swarming easily into the open, airy grounds of the palace, outnumbering the struggling defenders.

He could hear shouting and swearing all around him. Outside the open window of the room, there was a scream, and a Belthasian soldier dropped past for a heavy landing in the flower beds.

He ran back into one of the main halls on the third level, just as the last guard trying to hold the door was thrown back, and Belthasian soldiers poured into the room. Alex brought his weapon up into a guard position, but a soldier simply charged him, spear at the ready. With no room to get out of the way, Alex, small and light as he was, was simply forced back as the man slammed into him. Alex stumbled backward, lost his footing, and fell, and the soldier clambered over him, jabbing down with his short spear more as an afterthought than anything else.

The blow went wide, and Alex rolled onto his feet and lunged after the guard, who was heading toward the princess's room. The smakjab whirled and swept the man's legs out from under him, and he fell. On his own short spear.

The soldier screamed, rolling onto his back, the point having driven into his gut. He clutched at the wound, rolling, screaming, blood spilling. Alex was horribly reminded of the first time he'd had to kill a rabbit for the College, and been too weak with his first blow; the rabbit had writhed, screaming, suffering, and all he could think to do was stop it, stop it somehow. Bile and panic rising in his throat, he raised his smakjab to deliver a killing blow, trying to convince himself to do it. Footsteps behind him, over the screaming, and he turned barely in time to parry a spear point that would have ended his deliberations instantly.

The new soldier—an officer, judging by his finer tunic and bronze-bladed short sword—spared only a glance for his stricken comrade before throwing aside his spear and advancing on Alex, murder in his eyes as his sword was raised. Alex found his eyes drawn to the shining bronze, even as he struck and parried and was still forced to retreat back. It seemed ironic to be killed by more wealth than he'd ever owned (except once, very briefly). Mote chittered on his shoulder but all Alex could concentrate on was deflecting the reflecting, shining sword as it stabbed and swung and slashed toward him. Chips flew from the smakjab.

A wall bumped the back of his heels, and he could retreat no farther, only slide along the wall now. The stricken soldier on the floor fell suddenly silent, dead or unconscious. Alex heard other footsteps, saw other soldiers enter the room and come toward him. There was no retreat, there was no escape, there was—there was a window. He sprung for it, and glanced out.

A leap out this window would allow him to duplicate the king's famous accident years ago, not far from the same spot, but the outjutting support beams a few feet below offered salvation. Alex swung the smakjab in a wild arc, making his attackers jump back, and then vaulted out the window.

He landed on one of the wide beams, and quickly stepped along them to get away from the window. All those years of navigating the precarious upper reaches of the College had paid off. The enemy inside were shouting for bows but Alex tried to ignore them as he looked for a way up or down; this level seemed to be saturated with soldiers.

A sound made him look around, flattening his back to the wall with his feet braced on the wooden beam. The sound was a hiss, a shrieking knife blade of a hiss that struck some primitive primate chord and made one want to climb up a tree and gibber and throw things from the safety of the topmost branches.

Across the empty space of the air above the courtyard, on a wide walkway, the General stood at bay. Alex hadn't seen what had happened, but could guess: Surprised and beleaguered, the General had attempted to get the king to safety but had been outflanked, and had ended up here on the walkway between two of the towers. Behind him, a barred door shook under the assaults of the Belthasian soldiers behind it; in front of him, a group of wary warriors faced him, long spears down and at the ready. The General stood tense, the hiss dripping like venom through his bared teeth, his tail rod-stiff behind him, feet twitching with the memory of his vanished toe-claws. Blood stained his hands and feet and jaws. Almost invisible, huddled in confusion and fear behind him, was the small form of King Carawan.

Alex swore softly, and tried to find some way to bridge that distance between them, but the bare air was blank impossibility. On the walkway, one of the soldiers feinted with a spear; the General lashed out to try to grab it, but some of that blood on his hands was his own, and his grip slipped. His hiss spiked again in wordless threat and rage.

Alex saw a movement out of the corner of his eye, and glanced to see that several of the soldiers had gotten bows, and were leaning out the windows with them drawn; not aiming at Alex, but at the tableau across the way.

"Archers, General!" Alex shouted, and saw the General turn just as the snapping hum of bowstrings sounded. The massive Therop lunged, interposing himself between the arrows and the king. Arrows clattered on the stone and sunk into flesh, as the archers drew and reloaded and fired, and the General screamed and tore at the air. The solders darted forward, thrusting with spears; the General spun, his tail snapping one spear, his claws grabbing another and jerking. Mottled feathers flew. The soldier on the other end stumbled forward and the Therop's jaws snapped; the man stumbled away screaming, clutching the place where his face had been. Another spear flew like a javelin and the thrashing tail knocked it aside, but a second one darted in and stuck in the General's rib cage. There was a shout to "Fall back for archers!" and the men jumped back as the bows sang out again. The General, the spear still sticking from his side, grabbed up the king and leapt off the walkway, the arrows in a hail around him. There were the meaty sounds of arrows finding their mark.

Alex watched with sick vertigo as the General dropped; even above the shouts around him he could hear the crack of snapping bone as the Therop landed on his feet. Limping in a stumbling, hopping run, he staggered, a few more arrows flying after him but with no effect; he was out of range. But the effort had cost him too greatly. He took a last stumbling step forward on one leg, tried to catch himself on his broken leg, and fell over on his side with a hiss, his nictitating membranes closing like clouds over his eyes. He set the king down, gently, his arms failing. With his head, he nudged the king, urging him to run, keep running, but Carawan only wailed and tried to drag the General to his feet. The Therop was too heavy. His weight collapsed on the spear that still protruded from his side, pushing it in until it was forced out the other flank. King Carawan, totally unhurt, staggered back from the collapse as General Rhhuunn died.

The hail of arrows, useless at his distance anyway, slowed as shouts of "Cease fire!" erupted, and Alex thought of the soldiers hurrying now toward the courtyard, where King Carawan now was holding the head of his dead bodyguard in his lap and weeping like a child.

Perhaps they might only imprison the king. Perhaps Alex could still rescue him, somehow—

But some nameless unseen soldier, more enthusiastic, or callous, or hard-of-hearing than the rest, sent a single bolt deep into Carawan's chest.

The mad king didn't cry out, only grunted softly, and slumped over the General's neck.

Alex gave an involuntary cry of anguish, and then a much louder one of pain, as one of the archers shot him. The arrow sliced along the side of his head, tearing his ear and whistling over his shoulder an inch above Mote's head. He lost his balance and fell astride the beam, with painful results; flipped over on the beam as the universe contracted into a small world of pain. A sense of

panic fear love hope

forced itself into his consciousness, trying to shove back the pain, as Mote scrambled to hang on, climbing up his inverted form. His legs dropped off the beam, and he found himself hanging in front of another window. As he felt his splinter-filled grip on the beam failing and could almost hear the sound of another arrow being drawn, he swung himself back, forth, and then launched himself through the window.

His legs made it through, though his torso nearly didn't, and he landed awkwardly on the stone sill and had to grip it to keep himself from falling backward out the window; then he threw himself into the room. Mote fell off his shoulder, and he grabbed her and shoved her into his shirt, panting.

frightened worried

This was a small servant's area, long unused, with two open doorways through which the sounds of approaching feet could be heard. And a small cupboard door, closed.

There might be a weapon there; his smakjab had fallen when he had been hit by the arrow. He threw the cupboard open. Within was an echoing space, like a chimney, and two ropes that hung in the space. Without stopping to think, he grabbed the ropes and climbed into the empty space.

He started quickly to lower himself down the ropes, hand over hand, but weakness from pain and fear made him clumsy, and he missed one of the ropes. Still clinging to one rope, which was giving him scant resistance, he tried to stop himself on the walls of the shaft. He smashed down into a wooden platform, still gripping tight to the rope, which was now straining upward.

He abruptly remembered the pulley assemblies they'd used at the College, for getting bulky items up and down the higher levels, and realized that he must be in a similar arrangement. He slowly let out the rope in his hands, and found himself lowered gradually into the darkness. And it would have been an easy and safe trip, if the unseen pulley and rope, weak from long disuse, had not chosen to break suddenly and send Alex and Mote and the dumbwaiter all hurtling down the dark shaft.

ELEVEN

Alex landed with a crunch at the bottom of the shaft, shattering the flimsy wood of the dumbwaiter under his weight. He got to his feet painfully. It was dark. He'd expected to find himself in an ancient kitchen, but in fact—He looked up to confirm it; yes, he'd gone right through what must have been a trap door or something, down here into . . . a wine cellar, possibly, at one time. A few old dusty bottles still lay in their niches. As his eyes adjusted to the dimness, he saw that what the place was filled with now was Rodeni.

There must have been thirty or forty of them, watching him with wide eyes. A few had found crude weapons—sticks, broken bottles, even stones—and were holding them ready.

I didn't know they were living under the palace! Alex thought. *But then I didn't know they had the tunnels under the city, either, maybe miles of catacombs. They dug them out . . . but then Gleet said they built all the substructure of Belthas, too. They've been down here all this time and we never knew it . . . If Clak had been able to organize them, they'd have come up from nowhere, all around us . . .*

He spread his hands to show he carried no weapons, and tried to speak in Rodeni.

"Please, no harm, no fight. Find Flip, please, or Gleet—" Rodeni names were the same in Trade as in Rodeni, but when speaking Rodeni you had to say them fast, chirping on the vowels.

"We heard the soldiers come," said one small Roden, stepping forward cautiously and speaking in Trade. "Are we . . . are you winning?"

Alex looked down. "No. We've . . . we're losing. The king's dead. The General's dead." The Rodeni gave little meeps of shock at the news, whispering and chittering amongst themselves. Alex looked at them, suddenly thinking back to something the princess had said. Princess . . . no, Queen, now. If she was still alive . . . but she must be. Chernan would have made sure of that. An idea began to grow. With the desperation of one who has nothing left to lose, Alex jumped on it.

"But—we haven't lost yet," Alex finished, and the Rodeni looked at him in surprise. "Not yet."

The Roden who'd spoken to him jerked her head. "Everyone is this way. Come on."

Alex followed her down a long, low passage, lined thickly with Rodeni, who stared at him as he passed, and chattered amongst themselves. Alex could feel that tension in the air again, and suddenly thought to check—there *was* a faint glow hovering over the crowd of Rodeni, just a faint tinge, but it was there. Mote didn't seem to be disturbed, as she usually was in the presence of a greater spirit or a wizard, so Alex didn't allow himself to fear it either.

He stepped out into a vast hall, where several cellars and rooms had been broken down to make one large one, with careful support pillars left at crucial points. The hall, and galleries off it like the one he'd come from, all were packed full of Rodeni. The air was hot and humid with their thick presence, and filled with hushed whispering and chittering and chattering, milling aimlessly. Alex stared into the gloom, trying to guess how many there might be. Thousands, easily, perhaps even hundreds of thousands? They all seemed alert; the sick must be elsewhere, likely still packed into the odiferous, makeshift plague-hospital.

The plague! Or the curse, or whatever . . . Alex had to tell them that it was Chernan's doing. And the cure . . . but suddenly his heart sank. Temith must be dead. Temith, Valence, Serra. All the advisors, sworn to guard the king until death. Alex would have fallen with them, should have fallen with them, except that he'd failed them, gotten separated while trying to keep watch. He'd watched, all right, watched for magic, watched magic triumph.

With the allopathist dead, the cure was lost with him. That left only one person who could save the dying Rodeni. That was Chernan himself. If he had caused the Rodeni's sickness, as he'd caused the Humani's, then surely he could lift it. But how to find him, get him to bargain?

It would have to be through King Belthar, Chernan's new master. How to get *him* to listen, to bargain? What could Alex and the Rodeni ever manage to offer? Slowly, like leaves drifting down, pieces of a plan fell together.

His presence in the cavern had been noticed; Flip pushed his way carefully through the crowd, and a moment later Gleet shouldered up to him as well.

"The king's really dead?" Gleet asked, his voice a whisper. Alex nodded, then stopped.

"How'd you know? I only just told—"

"Word spreads," Flip replied, looking out over the seething throng. Gleet nodded solemnly. Alex thought of the crowd of Rodeni, packed in, prevented from their rage by the calming effect of the Deridal waters, and so kept hovering in indecision.

"What . . . what are you all thinking?" Alex whispered back.

There was a moment of silence. "Scared," whispered Flip. Alex was reminded of Mote's wordless emotions.

"Do you think you could manage bravery?" Alex asked.

Before they could ask him what he meant, Alex clambered up onto a pile of rubble, above the crowd. It took bravery of his own to do what he did.

"Listen! Listen to me!" Alex shouted in Trade, waving his hands over his head. His voice boomed in the acoustics of the cavern. The crowd of Rodeni stopped its milling and chattering, staring at him in surprise. He looked at them, saw the incomprehension on their faces, and looked quickly at Gleet. "Can you translate for me? Please?"

"I'll do my best," Gleet answered dubiously, hopping up onto a chunk of stone next to Alex. "But what—" Alex waved a hand to silence him, and cleared his throat.

"Listen! Deridal is doomed; we're overrun, the king's dead. You'll soon have no homes to go to, they'll break in here before long, and if Belthar doesn't kill you, the plague will. You only have one chance—attack!"

Gleet, who had been squeaking and cheeping along quickly with Alex's speech, stopped and stared at him.

"Are you mad!? There's thousands of soldiers, of—"

"Say it!" Alex demanded. "And tell them no, we will not attack them here. All their soldiers are here—and Belthas is almost undefended! We can take their city from behind them!"

Gleet squeaked along, his face showing none of the incandescent fervor that Alex was displaying, but the words had their effect. An eruption of chittering and clicking and squealing filled the room in a swelling wave, as those who spoke Trade heard the words first, then as others heard the translation.

A chorus of sound rose up; Alex got the general tone, but Gleet turned to him to say, "They don't believe it, and don't think it will work."

"It will! It has to! Listen! The person who started this plague, with his cursed magic! The one who made the Towers! His home is in Belthas!" There was a renewed outbreak of chatter at this news, but Alex continued, "And the king, who thinks you don't count. The king who wants you all dead . . . his family is in Belthas!"

"Hundreds of soldiers are in Belthas!" shouted an albino Roden, brandishing a broken bottle. It was Erk, Alex was sure. "You expect us to charge the walls and be slaughtered—like *rats?*" He spat the last word out. Alex could not help but flinch as the Roden threw the bottle, and it whizzed past Alex's head to shatter on the wall behind him. "We've seen what happens to those *you* lead, Human!" A chorus of shrill agreement erupted around him, and Alex felt hot shame welling up inside him.

"No! You hear him!" squeaked a new voice, and Alex saw Flip clamber up to a chunk of fallen stone. "We stay here, we die! Males, females, pups! Die like rats—here! You think you fly like birds? Swim the sea? You run ahead of soldiers? They own the island!"

"Better chance than running back to be slaughtered against the

Towers! That's a Humani way to die!" shouted Erk. The Rodeni around him seemed to agree with him, bouncing on their hind legs as they shouted in their own language.

"There's no Humani way into Belthas," Alex said, trying to keep his voice calm and steady. Luckily, even a calm Humani voice tended to be louder than a Rodeni's. "It's impossible. The walls and hills, the sea, the river, and there will be guards enough to protect her. Even if I could find any of the soldiers to go with me, we'd all be killed."

"He admits it!" cried a nameless antagonist. A chorus of chilling squeals began. Gleet looked in terror at Alex.

"Speak! Fast!" he hissed.

"Listen!" Alex held up a hand for emphasis, as the crowd started jammering again. "Listen! There's no Humani way . . . but I will bet my own life that there's a Rodeni way. Belthas was your city, once. You know its secrets, its bones. We can use that. It's your only chance—do you want to hide, and die, or do you want to fight!? Fight them, damn you! You can do it! We'll stop this war, we'll stop the plague, we'll give you back your lives, your freedom. You can do it . . . and you're the only ones who can."

There was crackling conversation a moment, and then a grizzled and graying black-and-white piebald spoke up. "He's right! There's ways in, under that wall. The old drains goes right under!"

"Yes! Come up unseen, unknown! Kill from inside, as they do to us!" squealed Flip passionately, his clawed fists clenched. He hopped in place, his tail lashing in fury. There was a clicking chorus of surprise as the Rodeni considered the possibility that the mad plan might actually have merit.

"You're forgetting something," sneered the albino, showing his long orange teeth. "The Screaming Towers! If we come within throwing distance of those city walls, we'll be driven mad by the sound! Sure, you can get under the city, but you'll never come up!"

"The Towers don't bother me," Alex replied, as the albino glared at him. He met the clear ruby gaze unflinchingly now. Flip's panting, helpless courage was too strong for Alex to fail him again. "I'll go with you. I'll go up, and I'll silence the Towers. If I fail, all you have to do is flee . . . as you would have done anyway."

"You will go?" Flip asked him, and Alex was conscious of all the eyes on him. He nodded.

"I'll go. I'll even lead, if you'll have me." He looked out into the sea of warm fur, the smell of fear, and was struck with the powerful memory of that day in the dry riverbed. He raised a hand aloft, and up his arm Mote scampered, to perch on his palm and survey the crowd. There was a chorus of awed gasps and squeaking as Mote's grey star-face looked down upon them.

"Some time ago, true, I led the small ones to doom. I carry that shame still. But I will put my life on the line now to redeem myself. I led your small kin away . . . now let me lead you home."

In a Humani discussion, there would have been a pause. Not so here. Flip bounded into the air and landed in front of Alex with a salute the General would have been proud of.

"Private Flip, Archer Third Rank, with you, sir!" he chirped loudly.

"Me, too. I can't fight well, but I'll go," added Gleet, watching Alex thoughtfully.

"And I! I also! Me! Me! We shall!" came the chorus of voices, cheeps, squeaks, until the room was filled with cries. The gruff albino stared a long moment, then nodded. Slowly, with formality but without malice, he looked at Alex and gave a salute.

Alex surveyed the dark chamber, full of squeaking sound, packed with eyes that glowed like coals. The squealing rushing sound filled his ears and he could see through Mote's eyes the flashing glow of the magic of the Rodeni community shining in the darkness of the Oether.

"You can make your way to the outskirts of the city, right?" Alex asked them. "Unseen, unattacked?"

"Oh, certainly," Gleet answered for them. "We've dug tunnels all the way to outside the walls, here and there. Never want a home you can't get out of . . ."

"Why didn't you all leave before?" Alex asked, puzzled.

"And go where? We're not . . . I mean, out in the open? In the fields? Thousands of us, milling around out, outside?" Gleet shuddered. "We don't like that. Dangerous to be out in the open like that.

Unless there's a better hole to duck for. We think you're going to give that to us." Again Gleet's dark unreadable eyes fixed him.

"I'll try . . . I will. I *will.*"

They scrambled through the dark passages for what seemed like an eternity before at last they tumbled out into the undergrowth on the high side of the city's hill. Beyond them rose the rumpled mountains, spanned by the low white zigzag of the aqueduct.

The Rodeni filed out like a furry flood; the sick and the old, the blind young and the nursing females were left behind, but still the Rodeni that clustered close were vast and almost frightening in their numbers alone. The gleam in their eyes and the flashing of teeth in the darkness was also a point to consider.

"We've got to hurry—I don't know how long Deridal will distract them," Alex said, looking at the light of flames and smoke from where parts of the city burned.

They fled out into the fields, keeping to the shelter of the thick stands of maize and the groves of citrus as long as they could. Once outside the cultivated areas, they made their way along, hiding as best they could.

From time to time they caught a glimpse of the river or the main highway; along the road more soldiers marched and carts rolled. Torches flickered in the darkness, and the glow that marked the city of Deridal dwindled in the distance.

At about halfway, they stopped for a break to allow the stragglers to catch up. They were by a small stream, and they all drank thirstily. Alex watched this, wondering how long it would take for the calming effects of the Deridal water to wear off. Then, exhausted, he fell asleep and had to be woken up again as they pressed on, but he felt better for the rest.

They avoided the fields of Belthas, and stopped in the surrounding hills and cliffs instead, which were rocky and uninhabited. Alex inspected his makeshift army. The Rodeni seemed, if not bold and courageous, at least cautiously determined. They were wincing and putting paws into their ears, or stuffing them with whatever they could find.

"You can hear the Towers?" Alex asked of Flip, who blinked up at him with his hands pressing his ears flat.

"What?" shouted Flip.

Alex managed to explain the plan to the Rodeni, who were quickly stuffing their ears with rags of clothing and mud and leaves. Alex had already bandaged Mote's ears along the way. Flip, Gleet, a small but burly Roden named Ket, and Pleep, and a grey-muzzled elder female called Noot were selected to lead Alex to the Towers.

They kept low as they crawled up to the walls. The Rodeni's ears were plugged tight, but still they cringed and clattered their teeth. Noot's recollections were uncertain, and they came up to the edges of the outer moat, and stumbled around there in the mud and stones, for what seemed to Alex to be a long time. At one point, Alex saw the light of a guard on the wall approaching; he threw himself flat, and the Rodeni followed suit. The light passed by, unknowing, and they kept searching.

At last they discovered a large earthenware tunnel extending from the muddy bank of the river. It was half-buried in rocks and mud and waterweed, and the grating of hardened wood across it supported a thick mass of rushes. It was massive, about four feet in diameter.

With Rodeni teeth and Humani leverage, they managed to cut loose the grating and pry it up to allow them to slip in; and slip they did, for the tunnel was full of mud and waterslime. Alex walked into the darkness bent over, and shuddered when slime dripped from the roof down the back of his neck. Ket and Pleep took the lead, and lit small candles which cast a flickering but welcome light in the squalid tunnel.

"Are these the sewers?" Alex whispered, as he crawled along.

Pleep clicked her teeth. "Some of. Most of them blocked now, since Rodeni stopped helping Belthas." Indeed, the pipes did have an unpleasant smell, but Alex knew from his stay in Belthas that most waste was dumped in the gutters of the city streets, where channeled outflow from the river would sweep it out to the sea. The subterranean sewers hadn't been used in a long time, and in the meantime had been scoured by storm runoff.

They proceeded into the depths. After every few feet, there would be a join in the pipe, stained and sometimes cracked, or with a small chunk broken free to show mud and stones beyond. From time to time, at these joins, Alex saw the wedge-shaped Rodeni script cut into the clay; he couldn't read it and didn't want to take the time to ask one of his companions to translate it. The marks must have been made before the clay was fired, though; another indication that these elaborate drains were Rodeni work. The joins allowed the pipe to angle slowly, curving, and soon the circle of night at the far end was lost.

As they proceeded, the Rodeni relaxed, and soon partially unstopped their ears. Alex could hear through Mote's ears that the noise of the Towers was silenced. He hoped that the other Rodeni had found the other pipes Noot had spoken off, and that they were out of the range of that maddening sound. He wondered if he could hear the other Rodeni scuffling in the pipes; but the pipe magnified and echoed even the sounds of their own group back to him.

The pipe ended in a four-way junction, full of sticks and debris. Noot thought a long moment, sniffing at the air of each tunnel, then chose one which led off in a new direction. This pipe at least was dry, though it was a foot smaller in diameter. Alex was obliged now to drop to his knees and crawl after his quick-footed Rodeni companions. His palms slapped loudly on the smooth ceramic of the pipe.

The passage was long and straight; their candlelight penetrated only a short, dim way, and ahead was only a receding blackness. It was surprisingly warm.

They came to another junction, and Noot led them more surely this time, down another long straight eternity, this of cleaner, whiter pipe, hard as stone. Alex wondered where they might be. What was above them? How far had they come? It was impossible to say; the stretched perspective of the pipe told nothing.

Here the joins in the pipe were more complex, made by collared rings so that each section of pipe fit into its neighbor as a lid fits onto a pot. And, as Alex gradually noted, this meant that the pipe was gradually diminishing in size. The Rodeni, impatient with his slow, crawling progress, were far ahead, just visible as dark moving shapes against the light. The clay walls grew closer and closer about him, and Alex wanted to ask the Rodeni to slow down and wait for him, but he did not want to admit he was uneasy.

His progress slowed, though, until Flip came back, followed by Gleet; they had no trouble turning around in this passage, while Alex would have had to bend double and contort himself to accomplish the same feat.

"It's getting narrow," Alex panted, as they came up to him. "Is it much farther?"

"Not long now," promised Flip. "Gets some smaller but opens soon, Noot says."

Gleet gave Alex an appraising look, and nodded. "Whrr, you should fit through all right. A bit of a squeeze, but you'll make it." Rodeni could fit through anything they could get their skulls past.

"I hope so," said Alex, and he crawled on.

The pipe continued to narrow. Alex was forced from his crawl to a slither, like an alligator, dragging himself along by his hands through the pipe. The Rodeni ran ahead, themselves forced to all fours, bounding along like rabbits with their strong hind legs. Alex found himself crawling through darkness, but there was nothing to see anyway. His eyes brought up the image of the tunnel in the candlelight on their lids when he closed them.

It was warm, and getting warmer, and stuffy. The pipe now pressed on his shoulders, forced down his head, hampered his elbows and his legs. Soon, he could no longer pull himself along but by his fingers and toes. He stopped again, as it enclosed around him, and lay there until Ket came back.

"You stop? Is not far now. Noot was wrong but we found where it opens soon."

"I can't crawl much more," Alex gasped, holding up his abraded palms for proof. "I don't have the leverage; I'm too squeezed."

"We help!" cried Ket, and he called back to the others. Pleep came down the pipe again, and Ket explained the situation to her. Ket then turned, and offered his thick furry tail to Alex. "You hang on, we pull you!"

"I don't want to hurt your tail!" Alex protested, despite his desperation to get out of the pipe. Ket slapped his tail into Alex's hands impatiently.

"It will not!"

Alex gripped the tail at the base, and Ket took hold of Pleep's in the same fashion. They pulled, and Alex slid forward. Once they got going, momentum along the slick pipe made it easy . . .

Until Alex jammed fast in the narrowing pipe, and could not budge. He oofed, and exhaled as the Rodeni tugged, but only succeeded in jamming himself further; and it was difficult to draw breath in again after that.

Ket eeped and squeaked, and Alex let go of the Roden's tail. The Roden tried to turn around in the pipe, and after much struggle managed it; Alex, stretched like a hung stoat, envied the Roden's flexibility.

"Is no good," panted Ket. "We must go back, start over." He leaned over Alex's outstretched arms, and put his paws on the Human's head, and pushed with all his might. The claws prickled Alex's scalp, but he did not budge. Ket squeaked, and Pleep turned around to help him push—to no avail.

"Go on ahead—see if you—can find a—rope or something," Alex gulped at them, struggling to draw breath in the tight confines of the pipe.

The Rodeni turned, with much squirming and kicking, and then scuttled back up the pipe, and were gone. "Leave a candle!" Alex started to call after them, but the darkness swallowed his words. He shut his eyes in the darkness, and couldn't help imagining himself dying here, smothered in the echoing warmth, unable to move or breathe . . . His heart started to pound in fear. He tried to struggle, couldn't, tried to breathe, couldn't, and felt a flood of panic . . .

comfort love reassurance

Mote wriggled out from where she'd been snuggled into his collar, and whuffled in his ear, all the while sending warm caring thoughts. Alex found himself calming, distracted by the soft fur tickling; Mote ran under his chin and back and forth, down to his hands where he stroked her; this motion, about all he was capable of, was comforting. Mote projected the Oether for him, without being asked. At least, it must be the Oether, but strange—silent and dark as he'd never seen it before, so very dark, free even of the drifting nature spirits he was accustomed to seeing as ever-present. Somehow, it was soothing, rather than frightening. The distraction was interrupted then by the sounds of returning Rodeni scuffling.

The Rodeni came hurrying back with a piece of rotten rope. Alex wrapped it tight around his wrist, and grabbed it. "Wait! Before you pull, let me try to get some more room here . . ."

Mote's teeth went to work at his suggestion. She gnawed and tore at the seams of his coat, and as each piece ripped free she pulled it loose and dropped it behind them. As his sleeves came loose, he called to Ket; the Roden grabbed them and tore them off. His shirt quickly followed. Soon there was space around him—only a few fractions of an inch, but enough. His skin slicked with sweat, the sweat of fear and heat, Alex gripped the rope, and closed his eyes, and wished he had someone to pray to.

The Rodeni hauled. And Alex slid slowly forward. And stuck again. He wriggled, the Rodeni pulled—he moved forward once more. And then, like a cork from a bottle, he tumbled out into a wider space. Freedom! To stretch and stand and move! The place seemed to be like the bottom of a well, a brickwork square four feet to a side, with tunnels in each wall; in one was a corroded grating around which the Rodeni had lashed their rope. Above him, the darkness ascended like a chimney.

"Is not far to Towers now, Noot says," said Flip, pointing to one of the tunnels from which Gleet's head peered. They were wincing and holding their ears again, and Alex guessed they must be close to the surface again. He shook his head.

"I'll go alone from here," he said, looking up.

"It might not be safe," Gleet warned, looking up as well. "Maybe we should try to find another way . . ."

"No more pipes," said Alex, firmly. "I'll go up here." Before they could argue, he began to scale up the shaft, bracing his feet on one wall and his back against the opposite. "You go find the others!"

"Good luck!" Flip whispered to him, and then they vanished below. Alex thought he saw the candles extinguished; the Rodeni would have no need of them.

The shaft ended at a flat circular ceramic slab, pierced through with many holes the size of Alex's fingers. Alex had seen these "Rodeni-hole" covers here and in Deridal as well. Deridal also had a system of drains and sewers, to carry away the waste water from the aqueduct. No wonder the Rodeni had been able to vanish into the city. But they'd have had trouble with this cover; it was terribly heavy, especially without anything to stand on to help him lift it. Fear of having to try and make his way out through the pipes gave force to his arms, and he managed to lift up part of the slab, bracing his feet and back against the shaft, and push it aside. From there it was easier to slide away, and then Alex cautiously poked his head up.

There was no one around; the street was empty. In the distance he could hear noises of revelry from some tavern; probably the impending victory of King Belthar was already being celebrated, but at this late hour most of the population had gone indoors. Alex climbed out, shivering now with the cool night air on his bare skin. He turned, listening, and caught the sound of the river, and the *clok-clok-clok* sound of the turning waterwheel, and headed toward it.

The first Tower loomed ahead in the mist. Alex glanced around, saw no one, and tried the door. It was locked and solid. He inspected it closely, but there were no holes or cracks that Mote could slip through. Besides, this close to the source of the sound, Mote was shivering, and broadcasting

fear unhappiness pain

at the noise of the Tower. Alex wanted to get her away from it, but quickly walked around to the side by the river, where the waterwheel churned in the current. The simple axle extended through a hole in the side of the Tower. Alex inched along the edge of the river, along the stone embankment, careful of the spinning wheel and splashing water, and put his eye to the hole.

There was little more than a quarter-inch of space between the axle and the opening—not safe passage for a rat, with the twisting axle taken into consideration. Within, the Tower was dark, but Alex thought he could hear a rhythmic hissing sound, like the pumping of a bellows, and the creak of wood, over the splash of the wheel.

Drawing back, he looked then at the wheel. It was solid wood, new-looking and well-constructed, built to withstand years of constant use. Nothing looked loose or easily breakable. If he'd had a good stone hatchet he might be able, with a lot of work, to chop through the axle, but he had no hatchet and nowhere to get one. Mote's complaints and unhappiness were loud in his mind, and he backed away from the Tower. As he did so, he stared at the river, thoughtfully gnawing on the knuckle of his thumb. And then, with an air of decisiveness, he jogged quickly away.

The Inflow Gate was guarded, even tonight. A few townsfolk wandered by, drinking and cheerful. They shouted jests to the guards, who waved back. This part of the wall was patrolled by five guards, half the usual number; almost all of Belthas's troops were participating in the attack on Deridal. Alex hid in the shelter of a shadow, and watched the men stand about. The river flowed in below them, through the gaping black maw of the Gatehouse. Over the top of the Gatehouse, below the wall, ramps led down to bridges to outside. He'd been to visit the Gatehouse with the watercourse men on that fateful day of his rat-charming, and knew that it was strongly built, the doors massive and reinforced with stone, nigh impossible to break into. The Gatehouse extended beyond the wall on both sides; on the inflow side, a strong grating prevented any entry that way, while the powerful flush of water would stop any attempt to enter from the other side. It reminded Alex of the aqueduct pipe, of Clak's pathetic body tied in the current.

Alex went back to the alleys and began to rummage. With the absence of the Rodeni, the trash and debris had begun to pile up in the streets—not filth, per se, but bits and pieces of things not really useful. Alex found what he was looking for, and wrapped it up in rags, and threw a piece of rough sacking around his shoulders.

The guards glanced at him as he wandered out of the gate and sat down by the river, but thought nothing of it; beggars and poor people were common here. Alex waited until their attention was elsewhere, and then gently pushed his unwrapped bundle into the current. He stood up and trudged back into the city again.

The bulk of the Gatehouse loomed ahead of him, blocking the view from the wall. Alex looked at the churning, frothing water, thinking about the storm, and the Delphini, and the choking, burning fire of water in your lungs, the pounding in your chest as you struggle to breathe, the dragging, *wet* weight of the water. It all frightened him far more than the confines of the tight tunnel. But then he thought back to the Rodeni, hiding and waiting . . . and to the mad king, dead just like that . . . to his friends and fellow advisors, all their hopes and plans destroyed . . . to the princess, who was surely even now suffering who could say what horrors.

Alex took a deep breath, and rolled the piece of sacking tight, tying it around his neck like a scarf, pressing the tense and trembling Mote to the back of his neck. Then he jumped.

The water was a cold smack, but he was braced for it, and the sound went unheard so close to the foaming gullet of the Gatehouse. He flattened out, head upstream, and kicked off the bottom, trying not to panic and flail at the water. He wished Rei were here, or that he'd made good on his promise to her to learn to swim. Still, perhaps this was as good a time as any to learn. First things first: got to breathe!

His head broke the surface and he saw, as the current rolled him back, the small chunk of wood floating in the water, skipping on the current but not following it. He lunged for it, missed, and was shoved downstream.

He managed to climb out a few blocks away, spitting water, and squelched back up to the Gatehouse to try again. This time, his grasping hands grabbed the wood and the rope it was attached to, and held on.

Struggling to keep his head above the water, Alex slowly pulled himself along the old rope, praying that all the pieces he'd had to knot together to make a rope this long would hold.

He hauled and hauled, thankful for the knots that helped him hang on, feeling the current tugging at his limbs, trying to spin him at the end of the rope. The Splicing Knots were holding. Slowly the walls of the Gatehouse enveloped him, and the sounds changed to an echoing roar. The water flowed through slick stone channels here, and though he hoped for a ladder or stairs out of the channel, there was nothing. He had to climb his rope all the way, to where the plank to which it was tied was jammed against the outside of the Gatehouse grill. Then he could get his fingers and toes into the grill, and climb wearily out into the cold mildewy darkness of the Gatehouse.

Feeling his way blindly along the walls, he at last found a bundle of matches and a small lamp, which he lit. The black void was lit with golden shifting shadows, the mossy vault overhead patterned with river-reticulation. Like guillotines for giants, the massive Gates hung above the channel, their chains and pulleys leading down to the massive counterweights on either side.

Alex had watched in fascination as the watercourse men had demonstrated their craft. At the time, he'd felt a secret desire to play with the massive machinery. Now he had his chance.

He gripped the first lever, and pulled it down. Below, something clanked, water rushed, and slowly the First Gate lowered into the rushing current, starting to push the water off to the sides. Was that a shout from outside? He had to hurry. He slowly pulled the next lever; there was a hiss of hydraulics and a clanking of chain as the Second Gate began to drop . . . yes, that was definitely a shout. Nothing for it then; he pumped the lever up then slammed it down. The Second Gate jerked and plummeted into its channel, jamming shut, blocking the way he'd come in.

The Third Gate was almost never used. The chains and gears were dull, in poor condition. With a great creaking screech of tortured bronze, the final Gate began to lower, then there was a crack, and shards of metal pinged past overhead as Alex ducked. The Gate fell, pulley screaming, smashing down into its channel with a ringing crash that shook the Gatehouse and echoed loudly in Alex's ears before dying into silence. A chunk of ancient bronze fell next to Alex; he used it to bash the levers into twisted ruin.

There was shouting loud now in the silence, and hammering at the doorway. Alex heard someone shout for a key. He looked around wildly, and grabbed the only weapon that came to hand—a broom, leaning in one corner. He tore off the head of bristles and held it at the ready, his back against the wall as he watched the door.

The Towers stood silent, and the river flowed around the city, split into twin channels that foamed past the outside of the walls. Swollen with the distant rains, the river rose, bubbling into the pipes and sewers.

People watching, later said that the Rodeni must have had some secret, silent signal that brought them forth in their fury. Others said they had been lurking, and it was only the abrupt silence of the Towers that gave them the courage to strike. In fact, it was the sudden gush of water through the pipes that drove them forth; the abrupt change of pressure and distant roar warned most of them in time to scramble for the surface. A few were sodden, caught too quickly, but they all came boiling up into the city; from drains and lanes, from ditches and dikes, cellars and sewers, a wild, squealing tide. They brandished sticks and staves and spears; those who had none grabbed stones and broken bottles and broken poles and anything they could find.

They were not organized, not disciplined, but they were full of fury, a mob-mind of anger and vengeance. Townsfolk ran screaming in terror, to hide behind barred and bolted doors. Tavern festivities were interrupted by the smash and crash, sticks flying. The people of Belthas had never known Rodeni as anything other than skulking, fearful creatures. Now they were suddenly seeing them bold and angry, and what was worse, wielding weapons with skill and ferocity. Surprise made up for what the Rodeni lacked in numbers and size, and they drove the Humani in panic before them. But they were not pursuing them; they had one goal in mind, one destination: the castle. Civilians fled before them. The soldiers of Belthas, few though they were, attempted to stop them. They died, often in shock and horror as Rodeni that should have fled before a shouted word and a brandished spear instead came leaping forward like demons, tails lashing, teeth slashing. Other soldiers, seeing this and deciding that no pompous king was worth being bitten to death for, threw down their own weapons and tore off their tabards, quickly opting for the civilian life; at least it was a life for which you were alive.

Alex was dragged from the Gatehouse, battered and beaten, still clutching the broken end of his broom. The guards hauled him into the night air, some of them glancing around at the sounds of screaming nearby, and then around the corner came a mob of Rodeni. Alex was thrown aside, and he sat up groggily to watch as the Rodeni, with swinging staves and leaping kicks and bites, tore into the Humani guards. Two Humani were hamstrung from behind by sharp teeth, three more staggered back clutching torn arms and fingers. Alex knew that the General had never instructed the Rodeni in these attacks; they must have worked on them themselves, in private. Several of the Rodeni were knocked back, and one collapsed screaming around the point of a spear, but soon the battle was over.

One of the Rodeni helped Alex to his feet. "Thank the gods we found you!" It was Chis.

"Have they reached the castle yet?" Alex managed to ask.

"Heading that way now," reported a rust-colored male, with an attempt at a salute. One of his ears had been torn off, but he seemed all the more cocky for it.

"Send runners and remind them about Chernan. He may have magically transported himself back here, now that the battle's been won. We've got to make sure we take him, and the queen and the prince, alive. Especially the queen and prince; they mustn't hurt them, not so much as a scratch, or it won't work."

The crowd of Rodeni led him through the city. Flames and smoke were already rising from the silent Towers, and there came a crash, as of a waterwheel bitten through by sharp gnawing teeth.

According to plan, several groups of Rodeni had emerged from the tunnels into the castle itself. As Alex and his comrades approached, a guard was flung from one of the parapets, screaming, to smash into the cobblestones below. Alex flinched at the sound and the shattered ruin, feeling sick. Inside, shouts of chaos and confusion reigned. Alex broke into a run.

"They've got to be careful!" he shouted. He'd explained this plan to the Rodeni, but had not counted on the enthusiasm they would show for battle once they had chosen to fight. Deridal's influence must be wearing off.

Inside the castle all was chaos. Rodeni ran past in small groups, waving captured spears (broken midway along the haft, to accommodate their smaller stature), driving fleeing servants before them. Alex was glad of his Rodeni escort; even with them, maddened Rodeni leapt out at him several times from side passageways, swinging wildly, until they noticed who he was. They were certainly enthusiastic; maybe too much so.

"You've got to calm down!" he told one group of them, who had just chivvied a butler into diving out a second-floor window. "You can't just kill everyone!"

"Why not!? It's what they'd do to us!" shouted one of them, and threw a vase out the window after the butler. It crashed below, and there was a scream, and the Rodeni gave a cheer.

"No! The whole point was, we'd capture the castle, take hostages, and force the king to negotiate. If you all act like savages, they'll think that the only way to stop you is to kill you all!"

The Rodeni seemed reluctant, but agreed. Alex made his way swiftly to the royal bedchambers, where Queen Ellin and the young Prince Belthar II were being held by several of the largest Rodeni. The queen was very pale, sitting up in her bed with the covers drawn up protectively under her chin. The prince was crying fitfully, and clinging to the apron of his nurse, a stout older woman who was glaring at the Rodeni with a much more stern and regal expression than the queen herself. The Rodeni didn't seem to pay them much attention, instead watching the single doorway. At first Alex thought they were just watching for guards, but then when a pair of combat-mad Rodeni came tearing down the hall and made as if to enter, one of the guarding Rodeni kicked him back with shouted reprimand. There was a quick curse and an apology, and the raiders left for other sport. These Rodeni seemed tense, caught up in the frantic fury of their community, but were holding themselves well. Erk was among them, Alex noticed. He was holding an ornate bronze sword he'd taken from one of the palace guards. He straightened up as Alex entered, and gave a curt nod.

"Well, you got us this far," he grunted grudgingly to Alex. "Wasn't expecting to even get into the city."

"What's happened to all the Humani here?" Alex asked him.

"Done for some of them; most we let leave, quick-like, before we closed the courtyard. A few we weren't sure of—guards, the like. Sent them down to the dungeons."

"Any sign of the wizard?" Alex asked and when Erk shook his

head, he looked at the queen. "Your Highness. Where's Che— . . . where's your royal wizard?"

"I . . . I don't know," she stammered. "I keep telling you things, I don't know! What's the meaning of this? Aren't you that boy who—"

"Did he come back from the battle yet? Tell me!" Alex demanded.

"I don't know!"

"She don't," Erk said. "We checked the room you said was his, too, no sign of him."

"Blastrafters!" Alex swore, and stomped out of the room.

The last stragglers of the Rodeni came up within the castle walls, through old sewers and drains. "It's impossible to get through the streets now," one of them reported proudly. Alex looked out the high windows to see smoke and flames rising above some of the rooftops. "We gave 'em what for, eh?" the Roden added, to cheers from surrounding fellows.

"Now what?" Flip asked Alex, who seemed to be going frantic.

"I've got to get ready to face Chernan, somehow," he said, Flip hopping after him as he ran through the halls. "He's the one who started that plague, he's got to know how to fix it. He's the *only* one who *can* fix it, with magic." Alex knew Mote was constantly aware of the Oether, and would warn him if Chernan or any other magist approached, but still he was nervous.

They'd found Chernan's study, with the bay leaves still scattered on the floor, but the desk had been cleared; the books and notes were gone, and the embers in the fireplace were warm.

"He knew we were coming," Alex said, looking at them. "How— oh, why do I ask. He's a wizard, of course he knew."

The Towers weren't the only structures the Rodeni had destroyed. They'd also set the barracks and guardposts aflame, broken into the city storehouses, and smashed the doors and windows of the tax collector's central agency. Out of fear and respect they'd left the temples of Jenju alone, but the bull-pit had been vandalized and the bulls themselves had been killed and piled into the rubble of their stalls, and set alight. Some of the Rodeni were gnawing smugly on chunks of charred, half-raw beef. (This later led to the totally false rumor that the Rodeni had eaten the Humani overseers of the bull-pits.)

This had been mainly just random aggression. Except for a few stones through the windows of some of the wealthier merchant buildings and a few other targets of opportunity, they'd managed to restrain themselves. Now, however, the general chaos had been taken up by the Humani populace; the Humani were already drunk and riled up from the war, and the Rodeni had killed or frightened away most of the city guardsman. There was looting and a sort of unspecified mayhem; some Humani were rebelling against the king who'd failed to protect them from this attack by the Rodeni. The majority, however, were more interested in the opportunities for redistribution of wealth afforded by the breakdown in law and order.

Alex, watching this from one of the high parapets of the castle, had an idea. The Rodeni had, after hours of hard work, finally broken into the king's treasury. It was mainly sacks and chests of the little ceramic tilecoins; most anything of real value had been traded away to other islands for bronze. Alex had the Rodeni carry the coins up to the audience platform that overlooked the plaza, from where the king made his announcements and speeches. Then, as the crowd of Humani milled below, he had the Rodeni throw handfuls of the ceramic coins down to the populace.

Much cheering and shouting greeted this largess; a good number of the coins shattered on the cobblestones, despite the best efforts of the Humani to catch them, until one wise woman thought to spread her wide skirts into a catching net; then there was quickly a thick pillow of shirts, coats, and clothing spread below. Despite some protests by the Rodeni, Alex had them disperse the entire store of hoarded tilecoins. This took quite some time, and a real carnival had started up in the plaza outside. Each reappearance of the Rodeni, burdened with clattering sacks, at the balcony was now greeted with cheers better than Belthar had received in many years. "It's symbolic," Alex explained, when the Rodeni asked him why.

There was still no sign of Chernan. Alex knew, though, that enough guards and soldiers had escaped that surely some of them had gone to report to their king, busy with the conquest of Deridal. Given some several hours for the messenger to get there at top strich-speed, then probably a short time to organize a retaliation, and then some more several hours for that retaliation to make its way back here . . . Time enough to rest, for the moment.

Several of the Rodeni seemed fairly competent in organizational skills; they'd already worked out a system of watches and patrols around the castle's perimeter. The wounded had been gathered into the big dining hall, scene of Alex's embarrassing meal. Despite past conflicts, Alex almost wished Clak were present now; a shaman to help comfort and heal the injured would have been very useful. Still, the Rodeni knew a bit of folk medicine themselves, and Alex helped where he could, stitching wounds and setting broken bones—not all that different from some of his training at the College. Even easier, he decided after a time, because at least a Roden could tell you where it hurt, and wouldn't just seek to hide its injury, as an animal would.

The first part of the retaliation came quickly; Alex didn't dare fall asleep, partly after what had happened the last time he'd allowed himself to sleep, and partly because, as an Animist, he would be the only one who could possibly see Chernan if the magist decided to infiltrate their ranks, but mainly because, as a Human, he was the only one in the makeshift counterattack who could see well enough at all to spot the approach of distant troops. At first he thought the glinting, flickering motion in the dim light of dawn was a hallucination brought on by exhaustion, but even after blinking and shaking his head it was still there. Pleep, who seemed to like him, was just bringing him another cup of coffee as he jerked away from the window; his sudden motion startled her and coffee went all over both of them. He apologized quickly and left her mopping at her splashed fur in annoyance as he staggered down the stairs.

TWELVE

It was a small group of about a dozen soldiers, mounted on striches, half with short bows with arrows knocked, the other half with spears. They wore no armor, to minimize the weight on their panting striches, and they looked nervously around at the broken and burning gates and Towers, and at the jeering citizens who greeted their return. Ignoring the Humani, they rode straight up to the castle; obviously one of the men who'd been allowed to escape had told the army where the Rodeni had taken shelter.

They stopped there. Alex, with Gleet and Erk on either side of him, raised a hand from the balcony above them, wary of the bows the men carried. In front of Erk, gripped by stern paws on his arms, was the prince, too tired to cry anymore, just whining and struggling feebly against the Roden's grasp.

"You go back, and tell King Belthar we wish to parlay!" Alex shouted at them. "We have something I think he wants to keep. Hardly a fair trade, one life for thousands, but it wasn't easy finding anything the king could care about more than his own self."

"Surrender at once, or we shall attack!" one of the soldiers shouted.

"You're the king, are you?" Alex asked sarcastically. "By all means, attack us if you like. Then go and tell your king how you killed his wife and only son." Alex actually had no intention of allowing the hostages to be killed, but with any luck these soldiers would think nothing was too evil or sadistic to be beyond the capability of Rodeni.

"Yeah, who do you think you are?" shouted one of the citizens, who'd now gathered like hopeful blackbirds every time someone came out on this balcony. He was glaring at the soldier with the belligerence of the truly drunk. "You and what army, now? You bully bastards all rompin' around poor dumb Deridal while we get overrun with Rodeni! Serves you right, I figger, they done outsmarted you and now you gotta deal with 'em!"

"I say we do better with the rats than with the royalty!" quipped a friend of his, making a mocking bow to the little group on the balcony. "Long life to the Rat King, I say!" Alex noticed a bag of coins that had missed the earlier dumping, and he scooped out a double handful and threw them down. There was a brief scramble among the citizens.

The soldiers stood there on their striches, watching this and muttering among themselves. One of the citizens, reaching for a coin, stepped too close to one of the striches, making it startle; the soldier mounted on it snarled and turned to swat the offending man with the butt of his spear, but the man swore back at him and grabbed the spear, yanking it out of his hands. There was a dangerous grumbling among the crowd.

The soldiers drew closer together, exchanging glances, and then quickly, without a word, they turned and rode back the way they came. A couple of Humani threw bits of garbage after them, but they were riding fast and already out of range.

Alex apologized to the young prince as they led him back inside, and the boy kicked Alex on the shin for his trouble. Back in the royal bedchambers, the queen was picking distractedly at a rich plate of pastries. Despite the Rodeni's appetites for all the delicacies in the castle larder, Alex made sure that the two hostages got nothing but the best.

He was a bit worried, though. The Rodeni were drinking normal water now (and wine, and beer, and anything they could find) and there were far too many of them filling the confined castle. Already some scuffles had broken out; only the tension of their position seemed to be keeping them together. Alex hoped the matter was resolved soon, or his careful plan would dissolve into chaos.

The sun was past its zenith when a much more impressive procession came into view along the road. Alex had finally submitted to wolf-naps, taking fifteen-to-twenty minute dozes in between getting up and making a quick search of the surrounding scenery. This approaching procession, with its carts and large military escort, could only have been the king's.

This time the citizens were not so quick to show open rebellion. Kings on Miraposa had a deep, almost mystical importance; hence the strange situation in Deridal, where their king had been retained even though he was no longer truly capable of governing the city. The citizens fell back to let the procession pass, but a crowd was gathering, a muttering, curious crowd, anxious to see what would happen.

The procession, a large number of guards and soldiers, fully armed and armored, mounted and on foot on all sides of two large covered ox-carts, slowly made its way up to the front of the castle, where the soldiers had stood before. Alex, peering through an arrow-slit, watched for any sight or sign of Chernan, but didn't see any. Again he and the Rodeni guards stepped out onto the balcony, with the prince. They didn't bring the queen, because she was a large woman, and prone to fainting; after Erk's friend Sut had almost been crushed underneath her, they found it was better to leave her in her chambers. The prince, however, was nicely portable.

The lead cart stopped, and the pavilion covering it was pulled back. King Belthar sat comfortably on a sort of portable throne, padded against the roughness of the road. He glared up at Alex, who was looking in his general direction, but with his eyes in the slightly unfocused gaze of one searching the Oether just as hard as he could. On his shoulder, Mote craned her head about in response. The king probably couldn't see these details, from this angle and distance. But he did see his son, held in the grasp of a filthy white Roden. The prince saw his father, and shouted, "Daddy! Make them lemme go!" and struggled with Erk a moment.

The king's face went white, then red. Obviously struggling to control himself, he looked up at Alex, and said, "So. First you lead our rats away, now you return to take our children? What price will you ask this time?" He paused, and smiled. "Perhaps we can arrange a . . . trade?" he suggested, and at a signal, someone pulled back the curtain from the second cart. There, tied into a similar throne arrangement and guarded by several soldiers, was Princess Celine. Her long hair was a wild mess, but she did not seem to be harmed, only furious. She looked up at Alex, and he forced himself not to look. *He won't kill her, he won't kill her,* Alex thought frantically to himself. *I know he won't. I didn't plan for this . . . I've got to work around it, somehow, then try some way to sneak in, get her free, get her away . . . after all the Rodeni have done, all they've suffered . . . I can't sell them away, not even for her. I can't.*

Alex blinked hard, and let himself come back into focus, knowing that Mote would warn him if there was any sudden appearance in the Oether. "King Belthar, my price is threefold. Your ears, your heart, and your words." He paused, trying to remember this speech; he'd been working on it, off and on, while trying to stay awake, and the details were a bit muddled. "Your ears I hope I have. I hope right now you're listening to me, and therefore, you're listening to a spokesman for a people whom you've never given a voice. It's tragic, as it is, that they had to get a Human to translate such basic concepts as decency and justice into words another Human would listen to."

"I assume you're referring to Deridal," said King Belthar.

"No!" Alex shouted. "Deridal was treated poorly, but the same as you've treated all these cities of Miraposa. Take them, tax them, torment them, conscript their sons to die for your glory. Sons that their families loved just as much as you love yours." The prince gave a sob at a surreptitious nudge from Erk. "But I was referring to the Rodeni. You treated them like animals, worse than animals. They're people. And yes, they've taken your castle, taken your son, taken your treasury. But had the situations been reversed, you wouldn't have captured their children; you would have killed them. Your orders to your soldiers have always been to kill the Rodeni on sight; males, females, blind infants. You should thank the gods above that these 'animals' have more compassion and mercy than you've shown."

King Belthar was fuming, but Alex was rambling on with the punchy assurance of one delirious with exhaustion. "That's why I ask for your heart. I know you've got one, and I want you to look into it now, see the fear and anger you feel when you see your boy up here—" he pointed to the prince, who made a half-hearted effort to bite his finger "—and know that the Rodeni felt that, lived that, when they saw you kill their families, their friends, their mates and children, when you drove them from their homes, when you sent them to die in bull-pits. They felt that same helpless terror and rage when you destroyed the last home they had, Deridal. They don't have any choice but to fight, as you would fight. Like trapped and cornered animals.

"But we're *not* animals—" (Alex hesitated, and was about to go into a long explanation that, well, yes, actually they *were* animals, mammals in fact, and—but he stopped himself. Animists weren't meant to make these kinds of speeches, he realized, but he pressed on.) "Not animals. Humani, Rodeni . . . we're Trading races. We're sapient, sentient. We can talk. We can listen. That's why I want, last but most importantly, your words. I want you to parley with us, with the Rodeni, with ourselves as representatives of Deridal, if you like, with Princess—with Queen Celine, whom you've brought to this meeting as well." He paused, looking down at her, hoping this would somehow all work out . . . "I want a truce, on your word of honor."

There was a long pause.

Then the king spoke. "Very well. On my word of honor, I declare a state of truce . . ."

"Until negotiations are completed," Alex said, just to make sure.

"—until negotiations are completed," snarled the king, looking helplessly up at his son. Gleet leaned over and whispered something in Alex's ear.

"—and a minimum of three days," Alex added.

"All right, three days!" shouted Belthar, shaking his fist. "Let us in. Let me see my son, my wife."

"You can leave your guards outside," Alex called down. Belthar shook his head.

"No! Do you think I'm a fool, to walk into a rat's trap that's already caught my family? My guards must come with me, to protect my self, and my interests." He waved a hand toward the captive princess.

Reluctantly, Alex conceded, and slowly the main gate was lowered, and the procession filed into the courtyard of the castle. Rodeni watched from the parapets and windows, wary but hopeful. All around the side gates and slit windows, Humani citizens crowded, as they had the day the pipe-playing stranger had come to town, eager to watch this latest drama. Most were hoping that the parlay would take place outside in the courtyard; this was quality entertainment. Alex thought to himself that a Deridal-style parliament would fit in quite well here.

The gate was shut behind the procession as the last soldier marched in. Alex noticed that the soldiers seemed to be rather more relaxed now, knowing that, for the moment, they wouldn't have to be fighting anyone. The Rodeni, they knew, were craven little creatures, and wouldn't dare to attack them, even in ambush. Alex knew better, but knew, too, judging from Flip and Gleet's stance beside him as they made their way to the courtyard, that the Rodeni now were feeling a cautious optimism, a readiness to sit back and see what might happen. Their tension at the crowded conditions was being bound tight by hope.

Which was why everyone was rather surprised when, as Alex stepped out onto a balcony one level above the courtyard, to greet the king's cart, Belthar snarled, "There can be no truce with vermin!" and shot him with a Deridal crossbow he'd had concealed in his lap.

Alex dropped, the force of the bolt punching him clean off his feet. Mote gave a shrill, screaming cry, as loud as the abrupt silence that followed it.

"Attack, you idiots, attack!" shouted the king, waving his arms frantically at his soldiers; they quickly drew weapons and obeyed. At the gates and windows, gasps and shouts rang up from the citizens of Belthas.

The Rodeni saw their friend fall, heard the cry of the *mookchee*. The pulse of rage washed through them. Hundreds of eyes narrowed, teeth bared, tails lashed, and the Rodeni sprung, like a single flowing organism. Part of the furry tide went washing over the Animist's body like floodwaters as they leapt from the balcony into the fray below.

Alex regained consciousness at the thudding of flat Rodeni feet bouncing over him, kicking and grinding the bolt that had skimmed his breastbone and sunk into his left shoulder. Lucky for him the king was a poor shot, even at close range.

The last of the Rodeni leapt past him and vanished over the edge of the balcony. He rolled into the shelter of the hallway, and tried to push himself up into a standing position. Mote was on his wounded shoulder, frantically alternating trying to clean the blood away and gnawing at the offending bolt, tearing out the bright blue fletchings in her fury. Alex stared blearily out at the scene in the courtyard, his left arm hanging uselessly.

The Rodeni were attacking in a milling mass, the air thick with the shouts of Humani and the shrill screams of the Rodeni. Outside, he could hear the roar of the citizens of Belthas; it was unclear for whom they might be cheering, or cursing. The soldiers were pressed right back against the carts, stabbing and slashing with their bronze swords, their bronze armor already red with blood. The Rodeni were many, but these were the elite of Belthar's army: loyal, well-trained, armored and armed in metal. It was still anyone's war.

Unseen by Alex, one single, huddled shape was trembling, shaking, his jaws working as he struggled against the compulsion that swept over him. Around him his kin and kind beat with a single bloody pulse, a lemminglike drive to death, in which there was no one, only all. But Flip fought it, fought to remain himself, to hope against hope that Alex his friend might be alive, might be up there, might need help. He could picture him, the Human, now suffering and dying slowly as Nuck had done, with no one to help him, no one to be with him. With slow, stumbling hops, like a fever-blind rabbit, he pushed his way against the physical and mental flood of Rodeni fury, and made his way toward the stairs, fighting with his will for every step.

Mote suddenly gave a warning squeak, and Alex spun as a flare in the Oether suddenly manifested itself. There was a smell, a powerful reek that reminded Alex, dizzy with exhaustion, pain, and lost blood, of his cool, quiet little garden back in Deridal. It was the smell of mint. Mote had clambered onto his head (he'd lost the Big Hat on the ride to Belthas) and was flattening herself against his scalp, concentrating, as Alex had taught her, on blocking any hostile magic with the force of the Animist bond.

The mint smell seemed to fade, and leaning against the opposite wall, in a possibly unintentional parody of Alex's own stance, was Chernan. He looked calm and unruffled as ever, and gave Alex a little smile and a wave.

"You," Alex managed. Not original, but it was the best he could come up with, given the circumstances.

"I suspected you'd be able to see me," Chernan commented, apparently oblivious to the screaming fury of the Rodeni below. He spoke in Trade, probably out of contempt for Alex, unwilling to treat him as a fellow Human. "They can't, of course," he added, nodding in the direction of the battle. "Right now they'd kill you, too, if you were down there. They aren't thinking anymore. Nothing fights like someone with nothing to lose."

"You . . . you . . ." Alex stammered, unable to formulate his thoughts any further than this.

"Me, yes. More than you can possibly know."

"I know enough . . ." Alex wheezed. "The king asked you to help him take Deridal, and to get rid of the Rodeni, too. So you combined them, drove them into our city, to drive them mad . . ."

"I did have some local help," Chernan admitted modestly. "But you had to meddle in that, as well."

"Clak! And when he failed you, you killed him and used him to poison the water, and you cursed the Rodeni with a plague—"

"Yes, yes," said Chernan impatiently. "Now. Aren't you curious why I haven't killed you yet?"

"Uh . . ." Alex managed.

"Alex. All this . . . This is power. This is magic. You see? Not just leading rats to dance, but making Rodeni, Humani . . . any race you care to, dance to the tune you call. Best of all, they don't even know you're playing." Chernan spread his hands and smiled.

"But . . . why?" Alex asked helplessly. "Why are you bothering with me? The Rodeni are trying to kill your king, and your . . . the princess!" Alex stammered, trying to ignore the coldness creeping over him. His blood was pattering on the stone and he could sense in himself the signs of shock.

"Princess?" scoffed Chernan. "She's nothing to me, no more than that idiot king, hells, *either* of those idiot kings, ever were. I imagine she made up some story about me to get you to follow her around, and stop protecting Carawan."

"She . . . did you charm her, somehow? Make her turn against Carawan? But I'd have seen . . ."

"No. I don't give a damn about her. Fool. You've seen what I can do. If I'd wanted her, I'd have had her, a thousand times over, and none of you could have prevented me."

Alex was shaking his head, trying to make the world stop spinning. "I don't . . . What's this all about, then? Whose side are you on?" he whispered.

"My side, as always," said Chernan, with a smile. "My side. And what's it all about?" He tilted his head. "It's fun. That's why. All this, all this blood, death, confusion, intrigue . . . it's all been marvelous fun to play with. I don't really care who wins, or loses, lives or dies, as long as it's interesting to watch."

"You . . . you're mad," Alex managed, staring in horror at the Oether-glowing wizard. "When I first met you, you seemed so Human, Temith's friend, with a pet cat. But now I see you're some kind of monster, who hides behind a Humani shell . . ."

Chernan's easy, cheerful air vanished, and his look became stern. "Silence, Animist . . . *boy*. And I'll tell you why I have let you live thus far. I've shown you power, shown you what it can do. And I can teach you—you have talent, wasted in your pathetic, clinging link to that pestilent beast on your head. Yes, my offer still stands. But now it's a simple choice. Join me, or die." He stretched out a hand, welcoming.

It was the Choice. They'd talked about it at the College. The talent that made Animists dangerous to magists, could be used by magists if the Animist chose to abandon his calling. To accept, for Alex, would mean freedom from slavery, from his dependence on Mote, from his weakness and guilt and failure. Alex felt his head bowing as

the wizard stepped closer. Just accept, let his defenses down, let the
wizard work his magic on Alex's mind . . . accept a new master.

"No!" Alex screamed.

anger fierce defend!

Mote squealed and bit Chernan's fingers; before Alex could
move, Chernan had snatched Mote off his head. She squeaked,

terror! fury! panic!

sinking her teeth into Chernan's hand as he gripped her; he didn't
even flinch, just inspected her closely.

"Well, I'm disappointed, but I suppose not that surprised," he
said with a sigh. Alex tried to grab her back, but Chernan gave him a
casual shove that knocked him sprawling back against the wall, the
bolt grinding in his shoulder. Alex gave a breathless, almost soundless
scream of agony.

"I take it this is the real one, this time?" Chernan added, holding
Mote up as she wriggled and writhed in his grip, biting and biting,
then starting to wheeze and struggle as he tightened his bloody fist,
not quite crushing her. Alex blinked hard, reaching helplessly out
again for his Anim. Chernan dangled her just out of reach, by her tail,
as he backed away. Alex followed, trying to grab her, stumbling and
sliding along the hallway. Chernan laughed softly.

"I'm tormenting you, aren't I? Tsk. As I said, it's been fun, but
I'm afraid like all good things, this must come to an end. Good-bye,
Animist . . . an Animist to the end. Your College would have been
proud of you. What a good little slave you are."

The wizard had arrived at the railing of the balcony, and he
hurled Mote away with a contemptuous toss of his arm. She sailed out
into space, a grey shape tumbling. Alex lunged helplessly, but his legs
gave way, and he fell to his hands and knees in front of Chernan. His
mind was full of the sensation of falling, tumbling end over end—he
gave a last thought of love to his faithful Anim, and prepared to die as
he sensed her swift descent toward the hard cold stone below.

Mote landed on the furry body of a dead Roden, and bounced, her
whiskers a-tremble. All around her were stamping feet; somewhere—

her head slowly tracked from side to side, her eyes unfocused. *There,* there was her Animist, her friend, her Alex. Concentrating, fixating on him, on his mind, his thoughts, she set off like a grey streak of lightning. She ran, weaving and jumping and dodging as feet thudded and pounded around and over her, a dying soldier falling like a massive felled tree barely missing her with an outflung arm.

Alex could have wept for joy and relief, but knew better. The pounding pulse of Mote's heartbeat was thudding through his head, as his vision took on the hallucinating overlay of hers; she was trying her best to shield him from Chernan's magic, but he knew she wasn't strong enough, and was too far away. He was doomed, and so was she; the brief stay of execution was strictly temporary. He slowly looked up into Chernan's face, saw the eyes watching him with a strange, totally inhuman coldness, a casual curiosity as one might display toward a microscope slide full of protozoan parasites. The voice spoke with the inflections of surprise, the eyebrows went up accordingly, but the eyes, the eyes were cold as the deepest depths of the sea.

"You're *still* alive?" Chernan said, with a sigh. "Dammit, I have to do *everything* around here," he grumbled, and his eyes narrowed. Even though Mote was still far away, scrambling toward him as best as her small body could, clambering over the dead and dying, Alex could sense the sudden crackling swell of power as Chernan's hands slowly traced gestures, preparing a final, devastating death spell.

Flip stumbled into the far end of the hallway, looking for Alex. The Roden saw the tall wizard looming over the huddled, helpless Animist, silhouetted against the open balcony. Without thinking, with only the sudden release of the fury that was trying to overtake him, Flip leapt forward on his powerful hind legs.

His first bound closed half the distance. Chernan looked up and saw him in the middle of the second bound, and the spell came smashing down as Flip leapt a third time, over Alex, right at Chernan's face, his mouth gaping wide. Crackling, arcing, spitting blue lightning exploded around them, baking brains, boiling blood. The pain, the noise, the light and the darkness . . .

Alex mercifully lost consciousness as his body went into seizures, the magic arcing through him, burning, destroying. Outside in the courtyard, Mote blinked, stopped, and fell over on her side, twitching.

Flip was struck dead in mid-leap. In the spasm of death his jaws snapped shut, his long yellow teeth meeting in Chernan's throat. They locked with a bulldog grip, buried deep, crushing artery and windpipe. Chernan struggled, staggered, his eyes burning, glazing as he died.

The wizard's death throes sent arcs of crackling magic out in snapping, sparking ripple-rings. In the courtyard fighting, where the Rodeni were just pulling down the last soldiers, and finally about to lunge for the cowering king, the magic swept across the combatants in a wave of pain and noise, knocking them down, shaking them like rags. The soldiers screamed and fell to the ground, shaking and trembling along with the Rodeni. King Belthar fell from his seat, rolled off the cart, thrashing helplessly; the princess writhed, straining against her bonds until they cut into her fine wrists, then snapped. She convulsed out of her chair, her body curling itself into a tight fetal position.

The magic scythed through the crowds outside, knocking them down as they clutched at their heads, fell to their knees. Along the road all the way to Deridal, it was said later, soldiers and citizens, prisoners and peasants staggered and stumbled as though the earth itself was shaking. Then slowly the power faded, draining away into the earth and sea and sky.

Chernan's body slumped against the wall. Still hanging from his throat was Flip, and at his feet lay Alex. All were spattered with blood.

The Rodeni and Humani in the courtyard slowly stood, looking around, blinking, as though wakened from a dream. But then quickly they remembered where they were, what they'd been doing, and they grabbed for their weapons. And it would have been a very short struggle, the stunned and staggering few Humani soldiers with their king groaning on the bloody ground against the massed Rodeni, still numerous although many, many of them had fallen in the attack. But the princess, looking around, got to her feet, and ran to stand over the king; he'd hurt his knee in the fall, and couldn't get up.

"Stop!" shouted the princess. "On behalf of Deridal, Queen Celine is willing to accept your surrender, King Belthar," she told him, her voice shaky but still ringing with command. "And you shall not be harmed, despite the custom. There has been enough death for one day."

Belthar looked around, looked at the surrounding Rodeni, their teeth and glittering eyes. He hadn't known there were so many; he hadn't known they would fight back, he hadn't known they could show courage or cunning . . . he'd never expected anything except a quick and simple slaughter, or he wouldn't have led his men into this ambush. But the slaughter he'd found was the wrong one entirely, and had almost been his own. Fighting to speak around the pain and fear and shock, he managed to speak.

"Yes. Yes, we accept," he gasped. The guards threw down their weapons gratefully, flinging their hands in the air, murmuring thankful prayers to Jenju and other gods that they'd been spared from death. The Rodeni took up the cry, in voices of gladness and surprise.

"Surrendered!" Outside, through the recovering crowd, the news spread, and there was confusion, some cheering, some shouting, but all craning to see as Queen Celine of Deridal gracefully helped her fallen adversary to stand, and to limp with her into the castle. The crowd of Rodeni swept along with them, loping and limping wearily, but some here and there leaping into the air in excited bounds. Along the way, one of the Rodeni paused, and stopped to scoop something up in her hands, then she went bounding after the others.

The king was reunited with his family; there were tearful embraces. The queen and prince were frightened but unharmed. They'd been left locked in their chambers when the Rodeni ran to battle, driven by their collective compulsion. This had surely saved their lives; Erk had felt and sensed the rage building as the word of Alex's death had swept the ranks, down the hallways, to where he and his friends guarded the prince and queen. He'd felt the urge to kill the Humani, but had fought it; he'd kicked his fellow Rodeni out and went with them, locking the door behind him before being swept instead into the mad rush to the courtyard. He was dead now, slashed through with a sword, on top of a pile of his comrades in the courtyard.

Pleep ran up to her brother, who was limping badly; a sword blow had severed his broad foot, and he was hobbling awkwardly on the stub of his ankle, hastily bound with the straps that tied his pants leg. She bounded up to him and almost knocked him over.

"Chis, Chis, look what I found," she squealed at him in Rodeni, her eyes wide. Chis looked at what she was holding up, a small limp furry thing. "It's the *mookchee!*" she exclaimed. It was indeed the grey small one with the star on its face, limp and still and bloody.

"We'll make sure they bury it with Alex," Chis began, sadly, but Pleep interrupted him, as the limp shape gave a deep, heaving breath.

"Chis, it's alive! Alive!" she said. Other Rodeni turned to hear what the young one was babbling about, and saw, and heard, and knew.

"It's alive? Then he must be—"

"But we saw—"

"We've got to find him!"

They found him. They shook him, tried to wake him, pulled him out of the pool of blood. He was alive, but barely.

Below them, in the castle, other Rodeni watched and whispered as the king and the princess debated. The princess had insisted that the gates be opened, and the citizens allowed to hear their discussion; now the main audience chamber was full of people, Humani and Rodeni.

Back in the upper hallway, Pleep had the idea of putting the *mookchee* on her master's head, where he always used to carry her. They held her there while others grabbed Alex's legs, others his arms, and with much swaying and cursing, they carried him downstairs to their makeshift hospital. More Rodeni came for Flip's body. They had to use a pry-wedge to free his teeth from the dead wizard's throat. The task was made more difficult by their reluctance to touch the wizard, but finally Flip's jaws released their grip. The Rodeni picked up Flip's body, and dragged it away. Rodeni had only minimal beliefs involving the disposal of corpses; typically they were interred in the deepest catacombs, set aside for that purpose. Humani had much more complex rites, and the Rodeni knew this; they left Chernan's body where it had fallen, and soon it had the hall to itself.

The blood-glazed eyes blinked.

Alex woke up with a familiar splitting headache; at least this time he hadn't fallen out a window as well as getting side-smacked with a death spell. He blinked, opened his eyes, but this didn't seem to make a lot of difference. But still, if he had a headache, that must mean he wasn't dead.

"You're awake," said a voice, a chirping Rodeni voice, thick with relief. Mote was a warm presence on his forehead, shifting slightly.

dizzy hungry

"Wha—what happened?" Alex asked, looking around. "Why is it so dark?"

There was silence, and a faint breeze in front of his face in the dim darkness. *Maybe I am dead,* he thought suddenly. Slowly memory was returning: the battle, Chernan, his face twisting in the focused concentration of a spell, a blur of motion, then pain, endless pain. "Am I dead?" he asked cautiously. You could never be sure. At least, he took some comfort in Mote's familiar presence.

"No," said the voice, a little more subdued now. "But you're blind."

Alex blinked, and squinted, and blinked again. "Uh. I guess I am," he said, shakily. "Who's that?"

"Pleep," said the voice. "We thought you *were* dead, but I found your *mookchee.*"

"Cher—the magist, where—"

"Flip, and the Human with you . . . both dead when we found you," reported the voice.

Alex tried to put his hands over his face, but his wounds hurt, and he couldn't move his left arm. He settled for pressing one hand over his eyes . . . he still *had* eyes, he could feel them, could feel the tears starting, not for himself, but for Flip, for Carawan, for all his friends and followers and everyone who'd had to die and suffer for Chernan's stupid game . . . the thought that the magist was dead didn't offer much consolation.

Even rubbing his eyelids didn't bring up any of the usual pressure-sparks. It wasn't even like having his eyes closed; everything was just a featureless, dark nothing.

On sudden impulse he checked . . . and the Oether opened up before him, as before, whisping lights in the darkness, oddly much clearer now that there was nothing to underlay the images. Mote stood up on his head, shifting, sniffing. Slowly the Oether faded, and light dawned, a dim, shifting grayness, shapes blurred and oddly skewed away in peripheral vision. Mote was trying to lend him her vision, poor as it was. Alex couldn't help but smile sadly, and he reached up to pat the rat on top of his head.

"Thanks, Mote," he told her. "But it'll take some getting used to."

Pleep filled him in on everything that had happened since they'd seen him shot; Alex, on realizing what had taken place, knew that he was lucky to be only blinded, and not killed, paralyzed, or driven insane and comatose by Chernan's spell. Flip must have somehow interposed himself, borne the brunt of it . . . must have killed Chernan, somehow. But the magist had died without explaining the secrets of his plague. The sick Rodeni had no hope, and Alex mentioned this sad fact to Pleep.

"No, no," she corrected. "They are getting better. A Human doctor came, and brought medicines . . ."

"A white-haired Human?" Alex asked in surprise. "Temith's alive?"

"Yes, he was hurt, was captured, but princess demanded all prisoners be freed. He gave medicines in Deridal, then came here, fixed your shoulder, and back again to Deridal, now . . ."

"How long have I been—"

"Several days you slept. The doctor said *coma*. Said you might wake before the wedding, but maybe not."

"Wedding? What wedding?" Alex asked, trying to sit up.

"The marriage for the alliance," Pleep explained, pushing and pulling to help him sit upright. "The princess of Deridal is to marry the prince of Belthas."

Alex was dismayed. "But he's just a child! And she's—"

"She suggested it! Says it is Humani political custom," Pleep added, with the tone in her voice implying that there was no further explanation needed when discussing the myriad idiocies of Humani behaviors.

Alex groaned, and sank back onto the bed. It made sense, and it was a common custom in these islands. But even so . . .

"But King Belthar says Rodeni will have full citizenship!" Pleep added quickly, trying to cheer him up. "Princess insisted. Not to be beaten and killed and harmed any more. To live free, just like Humani. King Belthar will let them stay in Deridal, or in Belthas, or in any of his cities, no more Towers. He knows," Pleep added smugly, "now, what we can do, what we will do, if he breaks his word again. And the Humani, they agree."

"I'm glad," Alex said, and he was. But he wasn't exactly happy.

The wedding was the next day, or some time after, or at night; Alex wasn't sure. He stayed in bed, on the excuse that he still felt unwell. His head ached, and his vision did not return. He heard the bells ringing from his bed in the infirmary, surrounded by other makeshift beds holding wounded and dying Humani and Rodeni. Day and night was more featureless blackness, with the smells and the sounds of the wounded and the dying all around him.

Some priests of Aescula came in to attend them that day of the wedding; apparently they came every day but Alex had been unconscious before and hadn't seen them. He watched warily in the Oether as the glowing shapes moved about from bed to bed, with the flares of magic as they worked their healing powers. Mote was a

wary, mistrustful

presence on his head.

One of them approached his bed; Alex could see the soft glow, not as bright as Chernan's had been at the peak of his powers, but bright enough. "Child," said a soft Humani voice, female, "I can heal you."

"I'm fine," Alex said, wishing he had the strength, and the sight, necessary to get up and run away. Mote was sitting on his head, bristling; he got the impression of a tall blurred shape, and a smell of incense and woman, but nothing clearer.

fear suspicion

As though she had read his thoughts, the priestess said, gently, kindly, "I can restore your sight. Just remove your Anim, let me help you. Open yourself to the light, to Aescula. Relax, let me—"

"Get *away!*" Alex screamed, suddenly terrified, as the light in the Oether flared, sparking too many memories; he flung himself backward out of bed and scrambled, stumbling over a cot and pulling it crashing down over him, its furry occupant yelping and struggling with him, hurrying footsteps, Mote squealing.

"All right, stop it, this is a sickroom, not a street brawl," snapped a familiar voice. Alex lunged toward it and fell across Temith's feet. There was a grumbling rustle as the injured Roden scrambled back into his cot. It was Chis, having the stump of his leg treated.

"I was only trying—" began the female voice, sounding hurt.

"Your concern is appreciated, but not, I think, by the patient," Temith answered her, politely. He helped Alex to stand. "If he decides he wants Aescula's help, I'll be sure and let you know," Temith told her, kindly but firmly, and led Alex away.

"I suppose you're well enough after all, then," he said, as soon as they were out of the room. "It's good to see you up and about again . . ."

"I want to go home," Alex said, shuffling his feet along, wary of anything that might trip him. He was weak and unsteady still, but determined.

"To Deridal? Not a problem. The royals are all moving into the palace anyway. King Belthar's to be king, seeing as we don't have one anymore, with Carawan gone . . ." Temith sighed sadly, "but with this new alliance, at least, things won't be too bad, for us, for the Rodeni, or for Deridal. And eventually, of course, Celine will be queen, and that's a way of a victory for Carawan, I suppose . . ."

"What about the other advisors?" Alex asked.

"Serra's all right; we had been holding the tower, barely, while the General tried to get Carawan away. After he'd left, they weren't as interested in attacking us. But Valence is dead. As for myself, well, I'm a bit of a mess . . ." Alex had stretched out a hand, trying to feel his way along, and Temith took it kindly to lead him. In the scientist's grip, Alex felt the bandaged awkwardness of two missing fingers.

"Lost an eye and an ear, too," Temith commented, as they went along. "But I was lucky, really."

"I don't want to go back to Deridal," Alex clarified. "I want to go back to the College."

"But Celine said she wants you to stay," Temith protested, helping him up a flight of stairs. "She says she needs a Royal Animist; as long as you can still see Oetherwise."

"Why? Chernan's dead," Alex said gruffly.

Temith sighed, and led Alex through a doorway. Mote stiffened and Alex looked up, uselessly, as the familiar

jealous sulk resentment

flickered through his mind.

"Alex!" said Celine's voice, and a patter of feet, then two cool, smooth hands caught his own. Mote gave a cheep of warning which the princess ignored.

"I'm so glad you're recovering!" Celine cried, squeezing his hands. "I need you, Alex . . ."

Despite everything, Alex still felt his heart rise a little. Temith cleared his throat.

"Oh, Temith," said Celine, in a much cooler tone. "Please, don't let us keep you from your work . . ."

"Thank you, Your Majesty," said Temith in equally cool tones, and his voice backed out, saying, "I won't be far, if you need me."

The door boomed shut behind him, and Celine leaned closer. He could tell by the way Mote tensed. "To tell you the truth, Alex, I'm a bit worried about him. He's been acting oddly, lately . . ."

"So's everyone," Alex sighed.

Celine insisted, "You might want to keep a close eye on him. He was one of Chernan's friends, after all . . ."

"But Chernan's dead," Alex protested wearily, gently freeing one of his hands from her grasp to grab Mote, who was tensing for a leap. "You don't need an Animist now . . ."

Celine sighed, and whispered, "No. We daren't let word get out. Only I know this, and Belthar, and his closest guards . . . and you, now, my closest guard. When we sent them back to find Chernan's body . . . it wasn't there." Her voice trembled.

"What?" whispered Alex, wishing he could comfort her, but he was scared, too. He thought of the wizard's words . . . *"She means nothing to me . . . made up some story . . . you'd stop protecting Carawan . . ."* But why should she have wanted Alex to stop protecting her father? Chernan, though, was mad. There was no point in trying to make any sense from his words or actions. Alex was reminded of the body of the magical assassin, who'd gotten up and run away from the General's men. Even death did not bind the magic-born . . .

"There were just some bloody footprints that kind of . . . fade out. It's not over, Alex. I need you more than ever, now."

When Alex had reluctantly conceded to stay, Temith was summoned and came back to lead him away.

"She did offer to pay me twice what I had been getting," Alex mentioned to the scientist, "but—"

"But. But you turned down the money."

"I had to! The country's in ruins, needs everything it has to try to rebuild, I can't in good conscience—"

"Alex! You got into this whole mess because you needed the money, and now you're going to throw it all away—"

"I can't help it. She needs me. She said so."

"Because of Chernan?"

"No—wait. How did you know about that?" Alex, paranoid these days, checked the Oether quickly, but all was quiet.

"I listened at the door. Sorry. Afraid I've always been nosy . . ."

Alex shook his head in irritation, but didn't force the issue. "Well, then you know what happened to his body."

"I do."

"And so you know I can't just walk away and leave her, if he, if that thing is still around, hiding, waiting."

"But you should get paid for it!"

"It's not about that. Cher—he terrifies me. This whole thing . . . but imagine how she must feel! I can't . . ."

"You still love her, don't you? You poor pup." Alex felt his face blushing. Temith opened a door and led him down a long flight of stairs.

"Where are we going?" asked Alex.

"I need your expertise," said Temith. He looked at the boy. Alex walked with a shuffling step and still turned his head constantly, this way and that, as though seeking some light that would be bright enough to penetrate the darkness.

Temith had examined his eyes and found nothing visibly wrong; they were still unclouded brown, and even now, as he passed next to the lantern, the pupils reacted to the light, contracting. But they remained unfocused, unseeing. Temith had to help him along as they descended into the lowest, coldest reaches of the castle's kitchens, and into the cold pantry. Alex seemed to be too wrapped up in his own misery to wonder what was happening.

"There you are," Serra welcomed them, relief in her voice.

"The princess *did* ask him to stay, but he turned down the pay," Temith reported, and Alex heard the sound of the dragging and shuffling of things being moved, and a door being unbolted. The room smelled of cold mildew and old onions.

"What! All this work for nothing?" Serra's voice said.

"Well, we're hoping, anyway." Temith, trying to be lighthearted. "What if she *does* have reason to fear?"

"Then we'll be the first to know, won't we?" Serra, tense.

"Well, he will." The unseen door creaked open, and Alex was led inside. It was much colder here, and water dripped from the ceiling onto Alex's head, and onto Mote, who jerked in response. The door creaked shut behind them.

Temith lit the lamps, fumbling from missing fingers. "Alex," he began, but his voice shook a bit and he caught himself, and restarted, slipping himself firmly into Lecture Mode. "Alex, I need you to watch Oetherwise for me. I don't expect you'll encounter anything, but . . . just in case."

"Certainly, sir." Alex nodded, the little rat on his shoulder looking up and around. Ever curious, Temith continued to watch Alex's eyes, as now they flicked about a bit, still without focusing. It reminded him of the eyes of a dreaming sleeper, though open and eerie.

"There's nothing," he reported after a moment. "Just you and me and Serra. Where are we? What's all this about?"

"No one else," Serra said, with relief in her tones.

"Not yet, anyway," said Temith, and there was a rustling as of fabric moving.

Alex heard Serra make a sound in her throat, and there was a smell in the air, a familiar smell but one he couldn't quite place. Mote had no trouble with it, however, and hid in his hair in fear.

"What . . ." Alex asked, blinking, squinting, wishing he could see. Oetherwise was very quiet, dark, and soothing as it had been before when he was far underground, but the smell of dried blood was strong. He heard the clink of tools, and Serra put her hands on his shoulders. Not to restrain him, but to lean on him, as though fearful or dizzy.

"It's Chernan's body," Temith said, matter-of-factly. Though he probably didn't notice it, his voice was a little higher than normal, from the stress. "I'm going to autopsy him."

Alex felt his gorge rise and forced it down. Behind him, Serra was shaking.

"I wish you wouldn't, Tem," she said. "Alex says there's nothing there, can't we just assume . . ."

"No! If Alex says he's really dead, then there's nothing to worry about, is there?" Temith demanded. "He's just meat now, all right? A corpse. A cadaver. You've butchered enough meat in your time, Serra, and I know you have, too, Alex. Stop acting like . . . like . . . a bunch of priests, or something . . ." Temith's voice was shaking, and he dropped something that clattered on the floor.

"Why?" Alex asked, wanting to back away but unable to do so with Serra behind him. "You know what killed him. It's probably pretty damn obvious!"

It was, to those who could see. Chernan's body was pale but marked with purple bruising where he lay. Most of the blood had been wiped away, but the deep double puncture wound was still there in the throat, the raw edges dark and drying now. The corpse had been kept in the cold room, but even so there was the faint stink . . . Temith handed him a cloth mask, scented with cedar, and Alex gratefully tied it on.

"I moved his body, so that Princess Celine would think there was still something she had to worry about," Temith explained, his own voice muffled a little by his mask. "Partly for you, Alex, I knew you still needed your money to buy your freedom. And partly for her. She's young, and headstrong. Alex, I know how you feel, but she can be ruthless, sometimes . . ."

"She doesn't like *you*, either," Alex said.

"I know. Believe me, I know. She never liked any of the advisors . . . except you, possibly. I'm not sure how much longer she'll let Serra and me stay. If we can put some doubt into her, it will help you keep your position, at least. And besides, I wanted to do this. No College has ever had a thaumaturgist to dissect."

"He was your friend!" cried Alex.

"He was my friend," Temith said, and his voice was unsteady. Alex thought he might be crying. "And yet he went from being a bit of a grump, to becoming a strange, evil, malicious, demonic bastard, who killed my king, my friends, my life. You can't tell me that's normal. He was sick."

"And so you're showing contempt by—"

"No! Respect, and pity, if anything. I think something happened to him. Something drove him mad . . . I knew him for years and never saw more than an ounce of the person he became at the end. When the king lost his mind, I couldn't do anything, because we know so little about how the brain works. If Chernan went mad, maybe I can learn something from that. Something that might save someone else's sanity, later on."

"It's affecting mine right now," said Serra. "And he smells, even through this mask. Come on. Get it over with."

Alex heard the flutter of pages and the scratching of a pen, as Temith quickly made notes, muttering to himself. "Humani male, age thirty-one, height five-ten, weight est one six zero . . . lividity present in . . ." He finally wrapped up with a terse description of the gory wound in the man's throat, and then there was a clink of a large glass scalpel being picked up, and the faint silken sound of slicing skin. Alex stepped back again into Serra, who stepped back twice. The smell was stronger now, but the Oether remained quiet.

"First incision—" Temith was muttering, and Serra interrupted,

"I thought it was his brain you were interested in. I don't think he swallowed it before he was killed."

"I have to do this right," Temith insisted. "I have to follow procedure. What if it turns out he went mad because, oh, he was in constant pain from an ulcer?" There were splopping sounds. "Or that his last meal of . . . what is this? Looks like rice . . . was drugged? Anything might be a clue."

"Glgh . . ."

Alex and Serra remained silent while Temith muttered, cut, noted, and plopped pieces into jars of preservative. Alex stared hard into the Oether, noting again how dark it was, how quiet. Too quiet. Something started dripping onto the floor with loud smacking sounds. Alex felt woozy.

"All right," Temith said at last, "hand me the saw."

More disgusting sounds followed. And then Temith gave a low whistle.

"What?" asked Alex.

"I think I may have found something. Look—oh, sorry. But Serra, you see?"

"Good gods . . . is that his shal?"

"Yes—Alex, you can't see this, but it looks like our friend's shal— you studied anatomy, right?"

"Yes, of course. It's that little kind of a livery thing in the front of the brain, isn't it?"

"Right, and the tendrils that wrap over the brain. All vertebrates have one. We used to think it worked as a liver just for the brain, fil- tering blood, but now we think it's where we keep our emotions. Because it goes over the top of the brain, like a direct road, and con- nects to the optic nerve. It's why, when we see something, we first have an emotion about it, and only later do we *think* about it." There were careful, moist sounds.

"Mote must have a big one, then," Alex said. "When she commu- nicates with me, that's mostly what it is, emotions."

"Not as big as Chernan's . . . the stem of a Humani shal is usually about the size of your thumb." Alex felt his own thumb gingerly. "Chernan's," said Temith, with a little grunt of effort, "is the size . . ." there was a sploshing sound of something going into a jar, "—of my palm," finished Temith. "Cancer, I think."

"No wonder he was unstable!" Serra said. "Full of huge emotions . . ."

"It was probably painful, as well," Temith added. "It had pushed through and overgrown parts of his brain." He sighed. "I have no idea what caused it, of course. When I found his body in his study I looked through the room for any of his journals or anything, but he'd apparently burned them long ago . . ."

"You mean you went through his study after you found him in the hallway," corrected Alex.

"No," Temith insisted, "I found him in his study, slumped against the wall . . ."

"Oh gods," Serra said weakly.

They all stared at the butchered corpse, two with eyes and two with Oether.

"Serra," said Temith, nervously, "and I ask in a spirit of purely scientific inquiry, do you think you could fire up one of the big fireplaces in the lower scullery? I find I'm rather chilled from working in here . . ."

"You mean those big ones for the laundry boilers, that are big enough to cremate a person in? I'll get right on it."

Alex was eventually moved back to Deridal, to his old room. Slowly his wounds healed, though his sight did not return. He got used to relying on the visions of the Oether, the dim shapes and shadows from Mote, and the gradual awakening awareness of sounds and shapes and smells. A lot of the time he'd spend sitting out in the main garden.

As he healed, he often talked about making a trip to the College, or at least arranging to have a tutor arrive to teach him Separation; but Mote wasn't even a year old yet, and everyone kept telling him that there would be plenty of time for that later. Alex suspected that they were really just reluctant to part with the sum in bronze he'd need to pay off his debt.

Len had recovered from the plague; his brother had not. But he and Pleep both came to visit Alex often; he was glad of their company. Temith, despite his wounds, was always going back and forth between Deridal and Belthas, tending the wounded in both places, with the aid of the priests of Aescula. Luken was missing, and presumed to be among the fallen. Gleet, too, was dead, and so were Ket and Noot, who'd helped him through the tunnels. It seemed like every day brought some news of another dead friend.

The princess came and talked to him from time to time; but only briefly, as she was very busy trying to put Deridal back into some form of order. Alex learned that the marriage to the prince was still only a formality at this point; the prince still stayed with his nurse in his own room, here in Deridal. King Belthar and his queen remained in Belthas for the moment, though they planned to eventually move into Deridal's palace as well. The young prince and his nursemaids and servants currently had Carawan's old rooms; the young prince seemed to enjoy playing with the mad king's toys, and perhaps Carawan would have been more than happy to have a playmate to share with.

As per tradition, a monument had been erected on the place where King Carawan had died; a stone plinth, with the circumstances on a small bronze plaque. By some unspoken need, the sculptors had also added another plaque on the opposite side, simply reading: GENERAL RHHUUNN. LOYAL UNTO DEATH. Alex had asked Pleep and Len to lead him out to "see" it, one bright morning. Slowly his fingers traced the words etched into the bronze, straining to make them out; it was possible, but took practice. He was learning. Len couldn't read at all, not even the Rodeni chops, and was rather impressed. While Alex was trying to make out an odd word on the plaque (it was "slayne"; one of the sculptors wasn't a very good speller), a voice called his name, sounding from an odd angle.

"Who's that?" he asked, tilting and turning to try to catch the sound.

"It is the Highness Princess waving from her window," Pleep reported, waving back. But the princess did not seem friendly; she looked worried, and angry. The Rodeni couldn't read these Humani expressions very well, though, especially not at this distance, and didn't notice.

"Alex! Come up here, quickly!" Celine called, and Alex nodded, and held out his hand. Len took it in his friendly warm paw, and led him back inside the palace, Pleep bounding along beside and warning him of where to put his feet.

When they got there, Alex could tell at once that there was something wrong in Celine's voice. She sent Len and Pleep away, rather brusquely, Alex thought, but they didn't seem to notice, and bounded off cheerfully enough. Mote sulked on Alex's shoulder, but at least she had stopped threatening Celine.

"Alex, thank the gods I found you," she said, as soon as they were alone. "Have you seen Temith?" she demanded.

Alex was, by now, able to give a rueful smile. "Well, no, not recently."

"I mean, do you know where he is?" Her voice was angry, and his joke didn't help her.

"Last I heard, he was back in Belthas . . . why?" he asked, concerned now.

"I've just had word from there. King Belthar is dead . . . Temith murdered him, and the queen as well."

"What?!" Alex was stunned.

"He was supposed to be treating the king's knee, the one he hurt in the fighting. Belthar's been spending most of his time in his room, and the pain had been bothering him. Temith always asked that he be allowed to help the king, he said he didn't trust any priests if you weren't around to make sure they weren't trying to put an Influence on the King." She paused, and took his hand; Alex still jerked a little at the touch, even though he knew she was married, even though he could no longer gaze on her beauty. Mote ground her teeth in his ear.

"The king must have called for him last night—we usually had guards go up with him but no one bothered this time—and Temith must have seen his chance. We think he poisoned Belthar and the queen somehow—probably told them it was medicine. No one's seen him since he went up to the king's room; after a while someone went up and found the king and queen dead, with expressions of horrible agony on their faces; and the window was open, with broken branches on the trellis outside . . ." The princess's voice stammered to a halt.

"I can't believe it," Alex said, dumbfounded. "I can't. He's an allopathist. They take vows . . . he wouldn't break them . . ."

"We can't be sure," Celine said, in a low voice. "But Temith might have done it in revenge for Carawan . . . I know he felt guilty that he managed to live, and my father didn't. Or he might have done it for me . . . after all, it means the prince, my husband, is the king now."

"I don't believe it," said Alex, unsure of everything, unsure what to know or to think. "Impossible."

"Maybe Chernan put an Influence on him?" Celine suggested. "Or—"

"No, it wasn't Chernan."

"How can you be sure?"

"I'm sure! Just as I'm sure Temith wouldn't poison anyone, not in the role of an allopathist, it would be a terrible act, he could never show his face again . . ."

"You're right about that! I've put word out, and a price on his head! We can't trust anyone!"

I don't know how long she'll let us stay, Temith had said.

Can't trust anyone . . .

"I don't believe it," he said again, and Celine's voice again:

"I'm telling you the truth, Alex! Who do you trust? Him, or me?"

warning anger dislike

He looked around, out of habit more than anything; there was nothing in the Oether, nothing but the typical blurriness of Mote's vision, and the warmth of the sun coming through the single window on his face in the darkness of his own world. Celine's breath was loud in the silence. Queen now, with nothing more to fear, no more General to cower her or advisors to shout her down . . . would Temith have wanted that? Had he really snapped, fallen into such a blatant disrespect of his physician's oaths? By his loyalty to Carawan, poor dead Carawan, whose monument Alex could have seen, could he see at all, out this same window that was shining warmth on his face . . .

"I don't believe it." He was sure now. "I don't. I don't think Temith killed them, or if he did, he didn't mean to." He took a deep breath. "I think you killed them."

"Alex!" A horrified whisper.

"Temith wouldn't have needed to kill them to help you . . . you were capable of helping yourself, and you did. You killed them. And," Alex added, slowly backing away, reaching behind himself so as not to stumble over anything, "and, you killed your father. You shot him, from that window—" he pointed vaguely, "—with a Deridal crossbow. That's why it wasn't out of range." He saw again how the archer's arrows had fallen short, and then that one, single bolt had sunk so deep. He thought of Celine, prowling through the towers, not lost and forlorn, but watching, waiting, with her crossbow and her deadly skills.

"How can you say that!" Celine's voice was angry, and hurt. "How dare you insinuate . . ."

"Your crossbow," Alex said, slowly. "King Belthar had it, after you were captured. You were good with it, and you were skilled enough with a staff to smack General Rhhuunn. The advisors . . . they were *afraid* of you, but they couldn't do anything about it! They still are. Temith hid Chernan's body to try to keep you from getting overconfident!"

"You . . . no, that's not true, they just never would listen," Celine stammered.

"You don't need to act with me," Alex said, warily. "I know how strong you are, inside and out. Just because you're beautiful and female doesn't mean you're weak or stupid . . ." *Manipulated again*, he thought sadly, *just like with Jeena . . .*

There was silence, and then he banged into the door; it had been closed. He was trapped.

"Chernan's really gone, then?" Celine asked, slowly.

Alex nodded, shuddering. "Temith . . . Temith made sure."

There was a faint clonk, as though someone in the room had just picked up a bronze-shod quarterstaff. "Then I guess I really *don't* need you anymore." Celine's voice again, changed now, hard and calm.

Alex rapidly checked the Oether, but there was nothing, no magic, no presence; Celine's words were entirely her own. He wasn't sure that this was any consolation. Mote, her eyes and ears and whiskers straining, managed to convey the impression of a shape moving toward him.

"You *did* kill your father," Alex whispered, horrified at the evil that could lurk in the human soul. *And now she's going to kill me*, he realized, but he couldn't bring himself to fight back.

"Do you know what it was like, having to watch him these past years?" she cried. "Watch him become a laughingstock, watch our city fall into decay and disrepair? I should have become queen after the accident. I could have turned things around, could have avoided all this, but people would rather have a fool than—"

"—than a murderess," finished Alex, and Mote gave him a vision of a sudden movement; he ducked wildly as the staff swung at him. It crashed into the door instead, with a boom.

"The General wasn't protecting you, he was protecting the king *from* you!" he shouted, feeling along, trying to find some way to unbar the door. "He warned me to stay away from you—"

"The other advisors knew well enough to give me room," she muttered, and he tried to duck again as he heard her faint intake of breath as she swung; but the staff caught him across the face, and pain and blood erupted from his nose. He staggered back against the wall, blood pouring down his face. "He wouldn't back off. I almost killed him, with the same crossbow. He was in my way. And now that you've decided to betray me . . . you're in my way, too."

"But I thought . . . you said . . ." Alex stammered. The whole thing was like a nightmare. Betrayed and stunned, he still loved her, he realized. He was going to be killed now, rather than harm her . . .

"You killed the shaman I hired to kill my father, and for that I wanted you dead . . . set Temith's traps for your rat, and a snake, that Valence would have been blamed for . . . but then I saw I could use you. I could lure you away from protecting my father, with some lies about Chernan. Of course he never cared for me—he never cared about anything but himself. And you believed it, and you loved me," she told him, knowing he was helpless. "I *did* need you, then. I could use you . . . and you were so easy to use."

Suddenly Celine had her hands around his throat, choking him. He couldn't breathe, the world was going red and black—he scrabbled, and as they struggled, something cold rolled down his arm like a bracelet.

"What a tragedy, poor blind loyal Animist falls down stairs, breaks his fool neck," she said, her voice still fearfully calm. He was trying to wriggle out of her grip, but she knew unarmed combat better than he did, and was strong under her beauty. "There's no doctor around to diagnose anything different, either." And Alex knew that his friend Temith was dead, and he himself was about to follow.

anger fury hate defend!!

Alex didn't feel Mote leap, but he heard her squeal and Celine yelp. The hands around his throat vanished and then Mote cried out again, as Celine snarled, "Stupid beast!"

pain! terror!

Alex wheezed and lunged blindly, striking now, grabbing her arm, yanking it back, prying at her fingers as she delivered rapid-fire punches into his kidneys. She dropped Mote, and then tried to turn Alex's grip into a painful hold, but Alex was ready for this and turned it into an escape.

The door flew open with a bang, knocking the two of them apart. Alex heard Rodeni voices: Len and Pleep.

"Alex? We heard noise . . . everything all right?" Pleep said.

"You're bleeding, Alex," Len commented. Tiny rat claws scrabbled up Alex's pant-leg; he scooped Mote up; she was shaken, but unhurt.

The princess was breathing hard, but silent. *She can't kill me if the Rodeni know about it,* Alex realized. *I'm their hero. She'd lose their support and then it would be war again . . .* But, he realized, as of right now, the island was in the hands of a ruthless ruler who, nevertheless, supported the Rodeni, was loved by the people, and by all accounts probably knew what she was doing. And she cared about the job enough to kill. To drag up the whole story, to open more conflicts now, would mean more fighting. More war, more death. All the cities would fracture, city against city, and Humani against Rodeni. Alex had the truth, but it would do more harm than good.

"The . . . queen was just explaining to me that she is dismissing me from her service," Alex managed, rubbing his bloody nose. "I don't have anything else I can say," he added, in hopes that Celine would catch his meaning, "so I won't. Say. Anything."

Len looked in surprise from Alex's face to Celine's rumpled clothing, and jumped to a conclusion. "Alex! She is married! Were you trying to—"

"Enough!" shouted Celine, her tone angry and haughty, but was there a hint of relief in it, too? "Get out of my sight, you bastard! If I see your face on this island again I'll . . . I'll . . ." She burst into realistic tears. Len and Pleep quickly grabbed Alex's arms, one on each side, and led him away, out of the palace, out of Deridal, forever.

"We had got word to fetch you, just after we left you with her," Pleep whispered in his ear, once they'd left the city. "Message came from . . . well, you will see."

Back along this horrible, memory-strewn road one last time. Back again to Belthas, with the roar of the waves on the cliffs, growing louder as they came closer. And this time, down a steep walkway with the cries of seagulls in the salt breeze. Rodeni voices on all sides, calling his name and patting him, whiskers tickling, teeth grinding. Pleep was warm and shy on one side, Len brave and confident at the other, and Mote rode proudly on his shoulder, showing him the glittering Oether clear and brilliant.

The Rodeni helped him onto a ship, and down into its hold . . .

"You found him!" shouted a familiar voice, and quickly followed with a chirrupping spatter of Rodeni in Humani accents. There was a rapid reply, and Alex heard the creaking of sails being raised.

"Alex! It's us!" It was Temith, and Serra with him. Alex sagged in relief. Len and Pleep wouldn't tell him where they were taking him, "They said, in case we get caught." The princess had apparently had some second thoughts, and had sent a few troops out to find Alex, but with the help of the Rodeni they had avoided them.

"Did they tell you? What did they tell you?" Temith demanded as he came running up. "I swear . . . I gave him a pain-draught, that was all, and a nerve tonic for the queen, she couldn't sleep, nightmares . . . that's all I *thought* it was . . . but then they started reacting. I did everything I could, but every single drug in my kit had been tampered, filled with—"

"I know, I know. I know too much, is what I know," Alex said. "And that's why I'm here. She wanted me dead, too. And you . . . I thought she'd killed you."

"I ran away when they died," Temith said, stammering, miserable. "I couldn't help them. I guess I killed them . . . and I ran. I found Serra—"

"I told him we needed to get away, get off the island," Serra spoke up. "But we knew you'd be in trouble, too. We weren't sure if it would be sooner or later, but I knew we couldn't trust her."

"None of us really did, but we couldn't say so to her face," Temith added, sadly. "And we couldn't tell the king . . . how do you explain, to a madman? I didn't realize how far she'd go, with this new alliance—"

"Royals killing each other . . . that's the way of things. But poor Carawan . . . he did love his daughter."

Alex said sadly, "I helped set her up to take the entire island away from Belthar . . . and I didn't even realize it. And there's more . . . I'll tell you all about it, but I think, finally, I really do need to get off this island."

"That's why we're on this boat," Temith agreed. "The Rodeni were grateful for the work I did to cure the plague . . . and I think some of them think I killed Belthar on purpose. In any case, I remembered how they helped you hide, and when I needed to hide, I found them."

"And I was along, helping him at the time," Serra added. "Celine isn't interested in keeping me as a minister of trade and finance, anyway. Since he speaks the language, he asked them to fetch you."

"I know you needed bronze or silver, to buy your way free of the College," said Temith, sadly. "I'm sorry we all had to leave in such a hurry that we didn't get anything of value. What are you going to do now?"

"I was wondering. Is this worth anything?" Alex asked, pulling the heavy metal thing he'd taken from Celine out of his shirt. Mote was clinging to it, and scrambled up onto Alex's shoulder. She was limping a bit, but her eyes were bright and her nose wriggled in greeting at them. "I can feel that it's metal, but I don't know what kind."

Temith and Serra saw it was a thin, three-quarter circlet of a strange, dark silvery metal, inlaid with gold, set with diamonds and emeralds. It was a crown; she'd probably been trying it on when she'd had her last encounter with Alex.

Temith took it reverently. It was the rarest metal of all. It came from the stars and tasted like blood and would shed orange-red powder if left to moisture. So much in one place . . . the few artifacts of it were the most precious treasures of the Physicists' College.

"Well, it's not bronze, but I imagine we can trade it, or parts of it, for enough to buy your freedom," Temith said, a bit weakly. "It's skymetal."

Alex frowned. "Never heard of it. Is it worth anything?"

"Uh. Yes. I don't know where Belthar got it, but . . . no wonder Celine sent troops out after you, after all. You've got enough here to buy your own island, I think."

"You'll need staff," said Serra. "Maybe a chef and an allopathist?"

"I'd be honored . . . Temith?"

"Certainly! I'd rather work for you than for Celine, any day."

"She'll be all right. And so will we, and the Rodeni." Alex sighed. "It's not a great, heroic ending," he said. "I wanted to save the king, uplift the Rodeni, win the princess, and live happily ever after . . . but . . . I suppose it could have been a lot worse. I just wish . . ."

"Yes, but wishes—"

"—only work for wizards, I know." The concept of wealth hadn't really sunk in, but he was relieved that he could go back to the College now. "As it is, I think I've done more than enough damage here, and I want to leave before the whole place sinks into the sea because of something I did."

"I'm looking forward to visiting your College," Temith said cheerfully.

"And I've never seen Lemyri before," put in Serra. "They sound fascinating."

"They'd be very interested in your studies of magic, I know that," Alex said to Temith.

"And I'd be interested in theirs." He glanced toward the open sea and the worlds beyond; Serra followed his gaze. Alex, meanwhile, was looking into the Oether, at the glowing world of spirits and magic, twinkling gently with the weather-promise of a fair day, good for sailing. Mote whiffled

happy

in his ear.

The Rodeni leapt and bounced around the ship as it pulled out of the port of Miraposa, and headed out to sea.